STAR WARS®

YODA
DARK RENDEZVOUS
(A CLONE WARS NOVEL)

By Sean Stewart

PASSION PLAY
NOBODY'S SON
RESURRECTION MAN
CLOUDS END
THE NIGHT WATCH
MOCKINGBIRD
GALVESTON
PERFECT CIRCLE
STAR WARS: YODA: DARK RENDEZVOUS

STAR WARS®
YODA
DARK RENDEZVOUS
(A CLONE WARS NOVEL)

SEAN STEWART

LUCAS BOOKS

DEL REY

BALLANTINE BOOKS • NEW YORK

For Caitlin and Rosie, bright and brave as any Padawans, and Christine, my swashbuckling companion and
guide to this galaxy, and all the others too.

CLONE WARS
TIMELINE

With the Battle of Geonosis (EP II), the Republic is plunged into an emerging, galaxywide conflict. On one side is the Confederacy of Independent Systems (the Separatists), led by the charismatic Count Dooku who is backed by a number of powerful trade organizations and their droid armies.

On the other side is the Republic loyalists and their newly created clone army, led by the Jedi. It is a war fought on a thousand fronts, with heroism and sacrifices on both sides. Below is a partial list of some of the important events of the Clone Wars and a guide to where these events are chronicled.

MONTHS
(after *Attack of the Clones*)

CLONE WARS
TIMELINE

MONTHS
(after *Attack of the Clones*)

+6   **THE HARUUN KAL CRISIS**
Shatterpoint (DR, June '03)

+6   **ASSASSINATION ON NULL**
Legacy of the Jedi #1 (SB, August '03)

+12   **THE BIO-DROID THREAT**
The Cestus Deception (DR, June '04)

+15   **THE BATTLE OF JABIIM**
Clone Wars III: Last Stand on Jabiim (DH, February '04)

+16   **ESCAPE FROM RATTATAK**
Clone Wars V: The Best Blades (DH, November '04)

+24   **THE CASUALTIES OF DRONGAR**
MedStar Duology: Battle Surgeons (DR, July '04)
                             Jedi Healer (DR, October '04)

+29   **ATTACK ON AZURE**
Jedi Quest Special Edition (SB, March '05)

+30   **THE PRAESITLYN CONQUEST**
Jedi Trial (DR, November '04)

+30   **LURE AT VJUN**
Yoda: Dark Rendezvous (DR, December '04)

+31   **THE XAGOBAH CITADEL**
Boba Fett #5: A New Threat (SB, April '04)
Boba Fett #6: Pursuit (SB, December '04)

+33   **THE HUNT FOR DARTH SIDIOUS**
Labyrinth of Evil (DR, February '05)

+36   **ANAKIN TURNS TO THE DARK SIDE**
Star Wars: Episode III Revenge of the Sith (LFL, May '05)

KEY:

DH = *Dark Horse Comics, graphic novels*
www.darkhorse.com

DR = *Del Rey, hardcover & paperback books*
www.delreydigital.com

LEC = *LucasArts Games, games for XBox, GameCube,*
PS2, & PC platforms www.lucasarts.com

LFL = *Lucasfilm Ltd., motion pictures* www.starwars.com

SB = *Scholastic Books, juvenile fiction* www.scholastic.com/starwars

1

The sun was setting on Coruscant. Shadows ran like black water, filling up the the alleys first, then climbing steadily higher, a tide of darkness rising to drown the capital. Twilight's gloom spread over retail districts and medcenters, and crept like a dark stain up the walls of the Chancellor's residence as the sun slipped below the horizon. Soon only the rooftops were gilded with the day's last yellow light; then the shadows conquered them, too, swarming up the pinnacles of the Senate Building and the spires of the Jedi Temple. The long day of the Republic had come to an end.

Dusk on Coruscant.

On a moonless night a million standard years earlier, perhaps even before the rise of sentient beings, sunset would have meant darkness absolute, except for the distant burn of the stars. Not now. Even during galactic war, Coruscant was still the blazing heart of the greatest civilization in the history of the galaxy. As the sun retreated, the great city began to sparkle with innumerable lights. Speeders darted between tall towers like glowflies dancing in meadows of transparisteel. Signs flared to life along every street, blinking bright promises at evening passersby. Lights came on in the windows of apartments and stores and offices.

So life goes on despite the gathering dark, Senator Padmé Amidala thought, looking out her window. *Each individual life burning bravely, like a candle raised against the night.* She kept her eyes on the spaceport landing platform nearest to the Jedi Temple. "It isn't a luxury," she said.

A handmaiden turned to look at her, puzzled. "Pardon?"

"Hope. It isn't a luxury. It's our duty," Padmé said.

The handmaiden started to stammer a reply, but Padmé cut her off. "Someone's landing," she said.

A ship settled like a dragonfly on the landing platform nearest to the Temple, lights burning at its tail and wingtips. Padmé grabbed for a pair of macrobinoculars and tabbed the night-vision settings, trying to read the designation on the courier's battle-scarred side. Searching the hooded figure climbing from the cockpit.

"M'lady?"

Slowly Padmé put the macrobinoculars aside. "It's not him," she said.

Chief Technician Boz Addle loved all the ships in his care, but he had a special affection for the sleek couriers. He ran a gloved hand along the metal flank of the Hoersch-Kessel *Seltaya*-class fast courier *Limit of Vision* that had just come home. "Electrical sparking, meteorite pocking, a couple of laser cannon burns," he murmured. His hand paused over a nasty gash where part of the ship's protective laminate had boiled away, showing a mass of fused wiring studded with shrapnel. "And unless I miss my guess, you took a few proton hits to boot."

Jedi Master Jai Maruk clambered out of the cockpit. His face was gaunt, stitched with shrapnel cuts, and puckered by a bad burn that lay in a bar of charred flesh across his cheek. Half healed on the frantic trip home, the burned skin had bubbled and turned stiff, pulling up one corner of his mouth. The chief technician regarded him gravely. "You promised you'd bring my ship back without a scratch, Master Maruk."

Grim smile. "I lied."

The duty medic bustled forward. "Let me check you out." He paused, squinting more closely at the slashing burn mark on the Jedi's cheek. "Master Maruk! What—"

"There's no time for that now. I must speak to the Jedi Council at once—as many as can be found, anyway."

"But Master Maruk—"

The Jedi waved him off. "Forgive me, medic, but now is not the time. I have a message to deliver that cannot wait, and I have been left, very much on purpose, in good enough shape to deliver it." Again the grim smile. He strode away, pausing only at the docking bay doors. "Chief Boz," he said more gently.

"Yes, Master?"

"Sorry about the ship."

The medic and the chief technician stood side by side on the landing platform and watched him leave. "Lightsaber burns?" Boz asked.

The medic nodded, wide-eyed.

The chief tech spat thoughtfully on the deck. "Thought so."

* * *

The Clone Wars like a mighty hand had flung Jedi throughout the stars, leaving only a few senior Jedi Knights in the Temple at any time. Yoda, of course, as Master of the Order and military adviser to the Chancellor, was nearly always on Coruscant. Tonight only two others had joined him to hear Jai Maruk's story: Jai Maruk's close friend Master Ilena Xan, nicknamed Iron Hand by the students—she taught hand-to-hand combat, and her specialty was joint locks—and Jedi Council member Mace Windu, who was too intimidating for nicknames.

"We were running recon in the Outer Rim," Jai said. "Began to think there was something funny going on in the neighborhood of the Hydian Way. Little drab transports kept popping up, like a mermyn-trail leading into and out of the Wayland region. Nothing so unusual about that, the Trade Federation has the whole region locked down . . . but these were popping in from strange coordinates. Deep-space vectors, not local traffic. I got a funny feeling about them, so I dressed up one of the clone transports in pirate's colors and sent it to intercept. Turned out that little commercial shuttle had legs on it like a Neimoidian jakrab. Dropped down a burst of plasma fire and jumped to hyperspace in a heartbeat."

Master Yoda's wrinkled brow rose. "In a nerf's coat, this krayt dragon was."

"Exactly." Master Jai Maruk glanced down at his right hand, which was trembling. An ugly char mark was burned across his palm. He regarded the hand steadily. The trembling stopped.

A young Padawan, a red-haired girl of perhaps fourteen, came into the room with a pitcher of water and some glasses on a tray. Bowing, she placed them on a low table. Master Xan poured a tumbler of water and gave it to Jai. He stared at the glassy, oozing skin on the palm of his burned hand, forced it to curl around the tumbler, and drank.

"So the Trade Federation was shipping something important into the Hydian Way," Jai continued. "Why? Not new ordnance; we don't have any significant troop concentrations out there. And why the disguise? They could wear their fleet colors proudly—it would scare off any pirates or casual raiders, like my poor clone troopers had pretended to be."

"There has to be something there we aren't supposed to know about," Ilena said.

Mace Windu studied the lightsaber burns on Jai Maruk's cheek. "Or *someone*."

Yoda tapped out a pattern on the Council Chamber floor with his cane. "One of these krayts, followed it did you."

"But you were caught," Mace said.

Jai's face tightened. "I tracked them to a rendezvous on Vjun."

Master Yoda stirred and shook his head. The others looked to him. "Strong in the dark side, Vjun is," he murmured. "Know you the stories?"

They looked at him blankly.

The corners of Yoda's mouth turned down. "A trial of being old is this: remembering which thing one has said into which young ears. But *he* knows; I remember we spoke of it when he was only a Padawan . . ."

The other Jedi stared. "Who knows?" Master Xan asked.

Yoda waved the question off with his stick. "It matters not. Master Maruk, continue."

Jai took another sip of water. "At first I remained sunside, hidden from my krayt, but when it stayed dirtside for longer than just refueling, I had to risk following it to the surface. I made a soft landing many kilometers away, I kept my heat and IR signatures crushed down, I swear it—" He slowed to a stop. His hand was trembling again. "It doesn't matter. She caught me."

"She?" Master Xan asked.

"Asajj Ventress."

A gasp came from the Padawan who had brought the water. Yoda glanced over, furrowing his face into a mass of stern wrinkles. Only those who knew him very well could have detected the light of amusement in his eye. "Little pitchers, big ears they have! Duties to attend to, have you not, Scout?"

"Not really," she said. "We've finished dinner, and there's nothing urgent I have to do before tomorrow. I mean, I was intending to practice in the training room, but that could—"

The girl flushed and stuttered to a halt under the massed gaze of the Jedi Masters. "Padawan Scout," Mace Windu said deliberately, "I am surprised to hear you have this much free time, given the upcoming Apprentice Tournament. I hate to think you might be bored. Would you like me to *find* you something to do?"

The girl gulped. "No, Master. Not necessary. As you say—practice—I should . . ." She bowed and backed out of the room, sliding the door almost shut, until they could see only one green eye. "But if there's anything else you need, don't hesitate to—"

"Scout!"

"Right!" And with a click the door slid shut.

Mace Windu shook his head. "The Force is weak in that one. I don't know—"

Master Xan held up her hand, and Mace fell silent. Xan's fingers truly were like iron, sheathed with muscle, the joints knotted from years of hand-to-hand combat training. She flicked her hand at the door in a gentle Force push. The door thunked and they heard a muffled yelp. A moment later, embarrassed footsteps pattered away down the corridor.

Mace Windu shook his head impatiently. "I don't know what Chankar saw in her."

"We'll never know now," Jai Maruk said. Together they paused in remembrance of Chankar Kim, another Jedi fallen in the ring at Geonosis. At first, there had been ceremonies and vigils memorializing that horrible slaughter. But time and the war had gone on, and the Temple was now bleeding from more than that one great wound. Every week or two, another report would come in of a comrade lost in a battle on Thustra, or blown up in high space over Wayland, or assassinated in a diplomatic mission to Devaron.

"Frankly," Mace said, "I was surprised she was ever chosen to be a Padawan."

The tip of Yoda's cane swirled slowly over the chamber floor, as if he were stirring the depths of a pond visible only to him. "To the Agricultural Corps she should be sent, think you?"

"Actually, yes, I do." A note of sympathy entered

Mace Windu's voice. "There is no dishonor in that. When you see how hard she has to fight just to keep up with children years younger than she is . . . Perhaps it would be kinder to let her work at her own level."

Yoda cocked his head and looked curiously at him. "See her struggle do I, as well. But if you make her stop, tell you it is 'kind,' she will not!"

"Maybe not," Jai Maruk said grimly. "But children do not always want what is best for them."

"Nor do Jedi Masters," Yoda said dryly.

The burned Jedi forged on. "Let's be honest. Not every pairing of Jedi Knight and Padawan will be Obi-Wan and Anakin, granted, but the truth is *we are at war*. To send a Jedi into battle with a Padawan who cannot be trusted to hold her own is to needlessly risk two lives—lives the Republic cannot afford to throw away."

"The Force is not as strong in Scout as it should be," Ilena agreed. "But I've had her in my classes for years. Her technique is good. She is smart and she is loyal. She tries."

"There is no *try*," Master Maruk said, unconsciously letting his voice slip into the Yoda imitation for which, a lifetime ago, he had been famous among the young boys of the Jedi Temple. "There is only *do*."

The other three Jedi in the room glanced guiltily at Yoda. He snorted, but laugh lines crinkled around his eyes. "Mm. Thinking of students, I am. Best then I should go to battle with him in whom the Force is strongest, hmm? With young Skywalker, think you?"

"He's not polished," Ilena said.

"And too impulsive," Mace added.

"Hm." Yoda stirred again with his stick. "Then best

of all would be the strongest student, yes? Wisest? Most learned in the ways of the Force?" He nodded. "Best of all, Dooku would be!" His eyes found the other Jedi, one by one: and one by one, they looked away. "Our great student!" Yoda's ears flexed, then drooped. "Our great failure."

The ancient Master hobbled over to the tray and poured himself a glass of water. "Enough. The rest of your story, tell us, Master Maruk."

"Ventress found me," Jai said. "We fought. I lost." His burned hand was shaking again. "She took my lightsaber. I composed myself for the killing blow, but instead she took me prisoner. She blindfolded me and bundled me into a speeder for a short ride, no more than an hour. Count Dooku was waiting at the end of it."

"Ah!" Mace Windu leaned forward. "So Dooku is on Vjun!"

"You escaped from Dooku and Ventress alive!" Ilena said.

A mirthless smile tugged on Jai Maruk's burned cheek. "Make no mistake, I am here because Dooku wanted me here. Ventress would have killed me if she could, she made that very plain, but Dooku wanted a messenger. One he could *trust*," the Jedi said, his voice heavy with irony. "One who would report here first, and not to the Senate. He was very particular about that—I was to deliver my message to Master Yoda, and only in the Temple, far from other ears."

"And what was this urgent message?" Mace Windu said.

"He says he wants peace."

Jai Maruk looked at the disbelieving faces of the Jedi and shrugged.

"Peace!" Master Xan spat out. "Bioweapons slaughter innocents by the millions on Honoghr and he wants peace! The Republic is falling like burned logs into the fire and he wants peace! I can imagine exactly the kind of peace he means."

"Dooku anticipated we might be, ah, *wary.*" Jai Maruk reached for a pocket under his cloak. "He would send me back, he said, with an offering and a question for Master Yoda. The offering was my life. But the question was this . . ." He drew his hand from his pocket and opened it. There on his shaking palm was a shell—a single, quite ordinary shell, such as a child might find on the seashore of a hundred worlds.

The Jedi looked at it in confusion, but Yoda, for once, was not so serene. He drew a sharp inward breath, and his brow furrowed.

"Master?" Jai Maruk looked away from the shell in his shaking hand. "I have carried this thing across half the galaxy. But what does it *mean?*"

Sixty-three standard years earlier. It is evening, and the sky is dark blue above the sprawling compound of the Jedi Temple. In the Temple's walled gardens, the twilight sky is reflected in the ornamental pond. Yoda's most accomplished student is sitting on a rock by the pond's edge, looking into the water. In one hand he holds a shell, running his thumb again and again over its bone-smooth surface. Before him, water-skeeters dance on the surface of the water, light-footed.

The apprentice's attention moves with them, dancing,

too, on the surface of silence; skating on the endless deepness of the Force. He has always been light-footed; the Force dimples underneath his attention, but holds him up, effortlessly. Only tonight, for some reason, he feels sad and strangely heavy. As if realizing for the first time how easy it would be to see his foot fall through, into that deep power—to sink into dark depths there, and drown.

Tick, tick, *tchak*. Tick, tick, *tchack*. Footsteps coming nearer, one, two, and then the *thunk* of a cane stubbed into the white-pebbled path. A glow light approaches, coming from the direction of the Masters' quarters, a blur of light moving through the garden's tangle of leaves and vines. The presence is a familiar one, and the student can feel Yoda, his old mind warm and bright as that glow light, long before the old one's silhouette rounds the last bend, and the great Master of the Jedi Order hobbles slowly up to join him.

The student smiles and dips his head. How many times Yoda has told him, in endless hours of meditation or lightsaber training, that while the outer form of a figure or an attack need not be displayed, one must feel its *intention* in every cell. So that little dip of the head, so casual, carries a lifetime of gratitude and respect. And fear, too. And guilt.

The Grand Master of the Jedi Order puts down his light and clambers awkwardly onto a rock, scrabbling for purchase and then hauling himself up to sit snuffling beside his student like some unfortunate garden gnome. The student's grin broadens, but he knows better than to offer to help.

Yoda settles himself on the stone in a series of grunts and shifts, adjusting the skirts of his worn Jedi robes, and letting his feet hang just over the surface of the pond. The water-skeeters zip under his ancient green toes, oblivious to the slightly hairy greatness dangling over them. "Pensive, are you, Dooku?"

The student doesn't attempt to deny it.

"No fear about this mission have you, surely?"

"No, Master." The student corrects himself. "Not about the mission, anyway."

"Confident, you should be. Ready you are."

"I know."

Yoda seems to want the light he has left on the ground. He turns his cane around and tries to hook the glow light's handle with it. Grimacing, he fishes once, twice, but the light slips off. He grunts, exasperated.

With the barest flick of his attention, the student picks up the lantern with the Force and sends it floating to his teacher. "Why not do it the easy way, Master?" he asks—and knows what's coming as soon as he shuts his mouth.

"*Because* it is easy," Yoda grunts. In the young man's experience, students get a lot of answers like this from Yoda. *He didn't send the light away, though,* Dooku thinks.

They sit together in the garden. Somewhere out of sight, a fish breaks the surface, then settles back into the water.

Yoda gives the student a companionable prod with the end of his stick. "So ready to leave, yesterday you were!"

"And last month, and last year, and the year before that." A rueful smile from Dooku lights and dies slowly away. "But now that it's really going to happen . . ." He looks around. "I can't remember a time I didn't want to leave—to go out, to travel the stars, to see the world. And yet I have loved it here. This place has been my home. You have been my home."

"And will be still." Yoda gazes at the sweet-scented darkness of the gardens approvingly. "Always be here, we will. Home, yes . . . they say on Alderaan, *Home it is, where when you come to the door, they have to let you in!*" He snuffs the evening air, laughing a little. "Hm. Always will there be a place for you here."

"I suppose so. I hope so." The student looks down at the shell in his hand. "I found this on the bank. Abandoned by a freshwater hermit crab. They don't have homes of their own, you know. They keep outgrowing them. I was thinking about that, how the Jedi found me on Serenno. With my mother and father, I suppose. I can't remember them now. Do you ever stop to think how strange that is? Every Jedi is a child his parents decided they could live without." Yoda stirs, but does not speak. "I wonder, sometimes, if that is what drives us, that first abandonment. We have a lot to prove."

A glow-fly comes flickering out of the tangled vines to zip over the surface of the pond, like a spark shot from a fire. The student watches it make its dizzy pattern over the quiet water.

Yoda has a question he likes to ask: *What are we, think you, Dooku?* Every time the student tries a different answer: *We are a knot tied in the Force* or *We are the agency of Fate* or *We are each cells in the body of History* . . . but tonight, watching the glow-fly hiss and flicker in the night, a truer answer comes to him. *In the end, what we are is: alone.*

With a faint *pop,* like a bubble bursting, a fish rises from the dark water and snaps. The glow-fly's light goes out and is gone, leaving no trace but one weak ripple that spreads slowly across the surface of the pond.

"I guess even then I was like that hermit crab," the student says. "Too big for my parents' house. So you brought me here, and it's been years, now, that even the Temple has seemed a tight fit for me. I guess . . ." The young man pauses, turning, so the light falling against the edge of his hooded robe throws a shadow across his face. "I worry that once I am out in the big world, I will never be able to fit inside here again."

Yoda nods, speaking almost to himself. "Proud, are you. Not without reason."

"I know."

"Not without danger, either."

"I know that, too."

The student rubs again at the hermit crab shell, and then drops it into the pond. Startled water-skeeters skitter madly from the splash, trying to stay afloat.

"Bigger than the Jedi, bigger than the Force, you cannot be," Yoda says.

"But the Force is bigger than the Jedi, Master. The Force is not just these walls and teachings. It runs through all life, high and low, great and small, light—" Awkwardly the student stops.

"—and dark," Yoda says. "Oh, yes, young one. Think you I have never felt the touch of the dark? Know you what a soul so great as Yoda can make, in eight hundred years?"

"Master?"

"Many *mistakes*!" Wheezing with laughter, the old teacher reaches out with his cane and pokes his student in the ribs. "To bed with you, thinker of deep thoughts!" *Poke, poke.* "Your Master, Thame Cerulian, says the most gifted Padawan he ever saw, you are. Trust in yourself, you need not. I, Yoda, great and powerful Jedi Master, will trust for you! Is it enough?"

The apprentice wants to laugh along, but cannot. "It is too much, Master. I am afraid . . ."

"Good!" Yoda snorts. "Fear the dark side, you should. In the mighty is it mightiest. But not yet Thame's equal are you; not yet a Jedi Knight; not yet a member of the Council. Many shells have we left for you, Dooku—as long as you can fit inside *this* one," he says, rapping his student's skin. "Tomorrow, go you must, into the darkness between the stars. But home always will this place be. If ever lost you are, look back into this garden." Yoda hefts his glow light, so shadows like water-skeeters dart away from them. "A candle will I light, for you to find your way home."

Sixty-three years later, Jai Maruk had been sent to the infirmary, and Ilena Xan had returned to her room, making preparations for the Jedi Apprentice Tournament. Mace Windu alone lingered with Yoda.

"Dooku asks to come home," Yoda said. "A trap, could this be."

"Probably," Mace agreed.

Yoda sighed and studied the shell. "A question, he called it. Yes, such a question! But ignore it we must, do you agree?"

Unexpectedly, Mace shook his head. "Dooku should be dead. I should have killed him on Geonosis. I could have stopped the whole war then. And still he is key. Could he come to parley in earnest? There is only a little chance. Could he come all the way back to us? Surely the chance is less than a little. But balance that chance, however small, against a million lives, and it's a chance we must take. So I think, Master."

Yoda grunted. "Hard it would be, to dare to hope again for this lost student!"

"Tough," Mace said. "Nobody said being a Jedi Master was easy—even for you."

Yoda grunted, glaring around at the Temple. "Pfeh. All too wise, you have become. Better before it was, when only Yoda was wise!" He glanced over at Mace and snickered. Mace would have laughed, too, if somewhere in the ring on Geonosis he hadn't lost the knack.

On the other side of the galaxy, the Order's most gifted apprentice reached out to tap a lightsaber with the toe of his boot. Count Dooku grimaced. The lightsaber was still attached to a hand. The hand was soot black and rimed with frost; it ended in a gory stump of frozen blood just above the wrist. Dooku was in his study, a place for reflection, and the severed hand hardly struck the contemplative note. Besides which, as hard as it had frozen in the bitter vacuum of space, it would be thawing out in a hurry now. If he wasn't careful, it would leave a stain on the tiles. Not a good thing, even though one more bloodstain on the floor of Château Malreaux would hardly be noticed.

On the other side of Dooku's desk, Asajj Ventress hefted a bag of foil insulation. "There wasn't much left of the ship, Master. The Force was strong, and I hit the reactor chamber with my first shot. It took me several hours to find that," she said, glancing at the frozen hand. "It occurred to me a magnetic scan might turn up the lightsaber. Funny to think he was reaching for his weapon when his ship blew up. Instinct, I suppose."

"He?"

"He, she." Asajj Ventress shrugged. "It."

When her first Master died, Asajj Ventress, scourge of the Jedi and Count Dooku's most feared associate, had tattooed her hairless head and left her girlhood behind. Her skull was striped with twelve marks, one for each of the twelve warlords she had killed after swearing their deaths. She was a dagger of a woman, slender and deadly. Even in a galaxy cluttered with hate, such a combination of speed and fury comes only once in a generation; Dooku had known that from the first moment they met. She was the rose and the thorn together; the sound of a long knife driving home; the taste of blood on one's lips.

Asajj shrugged. "I never found a head, but I did pick up a few assorted bits out of the wreckage if you want to take a look," she said, giving the foil bag a heft.

Dooku regarded her. "What a little cannibal you have become."

She said, "I become what you make me."

No easy answer to that.

With an expert Force tug, Dooku brought the severed hand, still clutching its weapon, to hang in the air before him, as easily as he had drawn up Yoda's glow light all those decades earlier. Before the starfighter explosion had ripped the hand so untidily from the rest of its body, Dooku rather thought it might have been olive-skinned. The charring made it hard to tell if it was even human. The dead flesh, unconnected to any spirit, was merely matter now—no more interesting than a table leg or a wax candle, and bearing no more imprint of its owner's soul and personality. Dooku always found this astonishing: how *transitory* the relationship was between one's body and oneself. The spirit is a puppeteer to make one's flesh limbs dance: but cut the spirit's strings, and nothing remains but meat and paint, cloth and bone.

A Jedi's lightsaber, now: that was something different. Each weapon was unique, built and rebuilt by its owner, made to be a pure expression of Self. Dooku ran one finger along the handle of the dead Jedi's weapon. The force of the explosion had stripped off half the casing and fused its works so it would never burn again, but the essential pattern was obvious still. "Jang Li-Li," he murmured. To his surprise, he found he was sad.

"I make that sixteen," Ventress said. "Seventeen, it should have been, if you had allowed me to kill that spy, Maruk."

Dooku turned. Released from his attention, the gory hand and the handle it clutched dropped with a wet *thump* and clatter to the floor. The Count walked to the window of his study. When he was very young, Yoda had told him Vjun's tragic story, and for years he'd had it in mind as a good place to make a retreat. The planet was heavy with the dark side, which made the study of the Sith ways easier. And more practically, Vjun's catastrophe—a plague of sudden madness that carried off most of the planet's population in a year—had left a great many nicely appointed manors empty for the taking. An old crab likes a comfortable shell, after all, and Château Malreaux was very comfortable indeed. The previous owner's sanity had slipped from him in sudden and spectacular fashion; except for the bloodstains, one might think the château had been built new expressly for Dooku's occupation.

Beyond the study window it was raining, of course—the same acid drizzle that had nearly eaten through the roof before Dooku had arrived to set things in better repair. In the distance, toward the seashore, a few twisted thorn-trees raised their claws at the dolorous sky, but the real ground cover was the notorious Vjun moss: soft, sticky, venomously green, and passively carnivorous. A two-hour nap on the stuff would leave exposed skin red, welted, and oozing.

Dooku watched rain run like tear tracks down his windows. "The last time I saw Jang, she must have been . . . younger than you, even. A handsome young woman. The Council was sending her on her first diplomatic mission . . . to Sevarcos, I think it was. She came to ask my advice. She had striking eyes, very gray and steady. I remember thinking she would do well."

Ventress picked up the bloody hand and tossed it into her foil bag. "Great are the powers of the Sith, but you're not much of a fortune-teller."

"You think not?" Dooku turned to consider the dead Jedi's murderer. "Jang lived in service, however misguided, and acted by the star of her principles, however incomplete. By that judging, how many lives are better?"

"Lots are longer, though." Ventress tied a knot in the foil bag and tossed it into the corner of the room. "If you ask me," she said, watching the bag hit with a wet *thud,* "that's not what winning looks like."

She licked her lips.

"You have a point," he said.

Asajj shifted unconsciously into what Dooku recognized as the echo of a fighting stance, shoulders squared, chin up and aggressive, hands high. *Here it comes,* he thought.

Ventress took a deep breath. "Make me your apprentice."

"It's not the time—" Dooku began, but Ventress cut him off.

"I'm not in it for the Trade Federation or the Republic," she said. "I don't care about flags or soldiers, sides or treaties, droids or clones. I'm not even in it for the killing, except for the Jedi, and that's not business, it's personal. When I work on my own, I do what I like. When I do your bidding, I don't need it to be right or reasoned or even sane: I do it because you ask it of me."

"I know," Dooku said.

Ventress strode to the window and stood before it, blocking Dooku's view. "Have I served well?"

"Superbly," he admitted.

"Then reward me! Make me your apprentice! Teach me the ways of the Sith!"

"Have I not taught you many secrets, Asajj?"

"Scraps. Little devices. Lesser arts. Not nearly what you would if I were your apprentice sworn in blood, I know. I am no fool," she said angrily. As if he didn't know that. As if she needed to convince him she was deadly. "I have learned much about the Sith. Their lineage and their greatness."

"But what of their natural history?" Dooku said.

Ventress blinked. "What?"

"The Sith, considered as a species. An insect, perhaps."

Asajj's thin lips got thinner. "You mock me."

"I have rarely been more serious." The Count paced over to a shelf of holocrons on the wall, plucked one out, and inserted it into the comm cube on his desk. "Behold: the sickle-back mantis of Dantooine." A glowing picture formed in the air over the desk, a glossy red-and-black mantis, all hooked forelimbs and wicked piety. "After mating, the female tears her partner's head off and lays her eggs in his body. When the broodlings hatch, they eat their way out and then attack one another."

"I am not given to parables," Ventress said impatiently. "If you have a point, make it."

"It is a tricky business, this making of apprentices," Dooku said. "The true Sith Lord must find a pupil in whom the Force runs strong."

"Sixteen Jedi dead is some testament to that," Ventress said. "Should have been seventeen," she added.

"But do I really want to make you so strong?" the Count said softly. "We are such pleasant company now, while you know your place. But if I were to make you my apprentice, if I were to take you by the hand and lead you down below the black water that is the dark side, then either you would drown, or you would grow far stronger, and neither option appeals to me. You burn so brightly now, I would hate to put you out."

"Why should you? What harm is there in teaching me to help you better?"

"You would betray me." He shrugged, cutting off her protests. "It is the unhappy hazard of embracing the dark side. I am old, and I have learned the limits of my ambition. You are young, and strong, and those two things have always led to one place in the history of the Sith."

"You think I would intrigue against you?"

"Not at first. But a day would come when you would disagree with my decisions. When you would start to dream of how much better things would be without my liver-spotted hand held over you."

"I disagree with your decisions right now," she said. "About that Jedi who—"

"Should have been number seventeen. I know." Dooku smiled. "I don't have your appetites. I can wait on my kills, and use them better. And for now, you might disagree, but you dare not disobey." And here, with a small smile, he lifted just one finger.

She blanched. "True," she said.

Dooku let his finger drop.

In the hologram on the desk, baby mantises were squirming from their father's body. They groped blindly about them with their spindly hooked limbs until one, a little larger than the others, chanced to find that the sickles on his hind legs fit like a collar around a sibling's neck. Driven by primitive instinct, he jerked and tore off his brother's head.

"In a perfect world," Dooku said, "one could feed an apprentice just enough to keep him growing—just enough to keep him wanting more. The Master could promise him fame, glamour. That's a good one to deliver on," he said. "He could do the Master's bidding, be his public face. Then if any of the Master's plans went wrong, why, he could take the fall." Dooku looked up, his eyes suddenly sharp and very much in the present. "Does that sound good to you, Asajj? Would you truly like to be my apprentice? I could make you the most feared woman in the galaxy. All the Jedi would come looking for you, while I sat safe and sound in Coruscant, biding my time."

Asajj licked her lips again. "Let them come," she said.

"Ah, to be young and full of hate!" Dooku chuckled. "You would be a star—great to everyone but me. But I'd have to keep you humble, you realize. I'd have to goad and needle and hurt you, to keep you in your place. Every secret the apprentice learns, he pays for dearly. Oh yes, he pays . . ." The Count paused, his eyes closing for a moment as if to shut out some terrible memory.

Asajj regarded him narrowly. "You don't think I'm worthy."

"You're not listening, are you?"

"You're not saying anything to the point," Ventress said angrily. "Was it that Jedi, Jai Maruk? Should I have killed him? I was following your orders, but perhaps that was the test." Her eyes narrowed. "I should have showed more initiative. That's what you're waiting for.

You don't need a . . . minion. Those you have in plenty. You need something more."

The Count watched her, bemused. "How strange it is, to know your every thought before you think it."

"Not even the dark side can give you that power," Ventress said, unnerved.

The Count smiled. "I have a power greater than the dark side, my pet. I am *old*. Your fresh furies are my ancient mistakes."

Mantises squirmed and hunted in the vision over his desk. He snapped off the holocron and consulted a monitor. "Ah. Our latest batch of guests is arriving. Loyal beings and true, for the Trade Federation cause and a ten percent profit. Go meet them at the door. You always make such an impression on visitors."

"Don't patronize me," Asajj said coldly.

Dooku looked around. "Or *what*?"

Her face went pale.

Dooku lifted that one finger, and this time he tapped it in the air, as if pushing a needle into a pincushion. Ventress crumpled to her knees. Her voice came out clotted with pain. "Please," she said. "Don't."

"It doesn't feel very good, does it? Like sharp stones in your throat and chest." Dooku made another little patting motion, and Ventress slammed to the tile floor. "It's the blood vessels I hate," Dooku said. "The way they *stretch* inside, like balloons about to pop."

"P-p-p-please . . ."

"But worse than anything is the memories," he said, more softly still. "They crowd around, like flies on meat. Every despicable thing, every petty vice, every little act of spite." A cruel, strange quiet stretched out as Ventress panted on the stone floor. Rain ticked against the window glass, and the Count's soft voice went dark and far away. "All the things you should have stopped, but *didn't,* and nothing will ever be right again. And the things you've done," he whispered. "By the pitiless stars, *the things you've done . . .*"

The comm on Dooku's desk beeped. He shook his head, like a man waking from a dream. "The Troxan delegation is at the door."

Ventress crawled to her feet. Her face was bruised and her cheeks were wet with tears. Both pretended not to notice. "Tell them I'll be right down," Count Dooku said.

Physically, the Count's age was rarely a handicap. Deft as he had become with the Force—unimaginably more subtle than the boy who had watched waterskeeters in the Jedi gardens all those years ago—he wore his eighty-three standard years better than most humans half his age. He was still in superb physical shape, senses keen, health undiminished by even the memory of a cold.

Only in this situation, stooped before the image of his Master, did he feel his years. Even via hologram, the flickering figure of Darth Sidious, hideous in blue and shadows, seemed to strip his false youth away, leaving his bones brittle, his joints worn thin and knotted with tension.

"These are the envoys from Troxar," his Master said. How could he know? Dooku didn't ask. Darth Sidious knew. He always knew.

"They are considering surrender," Dooku said. "They claim they have a resistance planned, ready to rise in insurrection when the clone troops withdraw."

"No!" the flickering figure said sharply. "The war has already damaged the planet too much to make it worth saving. Its only value now is to chew up more troops and resources. Tell them they have to fight on. Promise them reinforcements—tell them you will be deploying a new fleet of advanced droids to retake the whole system within a month, if only they can hold on. Explain that such weapons will not be put in the hands of those who surrender."

"And when the month passes, and no reinforcements arrive?"

"Help will come within another month at most. Promise them that, and make them believe it. I've shown you how."

"I understand," Dooku said. *How casually we betray our creatures.*

The hooded figure cocked its head. "Having an attack of *conscience,* my apprentice?"

"No, Master." He met the hooded figure's hideous eye. "It was their own greed that brought them to you," he said. "In their heart of hearts, they always knew what they were getting into."

The Château Malreaux was alive with eyes.

The spectacular security system installed by the seventeenth (and last) Viscount Malreaux in the final months of his descent into madness was one of the reasons Dooku had chosen the château for his current base of operations. Optic recorder studs littered the mansion, disguised as upholstery rivets in the parlor, screw heads in the kitchen cabinets, painkiller pills in the apothecary's pantry, and the black eyes of birds woven into the tapestries of the Crying Room. Top-of-the-line infrared swatches, originally developed as prosthetics for tongue-damaged Sluissi, were grafted into the cream-and-crimson Malreaux livery of the table linen and carpets and drapes. The faux walls that had been built at enormous expense to riddle the château with secret passageways were pocked with spyholes. Microphones nested like spiders in dozens of drawers and linen closets, under every bed, taped to the roof by each of the eleven chimneys, and even glued on the base of a priceless bottle of Crème D'Infame in the wine cellar.

The seventeenth (and final) Viscount Malreaux, convinced he was being poisoned, had murdered his kitchen staff and then fled into his secret tunnels, coming out only at night. The last anyone saw of him was a murky glimpse shot from a security cam hidden in a fake onion in a hanging basket in the kitchen: a thirty-second recording of a skeletal figure creeping from a hidden grate into the kitchen to drink two hurried gulps of tap water and gnaw a handful of raw flour.

If it hadn't been for the smell, the corpse of the seventeenth (and terminal) Lord Malreaux would never have been found.

Someone hidden in the secret passage that ran over the study, for example, would have been able to watch the whole of the conversation between Dooku and Asajj Ventress through a peephole gimlet in the ceiling. If that person had been patient, and waited until Ventress was well away, he or she would have seen the conference between Dooku and the hologrammic apparition of Darth Sidious.

And if the watcher had waited a good while after Dooku left the room, he or she might have seen a section of shelving swing out unexpectedly, admitting a small, quick, evil creature, a Vjun fox, its coat a brindled red and cream, with clever prehensile hands instead of paws.

After pausing a moment to sniff, it advanced warily into the room, speculatively at first, but almost immediately coming to the spot where Dooku had dropped Jang Li-Li's thawing severed hand. The floor was tiled in the Malreaux check, half fusty crimson, half dirty cream, like dried blood and curdled milk. The hand, landing with a wet *thud* on one of the dirty-cream tiles, had left a splotch. The fox sniffed, and its thin pink tongue showed between its lips.

"Not yet, my sweet." A wheezing older woman limped through the secret door. She was dressed in dirty tatters of what had once been fine clothing—a pink ball gown gone black at its raveled hems, torn stockings, and the remains of what had once been a pair of gold lamé slippers. Around her neck she wore a fur stole made from foxtails tied together. "Wait a bits. Which Momma wants to take a look-see." She lowered her bulk to the floor with a grunt and bent forward to peer at the stain.

She gasped. "Oh, precious," she whispered. She leaned over to stare more intently at the splotch, and her eyes, small and hard as little black marbles, went wet and shiny.

"Oh," she said. She sat slowly back on her haunches, rocking and rocking. "Oh, oh, oh!"

The fox looked up at her.

The old woman looked back with an expression of such savage triumph that the fox recoiled, baring its little yellow needle teeth. "Oh, such a day for Momma, sweetness! Which she's been waiting such a long time for this," she whispered. She met the foxy eyes. "Can't you see, honeypot? Can't you smell it? *The Baby's coming home!*"

She stood up. Emotion made her hams shake, and the thick flesh of her upper arms. "Time to get ready," she muttered. "Clean the Baby's room. Make his little bed." She limped quickly back into the passageway.

The fox waited with pricked ears until the sound of her mutters dwindled slowly into the darkness. Then it bent its head to the bloodstained floor, and with its long pink tongue licked the tile clean.

Count Dooku's meeting with the Troxan delegation went well. He made a cold kind of game of it, trying to see how little he could say, letting them do all the lying for him. "There are new battle droids in production," he had remarked. That was all it took; they did the rest.

"Surely you'll be sending them to our quadrant," said the under-palatine for patriotic liaisons.

"Really, we're key to the entire region," his assistant said.

"Of course, you understand our need," another said.

"What other planets have fought so bravely for the cause?" a fourth asked.

Each of these fine hopes he reinforced with a smile and pushed into their minds with the Force, like a seal pressed into warm wax, so it felt like certainty. In fact, using the Force was hardly necessary. What man—or Troxan, either—would choose to believe that with every sentence he was betraying thousands of his fellows to death, when he could see himself as a hero instead? So much for the urge to Do Good, Dooku thought. Shown up again as just another illusion blinding creatures to the stark universe the dark side alone showed in all its bitter clarity.

What are we, Dooku?

Alone. Alone. Alone.

Watching the Troxans hang themselves was middling sport at best, too easy to take much pleasure in. Dooku moved rapidly to bring the meeting to a close and send them back to their slaughterhouse. "Anything else?" he asked.

The delegates looked at one another. "Actually, there was one other curious incident," said the under-palatine, a portly middle-aged Troxan with a bulbous nose and purple gills. "As you may know, I was honored with the title of first diplomatic legatee, and sent to the second round of talks with Republican negotiators. Nothing came of it, of course; the Senate has dropped even the pretense of debate now, and it's all threats and bluster these days." He rippled his throat gills dismissively. "It hardly alters the impression, as I mentioned to the Senatorial committee years before hostilities even *began*—"

"The curious incident," Dooku said impatiently.

The flustered under-palatine sucked in his cheeks. "I was getting to that. At the end of the session, I was approached by Senator Amidala of Naboo, who asked me to deliver something to you." With plump, nervous hands he brought out a small box, marked with the Jedi seal. "Let me assure you, we have taken every precaution here, used the most advanced scanning techniques—"

"We thought it might be a bomb," his assistant volunteered.

"Or a bug," another said.

"I still think it could be poisoned," a fourth said.

"Believe me when I say, your safety, of course, has been *uppermost* . . ."

Dooku reached for the box. He found to his surprise that his hands were shaking. Odd. He had been almost as surprised as Ventress to see himself sparing the gaunt Jedi, Jai Maruk. It had been a sudden whim, sending him back. A hook dropped for Yoda, as he had told Sidious afterward. A hook baited with the pink squirm of an old memory.

Darth Sidious had given him a curious look, then, one that passed through him like a flush of fever, a weakness inside. "Do you still *love* him?" his Master said.

Dooku had laughed and braved it out. The idea was ridiculous.

"Ridiculous?" his Master had said, in that soft, terrible voice of his. "I hardly think so." And then, his voice like honeyed poison, "A good student always loves his teacher."

There was always a risk, talking with Sidious. Sometimes the conversation would go badly, and Dooku would fail to please somehow. It was a terrible thing, failing to please his Master.

He shook his head. These were a boy's weak fears. If Yoda had truly taken his lure, he would come, and if he did—what a gift for Sidious that would be, a nine-hundred-year-old head! That wheezing old half-crippled sage was stuck in the Republic like a cork; pull him out and, with a *pop*, the dark side would come rushing through. Then his Master would see how loyal a servant Dooku truly was.

He grabbed the box. He could feel Yoda's touch still lingering on the edges like a distant echo. Vividly his mind went back to their last meeting, on Geonosis: swords drawn at last, and finally *equal*. What a bittersweet moment—to see Yoda again, and be a match, or more than a match for him . . . but not to be seen by him. No, they had gone their separate ways, and Yoda had newer Jedi to look after. Kenobi and, worse yet, young Skywalker.

Oh, yes, and wasn't everyone watching *him*. Even Darth Sidious, with a gleam in his eye, mentioned the boy as one strong in the Force. "Just a little piece in a great game," his Master had said; but a stab of jealousy had gone through Dooku when Sidious lingered over the name. *Skywalker, yes . . . The Force is strong in him.*

The same Anakin Skywalker who, he had learned, had recently killed a clone of Count Dooku of Serenno. Poor foolish clone. Another changeling, another Dooku abandoned by his parents, left to be chopped up by some upstart Jedi butcher in the name of a corrupt Republic.

Dooku rather thought that if he weren't so old and wise, he would probably hate this Anakin Skywalker. At least a little.

His flipped back the clasps on the box. Strange that his hands should still be shaking so.

The under-palatine for the Bureau of Patriotic Defense looked over his shoulder. "We studied it exhaustively," the diplomat said, flapping his gills in puzzlement, "but all our experts agree it's nothing more than a plain wax candle."

2

On the top of a dilapidated skyrise in the Temple district of Coruscant, two droids were playing dejarik in the rain. They played extremely fast, moving each piece with blinding speed and precision; their fingers fell and rose like sewing-machine needles plunging through reams of syncloth.

The two droids were built to an identical design, humanoid and tall, but there the resemblance ended, as if they had been twins separated at birth, one to live in a palace, while the other was doomed to be an outcast, scraping out a hardscrabble existence in alleyways and gutters. The first droid was immaculately painted in an ornate livery, cream with crimson piping on his limbs, the blood-and-ivory colors repeated in a formal checker on his torso. The red was somewhat light and shaded with brown, like the color of fox fur, or dried blood. The cream was tinged with yellow; the color swatch at the store where the droid had last retouched his paint had called the tint "animal teeth."

The outcast droid had long since worn down to bare metal, and never been repainted. His scratched face was gray, scuffed as if from countless years of hard service. He paused to look up into the rain. He was careful to scour himself every night, but still the rust crept into his joints and scratches, and his face was pocked where flakes and patches of metal had started to rust and been ruthlessly rubbed away.

The droids sat at the edge of the roof. The scuffed one kept his visual receptors on the game, but his richly painted partner was constantly glancing up, looking out onto the canyon between buildings, the busy slidewalks and the constant flow of fliers humming by, and, farther off, the wide entrance and towering spire of the Jedi Temple.

Of course, from this little terrace, it would be very difficult to observe much of anything happening at the Temple. At such a distance, and with the rain falling, too, it would have required the eyes of a Horansi to see a bedraggled figure come splashing up to the Temple's front doors. To resolve that figure as an angry Troxan diplomat carrying a curious-looking diplomatic pouch would have taken something far beyond biological sight: something on the order of the legendary Tau/Zeiss telescopic sniperscope—etched transparisteel or neural implant reticle available on request—whose ability to hold its zero through a full range of adjustment from X1 to X100 had never been matched in the four hundred standard years since the last T/Z production line fell silent.

The cream-and-crimson droid paused, its fingers motionless over the board. Several kilometers away, through a shifting curtain of rain, the Troxan diplomat was arguing with the young Jedi standing sentry duty at the Temple doors. The packet changed hands.

"What are you doing?" his drab, gray partner asked.

The diplomat splashed back through the rain to a waiting flier. The youngster disappeared into the Temple.

The liveried droid's fingers bent down through the holographic warriors on the circular gameboard to move a piece. "Waiting," he said.

The xeno-ethnologists of Coruscant have estimated the number of sentient species in the universe at around twenty million, give or take a standard deviation or two depending on just what *sentient* means at any given time. One might ask, for instance, if the *Bivalva contemplativa*, the so-called thinking clams of Perilix, are really "thinking" in the usual sense, or if their multigenerational narrative semaphores reflect something less like conversation and more like hive building. Still, twenty million is the usual number.

Of all of these species, an observer watching Jedi Master Maks Leem lift the hem of her robe and go hurrying through the Jedi Temple, late in the evening some thirty months after the Battle of Geonosis, might argue that it was the three-eyed, goat-headed Gran whose faces were most particularly suited to expressing *worry*. The three shaggy brows above Master Leem's anxious eyes were tensely furrowed. Her jaw was long and narrow, even by Gran standards, and when she was anxious she had a tendency to grind her teeth, a ghostly holdover from the Gran's cud-chewing ruminant past.

Master Leem was not normally of a nervous disposition. Gentle, motherly, and placidly competent, she was a great favorite of the younger acolytes, and very difficult to rattle. A Mace Windu or an Anakin Skywalker might grow restless at the Jedi's essentially defensive posture, but not so Maks Leem. The Gran were a deeply social, community-oriented folk, and she had gladly given her life in service to the ideal of *peacemaker*. What she hated was that now, by slow but seemingly relentless degrees, she and the Jedi were turning, contemptibly, into *soldiers*.

She had thought the Republic's civil war was the worst thing that could happen. Then came the slaughter on Geonosis, claiming the flower of a Jedi generation in a single day. The flash of plasma bolts, the taste of sand in one's mouth, the whine and shriek of battle droids— it seemed like a nightmare now, a confused blur of grief and pain. She had lost more than a dozen comrades, all closer to her than sisters. That had brought the war home as no distant newsvid could.

On the way back to Coruscant, Master Yoda had spoken of healing and recovery, but for Maks Leem the last thirty months had been hard, hard. For her, it was easier to face memories of the battle than to cope with the terrible *emptiness* in the Temple. Forty places set for dinner in a hall made to hold a hundred. The west block of the kitchen gardens left fallow. The rhythms of Temple life cut away for lack of time; no time for gardening now, or mending robes by hand, or games. Now it was hand-to-hand combat, small-unit tactical training, military infiltration exercises. Food made in a hurry from ingredients bought in the city, and grave-eyed children of twelve and fourteen suddenly monitoring comm trans-

missions, running courier routes, or researching battle
plans.

The children worried Leem the most. The Temple,
nearly empty of adults, felt like a school the teachers
had abandoned. Suddenly orphaned Padawans, acolytes
with too few teachers and too many responsibilities:
Maks Leem feared for them. As hard as Yoda and the
other teachers tried to instill the ancient Jedi virtues, this
generation could not help but be marked by violence. As
if they had been weaned on poisoned milk, she always
thought. For the first time since the Sith War, there
would be a generation of Jedi Knights who grew up surrounded by a Force clouded by the dark side. They were
learning to feel with hearts made too old, too hard, too
soon.

It was one of these children, the gentle, graceful boy
named Whie whom she had taken as her Padawan, who
had called her to the Temple entrance. Maks had arrived
to find the boy remaining (as always) remarkably serene,
while enduring a good deal of moist bluster from a pompous, overbearing, and furious Troxan diplomat, who
could not believe he was to be stopped at the Temple
doors by a mere boy. This purple-faced being with furiously vibrating gills claimed to have a dispatch to be delivered to Master Yoda personally.

Maks came to Whie's rescue at once, using the Force
in the way that came most naturally to her, soothing
the Troxan until his gills lay still, pink, and moist, and
seeing him off with the promise that she would personally deliver the package to Master Yoda. Whie could
have done the same—the Force was strong in him—but

Padawans were not encouraged to use their powers lightly. The boy's gifts had always been great; perhaps in consequence, he always took special care not to abuse them.

Whie handed her the packet. It was a high-security diplomatic correspondence pouch, of a type in common usage by many Trade Federation worlds. A mesh of woven meta-ceramic and computational monofilaments, the pouch was both a container and a computer, whose surface was its own display. Most of that surface was presently covered with a bristling array of letters, the same message repeated in Troxan and Basic.

BENEVOLENCE OF TROXAR

BUREAU OF DIPLOMATIC LIAISON

Incendiary Packet

MOST CONFIDENTIAL COMMUNICATION FOR:

YODA,

"Grand Master of the Jedi Order"

&

Military Attaché to the Supreme Chancellor

of the Galactic Senate

WARNING!

Listed Recipient Only!

This Diplomatic Pouch Is Actively Enabled:

Without Positive Identification

Contents Will Plasmate on Packet Rupture!

The bag seethed in her hand, not unpleasantly, as computational monofilaments shifted and flowed under her touch until they cradled the palps of her fingers. It was rather like standing on the shore at the seaside and feeling the outflow of each wave pulling the sand gradually out from under her feet. A brief topographic map of her fingerprints appeared on the packet's surface. Another part of the packet cleared to a small mirror surface, with the ideogram for "eye" marked neatly above it. Master Leem blinked at her own reflection, then blinked again as the packet flashed briefly with light.

   *Gill Pattern: **Not Applicable**
   Fingerprint Identification: **Negative**
   Retinal Scan: **Negative**

Current Bearer cannot be identified as the intended recipient of this Bureau of Diplomatic Liaison Incendiary Packet.

WARNING!
CONTENTS WILL PLASMATE ON PACKET RUPTURE!

Maks and her Padawan exchanged looks. "Better not drop it," the boy said, deadpan. Maks rolled her eyes—another remarkably expressive gesture among the three-eyed Gran—and padded back into the Temple, looking for Master Yoda.

She found him in the Room of a Thousand Fountains. He was perched on a boulder of black limestone that jutted out of a small pond. Approaching him from behind, she was shocked by how small he looked, sitting there, dumpy and awkward in his shapeless robe. Like a sad swamp toad, she thought. When she was younger, she would have suppressed the thought at once, shocked at herself. With age she had learned to watch her thoughts come and go with detachment, and some amusement, too. What an odd, quirky, unruly thing a mind was, after all! Even a Jedi mind. And really, with that great round green head and those drooping ears, a sad swamp toad was exactly right.

Then he turned around and smiled at her, and even beneath Yoda's weariness and his worry she felt the deep springs of joy within him, a thousand fountains of it, inexhaustible, as if he were a crack in the mantle of the world, and the living Force itself bubbled through him.

The shaggy brows over Master Leem's three warm brown eyes relaxed, and her teeth stopped grinding. She picked her way down to the edge of the pond, gently brushing aside long fronds of fern. The sound of water was all around, rushing over pebbled streambeds, bubbling up through the rock, or dripping into small clear pools: and always from the far side of the enormous chamber, the distant roar of the waterfall. "I thought I would find you here, Master."

"Like the outdoor gardens better, do I."

"I know. But they aren't nearly so close to the Jedi Council Chamber as this room up here."

He smiled tiredly. "Truth, speak you." His ears, which had pricked up at the sight of her, drooped again. "Meetings and more meetings. Sad talk and serious, war, war, and always war." He waved his three-fingered hand around the Room of a Thousand Fountains. "A place of great beauty, this is. And yet . . . we made it. Tired I am of all this . . . *making*. Where is the time for *being*, Maks Leem?"

"Somewhere that isn't Coruscant," she answered frankly.

The old Master nodded forcefully. "Truer than you know, speak you. Sometimes I think the Temple we should move far away from Coruscant."

Master Leem's mouth dropped open. She had only been joking, but Yoda seemed completely serious. "Only on a planet such as Coruscant, with no forests left, no mountains unleveled, no streams left to run their own course, could the Force have become so clouded."

Maks blinked all three eyes. "Where would you move the Temple?"

Yoda shrugged. "Somewhere wet. Somewhere wild. Not so much *making*. Not so many machines." He straightened and snuffed in a deep breath. "Good! Decided it is! We will move the Temple at once. You shall be in charge. Find a new home and report to me tomorrow!"

Master Leem's teeth began to grind at double speed.

"You must be joking! We can't possibly do such a thing now, in the middle of a war! Who could we find to—" She stopped, and the three eyes that had been so very wide went narrow. "You're teasing me."

The old gnome snickered.

She had half a mind to pitch the Troxan packet at Yoda's smirking face but, remembering all the scary legal warnings on the side, she held her hand. "I promised I would give this to you."

Yoda scrunched up his nose in distaste. He gathered the hem of his robe up above his wizened knees and slid off the rock with a splash. It was an indoor garden near the top of a mighty artificial spire, after all, and the water in the pond was only shin-deep. He stumped to the shore and took the packet. Wrinkles climbed up his forehead and his ears twirled in surprise as the Incendiary Packet took its fingerprint scan.

Fingerprint Identification: **Positive**

The reflective mirror appeared on the packet's surface. Yoda stuck his tongue out at it and made a face.

Retinal Scan: **Inconclusive**
Please present intended recipient's face or equivalent bodily communication interface to the reflective surface.

"Machines," Yoda grumbled, but he stared glumly into the packet.

Retinal Scan: **Positive**

Current bearer has been identified as the intended recipient of this Bureau of Diplomatic Liaison Incendiary Packet. Destruct device disabled.

A microperforation appeared around the edges of the packet and then the pouch peeled back, revealing the charred and battered handle of a Jedi lightsaber. Yoda's stubby green fingers curled lightly around it, and he sighed.

"Master?"

"Jang Li-Li," he said. "All that is left of her, this is."

Water dripped and whispered all around them in the garden.

"Thinking of the dead, have I been."

"The list grows longer every day," Master Leem said bitterly. She was thinking of the last time she had seen Jang Li-Li. They had shared dinner duty not long before she left, and the two of them had gone down to the gardens to pick vegetables for the evening meal. She remembered sitting on an upturned bucket, Jang making a droll face at her and asking if Maks thought using the Force to shell Antarian peas was an abuse of power. Laugh lines around her almond eyes.

Yoda's face, dark in reflection, looked up at him from out of the pond. "Some believe it possible to enter completely into the Force after death."

"Surely we all do, Master."

"Ah—but perhaps one can remain unique and individual. Can remain oneself."

"You are thinking of Jang Li-Li," the Gran said with a sad smile. "I would love to believe she is safe and free and laughing still, somewhere in the Force. I would love to, but I cannot. Every people longs for the hope of something after death. These hands and eyes have been knit into a shape by the universe, will hold it for a few score years, then lose it again. That must be enough. To enter more completely into the Force: one would dissolve, like honey mixed into hot stimcaf."

Yoda shrugged, looking down at poor Jang Li-Li's lightsaber handle. "Perhaps you are right. But I wonder . . ." He picked a pebble from a crack in the rock on which he was sitting. "If I drop this pebble into the pond, what will happen?"

"It will sink."

"And after?"

"Well," Master Leem said, feeling out of her depth. "There will be ripples, I suppose, spreading out."

Yoda's ears perked up. "Yes! The pebble strikes the water, and a wave carries out until . . . ?"

"It reaches the shore."

"Just so. But is the water in the wave where the pebble drops the same as the water in the wave that touches the shore?"

"No . . ."

"And yet the wave is the same wave?"

"You think we can become . . . *waves* in the Force, holding our shape?"

Yoda shrugged. "Speak of this once, Qui-Gon did."

"I miss him," Maks Leem said sadly. She had never really approved of Qui-Gon Jinn; he was too quick to rebel against the Order, too ready to oppose his solitary will to the good of the group. And yet he had been a brave and noble man, and kind to her when she was young.

She turned her attention back to Jang's broken lightsaber. "Who sent it, Master?"

Maks wasn't sure Yoda had heard her question. For a long time he was silent, stroking the handle with his blunt old fingers. "Have you now a Padawan, Master Leem?" She nodded. "Your second?"

"Third. Rees Alrix was my first. She is fighting with the clone troops at Sullust. My second . . . my second was Eremin Tarn," she said reluctantly. Eremin had become a follower of Jeisel, one of the more outspoken of the dissident Jedi, who believed the Republic had lost the moral authority to rule. Eremin had always resisted authority—including hers when she was his Master—but he was fiercely principled. Intellectually, Maks could understand his decision to withdraw from the Order, but it had torn a hole in her Gran heart to see her very own Padawan, one she had taught from thirteen years to the status of a full Jedi Knight, deliberately cut himself out of the Order.

As if reading her mind, Yoda asked, "Does he fill that empty place in your heart, this new Padawan?"

Maks flushed and looked away.

"No shame in this, there is. Think you the relationship between Master and Padawan is only to help *them*?" Yoda cocked his head to one side and looked at her with ancient, knowing eyes. "Oh, this is what we let them believe, yes! But when the day comes that even old Yoda does not learn something from his students—then truly, he shall be a teacher no more." He reached up to give her hand a little squeeze, his three fingers around her six. "No greater gift there is, than a generous heart."

Tears came to Maks Leem, and she let them come. "Attachment is not the Jedi way, I know. But . . ."

Yoda gave her hand another squeeze, and then returned to considering the handle of the lightsaber. For a moment she saw his finger stop on a little piece of metal, surprisingly clean and fresh looking, as if it had escaped the blast or been added afterward. Yoda frowned. "This Padawan of yours—ready for the wide galaxy, is he?"

"Whie? No! And yes," she said. "He is young. They are all so young. But if any of them are ready, he is. The Force is strong in him. Not so strong as in young Skywalker, but in the next level down: and between you and me, he carries it better than Anakin ever has. Such calm. Such serenity and poise; truly it is incredible in one so young."

"Truly."

Something in Yoda's voice caught her ear. "You think it impossible?"

"I think he wishes to please you very much," the old Master said carefully.

Before she could ask him what he meant, a gong sounded the hour. "Ah—my class!" Maks said, slapping one hand against her forehead horns. "I am supposed to be teaching hyperspace navigation in Tower Three."

Yoda bugged out his eyes and made little shooing motions with his hands. "Then engage your hyperdrive you must!" He watched, chuckling, as she ran from the chamber with the hem of her robe flapping excitedly around her hairy ankles and her boots thudding into the distance.

When he was sure he was alone, he tabbed the power switch on what had once been Jang Li-Li's lightsaber. As he had suspected, the weapon had been modified; instead of Jang's blue blade humming to life, a hologram appeared: Count Dooku, ten centimeters tall, as if standing on the lightsaber handle. He looked old . . . much older than he had on Geonosis. Careworn. He was sitting at an elegantly appointed desk. There was a window behind him spattered with rain; behind it, a cheerless gray sky. Before him on the desk lay the candle Yoda had sent.

"We should talk," Dooku said. He did not look at the holocam, as if, even across weeks of time and the endless black chasm of space, he was afraid to look his old Master in the eye.

"There is a cloud around me now. Around all of us. I felt it growing in the Republic years ago. I fled it then, and tried to bring the Order with me. You wouldn't come. Cowardice, I thought then. Or corruption. Now . . ." He rubbed his face wearily. "Now I don't know. Perhaps you were right. Perhaps the Temple was the only lantern to keep the darkness at bay, and I was wrong to step outside, into the night. Or perhaps the darkness was inside me all the time."

For the first time he looked up. His eyes were steady, except for a faint flicker of pure anguish, like the sound of weeping from a locked room. "It's like a sickness," he whispered. "A fever in the blood. War everywhere. Cruelty. Killing, and some in my name. Blood like rain. I feel it all the time, the cries of the dying in the Force, beating in me like a vein about to burst." He gathered himself;

shrugged; went on. "I have come to the end of myself. I don't know what is right anymore. I am tired, Master. So tired. And like any old man, as the end nears, I long to go home."

The tiny hologrammic Dooku touched the candle Yoda had sent, turning it over in his old fingers. "I want to meet. But nobody outside the Temple must know. I am always watched, and you are betrayed more profoundly than you guess, Master. Come to me; Jai will show you the way. We will talk. I promise nothing more. I cannot think you corrupt, but even you, Master, are snared beyond your understanding. If word reaches my allies of your coming, they will stop at nothing to kill you. If they guess *why* you are coming, they will stop at nothing to destroy me."

His eyes came fully back into the present: shrewd and practical. "I would be disappointed if you took my invitation as a tactical opportunity. If I see even the slightest sign of new forces deploying in the direction of the Hydian Way, I will abandon my current location, and carry the war forward until droid battle cruisers burn the life out of Coruscant with a rain of plasma fire. Bring none but Jedi with you." He gave a sad, crooked smile. "There are some things that should be kept inside the family . . ."

Count Dooku of Serenno, warlord of a mighty army, among the richest beings in the galaxy, legendary swordmaster, former student, notorious traitor, lost son, flickered in front of Yoda's ancient eyes, and went out.

Yoda tabbed the lightsaber's power switch and watched the recording again, three more times. He clambered back onto his favorite rock, deep in thought. Somewhere above him, in his private quarters, messages from the Republic would be piling up: dispatches from military commanders, questions from far-flung Jedi about their various assignments and commands, perhaps a summons from the Senate or a meeting request from the Chancellor's office. He had come to know the weight of all those anxious eyes far too well. Today they would have to wait. Today, Yoda needed Yoda's wisdom more than anyone else.

He breathed deeply, trying to clear his mind in meditation, letting thoughts rise up before him.

Dooku's hands on that candle, the hum of emotion like a current, making his fingertips tremble.

Jai Maruk giving his clipped report in the Council Chamber with the charred welt of a lightsaber burn on his gaunt cheek.

Farther back, he and Dooku in a cave on Geonosis. The hiss and flash of humming lightsabers, darkly beautiful, like dragonflies, and Dooku still a boy of twenty, not the old man whispering on top of poor dead Jang's blade. Yoda's ears slowly drooped as he sank deeper into the Force, time melting out beneath his mind like rotten ice, setting past and present free to mix together. That proud boy in the garden sixty years ago who murmured, *Every Jedi is a child his parents decided they could live without.*

Little Jang Li-Li, eight years old, misting the orchids in the Room of a Thousand Fountains. A bright day, sunlight pouring through transparisteel panels, Li-Li making puffs of water with her mister and shrieking with laughter as every little cloud she made broke a sunbeam into colors, fugitive bars of red and violet and green. *Master, Master, I'm making rainbows!* Those colors hadn't come to mean military signals, yet, or starship navigating lights, or lightsaber blades. Just a girl making rainbows.

Dooku newly brought from Serenno, grave-eyed, old enough to know his mother had given him away. Old enough to learn one can always be betrayed.

Water bubbled and seeped and trickled around Yoda, time past and time present, liquid and elusive: and then Qui-Gon was beside him. It would be wrong to say the dead Jedi *came* to Yoda; truer would it be to say Qui-Gon had always been there, in the still point around which time wheels. Qui-Gon waiting for Yoda to find his way down the untaken path and pass through the unopened door into the garden at the still heart of things.

Yoda opened his eyes. The feel of Qui-Gon in the Force was the same as always: stern and energetic, like a hank of good rope pulled into a fine sailor's knot. *Become a wave he has,* Yoda thought. *A wave without a shore.*

Yoda tapped the handle of Jang Li-Li's lightsaber. "You saw?"

I did.

"Cunning, it is. If I move to see him, I must keep any Republic ships away from the Hydian Way. Deny the chance of peace utterly, must I, or else give him extra months unharried in his lair."

He is a fencer, Qui-Gon agreed. *Leverage, position, advantage—they are as natural to him as breathing.*

"My old student—your old Master, Qui-Gon. The truth he is telling?"

He thinks he is lying.

Yoda's ears pricked up. "Hmm?"

He thinks he is lying.

A slow smile began to light Yoda's round face. "Yessssss!" he murmured.

A moment later Yoda felt a vibration in the Force, a ripple rolling out from the student dormitories far below, like the faint sound of distant thunder. Qui-Gon shivered and was gone, as if the Force were a pool of water and he a reflection on its surface, broken up by the splash of whatever disturbance had just struck the Temple.

They didn't happen often, the true dreams. To be honest, Whie tried not to have them.

They weren't like regular nightmares at all. He had plenty of those, too—almost every night for the last year. Rambling, confused affairs, and in them he was always failing: there was something he should have done, a class he was supposed to attend, a package he had meant to deliver. Often he was pursued. Sometimes he was naked. Most of these dreams ended with him clinging desperately to a high place and then falling, falling: from the spires of the Temple, from a bridge, from a starship, down a flight of steps, from a tree in the gardens. Always falling, and down below, waiting, a murmuring crowd of the disappointed, the ones he had failed.

The true dreams were different. In those he came unstuck in time. He would go to sleep on his dormitory cot, and then wake up with a jerk in the future, as if he had fallen through a trapdoor and landed in his own body.

Once, going to sleep when he was eight, he had woken to find himself eleven years old and building his first lightsaber. He worked on it for more than an hour before another boy entered the workshop and said, "Rhad Tarn is dead!" He tried to ask, "Who is Rhad Tarn?" but heard his own voice say something quite different. Only then did he realize that he wasn't the Whie building the lightsaber—he was just riding around in his head like a ghost.

There was nothing—*nothing*—worse than the horrible feeling of being buried alive in his own body. Sometimes the panic was so intense he woke himself up, but other times it would be hours before he jerked upright in bed, weeping and gasping with relief at the sound of an alarm, or the touch of a friend's hand.

This time he fell through the true dream and landed in a strange room, richly furnished. He was standing on a deep, soft rug embroidered with a tangled woodland pattern, thorn-trees and thorn-vines and venomous green moss; in the shadows, the glinting eyes of evil birds. The rug was spattered with blood. From the burning pain in his left arm and the slow dull ache in his ribs, he guessed some of the blood was his.

An ancient chrono, hanging in a metal case crafted to look like a tangle of thorns and brambles, ticked dully in the corner of the room. The beats seemed slow and erratic, like the beating of a dying heart.

There were at least two other people in the room. One was a bald woman with stripes painted on her skull and lips the color of fresh blood. He could smell the dark side on her like wood smoke, like something burning on a wet night. She scared him.

The other was another Jedi apprentice, a red-haired girl named Scout. In waking life she was a year older than Whie, bossy and loud, and had never paid much attention to him. In the dream, blood was dripping down her face from a cut on her scalp. She was staring at him. "Kiss her," the bald woman whispered. Voice soft. Red teardrops crept from the girl's cuts, spilling by her mouth. Blood trickled in a red line down her throat to soak into the lapels of her tunic just above the tops of her small breasts. "Kiss her, Whie."

The dreaming Whie recoiled.

The waking Whie wanted to kiss her. He was angry and sick and ashamed, but he wanted to.

Blood dripped. The chrono ticked. The bald woman grinned at him. "Welcome home," she said.

"Whie!"

"Hnn?"

"Wake up! Whie, wake up. It's me, Master Leem." Her kind face was looming over him in the darkened dormitory, all three eyes worried. "We felt a disturbance in the Force."

He blinked, gasping, trying to hold on to a *now* that still felt slippery as a bar of wet soap.

The boys who roomed in the dorm with him were clustering around his bed. "Were you having one of those dreams again?"

He thought of the girl, Scout—another Jedi apprentice!—the trickle of blood along her throat. His guilty desire.

Master Leem laid her six fingers on his hand. "Whie?"

"It was nothing," he managed to croak. "Just a bad dream, that's all."

The boys around the bed began to drift off, disappointed and disbelieving. They were still young enough to want to see miracles. They thought having visions would be *fun*. They couldn't understand how terrible it was, to see a moment loom out of the future like a pillar suddenly revealed on a foggy road, and no way to keep from hitting it.

Who had the bald woman in the vision been? She stank of the dark side, and yet he hadn't been fighting her. Would some strange fate make them allies? And the girl, Scout—how would blood come to spill red onto her red lips, and why would she—someday— look at him with such intensity? Perhaps Scout would become an ally of the evil bald woman. Perhaps she would give in to her desires, her anger, her lust. Maybe she would try to trap him, too; seduce him; deliver him to the dark side.

"Whie?" Master Leem said.

He gave her hand a reassuring squeeze, trying to sound more normal. "Just a bad dream," he said again. He kept insisting, politely and gratefully, that he would be fine, just fine, until she finally left the dorm.

Another interesting thing about the true dreams: they had haunted Whie like a curse all his life, but this was the first time he had ever woken into a place other than the Jedi Temple. And never once, in a score of visions, had he found himself in a body much older than the one he had now.

His death was coming. Soon.

3

The white walls of the Combat Training Chamber in the Jedi Temple had been newly cleaned, the white floor scrubbed, and new white mats laid down in preparation for the day's tournament. Nervous Jedi apprentices in sparkling white tunics prepared for the upcoming test, each according to personality. In her mind, Jedi apprentice Tallisibeth Enwandung-Esterhazy—nicknamed Scout—had them loosely grouped into four categories:

Talkers, who clumped together, murmuring in low voices to distract themselves from the mounting tension;

Warm-ups, who stretched their muscles, or ligaments, or pulse-fibers; cracked various numbers of knuckles; and jogged, or hopped, or spun in place, according to their species-specific physiological needs;

Meditators, whose usual approach to sinking into the deeper truth of the Force, in Tallisibeth's opinion, mostly involved keeping their eyes shut and assuming an affected expression of smug serenity; and

Prowlers.

Scout was a prowler.

Probably she should try a little meditation. Certainly her history suggested that getting too tense and excited was her worst problem. At the last tournament, back before the devastation on Honoghr and the Rendili Fleet Crisis, she had gone out in the first round, losing to a twelve-year-old boy she nearly always beat when they sparred. The defeat had been all the more humiliating because the boy was nursing *a broken leg* at the time, and had been fighting in a brace.

She stalked past a little clump of Talkers, face flushing painfully at the memory. "Hey, Scout," one of them said, but she ignored him. No time for talking today. Today was all business.

Anyone with the brains of a Sevarcosan prickle-pig could figure she was out of chances to screw up. The fact was, the Force was weak in Tallisibeth Enwandung-Esterhazy. Oh, it was there, all right. Strong enough to make an impression on Jedi talent scouts when she was a toddler—although from something one of the Masters once said, her family had been dirt-poor, and her parents had begged the Jedi to take their daughter away from a life of grinding poverty. She was haunted by the idea that her mother and father, her brothers and sisters—if she had them—were all trapped in the slums of Vorzyd V while she alone had escaped. She alone had been given this one incredible chance to make good. It would be unbearable to fail.

But somehow, as she grew in body, she had not grown in the ways of the Force. She did have a gift for anticipation. When she was sparring, for instance, and open to the Force, she would have flashes where she knew what opponents were going to do next even before they knew it themselves. Her habit of scoping out a situation and reading it just a little faster than everyone else had earned her her nickname. But even that could fade out on her if she was flustered or upset, and as for the rest of the Jedi's traditional abilities with the Force . . .

Some days she could pull a glass off a counter with her mind and bring it to her hand . . . but more often it would slip on the way and smash on the floor. Or explode as if squeezed. Or go rocketing into the ceiling and fall in a shower of blue milk and splinters. You didn't have to be a Mrlssi to catch the way the Jedi Masters talked together in low voices when she went by. You didn't have to be very smart—and Scout *was* smart—to notice how the other apprentices rolled their eyes at her, or laughed, or, worst of all, covered up for her mistakes.

By the time she turned thirteen, she had all but given up hope of becoming a Jedi. When Master Yoda summoned her for a private talk in the Room of a Thousand Fountains, she had dragged up there with feet of permacrete, stomach churning, waiting to hear which branch of the Agricultural Corps they would assign her to. "Worthy work," people always said. "Honorable work." The hypocrisy of it made her furious. As if it weren't humiliating enough to fail at the only thing she'd ever wanted, they had to make it worse by pretending a hoe was the same as a lightsaber, and the mud of a potato field was as exciting as the dust of a hundred planets beneath her feet.

By the time she'd entered the room, her face had been slimy with tears and there was a big wet splotch on the arm of her tunic where she kept wiping her sniveling nose. Master Yoda had looked at her, his wizened, round face wrinkled with concern, and asked why she was weeping. "Only Jedi have to strive for nonattachment," she'd said defiantly between snuffles. "Farmers can cry all they want."

Then he'd told her that Chankar Kim had asked that she be her new Padawan, and Tallisibeth Enwandung-Esterhazy, known as Scout to her friends, was left with what she later decided was the classic post-Yoda feeling: breathtakingly stupid, heartbreakingly happy.

Three months later Chankar Kim was dead.

If her whole life hadn't been a struggle, Scout thought, that would have broken her. It was sheer will that kept her going, sheer bloody-minded un-Jedi-like rage, against the Trade Federation, against Fate, against herself. "I'll let you come along on the next mission," Master Kim had said with a smile. "Let's polish off a few more of those rough edges first. You can come next time, I promise." Only here was the joke: Chankar Kim bled her life out on a distant planet, and *next time* was never going to come.

And so Scout was an orphan, an aging apprentice with no Master anymore. The only way she could become a Jedi was to be made a Padawan, taken on missions, given a chance to prove that she could make a difference. And the only way to do that was to gain the other Jedi's trust.

She drove herself to the top of class after class, practiced joint locks on herself until her wrists were numb, went sleepless late into every night until star maps danced before her aching eyes. She trained harder than she had ever trained in her life—astrocartography, unarmed combat, hyperdrive math, comm installation tech, lightsaber technique. She was slightly built, and her girl's body was agonizingly slow to gain muscle, but she worked out until the sweat ran in rivers down her back because she *had* to, she had to: she couldn't rely on the little cheat the rest of them had, the Force.

And still every day there was the torment of classes in using the Force; Scout grouped together with the eight- and nine-year-olds, looming among them, an awkward bumbling giant: and every day, as hard as she tried to fight back despair, her footsteps came more heavily, as if she were already slogging through the muddy potato fields that were her destiny.

"Hey, Scout—relax!" The voice pulled Scout's attention back to the here and now: combat chamber. Tournament day. It was Lena Missa calling, a good-natured Chagrian girl Scout's age. "You're wound so tight I can hear you squeak when you walk."

Easy for Lena to say—she, too, had lost a Master in the last year, but Lena was witty and well liked, and her touch with the Force was deft; Jedi Masters had been lining up for the right to choose her as their Padawan as soon as an appropriate grieving period was up. Scout forced a tight smile. "Thanks. I'll try," she said.

Lena leaned in confidentially, so her forked tongue flickered between her blue lips, and her soft lower horns swung forward. "Scout, don't worry. You're really good at combat. Just relax and use—" She hesitated. "Just trust your ability."

Scout forced a smile. "You're only being nice to me in case you end up in my bracket."

Lena grinned back. "You bet. My elbow is still tingling from that arm bar you put on me last week. You wouldn't hurt a friend, right?"

There were thirty-two apprentices entered in the tournament. An apprentice had to be at least ten years old to enter, with the majority of entrants in the eleven- to twelve-year-old range. The younger kids weren't quite ready to encounter the big kids in full-contact sparring, and the older ones who had made Padawan were mostly busy with their duties. Lena hadn't originally meant to enter, but they had needed one more to make an even number.

The apprentices had been given the choice of a layered tournament or a sudden-death elimination format, in which the first loss meant you were done. Scout had been strongly in favor of single eliminations. In the real world, she had argued, no enemy offered to go best three matches out of five. Privately, she also felt the win-or-go-home format would play to her strengths. As good as she was at the physical elements of combat, the Force was weaker in her than in anyone else in the field. For her to do well, she would need to out-think her opponents. Trickery was usually most effective the first time you tried it; the fewer matches she had to fight, the better her chances of winning.

Master Iron Hand adjusted her tunic and picked her way to the center of the combat room, passing the Talkers and the Warm-ups sprinkled around the white chamber. *We look like so many weevils wiggling in a box of flour,* Scout thought. Where the Master passed, the apprentices fell silent. In the center of the room she announced that the first two rounds of the tournament would take place here, but when they were down to the Round of Eight, the remaining matches would be moved to less artificial environments. Students looked at one another, eyebrows raised. "You wanted lifelike," Iron Hand said dryly. "We decided you should get it. Now— to determine the first-round matches." She consulted her datapad. "Atresh Pikil and Gumbrak Hoxz."

Atresh, a lithe black-skinned girl of twelve, stepped forward, along with Gumbrak, a thirteen-year-old Mon Calamari boy whose salmon-colored skin was already speckled with excitement. The Mon Calamari was stronger, but he had grown a lot in the last year and still had a tendency to stumble over his webbed feet. If Atresh used her quickness to keep dancing out of range until he tripped, she should be fine. Of course, Atresh wasn't a very calculating fighter. Like many of the more gifted apprentices, she tended to trust to her own strengths instead of doing the kind of detailed preliminary observations that had earned Scout her nickname. The other kids used to laugh at her relentless calculation, but then, they could afford to. Scout needed to do her homework. She had spent many hours over the last six weeks watching the other combatants spar, sometimes openly and sometimes in secret. She had a plan for tackling each of them, and, if not confident, she was at least *prepared*.

"Flerp, Zrim," Master Xan called. "Page, Gilp. Horororibb, Boofer."

Scout wondered if the matches had been assigned by computer simulations designed to find the most even contests, or by some other criteria known only by the Masters, designed to test each student's weaknesses.

"Chizzik, Enwandung-Esterhazy."

Scout's heart sank. Pax Chizzik was an eleven-year-old boy of enormous spirit and charm. As a fighter he was strong in the Force, smart, a little chunky, and without the best footwork, but with exceptionally quick wrists. He had a very fast parry, and most kids his age with that gift scored their points on the counterattack, but Pax was also imaginative on the attack, with the hand speed and creativity to launch complex and rather beautiful feint-and-cut sequences. High-spirited and good-natured, he was a natural leader, born to play a dashing prince in some romantic epic of the last age. Everybody liked Pax. Scout liked him enough that she had taken time out of her relentless study to help him practice the Twelve Intermediate Knots when he was having trouble in Master Bear's Climbing and Ropework class. She had several ideas for how to beat him in the tournament, but some of them weren't very nice things to do to a kid, and she had really been hoping she wouldn't have to face him.

Which is probably why they'd been paired, she thought sourly. She shot a suspicious glance at Iron Hand. The Master met her eyes blandly and went on with her list.

The matches were open combat, no holds barred, with sparring to continue until one person surrendered by tapping the floor three times or took three burns from the training lightsabers, which were dialed to their lowest power settings. Even at low power a cut from a training lightsaber was no joke. The touch of the blade was shockingly painful, a searing kiss that made one's muscles jerk and one's nerves howl, and it left a red welt that took days to heal. Scout knew because every day for the last three weeks she had gone to a private spot in the unused kitchen gardens and touched herself on the flank or shoulder or leg with her own lightsaber at low power. Pain, as Master Iron Hand was fond of pointing out, was extremely distracting, and Scout, knowing she was likely to get hit, was determined not to let the pain make her lose focus.

She couldn't afford to lose.

The first matches began. Scout tried to pay attention, watching for any obvious weaknesses in case she met the winner in a later round, but the cramping anxiety in her stomach made it hard to focus, and after a couple of bouts she joined the ranks of the Meditators, thinking only of her breath, of silence, of the deep calm of blood washing through her body like a hidden tide. She could feel the Force there, too, filling the room like a fat electric charge. Twice it jumped like a spark from one fighter to another, leaving the victor and the vanquished both blinking as if struck by lightning. Scout didn't even try to open herself to it. The Force was not an ally she could trust, not when so much depended on this.

Her lips were dry and there was a bitter, metallic taste in her mouth. *Get a grip,* she told herself. *Come on, Scout. Breathe in. Breathe out. Breathe in. Breathe out.*

Suddenly it was time. Her palms were sweaty and her legs felt like jelly underneath her as she walked into the center of the chamber. Her lightsaber handle dangled from a loop on her tunic, bumping against a welt on her

thigh. She went through the opening rituals, bowing to
Master Xan and presenting her lightsaber for inspection. The Master checked the power settings and handed
it back to her. Pax bowed deeply in his turn, then presented his weapon with a theatrical flourish. As Iron
Hand looked it over, he shot a merry glance at Scout and
tipped her the slightest wink. It was impossible not to
smile. *I'm glad it's you,* he mouthed.

They reclipped their weapons, parted, faced one another, and bowed. "May the Force be with you," Pax
said, and she knew he meant it.

The murmur of conversation in the chamber died away
as Iron Hand held up a small red handkerchief. Now
that the horrible waiting was over, Scout was calmer.
She felt her attention relax and grow broad, seeping into
the whole room. Her breathing slowed down, and she
was aware of everyone in the room, even the ones standing behind her back. At the back of the room a door
opened, and she felt the presence of Master Yoda, glowing like a lamp.

Master Xan let the red cloth slip between her fingers.
Down it fell, fluttering, dipping, ever slower as time
stretched out for Scout and Pax, until at last, gentle as a
snowflake, the first edge touched the floor.

Two lightsabers blazed to life; clashed; whirled; clashed
again; held motionless, humming and sizzling in the middle of the room. Pax laughed, and Scout could feel herself smiling back. She felt a little ashamed of all her
scheming. It was hard not to wish Pax well.

I could let him win.

Scout blinked, turning over this new idea. She could

throw the match. If she made it just obvious enough that she had "let" him win, it would imply that she *could* have beaten him, if she really wanted to. It wouldn't be as if she'd actually *lost*.

I could let him win.

Relief flooded through her. Pax would advance to the next round, enjoying himself hugely, and for the first time in six weeks Scout would be able to stop worrying about this tournament and join in the celebration of his victory.

Pax cut a little flourish in the air with the humming green blade of his lightsaber. "Ready, Scout?" he said, and he let his tip drop just a little, as if inviting her in.

I should let him win.

The humming silence was broken by a small horking noise from the corner of the room: Master Yoda's testy snuffle.

Scout blinked again, as if waking from a dream. "By the black stars," she whispered. "You almost had me."

Pax had been using the Force on her.

She shook her head to clear out the cobwebs. Pax was no sly manipulator—he probably wasn't even aware of what he was doing. But make no mistake, he *willed* people to like him. Always had.

Scout laughed and made a mystical pass with her fingers. "This is not the victory you were seeking." Pax looked at her, baffled. "Yeah, I'm ready," she said. Then she attacked.

She ran in fast on a slant, testing his footwork. She got in with a bind that locked their blades together and let her use her size and weight to shove him hard. He stumbled backward, and she tried to drive home her advantage. He let his body go loose and tumbled backward, his blade slipping out of her bind and slashing up at her neck. She barely managed an awkward parry. It wrecked her balance and she pitched forward over his tumbling body. She somersaulted over him, hit the floor with a shoulder roll, and bounced to her feet, whipping her lightsaber around in a high parry that caught his blade in a shower of sparks.

Oh, boy. That was too close.

He fell back en garde, grinning hugely. Clearly this was the best fun he'd had in ages. It was only a game to him, of course. Nobody was ever going to send Pax Chizzik to the Agricultural Corps. No, twenty years from now they'd all be reading breathless accounts of his daring deeds as a Jedi Knight. Written by love-smitten journalists, no doubt.

It was enough to make her want to spit.

He attacked.

Usually they were evenly matched, but Pax was clearly feeling the Force today. His attack was long and fluid, a series of feints and cuts that came blindingly fast, each disguised as the other, so the real attacks melted in and out of the fake ones. Scout parried the first three with increasing difficulty, gave ground, felt herself becoming lost in the swirls of humming light, and finally broke back in full flight, using her speed to plain run away until she could escape the maze of humming green light he had almost trapped her in.

Another pause.

They stood five paces apart. Scout was breathing hard. Glancing down, she saw a char mark on her tunic where his blade had come too close. The smell of burned cloth tickled the back of her throat.

Pax looked down at his own saber, wide-eyed. "Did you recognize it, Scout?"

"What?"

"The Mrlssi half-hitch. The knot you taught me. I was feeling for you with the Force, you know, the way they teach us, and suddenly it was like I was making the Half-Hitch around you, but all in light."

Murmurs throughout the room, and scattered clapping.

So much for trying to beat him straight up, Scout thought grimly. *Time for Plan B.*

Pax looked up at her in wonder. "I've never done anything like that before," he said, delighted. And he stepped toward her with renewed confidence, eager to dissolve once more into the calm fury of the Force.

Scout dropped her lightsaber on the ground.

Pax stopped, puzzled. Scout held out her hands, palm up, and bowed.

Understanding dawned. Pax clipped his lightsaber to his belt and returned her bow respectfully. Now that the combat fire was draining from him, Scout could tell he was anxious that she not lose face. "Well fought," he said. And then, taking a step nearer, he whispered, "This isn't going to mean they send you to the corps, is it?"

Scout tried to smile reassuringly, and held out her hand to shake. "Don't worry about me," she said soothingly, as his hand entered hers. "I'll be—"

In the middle of her sentence, as soon as his grasp was in hers, she flipped it over into a wrist lock. Pax blinked in surprise, then went quickly to his knees as Scout upped the pressure.

"Oh, man," he breathed. "You got me." And with his other hand he tapped three times on the floor.

Scout instantly let him out of the wrist lock. "Sorry!" she said.

Hanna Ding, an Arkanian apprentice Scout's age, shouldered past her to get to Pax. "That was ill bred," she said. At the best of times, Hanna had more than her share of Arkanian hauteur, and now a single glance with her milky white eyes made it clear that, as little as she had ever expected from Scout, she had expected more than this.

Master Iron Hand approached Pax. "Are you all right, Chizzik?"

"My pride is a little bruised," he said ruefully, shaking the tingles out of his right hand, "but otherwise I'm fine."

"Of course you'll disqualify Enwandung-Esterhazy," Hanna said.

"With all due respect," Scout ground out, forcing herself to meet Master Xan's eye, "the conditions of the match were plainly laid out."

"Combat to continue until one competitor surrenders, or receives three cuts," Pax said. "It's not Scout's fault I was dumb enough to forget the rules. She tricked me fair and square."

"I see no reason to overturn the result of the match," Master Xan said, and she walked back to the center of the room.

Hanna Ding watched her go. "Well done, Scout. You

proved you can beat up little boys, as long as you are allowed to cheat." She turned her milky eyes on Scout. "How proud you must be."

Somehow Scout wasn't surprised to find she would be sparring with Hanna in the second round. It was so very much the Jedi style to throw the two of them together and see who would be able to retain her composure the best. Hanna's proud, pale features took on an expression of distinct pleasure when she heard Scout's name called after her own. "I am looking forward to this," she said.

I bet you are, Scout thought grimly. Realistically, Hanna was much the better fighter. Physically, Scout gave herself a very slight advantage in speed and strength, thanks to her extra training. Technically they were comparable— Hanna possibly stronger with the lightsaber, while Scout was definitely ahead in the unarmed techniques that Master Iron Hand taught. But when the Force was added into the equation, the contest wasn't even close. Hanna was fourteen, and her use of the Force was on an entirely different level from Pax Chizzik's: polished, strong, and supple. Scout watched her warm up across the chamber, leaping ridiculous distances into the air and then drifting down, light as a snowflake falling.

"Good luck," Lena murmured, watching Hanna warm up.

Scout grunted. "On the bright side, at least I'll be fighting someone I really want to hit."

It was time for their bout. They bowed to Master Xan, presented weapons, got them back, bowed to one another. Master Xan said, "Some of the apprentices were very vocal in lobbying for a tournament that was 'more like real life.' " Was Scout imagining it, or did Master Xan look directly at her? "In real life, we rarely get optimal combat conditions. One might find oneself attacked in null gravity, for instance. Or by surprise, or by a droid or other creature whose physiology made certain techniques difficult or impossible. Of course, introducing a Gorax into the Temple is not practical. But there are some things we can do. For instance, in real life—" Scout would swear the Master's eyes were lingering on her again. "—it is often *dark*."

And the lights went out.

Oh, great, Scout thought. *No problem. I don't need to trust my eyes, after all.*

I can trust the Force.

It was pitch black. In the darkness, Scout could just hear the audience breathing, and the sound of her own blood beating in her ears. A soft rustle of cloth from the direction Master Xan had been standing in. She would be lifting up the red handkerchief—*and Scout had no way of telling when she was going to let it go.*

Oh, boy.

She tried to use the Force, tried to let her awareness seep out into the dark room. She could feel the presence of the watching acolytes, Master Yoda back in the corner, Master Xan. But she couldn't find the little scrap of red cloth. For that matter, she had only a vague idea of where Hanna was. It was as if the Arkanian were muddying the Force, the way a Quarren might squirt ink into the sea.

Well, there was nothing for it. She couldn't draw before the handkerchief touched the ground, and she couldn't tell when that was going to happen. She would just have to stay alert, ready to spring backward at the first instant Hanna made any move.

Scout stared into the darkness. Her eyes felt wide as saucers, and she was straining to hear every creak and whisper. The little hairs on her arms stood up, as if she could listen with her skin.

And then, a gift from the Force: the sudden electric knowledge that Hanna was going to lash out—

Now!

The Force told Scout when the attack was coming; her own hard work told her what it would be. Scout had watched Hanna fight many times in the last six weeks. She *knew* Hanna would start with a high, Force-aided leap, to get out of Scout's plane of vision, hoping to drop down like a bird of prey from above. The Arkanian's blade blazed to life, a stroke of green lightning crackling down from directly overhead: but Scout's blade, a wand of cool blue flame, was there to meet it. The weapons clashed in a jarring burst of sparks, but Scout had the floor to brace against, and the force of her parry sent Hanna tumbling backward through the air. The Arkanian twisted into a perfect backflip and landed in a balanced fighting stance.

A scatter of applause drifted around the room.

Blue and green reflections hissed and spat in the milk-white surface of the Arkanian girl's eyes. "Come now, Esterhazy. Aren't you going to try one of your dirty tricks on me? You didn't use them all up on poor little Pax, did you?"

Scout grinned. "Not even close."

If Hanna had a weakness, it was that she was too in love with her lightsaber. There was something in her fastidious nature that made the sweaty grappling of hand-to-hand combat distasteful to her; she was really much happier standing two paces from her opponent and letting her blade do the fighting for her. "You know, Hanna, there's one thing I've always wondered. How exactly do you manage—"

Scout exploded into a flying flèche in the middle of her sentence, hoping to catch the Arkanian off guard. Hanna snapped to parry, Scout disengaged, Hanna caught her blade triumphantly and slid it down to the side. Scout's blue lightsaber passed harmlessly by as Hanna spun like a matador to let her go by, but that was all right, since Scout had only meant the swordplay to be a distraction, something for Hanna to feel superior about, right up to the moment Scout's body was nearly past, when her whip kick knocked Hanna off her feet.

They both hit the mat hard.

Scout tried to push her advantage, but by the time she was back on her feet the Arkanian was flashing forward in a lunge of her own. Hanna had a humming, buzzing, circular style of swordplay, fast slashes that changed angle continuously. Only Scout's little Force talent saved her, subtly prompting her to ignore the feints and parry the real blows.

Remember, you are the weapon, Scout told herself. *Don't get caught thinking about the lightsaber alone. Be the weapon.*

Slash, parry, slash, parry, slash—and this time instead

of making the expected parry high, Scout dived in low under the blade, trying to tackle Hanna around the knees. The Arkanian flipped up, sending Scout between her legs as she somersaulted in the air, twisted, and landed in a fighting stance. Scout tucked, turning her dive into a roll, and bounced up. They were both breathing hard now. Lightsabers buzzed, blue and green.

Hanna lunged again, but this time she used the Force as well, dragging on Scout's sword arm so her parry came too late and she had to throw herself wildly backward out of the center circle of mats to evade the blow. Regaining her balance, she skipped in among the surprised spectators, who scrambled out of her way.

"Hey!" Hanna cried. "You can't go in there!" She swung around to face Master Xan. "She can't go in there. One of the bystanders could get hurt!"

Scout edged behind Lena Missa. "Bystanders get hurt sometimes," she said with a shrug.

"Master Xan!"

Scout rather thought there was something like a smile tugging at the bottom of the Jedi Master's mouth. "This is real, Master Xan." Scout tapped Lena lightly on the shoulder. "This is the terrain."

"Perhaps so," Iron Hand said dryly. "But I think we'll try to keep the mayhem at least a little contained today, Scout. Fighting in the central circle only." She held up her hand even as Hanna's mouth started to open. "That does not constitute reason for Enwandung-Esterhazy's disqualification. I have made the ruling in flow, and she may recommence inside the boundaries at no penalty. You will both be satisfied." It wasn't a question.

"Of course," Scout said immediately, with a low bow.

"Of course," Hanna grated out.

Hanna stood aside. With all the composure she could muster, Scout walked back into the circle of mats.

"Begin."

Hanna's sword point dropped and she leapt forward, slashing for Scout's head.

And Scout ran behind Master Xan.

Hanna's lightsaber blade got to within a hand span of the Jedi Master's face, froze, and snapped back like a child's finger from a hot stove.

"Whoa there," Scout said. "You nearly hurt an innocent bystander."

Hanna's mouth opened in something like a snarl. She lunged behind Iron Hand.

Scout scurried out in front.

"Stop!" Master Xan said.

"It's not my fault," Scout said. "You're in the terrain."

Hanna made furious gurgling noises.

Iron Hand was definitely trying not to smile. "True, Scout." She walked to the edge of the circle of mats, with Scout and Hanna in orbit around her like two eccentric moons. "But sometimes, the terrain changes."

"I was afraid you'd say that," Scout sighed, leaping backward to avoid a slash as Master Xan left the ring.

Hanna stalked after her. "Any more cute ideas?"

"I'm working on it."

At least she had the Arkanian mad enough that she wasn't bringing the Force to bear with quite as much finesse as she had at the beginning of the bout. On the downside, she was running out of tricks to deal with Hanna.

The other apprentice knew it, too. Once more she attacked, methodically this time, step after step, driving Scout toward the edge of the ring. *Can't let it go like this,* Scout thought. She couldn't let herself get trapped purely on the defensive. She fell back, parried a slash and whipped her wrist around to bind their blades, then leaned as if she was going to charge forward as she had with Pax. This time she reached up with her left hand and made a jabbing two-finger pop to the pressure point under Hanna's left elbow.

It was perfect. As the Arkanian's forearm went temporarily numb, her nerveless fingers opened just as Scout kicked up at her hand as hard as she could, sending Hanna's lightsaber spinning through the air. With a snarl of triumph Scout charged forward with a roundhouse slash . . .

. . . and impossibly Hanna jumped *over* her blade. Scout pitched forward through the space where Hanna ought to have been, stumbled, got her balance, and turned just in time to see Hanna, her mouth set in a grim line, use the Force to grab her lightsaber out of midair. It smacked back into the Arkanian's hand with a sharp *thud.*

Hanna came forward again, relentless. "That was your last chance." She fell on Scout like a storm, her limbs flashing like whirlwinds, her long, humming blade falling like green forked lightning.

Slowly, irresistibly, Scout was being overwhelmed. She could see the attacks coming, she knew which ones were real and which were feints, but now Hanna was bending all her will to Scout's sword hand, using the Force to slow it down until it felt as if Scout had to drag it through water, or mud. Feint, slash, feint, cut, cut, and then a hard blow, a dipping slash to the leg that cut through the cloth of Scout's robes and left a red welt across her thigh.

The pain dropped her to the floor. She rolled sideways and came up parrying, stopping Hanna's blade a finger width from her face. The lightsaber hissed like a furious serpent, spitting green light in her eyes. With a grunt Scout spun sideways again and tried to make a cut, but Hanna was inside her blade, slamming it flat to the floor, so hard Scout's fingers loosened for just an instant. Hanna used the Force to grab her lightsaber, that line of blue heart's fire. Then she ripped it from Scout's grasp, and flung it to the far side of the room.

Grab me, Scout prayed. If Hanna would just grapple, there was still a chance. If she would just try a joint lock, an arm bar, *anything . . .*

The Arkanian stood up.

As soon as the weight left her hand Scout rolled over on her back, lashing out with her legs, but Hanna was already out of range, cool and composed, holding her lightsaber so the green tip hummed and buzzed a hand width above Scout's heart. The Arkanian looked down on Scout from what seemed like a vast height, an impossible height. The distance from a farmer's field to the stars. "Yield," she said.

Scout lay under her blade, gasping for breath. Her leg burned and throbbed.

Hanna looked at her impatiently. "Yield!"

"No."

The Arkanian blinked. "What?"

"No." Scout coughed and spat. "I said no. I'm not giving up."

Hanna looked at her, genuinely baffled. "But . . . I won. Now you yield."

Scout shook her head. "Don't think so." She thought about trying to use the Force to drag her lightsaber back while Hanna wasn't paying attention, but the pain in her head made it hard to concentrate. And she was tired. So tired. "I'm not ready to give up yet."

"But *why*?"

Scout shrugged. "Doesn't hurt enough yet."

Hanna shook her head in disbelief. "You're crazy. What am I supposed to do? Just cut you while you lie there?" Her lightsaber buzzed and sputtered in frustration: and right then Scout saw how she was going to win this fight.

She smiled. "We go until one of us surrenders or takes three burns. You got me once. That means I've got two left. Here's one," she said, and gritting her teeth she grabbed Hanna's lightsaber blade with her naked left hand.

"You can't do that!" Hanna yelped.

"Want to bet?" The blade burned and spat, but Scout held on to it for dear life and jerked down. Unable to believe what she was seeing, Hanna couldn't bring herself to let go of her weapon fast enough, and down she came, falling on top of Scout, who was already rolling, her right hand already sliding up to the neck of the Arkanian girl's tunic.

The two of them rolled over and over across the floor, and then Scout was on top with her left hand still tight around Hanna's blade and her right hand clamped around the Arkanian's throat. Scout was Iron Hand's best pupil; her choke holds were very precise, always centered beautifully on the carotid triangle, and they invariably induced unconsciousness within ten seconds. Scout bore down, counting off the seconds she still had to hold on to Hanna's lightsaber. One, two, three . . .

A film swam over the Arkanian's milky eyes, like frost creeping over a pond.

Four, five.

"It's not . . ."

Six.

"*Fair,*" Hanna whispered.

Seven.

And she surrendered.

Scout yelled and threw away Hanna's lightsaber. She rolled off Hanna's limp body and forced herself to her feet and swore a long stream of words that were absolutely not to be uttered inside the Jedi Temple, shaking out her poor burning left hand. Her legs were trembling so badly she thought she would fall down again, but she managed to bow to Master Xan.

Iron Hand regarded her. She wasn't smiling anymore. "You know, Esterhazy, if this had been a real fight—"

"With respect, Master . . ." Scout stopped to catch another breath and wipe the sweat out of her eyes. "With all due respect, that was a real fight. This is real," she said, waving at the room. "Lightsaber was real, set to a real setting." Behind her, Hanna began to moan softly.

"She's real." Scout looked toward Hanna. "It was a real fight."

After a long moment, Master Xan finally nodded. "I guess it was, at that."

Some heartbeats later the clapping started. The applause was still mounting as Scout walked out of the chamber, shaking off offers of help, and limped toward the infirmary.

4

The Jedi Temple rectory was buzzing with commentary on the tournament as apprentices and Masters alike sat down for their midday meal. Even Master Yoda, who usually took his meals alone or in the Jedi Council Chamber, had hobbled up to one of the long trestle tables and clambered, grunting and snuffing, up onto the bench, where he sat benignly surveying the hall. "Master Leem!" he called, waggling his cane as she came into the hall. "Mm. Sit with me awhile, will you not?"

Maks's long jaw made tiny chewing motions. She had really wanted to find her Padawan, Whie, and give him a couple of tips before the afternoon bouts resumed. But in truth, that was more to calm her own nerves than to help him; the boy had gone through his first two matches effortlessly, disarming his first opponent, who then tapped out, and putting the neatest little wrist lock on the second, so they were both barely inconvenienced by being beaten. The boy had always been smooth that way, like a diver who hit the water so cleanly he barely left a splash. He didn't need her help.

Besides, when the Grand Master of the Jedi Order invited one to dine, one could hardly turn him down. Even if she wanted to.

Frankly, even beings who would follow Yoda to the gates of Death preferred not to share his meals. Perhaps traveling the length and breadth of the galaxy had given the Master a more wide-ranging palate than mere mortals, or perhaps he was so evolved a being that he didn't care what he put into his body; or perhaps when one lived eight-hundred-odd years all one's taste buds died. Whatever the reason, the old gnome's preferred foods were notoriously disgusting. He was fond of hot, swampy stews that smelled like boiled mud; small dirt-colored appetizers that jiggled uneasily on the plate; and viscous drinks, both hot and cold, that ran the gamut from burned syrup to grainy sludge. As Master Leem settled on the bench beside him, the oldest and greatest of the Jedi was peering happily into a bowl of dark brown-and-gray stew, studded with little floating chunks of what looked like raw animal fat and spackled with the scales of some small reptile. The whole concoction smelled like dead womprat that had been left out in the sun.

"Fought well this morning, your Padawan did," Yoda mumbled around a mouthful of stew.

A moment earlier, Master Leem had been looking forward to a platter of dry grain with a side of dried candleberries and a mug of fragrant naris-bud tea, but as the smell of Yoda's lunch reached her, she abruptly lost her appetite. "Yes, Whie did very well," she said, eyes suddenly gone glassy.

"Had a nightmare last night, did he?"

"He said it wasn't one of the . . . *special* dreams."

Yoda gave her a sharp glance from under his ridged eyebrows. "Believe him, did you?"

"I'm not sure," she admitted. "It's not like him to lie about something like that. It's not like him to lie at all. But he was badly scared. And there was . . ."

"A stirring in the Force."

Master Leem nodded unhappily. "Yes, I felt it, too." It had woken her in the middle of the night, like a distant scream, so faint that at first she couldn't think what had jolted her upright in her bed, with the hair prickling around her neck.

Yoda bent back to his bowl, slurping and gobbling. "Told you of how he came to us, have I?"

"No, actually. I was on a long mission when he came to the Temple. I think he had been here three years before I ever saw him." She could still remember the occasion. She had agreed to take a class of five-years-olds into the garden for a botany lesson, learning the names of plants and their uses. Even then the Force had been strong in Whie. He had fallen behind the others, and when she went to look for him, she found him stroking the buds of a Rigelian iris, which opened and flowered at his touch, as if he were softly pulling the very springtime through them.

Still smiling at the memory, she turned to look for him in the crowded room, partly out of fondness, and partly to get her nose away from the appalling stench of Yoda's gumbo. Whie was three tables over, sitting with his agemates and yet a little apart, not fully joining in the raucous conversation around the table. There was always a little reserve to him, as if he saw something others couldn't see and didn't know how to share it. Then again, he was one of the eight apprentices still standing in the tournament, so perhaps it wasn't surprising that he kept to himself, to gather his thoughts and keep his concentration focused. As if feeling her gaze on the back of his neck, he turned and met her eyes with a half smile and a respectful nod.

A good Padawan. The best she'd had, though of course one wasn't supposed to have favorites.

Yoda followed her gaze. "Born on Vjun was he." His ancient tongue crept out to wipe brown and gray stew-slime from around his wrinkled mouth. "Insane, the father went. And his mother . . . very strong she was. Very strong."

Maks felt her three eyebrows furrow. "I had no idea."

"Mm. Begged us to take him, she did. 'Take him from the slaughterhouse.' Her words those were. Drunk she was, and half out of her mind with grief, for there was murder in the house that day."

"Good heavens."

Yoda nodded. "Not clear to me, our path that day was. Knew even then the mother could change her mind. But the Force was strong in him . . ." The old Master shrugged and snuffed. "We guessed. We dared. Wrong or right, who knows? Sometimes wrong and right only have meaning in small time. In big time, in decades, in centuries . . . then we see that things are as they are. Each choice, the branch of a tree is: what looked like a decision, is after only a pattern of growth. Each act, you see, is like a fossil, preserved in the Force, as—*aiee*!" Yoda broke into a sudden squawk as a rectory droid came to the end of the table and took his bowl, still half full of stew. "Stop! Stop! Eating this, I am!"

"This bowl contains a substance my sensors cannot identify as food," the little round droid said. "Please wait here, and I will bring you one of today's specials."

Yoda grabbed on to the edge of his bowl. "Ignorant machine! Not on menu, my food ever is. Made special for me, was this!"

The droid's servos whined as it fought to pull the bowl from the table. "Preliminary readings cannot confirm the edibility of the contents of this bowl. Please wait here, and I will bring you one of today's specials."

"Back!" Yoda cried, whapping the droid on the arm with his cane. "Mine! Go away!"

"You are bound to enjoy today's special," the droid said. "Baked dru'un slices in fish sauce. Wait here, and I will bring you some."

Yoda fetched the droid another thump with his cane, yanking on the bowl. The droid yanked back. The bowl shattered, sending flying stew everywhere, most particularly on the robes of Jedi Master Maks Leem.

"Oh, dear, a spill," the little droid said with satisfaction. "Let me clean that up for you."

Yoda's round eyes grew wide, and he stared at the droid with great intensity. "Bah!" he said, with an explosive grunt. "Droids!" The Master of the Jedi Order, quivering with frustration, stuck out his tongue at the droid, which was now happily picking gobbets of what looked like stewed tendon off Master Leem's robes.

Ten minutes later Master Leem had returned with fresh clothes, and Master Yoda was staring glumly at a plate of baked dru'un slices in fish sauce. He brightened as Jai Maruk entered the refectory, and summoned the lean Jedi to their table with a waggle of his stick. "Come to watch, have you?"

Master Maruk joined them with a grave bow to Yoda and a courteous nod to Master Leem. "Master Xan gave me a tip."

"Tip? Tip about what?" Maks Leem said.

Jai Maruk plucked a mug of steaming stimcaf from the tray of a passing droid, which Yoda eyed with disfavor. "You have a Padawan still alive in the tournament, yes?"

"That wasn't really an answer," Master Leem observed.

Master Maruk permitted himself a rare, small smile.

"Eight alone remain," Yoda remarked, glowering at the back of the beverage droid as it rolled away across the room.

"Seven, surely," Maruk said. "The weaker girl, Esterhazy—I heard she went to the infirmary with burns on her leg and hand."

At that moment, a murmur rippled through the benches nearest the eastern doors of the big hall as Scout limped in. Yoda glanced at the tall Jedi with a sly smile. "Went, yes."

"Did you know she was coming back?"

"Guessed it only, did I."

"She doesn't have any business fighting," Maruk said, shaking his head. "Left hand badly burned and bandaged, limping on her right side—another lightsaber burn, probably. What did you think of the way she competed this morning?" he asked Yoda. "Not quite in keeping with the Jedi ideals, I would say."

Yoda shrugged. "Which ideals mean you?"

"Too much trickery."

"Resilience, though," Master Leem said. "Lots of that. And courage."

"Mm. One more, too," Yoda murmured. The younger Jedi looked at him. "She never gives up," he said. Yoda's old eyes went narrow and crinkly. "Think you still to the Agricultural Corps she should be sent?"

"It's not for me to question you as to the development of our apprentices."

Yoda tapped him on the shins with his stick.

"All right," Jai said testily, "Yes, I do. I think she is smart and determined, and in the Agricultural Corps she could do a lot of good for many years. A Jedi Knight has a different kind of mission, and in the work we do, I think she would be dead in six months. How glad will we be that we let her dream live, when the dreamer is dead?"

"That she is not so strong in the Force as some surely requires an extra effort from her," Master Leem said thoughtfully. "But perhaps it also places a greater responsibility on us." She was a kindhearted Gran, and she hated the idea of sending Scout to the Agricultural Corps. "Perhaps we should exert ourselves even more in her training. Nobody can say Scout hasn't brought her all to being a Padawan; can we say we have worked as hard to make her a Jedi Knight?"

Yoda cackled. "A kind heart and a cunning have you, Master Leem. Jai Maruk, take a little wager with me, will you?"

Jai looked pained in the extreme. "Of course, Master, if you wish it."

"Watch the tournament, how it finishes. Of the eight

remaining, should the young one finish in the bottom four, then to the corps will I send her."

"After beating out three-quarters of the other students to get this far?" Master Leem exclaimed.

Yoda shrugged. "Worse tests must any Jedi face, against far more terrible odds. And as Master Maruk says, not strong is the Force in this one."

"And if she finishes in the top four?" Master Maruk said suspiciously.

"Second, third, fourth: then an apprentice she remains. But if she *wins*," Yoda said, poking Jai Maruk in the chest with his stick, "*your* Padawan she will be."

"Mine!" Maruk blurted. "Why me?"

Yoda snickered. "Why, then would you have lost, Jai Maruk. And need to learn about winning from one who knows how."

Master Maruk, looking singularly as if he had just had one of the spiny-collared toads of Tatooine shoved forcibly down his throat, was spared having to answer as Master Xan clapped her hands for attention. The tables of Jedi apprentices, well trained to pay immediate attention—not for nothing did they nickname her Iron Hand—fell silent at once.

"Apprentices, Padawans, Jedi Knights, and Masters: the first half of today's tournament has been extremely enlightening. The participants have fought with skill and courage—sometimes with great beauty . . ." Her eyes rested for a moment on Whie. "And sometimes with remarkable, ah, ingenuity." This remark accompanied by a dry sideways glance at Scout, who colored but kept her chin fiercely upright.

"I said earlier that the apprentices who were to spar in

this contest made it clear to me that they wanted the tests to be more lifelike; more closely resembling situations they might find if they were dispatched outside these walls into that larger world where even now a war is raging." Heads nodded around the refectory tables. *How serious they are,* Master Leem thought, and once again her heart went out to this generation of children raised not as keepers of a Republic's peace, but soldiers in a galactic war.

"I commonly hear our apprentices talk about Coruscant, and the stars beyond, as 'real life.' I wonder, sometimes, if they think what we teach them is merely pretend," Master Xan continued. "I assure you, it is not. The living Force you come to see here, under Master Yoda's guidance, is the truest reality; beyond these walls it is the truth, masked by hope and fear and treachery, that is hardest to see."

Yoda's old head nodded agreement with these words.

"But it is true that in real life we rarely face our enemies one by one, in a closed room, with comfortable mats on the floor," Iron Hand said. "Out there, situations are more chaotic. Instead of fighting in a sparring room, you might find yourself drawing your lightsaber in a docking bay, or a library, a city street, or even . . ." She paused, lifting her eyebrows. "Even in a dining room, for example. Under the impression that you had hours before your next exertion, you might have just eaten a large meal," she said, looking at Sisseri Deo, a tall golden-skinned Firrerreo who was one of the eight remaining combatants. He looked down at his plate, and the nictitating membranes of his eyes flickered rapidly with dismay.

"Out there, you might not have remembered to pay attention closely enough earlier in time, leaving you confused as to who, exactly, your opponents were," she continued, glancing at Lena Missa. The Chagrian girl wet her blue lips with her forked tongue and looked quickly around the room, trying to remember who all the morning's victors had been.

"Out there, it's rarely so easy as single combat at a defined time and place. More likely it is a barroom brawl, a fistfight in a back alley." Iron Hand lifted up the red handkerchief. At the sight of it, nervous apprentices scrambled up from their benches. "Or even a dining room free-for-all. Eight contestants remain. May the Force be with you," Master Xan said, and she let the red cloth slip from her fingers.

As soon as Master Xan started talking about "real life," Scout guessed what was coming. She scanned the room, locating the rest of her comrades in the Round of Eight, checking to see who might make the best opponent. Not Lena—Lena was a friend; besides, the Chagrian was looking straight at her.

Sisseri Deo, all 2.3 golden-skinned meters of him, was sitting with his back to Scout just one table away. As Master Iron Hand continued her little lecture—wasn't she enjoying herself, that grim old lady!—Scout slid from her bench carrying her cup of muja juice, and shuffled forward a few steps as if trying to make out what the Master was saying.

The red handkerchief went up. Everyone who didn't want to get caught in the crossfire of lightsaber blades and dirty dishes jumped to their feet. Scout glanced over

at Lena, checking to make sure the Chagrian wasn't
sneaking up on her. So far, so good. She edged casually
over until she was right behind Sisseri. In purely physical terms, Sisseri was by far the strongest remaining combatant, a huge boy with muscles like tree roots
under his gleaming skin. Scout had watched his second-
round match, when his roundhouse kick had taken out
Forzi Ghul, and she had no interest in going up against
him.

By the worst luck, just as the red handkerchief slipped
from between Master Xan's fingers, Sisseri spun around
to face Scout.

She swore.

The handkerchief hit the ground.

Sisseri grabbed for his lightsaber.

Scout tossed her cup of juice in his face.

Up snapped his hands, the lightsaber a beam of blue
light humming wildly over Scout's head as he frantically
tried to wipe the juice out of his eyes. Ignoring her
lightsaber completely—there was no point in trying to
duel Sisseri, he was far too good for her—she charged
straight into his chest, letting her hands find the neck of
his tunic. She found the sweet hold, her strong wrists
cranked, and she felt the old familiar pressure of fingers
and cloth cutting into her opponent's neck. *Great,* she
thought. *Now all I have to do is count to ten and hold
on. One, two . . .*

The muscles in Sisseri's legs bunched, and with a little
Force tingle Scout knew what was coming next. He
launched himself backward, twisting in midair like a
dragonsnake in its death throes so as to come crashing
down on the tabletop with Scout underneath him, but

she had felt it coming and wiggled around him in mid-flight, so she was on top again when he hit the table with a *whump*.

Three, four . . .

The Firrerreo kept rolling. His giant hands flexed, but for some reason the Force was flowing easily for Scout now and she knew he would try to pull her hands away before he knew it himself. Keeping the choke hold on with her right hand and forearm, she reached down with her left and popped the pressure point in his elbow, so his arm went numb and tingly.

Five, six . . .

Sisseri stopped thrashing and lay on the tabletop, blinking as if trying to summon the Force, but his eyes were glazing over. He gave a long, despairing hiss and glared at her with bulging eyes, his face congested and still running with juice. "I hate . . ."

Seven . . .

"I *hate* muja juice," he gasped, and yielded.

Scout rolled off him and crouched beside the table, peering around the refectory. There seemed to be six combatants left. Pirt Neer and Enver Hoxha were taking up most of the attention with a scintillating lightsaber duel. Whie and Hera Tuix were fighting hand-to-hand, but still at range, trading kicks, punches, and blocks. That wouldn't last; no matter how elegant one was at range, unarmed fights always went to ground in the end, where it was all grappling skills and joint locks. Lena was just standing up over Bargu, the skinchanger, who was clutching her arm with one hand and bowing in defeat.

Lena's eyes met Scout's, and they exchanged weary, wary smiles.

There was a gasp from the crowd. Whie had just caught Hera Tuix in a very elegant little wrist lock, and although Hera was trying to come up with a counterattack, odds were she would have to tap out at any second. Scout found Lena's eyes. "Now!" she said, and charged, with Lena right on her heels. Whie was stronger than either of them, but if they could take him now, together, while his back was turned and he was holding on to Hera, they might get him out of the equation.

They were at his back. Lena leapt in, but something about the set of Whie's body whispered to Scout that he knew exactly where they were.

Hera yielded.

Whie leapt into the air, five effortless meters, turned a backflip, and landed gently on a tabletop behind them. Lena ran into the table where he had been standing, and if Scout's one Force talent hadn't come to her aid she would have done the same, leaving them both at Whie's mercy. Instead, she was waiting with a whirling lightsaber slash at his legs as he landed on the table. He met her blue blade with his green one in a shower of sparks.

Then something strange happened. Whie stared at Scout, his mouth dropped open, and he recoiled.

"What's the matter?" Scout growled. She swiped across her face with her injured left hand. A few spatters of muja juice showed on the bandage, but that hardly seemed like a reason for him to be staring at her as if he had seen a ghost.

Lena hissed, recovered herself, and darted in to attack. Scout knew she would thrust low, and slashed high, hoping Whie couldn't parry both attacks. Instead of jumping back like any normal person, though, and falling off the table, Whie leapt *forward,* over their heads. A Force shove in her back sent her sprawling into the table he had been standing on, sending up showers of baked dru'un slices, a sleet of fish sauce, and a rain of juice and water.

She rose and shook her head, sending little bits of lunch out of her hair. A line of lightsaber cuts went pinwheeling across the room, followed by a round of spontaneous applause. Lena's feet raced by her table. Then a lightsaber came hissing and spitting through the air, bounced on the floor, and rolled to a stop less than a meter away. An instant later Enver Hoxha appeared, his face contorted with desperation, lunging for his weapon.

Scout reached out and grabbed it. "No!" Enver shrieked as Pirt Neer caught up and held her blade to his throat. "Well?" Pirt's voice said, somewhere high above.

Enver stared daggers at Scout.

"Thanks a lot, Scout," Enver snarled, and surrendered. He stood, to a round of applause, and brushed off his pants. "Well done, Pirt. You may as well collect Esterhazy so I can get my lightsaber back."

"Not a bad idea—*ulp*!" Lena had come up behind Pirt while she was accepting Enver's surrender, and put a sturdy arm bar on her. Pirt sighed and yielded.

Lena's cheerful blue face beamed at Scout. "Are you just going to sit there, or are you going to come out and play?"

There was a whirring buzz, lightsabers clashed and

sparked, and Lena disappeared in a dance of fancy foot-work across the refectory tables. Scout groaned. She should, she really should go help.

She edged out into the open. Lena and Whie were the only two combatants left. They were going at it in the wide clear space in front of the swinging kitchen doors. Whie was pressing Lena hard, his lightsaber spinning a cage of green light around her. Scout sprinted toward the pair.

Too little, too late. As she watched, Lena went through a parry-feint-beat attack-flèche combination, trying for a straight thrust into Whie's chest. He sidestepped, limber as a whipcord. He used his blade to guide hers harmlessly by while at the same time letting his free hand clamp on to her sword hand. He continued to pivot, sinking his weight exactly as Master Iron Hand always taught them, and now Lena's sword hand was caught in a thumb lock that her own momentum was making worse. An instant later they finished like a pair of dance partners: Whie behind the Chagrian girl, pinning her arm behind her back with her thumb folded up at an unnatural angle. He gave the slightest upward pressure on her thumb, and the lightsaber dropped from her hand. One more little nudge had her on her tiptoes. She yielded.

He smiled, let her go, and accepted her surrender with a grave bow. She answered with a curtsy and a laugh, amid the applause of those watching.

Oh, well, Scout thought. So much for tackling Whie two-on-one. She had a plan, but she had really, really been hoping she wouldn't have to use it. She sighed and switched her lightsaber over to her left hand. She trained left-handed often enough that it wasn't completely implausible that she would do such a thing as a desperate ploy to throw him off. For that matter, he might even think she was left-handed. The brutal truth was, she had probably spent a whole lot more time worrying about him than he had ever spent studying her.

She thumbed the power switch, and her lightsaber came on. Stars, how she loved its sound, the weight of the handle in her hand, and the pale luminous blue blade, clear as the sky at first light. She might not be the greatest Jedi apprentice ever, but she loved the Temple and her weapon and this life, and if even Yoda himself tried to take that away from her, she would go down kicking and screaming to the very end.

A small serving droid wheeled through the swinging doors from the kitchen area and surveyed the refectory, emitting a series of dismayed beeps and whistles as it took in the shattered crockery and the food spattered over half the floor and some of the walls. Several tables showed scorch marks from stray lightsaber strokes.

Tallisibeth Enwandung-Esterhazy—Scout to her friends—cut a little figure in the air to catch Whie's attention. "I guess that leaves you and me, sport."

Whie turned. His face fell. "You're still—I mean, I thought I was done."

There was something insulting about the way he stared at her and then looked away. "Hey, we don't have to fight," she said.

His shoulders sagged with relief. "I would prefer that. It's just—"

"—You can always surrender," she finished sweetly.

Scattered laughter in the room. The serving droid

scooted forward, its round head spinning anxiously from side to side.

"*Me*? Surrender to *you*?" Whie struggled to master himself. "I don't think so." Drawing himself up with cool formality, he drew his lightsaber and bowed to her, Master Xan, and Master Yoda.

Scout drew herself up to do the same, but as she dipped toward Whie, the little serving droid buzzed up to her. "Oh, dear, a spill," it said, peeling a slice of mashed dru'un in fish sauce off her hip. "Let me clean that up for you."

Laughter roared around the room. Scout blushed to the tips of her ears. So much for her dignified entrance. "Let's go," she said, and she leapt in.

With the lightsaber in her left hand she made a hard, straight lunge with a single disengage around his first parry, easily blocked by his second. He was sliding her along exactly as he had done Lena . . . his free hand dropping onto her sword hand and twisting it around, using the lightsaber handle as a lever to create the initial thumb lock. The whole thing was incredibly smooth: the fighter in Scout couldn't help but admire his balance, his precision and body awareness. She would have had a hard time countering the technique, even if she had wanted to.

Three seconds into their fight, and it already looked to be over. He was standing behind her, just as he had been with Lena. A single nudge, exactly placed, sent pain shooting up her thumb and into her wrist. She dropped her lightsaber with a clatter. "Let's stop," he said. Pleading.

It was the strangest thing—he hadn't been nearly this flustered dealing with Lena, and Lena was a more dangerous opponent than Scout by anyone's reckoning. Scout had seen boys with crushes seem this nervous around the girl of their dreams—it made sparring practice acutely embarrassing for everyone—but she had been working through arm locks with Whie only yesterday, and she would swear on every star in the Republic there hadn't been anything unusual about his behavior then.

He gave her thumb another nudge, and she found herself standing on tiptoe, as if somehow she could climb away from the little needle of pain shooting through her thumb. *"Yield!"* he whispered.

"Not this time," she said. And then, gritting her teeth, she dropped down, into the pain, and back, driving straight into the teeth of his hold. All he had to do was keep it steady, and her thumb would snap like a dry stick.

But he let go, as Scout had known he would. He was too nice, too sporting to hurt her that badly, and the Force was with her now, and the element of surprise. She turned into him, unwinding the arm he'd had pinned against her back as he loosened his hold. The instant before he decided to leap clear she felt it coming, took his arm like the spoke of a wheel so that when he made his jump she could swing him fluidly into a perfect shoulder throw.

Three seconds later it was over. Whie was lying flat on his back on the floor gasping for breath, while Scout sat on his chest and grinned. She had her right hand twisted in the collar of his robes, which she bunched as he started to twitch. "Un-unh," she said, tightening her hand just a little to show she had the choke hold if she needed it.

Whie glared up at her, sighed, and yielded. Scout let go of his robe and stood up.

The little serving droid rolled back and forth in dismay. "Oh, dear," it said. "There's been a spill."

Someone laughed, and then the clapping started. Master Leem ran by her to attend to Whie, but Master Xan gave Scout a small, wintry smile.

Lena skipped out of the crowd. "Scout! That was incredible!" she cried, grabbing both Scout's hands to swing her around in a victory dance. "That was great! Who would have guessed in a million—Scout?"

"Hand," Scout whimpered. "Not the left hand."

"She did it on purpose, you realize," Hanna drawled. The Arkanian girl regarded Scout coolly. "She was counting on Whie's good nature, guessing he'd be so worried about hurting her he would stop fighting and she could catch him off his guard."

"It wasn't a guess," Scout said.

"I don't see why you have to sound so contemptuous about it, Hanna," the Chagrian said. "It was a smart idea and it took a ton of guts to go through with it."

Hanna shrugged. "Oh, absolutely! Who am I to deny Esterhazy her moment of triumph? And, like grabbing my lightsaber, it should be such a useful tactic in real combat. As long as she's fighting only the very nicest Trade Federation combat droids, of course—and until she runs out of thumbs."

"Look, I'm sorry," Scout said, in a low voice. "I just did what I thought I had to do. I didn't mean . . ." But Hanna had already turned her back.

"Don't you apologize to her!" Lena said. "Vindictive stuck-up Arkanian prig. She's just mad because you beat her, fair and square."

"I beat her," Scout said tiredly. The little droid was still picking bits of food off her robes. The lightsaber burns on her leg and hand were throbbing with dull red fire. "I don't know about fair and square. Some days it's hard to believe I'll ever make any kind of a Jedi."

"Hey. Tallisibeth?"

Scout turned to find Pax Chizzik, the stocky eleven-year-old boy she had beaten in her first match, crouching beside her. "Tallisibeth," Pax said firmly, "being a Jedi is about being resourceful, keeping your eyes open, and never, ever giving up. You taught me a lot about being a Jedi today."

Scout looked at him, speechless. "Oh. Oh, you're so . . . so *good*," she said, sniffling, and then she burst into tears.

5

Yoda and Jai Maruk found Scout in the infirmary, where Master Caudle was putting bacta patches on her burned hand. "Though I don't know why I should bother fixing her up, if she's going to make a habit out of grabbing people's lightsabers." Master Caudle looked dryly at Yoda. "Three days and she'll be fine."

"It's not a big deal," Scout said. "I made sure it was the left hand that got, um . . . sacrificed." She looked anxiously at Master Yoda. "I'm in trouble, aren't I?"

Slowly he nodded. "No more can we watch you struggle as an apprentice in the Temple," he said gently.

Deafness rushed in on Scout—a numb feeling, as if she had gone stiff inside. She closed her eyes and shut out what he was saying. *I won't hear this. I won't hear this. It's not* fair.

"—Padawan, and send you off Coruscant."

Scout opened one eye. "Um, sorry, what was that?"

Master Yoda prodded her shoulder—very carefully!— with his stick. "Ears bruised, are they? To be Jai Maruk's Padawan are you, and come with him on a mission beyond Coruscant."

She gaped.

Master Yoda snickered. "Look like a fish, do you, Tallisibeth Enwandung-Esterhazy. Little pop-mouth, gulp, gulp, gulp!"

She looked wildly at Jai Maruk, the gaunt, fierce Jedi Master who had come back from his last mission with a lightsaber burn on his cheek. The burn had healed, but he still had a livid white scar running from his jaw to his ear to show for his encounter with the infamous Asajj Ventress. "You're making me your Padawan?" She turned back to Yoda. "You're not going to send me to the Agricultural Corps?"

He shook his old green head. "A reward for your fighting technique, it is not. Too few Jedi have I already. But even had I a crop of thousands, small one, I would not let you go without a fight. Spirit and determination you have. Between the stars, so much darkness there is. Why would I throw away one who burns so bright?"

Scout stared. All her life, it seemed, she had been trying not to let Master Yoda down. Clearly they all expected her to bubble with joy, but instead her eyes grew hot and filled with tears.

"What's wrong?" Jai Maruk said. He turned to Yoda, mystified. "Why isn't she happy?"

"She will be," Master Yoda said. "A band around her heart has there been, years on years. And now she feels it loose, and the blood running back into her heart: stings it does!"

"Yes!" Scout cried between sniffles. "Yes, exactly! . . . How did you know?"

Yoda scrambled up onto the bed and sat beside her, letting his little legs dangle in space. His ears perked. "Secret, shall I tell you?" He leaned in close, so she could feel his whiskers rasping against her face. "Grand Master of Jedi Order am I!" he said loudly right in her ear. "Won this job in a raffle I did, think you?" He snuffed and waved his stubby fingers in the air. *"How did you know, how did you know, Master Yoda?"* he said mincingly, followed by another snort. "Master Yoda knows these things. His job it is."

Scout laughed, and now, finally, the happiness started to hum in her, and she was fine and sharp and humming, her spirit switched on and glowing like a lightsaber blade. That sharp, and singing inside.

The holomap room in the Jedi Temple was a large domed chamber given over to celestial navigation. Here hologrammic projectors created three-dimensional star maps for students to walk through. These could be set to almost any scale, so a student might examine, say, one solar system in great detail, with each planet and satellite displayed in increasing resolution, showing every mountain and sea. Or the entire galaxy might be compressed into the space of the room, so nebulae of a thousand blazing suns were only pinpricks in the deep reaches of black space.

Whie had always liked the Star Room. No place in the Temple was more magical. When he was upset, or frustrated, or just needed time to himself, he would come here to walk among the stars. This afternoon had been trying. He had walked Scout to the infirmary and stayed to hear Master Caudle say the thumb she had sprained was not a serious injury. Then he had returned to accept polite congratulations from Master Xan and his fellow students for his performance in the tournament. He had done these things gracefully and well, because that was the standard to which he held himself; but it hadn't been easy, and he had slipped away as soon as he felt he could gracefully do so.

For a while he inspected his lightsaber, making sure it hadn't been damaged in the sparring, and carefully taking out a blemish on the handle where a stray blow had left a char line. Then he had tried to force himself to do some studying, sifting through the news dispatches to try to form an accurate picture of the war since the Honoghr disaster. The older apprentices talked about it all the time, and some of their instructors were very direct about using Clone War scenarios for their training. Last week Master Tycho, who was teaching military strategy this term, had demanded a rigorous evaluation of what had gone wrong on Honoghr, along with a set of recommendations from every student about what could have been done to prevent the debacle.

Whie had done well on the assignment—he always did well; that, too, was a standard to which he held himself—but in his heart, he wasn't sure that implementing his suggestions would have saved the day. He had the uneasy feeling that the reality was both more complicated and more simple than even Master Tycho wanted to believe. More complicated, because the lesson of the catastrophe was that no plan, however beautiful, long survives the harsh chaos of war.

More simple because Whie was coming to believe that situations, like people, could give in to the dark side: and once the dark side had one in its grip, it never, ever let one go.

After an hour of inefficient studying he had given up

and come here, to the Star Room. The last person to use the room had been studying the Battle of Brentaal—with key terrain color-coded by which side currently controlled them, watery blue for the Republic, and gleaming machine silver for area the Trade Federation's battle droids had held at the decisive moment of the conflict.

Whie deleted Brentaal and set the chamber's projectors to show the whole galaxy, running at a million years per second. Through these deeps of history he paced, watching stars form and burn and go out, feeling the wheel and swing of the whole spinning galaxy around him. From this view, none of it mattered—not his dream last night, not the war today, not the whole long watch of the Jedi Order. Indeed, the rise and fall of sentient life passed in an eyeblink, a barely perceptible ripple in the grand pavane: comets and constellations dancing in the dark; the Force the music and the dancing, too.

The door of the Star Room cracked open, and a voice disturbed the great impersonal whirl of time. "Whie?"

"Master Leem." So much for his private time. Even so, Whie smiled. Master Leem was fond of him, and he of her. She was older and wiser than his fellow apprentices, of course; she was the only one he dared complain to about the difficulties that came with being enormously talented. The responsibility. The pressure.

"I thought I might find you here." In the darkness she, too, was swimming in stars. The constellation of Eryon, which on Coruscant was called the Burning Snake, spun slowly across her shoulders and drifted away. "I hope you don't feel bad about that last match. You were perfectly right to stop."

He shrugged. "Was I? But maybe that's the difference between the dark side and us. So long as they allow themselves to do things we will not, they will always have an advantage."

He faltered at the end of the sentence, struck by an overwhelming sense of recognition. He had been here before. Said this before . . .

Ah—last spring he had dreamed this moment. Did that mean that even now, the self from last spring was trapped inside his head somewhere, watching the conversation unfold? Whie felt cautiously inside himself, but it was like putting his hand down a snake hole—a panicking dreaming Whie, locked up in his skull like a boy being buried alive, was the last thing he wanted to find.

"Ah, but the dark side eats its young." He listened as Maks Leem said, word for word, all the things he had already heard her say. "After all, if you and Scout were to fight again right now, who would be better able?"

"Oh, that doesn't signify," Whie said. To himself, his voice sounded perfectly calm and reasonable, but it felt mechanical, as if he were producing the lines of a play. It was almost as if his current attention was mingling with his dreaming self, leaving him nothing but a spectator of the present, unable to change what was about to happen. "*What If* is a game you can always win. In the real encounter, the one that mattered, she wanted it more, and she won."

"Perhaps," Master Leem said. "But I'm just as glad not to be patching up your thumb. Speaking of which—"

"Master Yoda wants to see us in the infirmary."

Master Leem blinked all three eyes. "How did you know?"

"I dreamed this moment last year. Just recognized it now. I wondered for months who we would be talking about; who it was that would have bested me. Now I know."

And that was two dreams, now, in which Tallisibeth Enwandung-Esterhazy had figured. A fragment of last night's dream came back to him—Scout staring at him, blood running like tear tracks down her face. Eyes bright with longing.

He forced his mind away. The dark side lay down that path; he could feel it there, waiting for him like a beast in the jungle.

Maks Leem's three brows furrowed, and her long, thin jaw began its customary chewing motion. "We should go, Whie. I don't want to keep Master Yoda waiting."

"End program," Whie said, following her. At his words the whole galaxy of stars like birthday candles flickered and went out.

Footsteps hurried across the infirmary, and a moment later Master Leem joined Jai Maruk beside Scout's bed. "This is fun," Scout said giddily. "Like being a languishing princess and having my courtiers come stand attendance around my bed." Whie appeared a moment later, standing at Master Leem's side. He was Leem's Padawan, of course—just as Scout was Master Maruk's. The thought made her absurdly happy. Truthfully, she hardly knew Master Maruk, but that didn't matter. What mattered was that she was going to be a real Jedi after all. *Now all I have to do is go on missions, battle against terrible odds, and carve my way through the armies of the Trade Federation! Nothing to it!*

Scout found herself grinning so hard her face ached. She laughed.

Master Leem looked dubiously at the bandaged girl lying on the infirmary cot. She turned to Jai Maruk. "Is she drugged?" she murmured to the Master.

"No, ma'am!" Scout chirped. "I'm just a little beam of sunshine."

Master Leem's shaggy eyebrows climbed slowly toward her hairline.

"Glad you are here, am I," Yoda said. He shifted around until he was sitting cross-legged at the bottom of the bed. "News for you I have, Tallisibeth and Whie. Master Leem and Master Maruk, going on a mission for the Temple, they are. As their Padawans, you will go with them."

"Already?" Scout said, shocked.

"They made you a Padawan?" Whie said, no less shocked.

"Where are we—" Scout checked herself, and glared at Whie. "What did you mean by that?"

"I mean, *congratulations*!" Whie said smoothly.

Jai Maruk's mouth quirked in a little smile. "Your boy *is* agile," he murmured to Master Leem.

Yoda snuffed and waved all bickering aside with his stubby old hand. "This may you tell your friends, when they see you making ready for the journey. What you may *not* say, is that Master Yoda with you also will be coming."

"You wouldn't be leaving the capital unless it was for something extremely important," Scout said.

"Something to do with the war," Whie added.

Yoda's ears drooped. "True it is, what you say. Better things than fighting, should a Jedi Master be doing! Seeking wisdom. Finding balance. But these are the days given to us."

"Where are we going?" Whie asked. It seemed to Scout there was something strange in his voice—as if he knew the answer already, and was hiding his fear of it.

Yoda shook his head. "Tell you that, I will not yet. But a problem I have for you. Yoda must leave Coruscant—but in secret. No one must know."

In the silence that followed, a little medical droid rolled out from Master Caudle's dispensary and approached Scout's bed, bearing a tray with a pot of the healer's cut and burn ointment.

"It can't be done," Master Leem said. "The Senate and the Chancellor's office expect to hear from you every day."

"Make a feint," Whie said. The Jedi Masters turned to look at him. "Tell everyone you are leaving. Make a show of it, Master. Show pictures of you getting into a Jedi starfighter."

"—But the pictures are a deception," Jai Maruk said, picking up the boy's thought. "While the world watches you go on a very public mission, in reality you will slip onto a different ship with us. A clever idea, boy."

"But . . ." Scout waited for someone else to say the obvious. The little medical droid pulled up to a stop at her bedside and handed over a pot of Master Caudle's balm.

Master Yoda's green moon face tilted toward her. "Yes, Padawan?"

"Well, Master, it's fine to say you should sneak off in secret, but the truth is, you're, um, very recognizable."

Master Leem nodded. "What the girl says is true. Everyone on Coruscant recognizes the face of the Grand Master of the Jedi Order. Your addresses to the Senate have been broadcast many times, and pictures of you conferring with the Chancellor are routinely produced by every journalist in the capital."

"As a child, disguise me, could we not?" Yoda asked. "Perhaps Masters Leem and Maruk, traveling as a family with their three children—Yoda a sweet stripling of five or six?" His old face crinkled into a hideously unconvincing childish smirk. The others involuntarily recoiled.

Scout struggled with the lid of the pot of ointment and then gave up; it was screwed on too tightly for her to manage with her damaged hands. "Open this for me, would you?" she said, handing the jar back to the medical droid. Its gears and servos whined as it extended its metal claws and popped the lid smartly off the jar. The smell of beeswax and burned oranges stole into the room. "I can't imagine how we could smuggle you off the planet. Unless . . ." Her eyes flicked over to Yoda. An idea bloomed in her eyes, and she choked back a snort of laughter.

"Unless *what*?" Jai Maruk, her new Master, said impatiently.

Scout choked back another laugh and shook her head. "No. Nothing. It's a terrible idea."

"Let me be the judge of that," Master Maruk said, his voice gone alarmingly soft.

Scout looked pleadingly at him, then at Master Yoda. "Do I have to say?"

The ancient green-faced humpbacked gnome was staring at her with narrow eyes. "Oh, *yes*."

It was raining again on Vjun, harder than usual. A wind had come up, shaking the blood-and-ivory rosebushes in the gardens of Château Malreaux. Ugly weather. Count Dooku watched the acid raindrops hurl themselves against his study windows, like the Republic troops who every day flung themselves against his battle droids and computer-controlled combat installations across the length and breadth of the galaxy. Each little splotch leaving the imprint of its death on the glass, then dissolving into a featureless wet spill and trickle.

The half-mad old woman Dooku had found haunting the château when he moved in claimed to be able to read the future in the fall of broken plates, the spill patterns of drinks carelessly overturned. An amusing mania. He wondered what she would see in the pattern of raindrops. Something ominous, no doubt. *Beware: one you love is plotting your betrayal!* or *You will soon hear from an unwelcome guest.* Some such claptrap.

Outside, the wind picked up another notch, shrieking and groaning among the eleven chimneys, as if to announce the arrival of a hideous guest.

Dooku's comm console chimed. He glanced over, expecting the daily report from General Grievous, or perhaps a message from Asajj Ventress. He reached over to open the channel, recognized the digital signature of the incoming transmission, jabbed the channel open, and snapped to his feet. "You called, my Master?"

The hologrammic projector on his desk sprang to life, and the wavering form of Darth Sidious regarded him. As always the picture was oozy and unclear, as if light itself were uneasy in the presence of the Lord of the Sith. Dark robes, purple shadows—a patch of skin, pale and mottled under his hooded cloak like a fungus growing under a rotten log. From under heavy lids the Master's eyes, snake-cold and serpent-wise, regarded him.

"What would you have from me, Master?"

"From you? Everything, of course." Darth Sidious sounded amused. "There was a time when I wasn't sure if you would be able to overcome that . . . independent streak of yours. After all, you were born to one of the wealthiest families in the galaxy, with gifts and abilities far, far greater than any amount of wealth could bestow. Your understanding is deep; your will, adamant. Is it any wonder you should be proud? Why, how could it be otherwise?"

Dooku said, "I have always served you well and faithfully, my Master."

"You have. But you must admit, your spirit was not made for fidelity. After all, a man who will not bow to the Jedi Council, or even Master Yoda . . . I wondered if perhaps loyalty was too mean, too confining a thing to ask from so great a being as yourself."

Dooku tried to smile. "The war progresses well. Our plans are on schedule. I have dealt out your deaths, your schemes, your betrayals. I have paid for your war with my time, my riches, my friends, and my honor."

"Holding nothing back?" Sidious asked lightly.

"*Nothing*. I swear it."

"Excellent," Darth Sidious said. "Yoda came to the

Chancellor's office this morning. He is going on a very special mission. Top secret." He laughed, a harsh sound like the bark of a crow. The wind rose again, shrieking around the mansion like a creature in torment. "When he arrives, Dooku . . . see that you treat him *as he deserves.*"

Darth Sidious laughed. Dooku wanted to laugh along, but couldn't quite manage it before his Master cut the connection and disappeared.

Dooku paced in his office. With the end of Sidious's call, the storm had slackened, and the shrieking wind outside now only sobbed quietly under the gables of Château Malreaux.

He paused by his desk and examined the small red button he'd had installed the day after he first heard Yoda was intending to come to Vjun. It held a very considerable importance for such a small button. A last card to play.

Dooku found his hand was shaking.

He was still looking at it when the study door slid open, revealing a tattered pink ball gown. "Ah—Whirry. I was about to—"

"Call a droid to bring you a hot cup of stimcaf, sure you was." The madwoman waddled through the door with a lovely old tray in the blood-and-ivory Malreaux check, on top of which sat a silver pot of stimcaf and a cup already poured into a demitasse of finest boneshell china, also in the Malreaux colors. Her evil-faced pet, the brindled fox with the cunning hands, loped in behind her. "Which I saw downstairs when the chambermaid broke an egg on accident, didn't I. Slapped her nasty knuckles; if we be wasting eggs, that's a short stop and a long drop down into ruin, isn't it, sir? Sir?" she said.

Dooku let her live in the old house mostly on a whim; she seemed to give it a quaint touch of madness perfectly in keeping with its setting. But for some reason the Count found himself on edge. It was clear the old hawk-bat wanted something from him, but he had no interest in letting her try to flatter and wheedle favors out of him. "Hustle along, now," he said. "I have important work to—"

Crash.

"Oh, Count, ever so sorry! I don't know how come Miss Vix got a-tangled up in your feets! And your lovely cup of stimcaf all over like that!"

There was something undeniably comical about the whole scene, Dooku thought. Him tripping over the fox, the cup smashed on the tile floor. He rather suspected Whirry had arranged the whole incident. Already she was crouching greedily over the fragments of the shattered cup, staring at the patterns of china and spilled stimcaf on the tile floor. It cleared his head, to see her scheming so nakedly below him; restored the proper sense of perspective. "Well, Whirry?" he asked, amused. "What does the future hold for us, eh?"

"Death from a high place," she said, her fat pink fingers fluttering over the spill, her black eyes greedy. "And here's the Footman, which stands for the easy destruction of a faithful servant." She glanced sideways. "Not me, I hope and pray, Your Honor. You wouldn't be a-doing that to old Whirry, now, would you?"

"Please me, and don't find out," he said, half mocking; and then, unbidden, a thought returned to his mind: *How easily we betray our creatures.*

He stirred uneasily. "Clean this up," he said abruptly. The comm console chimed, and he sat down to read General Grievous's daily dispatch, dismissing the old woman from his attention. So it was he didn't see her verminous companion, Miss Vix, start lapping at the stimcaf. Nor did he hear the old lady as she put her finger on the china cup's broken stem, lovingly tracing the curled handle, and said, "And here's the Baby, coming home, my love. Coming home at last."

Palleus Chuff was, almost certainly, the greatest adult actor on Coruscant under one meter tall. As a boy, he had loved pretending to be a starfighter pilot, a Jedi Knight, a swashbuckling hero. That's why he'd written *Jedi!* when he grew up; when one was a single meter tall, one didn't get many chances to play the dashing hero. Mostly villainous scheming dwarfs, or comic relief. Not much that spoke to that boy who had pretended to be a space pirate so long ago.

Of course it was the *pretending* he really loved. The acting. The flying he wasn't so keen on. When the government had approached him about doing his terrific Yoda impersonation ("An astonishing re-creation of the Grand Master himself—the Force is with this 4-star performance!" as the *TriNebulon News* had been kind enough to put it) on behalf of the war effort, he had been flattered, and perhaps a bit intimidated. When people wearing uniforms and carrying blasters ask one for a favor, one says yes.

But now, standing on the Jedi Temple landing platform about to get into a real starfighter, which was going to launch his body into Outer Space at some unspeakable multiple of the speed of light, he was beginning to have very serious second thoughts.

The Jedi handlers gave him his cue. Chuff swallowed. "Showtime, it is!" he murmured to himself.

He stumped out of the docking bay and onto the flight deck of the Jedi Temple landing platform. A volley of questions came from the throng of reporters in the roped-off press area twenty meters away:

"Can you tell us the nature of the mission? What's so important about Ithor?"

"When will you be back, Master?"

"Are you worried that an abrupt change in the front might cut you off from communications with the Chancellor's office?"

Palleus waved his walking stick at the reporters and waggled his ears. The ears were very good, top-notch prosthetics, and he was expert at using them. *Keep smiling, Chuff,* he told himself. *Don't think about the pressure, just look your audience square in the eye and sell it.* Palleus had Yoda's smiles down pat: the Gleeful Cackle; the Sleepy Grin; the Slow Almost Menacing Smirk; the Gentle Joy that came so often to the Master's face in the presence of children. But he wasn't going to try the voice: he didn't dare risk missing an inflection, getting a flaw in tone that would cause someone to take voiceprint sonograms and go around claiming that the Yoda clambering into the *Seltaya*-class courier today was not the real Yoda.

He reached the transport and clambered in. This was

the part he was dreading. He'd never been a fan of enclosed spaces. Or starflight. Or rapid acceleration. They had promised him the ship's R2 unit would do the actual piloting. They also had an emergency override that would allow them to fly the ship from the control tower, they said. Well, maybe they did. But what if the Trade Federation had gotten to the little R2, eh? After all, why wouldn't a droid side with the other droids? Maybe it was part of some sort of mechanical fifth column. A traitor droid would probably sacrifice itself in a heartbeat for the sake of getting rid of the senior member of the Jedi Council.

The starship canopy swung up and over him and then snapped shut, cutting out the crowd noise and leaving Palleus Chuff feeling suddenly very alone.

The cockpit was supposed to be climate-controlled, but he felt hot. Hot and sweaty. The starfighter's engines rumbled to life, and he found himself thinking that this craft had been rushed through assembly on a wartime production schedule; every single piece of it, from the seat straps to the canopy rivets, had been built on contracts to the lowest bidder.

The ship lurched queasily and rose a meter into the air to hover over the landing platform. Palleus gave the crowd a grin and a wave.

Under his breath, he began to pray.

Meanwhile, back on the roof of a skyrise overlooking the Temple district, the two droids were finishing up another hologame match. Solis, the plain droid, watched his pieces get systematically run down and destroyed by those of his livery-painted companion, Fidelis. The two of them had played every conceivable variation on dejarik many, many times. Solis nearly held even, where chance and brutality were great equalizers, but they both preferred courtier, an entirely skill-based strategic variant. The difficulty was that Fidelis, having been continuously in service, had been routinely upgraded. Solis, on the other hand, had been fending for himself for a long, long time, and advanced hologame software had not been his highest priority.

As a result, he lost. Not inevitably, not every time: but steadily, in a trend that would never reverse. So it went: those in livery prospered. Those without . . . didn't.

"Another game?" Fidelis inquired politely, resetting the board.

"I think not."

"Are you sure? We could make it best nine hundred sixty-seven thousand four hundred and thirteen games out of one point nine million thirty-four thousand eight hundred and twenty-four."

"I don't feel like it."

"Don't *say* that. It doesn't even mean anything. You're very free with these organic expressions," Fidelis said primly. "I'm certain your initial programming did not support this sort of . . . sociolinguistical slovenliness."

"Yeah," Solis said. "Whatever."

Fidelis claimed that the range of emotions for which they had been programmed was very narrow—consisting, of course, of loyalty, loyalty, and loyalty—and that the semblance of organic states such as *annoyance* or *pique* was sheer affectation, and in dubious taste. Nonetheless, he played a game of solitaire dejarik with a markedly peevish air.

Solis wandered over to the edge of the roof and looked down, watching beings streaming like insects in their hovercars and pedways. A being lying flat on this rooftop and sighting down the barrel of a SoruSuub X45 sniper riflette would be able to pick off his or her choice of targets nearly invisibly. Death from above.

As if in answer to his thoughts, a spire falcon appeared overhead, drifting wide-winged on the column of warm air squeezing up between the ferrocrete towers. What people usually thought of as "Nature" had been banished from Coruscant long ago: to a casual eye, the planet had become one continuous city, with no room left for anything but urban sentients. But life was adaptable—how well Solis knew it!—and even in so strange a habitat as the city-world, there were plenty of creatures that did not realize the streets and towers of the capital had not been built for their convenience. Small birds, mammals, and reptiles were brought to Coruscant all the time as pets, and as regularly escaped into the sewers, the streets, and the rooftops, as if the city were a ferrocrete jungle and they its natural denizens. Then, too, there were always vermin that thrived on the heat and waste of sentient life: gully rats, grate toads, ferro-worms, the blind snakes that nested inside buildings, and the clouds of trantor pigeons that roosted on their ledges. And above them all, at the top of this alternate food chain, the spire falcons.

This was a female, blunt-winged, her soot-and-concrete plumage beautifully camouflaged against the buildings.

Like a flake of ash she drifted on invisible currents of wind; stuttered in midair; and then dropped like a thunderbolt to pounce on something below. Solis watched her drop, tracking her fall through bands of light and shadow, magnifying her image smoothly as she fell until he could make out the yellow band around the edge of her mad eyes, and see her prey, a scrap mouse nosing around a pile of slops in a back alley 237 stories below. Solis's eyesight was without exaggeration the equal of anything in the galaxy. Upkeep on the Tau/Zeiss tac-optics had been a higher priority than keeping current with the latest hologame programming. When one wasn't in livery, one had to make some cold calculations about the kind of work one was best at, and the steps one had to take to keep oneself employed. The tracking cross-hairs centered over the mouse's head as its little mouth opened, a single shocked squeak as iron talons drove like hammered nails through its tiny side.

Death from above.

Solis looked away from the falcon's kill, sparing a reflex glance at the Jedi Temple as he did so. "Hey."

"What?"

"Your target's leaving the Temple," he said.

Fidelis's head snapped around. He stared transfixed at the steps leading down from the Jedi Temple 1.73 kilometers away. "Oh," he said.

"Two Jedi, two Padawans, and an artoo unit," Solis said. They were both standing at the edge of the roof now. Solis looked at his comrade. "There's something funny about that artoo, don't you think? It's not moving quite right. Maybe a servo out of whack . . ."

No answer from Fidelis, who only continued to stare at the little party sallying forth from the Temple, watching them with the hungry intensity of someone lost in the desert who has just seen water for the first time in days.

Weeks.

Years.

It had been so long since Solis was in livery, he could barely remember the shock of loyalty, that hardwired current of connection that moved through one like religious awe in the face of Family. Really, it made Fidelis look rather foolish, standing there gripping the rooftop railing so fiercely he was leaving crimp marks in the duracrete . . . and yet it was hard not to envy him. It would have been nice, just one more time, to feel that thrill of connection.

If droids could feel envy, that is. But as Fidelis was quick to point out, they hadn't been programmed for it, had they? Envy, disappointment, regret. Loneliness. Affectations, every one of them. Not real at all.

"Let's go," he said, taking Fidelis roughly by the arm. "Time to hunt."

There's no such thing as *above* in space. Of course, any sufficiently massive object—a planet, a star—exerts a gravitational pull, but unless one is falling right down its gravity well, the pull feels more like *toward* than *down*. So, in a strictly technical sense, Asajj Ventress, hovering in deep space in the *Last Call,* a Huppla Pasa Tisc fanblade starfighter so sleek and deadly as to seem like her own lethal self reconsidered, with transparisteel for skin and laser cannon eyes, could not be said to be circling above Coruscant like a spire falcon waiting for her prey.

But to a less scientific observer, one who knew little about physics and saw only the cruel, satisfied light in her eyes as Yoda's ship cleared local space, that's exactly what she looked like.

As Palleus Chuff, doing his duty as a patriotic actor, was accelerating to escape Coruscant's gravity well, the real Yoda was waiting in a seemingly endless line along with what could easily have been the population of a frontier planet, all shuffling glumly through the cavernous new Chancellor Palpatine Spaceport and Commercial Nexus.

Nobody was supposed to know that, though.

The trouble with undercover missions, Jai Maruk was thinking, was that one gave up so many of the perks of being a Jedi. Under normal circumstances, dashing off to face death for the good of the Republic was a fairly straightforward business. Packing for even the most extended trip took him less than an hour. A quick bite of food in the refectory, then up to the Jedi Temple's private launch bay. A few words with the tech chief, an eye and thumbprint required for him to take out the preapproved choice of starcraft, a simple preflight checklist, and he was away.

A considerable improvement over *this*.

They were to travel in disguise, taking commercial starship flights all the way out to Vjun, and the whole process so far had been excruciatingly boring. After taking an hour to drop off their baggage and another hour getting tickets, they had been standing in this monstrous security line for nearly *three* hours. It was all very well for Maks Leem—she was a Gran. Gran were descended from herd animals; they *liked* crowds. Jai singularly didn't. He was a private man at the best of times; the muddy wash of emotions slopping around him—anxiety, irritation, pre-flight nerves, and sheer shrieking boredom—was foggy and irritating at the same time, like being swaddled in an itchy bantha blanket. On top of which, their position was ridiculously exposed. A would-be assassin could loom out of the crowd at any instant. Even if he had time to react, simply drawing his lightsaber in the crush of this crowd would probably lop the limbs off a couple of innocent bystanders.

On top of which he was supposed to look after his new Padawan, Scout. Not that she had done anything wrong so far—if you didn't count her annoying tendency to contradict his judgment, more than a little off-putting in a fourteen-year-old girl. But she still had her left hand in a bandage, and bacta patches on her burned leg. Not only was the Force weak in her; the truth was, she ought to have been lying in the infirmary sipping Hillindor fowl soup.

And to be honest—which Jai Maruk was, even to the one audience to whom people tell their worst lies, himself—Jai didn't feel ready to deal with a Padawan. He was a doer still, not a teacher. He wanted to get back to Vjun and make good his last miserable interview with Count Dooku, and he didn't want to drag a teenage girl across the galaxy at the same time. Clearly Master Yoda had a reason for forcing the Padawan on him, but Jai hadn't learned to be happy about it.

And as for Master Yoda himself . . .

Jai glanced uneasily at the little R2 unit traveling with them and caught it starting to sidle out of line again, slipping under the security ribbons. "Scout, check the artoo," he grated. "It seems to be having a little difficulty *staying put.*"

The girl clapped her hand on top of the R2's caparace, which gave an odd ringing thump, as if she had whacked the side of an empty metal barrel. "Don't worry, Father," she chirped. "I've got an eye on him. On it, I mean."

"At least we're nearly at the head of the line," Master Leem said soothingly.

A little knot of security officers in the tan-and-black colors of the Republic were directing people into a dozen different security scanners, so the one mighty line splintered at the end of its journey like a river dividing into a dozen channels to run into the sea. Each station was staffed by a pair of weary, irritable security personnel; behind them, additional squads were performing random security checks, opening people's carry-on luggage and making them empty their pockets and performing pat-down searches.

"You should have packed your lightsaber in your luggage," Scout murmured to Jai Maruk.

He gritted his teeth and made a grab for the R2, which had skittered forward and bumped into the Chagrian in front of them. "Terribly sorry," he ground out.

They got to the head of the line. "Line seven," the security guard said to Jai Maruk. "You to line eleven, and you're in line two," he said to Maks and Whie. "Line three for the girl. Who's the droid going to go with?"

"Me," all four of them said at once.

The security guard raised an eyebrow.

"I'll take the artoo," Jai Maruk said. "We are all traveling together. You should let us go through the scanners together," he added, slowly and with emphasis.

The security guard started to nod, caught himself, and glared at Jai Maruk with redoubled suspicion. "Like the song says, you'll meet again on the other side, Twinkletoes. But you just earned yourself a completely random Deep Tissue Inspection. DTI on number seven!" he bellowed.

"But—" Master Leem said.

"No time for that," the guard said, shoving her toward line number eleven.

"But—" Scout said.

"No time for that, either!" The guard shoved Scout toward line three. "And take the artoo with you."

A couple more security guards stepped forward. Behind them, the crowd began to mutter darkly about the delay. The four Jedi exchanged glances, and split apart.

"May I ask why I am being subjected to this extra search," Jai Maruk said icily.

"Random search, sir, completely random, completely for your protection," said the guard on station number seven, a briskly competent middle-aged woman. "Plus you look like a Druckenwellian."

"That's because I was born on Druckenwell," Jai grated.

"But Coruscant papers, I see. Neat trick," the guard said.

"I've lived here all my life—"

"Except for the part where you were born there? In

case you didn't know, sir, Druckenwell is an avowed member of the Trade Federation, with which—perhaps this escaped your notice as well—we are currently at war. Oh *ho!*" she said, laying a hand on the hilt of his lightsaber. Instantly Maruk's hand was covering hers, a dangerous light in his eye.

The guard met his glance. "Are you interfering with a security guard in the line of duty, sir?"

"I am a member of the Jedi Order," Jai said quietly. "That is the handle of my lightsaber. I prefer others not touch it."

"Should have packed it in your luggage then, shouldn't you?" she said perkily.

"And if pirates were to attack the liner, I'm supposed to run to the cargo bay and find my weapon somewhere between my shirts and socks?" Maruk hissed.

The guard smiled at him indulgently. "Look, sir—you and I both know the Jedi Order has its very own starships. If you were really a Jedi Knight, you wouldn't be flying out of Chance Palp, would you?"

"But—"

"You can always explain it to my manager. Rumor has it the wait is less than two hours!"

The guard at security point three was a dull-eyed young man with a lip full of Chugger's Chaw. "Walk directly beneath the scanner beam with your hands at your sides," he mumbled.

"Sure," Scout said. She gave the R2 a little nudge and they went at the same time, Scout passing underneath the scanner while the R2 lurched uneasily around the outside.

No lights, no sirens. *Whew,* Scout thought. Glancing over at security point seven, she saw Jai getting a lecture from the security staff. He looked like he was going to pop a vein right there on the concourse. Scout congratulated herself once more on stashing her lightsaber in her luggage.

Her guard paused to eject a long string of brilliant green spit into an empty stimcaf cup. "Sorry, ma'am. The droid has to pass through the scanner, too."

"The droid? He can't," Scout blurted.

The guard blinked. "Regulations, ma'am. The Trade Federation is spreading madware through our droids. We start letting them skip the cleaners, one day you'll wake up in your very own home and find it's been conquered by the smartvac and the laundry droid."

"Are you serious?"

"They use *microwaves,*" the guard said, jetting another stream of spit gravely into his cup. "The artoo's got to go through. Come on, little fella," he said, making a chucking sound in his throat, as if calling a faithful hound.

The R2 gave a weird, croaking wheep and shook its head.

"He can't go through," Scout said desperately. "He's afraid of scanners."

"Afraid of scanners?"

"It's his eyes. Video sensors, I mean. Very delicate, specialized," she babbled. Next to her, Whie had breezed through line two. She gave him a beseeching look. "This little fellow actually belongs to my grandfather," she said, giving the R2 another hollow-sounding slap on the carapace and then wishing she hadn't. "He's a Seeing Eye droid. That's why his sensors are so, so . . ."

The guard's mouth was hanging open, and a little line of spit was dangling from his lower lip. "Seeing Eye droid, my *butt*," he said. His eyes narrowed. "Let me see those papers again, and get that tin can back behind the red line so he can go through the scanners proper!"

Whie picked up his carry-on and stepped over to rejoin Scout. "You don't need to scan the artoo again," he said casually.

The guard blinked.

"It went through with the girl," Whie said. "They both checked out fine."

Splotch. The trickle of green spit soaked slowly into the guard's uniform shirt. He looked down at it and swore. "Git on," he said, waving his hand irritably. "I don't need to scan the artoo again."

Scout looked from Whie to the guard. "So . . . we checked out all right?"

"You checked out fine. Now, git! Can't you see I'm busy over here?"

"Yessir. Thank you, sir." Scout walked quickly away from the guard station. Whie followed behind, checking the heft of the lightsaber on his hip and grinning at her.

"That was impressive," Scout whispered. "Must be nice, to just make people do what you want."

"It comes in useful every now and . . ." For some reason, looking at her, he trailed off, and the smile left his face.

"What's up?" Scout said. And then, "Hey—aren't we missing someone?"

* * *

In a crowded spaceport concourse, a standard R2 unit is easy to overlook. First, there is the issue of size. At just over one meter in height, an R2 is quickly obscured in a dense crowd of humans, Chagrians, Gran, and assorted other humanoids. Then, aside from a lack of *physical* height, there is the issue of a droid's comparative lack of *psychological* size. To a sentient organic, another sentient organic is an object of great interest: will this new person be my friend or enemy, help me or harass me, thwart me or save me a place in the stimcaf line? Droids, on the other hand, occupy a spot in the consciousness of the average sentient being roughly analogous to, say, complicated and ingenious household appliances. A programmable food prep, for instance, or a smart bed. To a humanoid, a droid—unless it's a battle droid approaching with laser cannons on autofire—just doesn't *matter* very much.

To a droid, on the other hand, another droid is exactly life-sized.

Which might explain how it came to be that one little R2 unit, still in its original drab factory colors, could go lurching and wheeping through the dense crowds thronging Chancellor Palpatine's Delta Concourse almost completely unnoticed, despite the fact that it kept banging into shins, walls, and water fountains as if, instead of sensors and a fine computer brain, it was being navigated from the inside by a hot, grumpy, and increasingly exasperated person with only four tiny eyeholes to look out of.

It might also explain why, in the midst of so much obliviousness, this same droid was being pursued, quite relentlessly, by a second R2, this one painted in the smart crimson color of the Republic, with the fine insignia of security painted on its carapace . . .

"Ma'am?" The guard on security point eleven was a perspiring middle-aged man with a double chin. His hair was grizzled black and white, cut to a military buzz under the sweat-stained edge of his uniform cap. "Ma'am, I'll have to ask you to step to one side with me here."

Master Leem's jaw began to work. "But, why, Officer? Have I done—"

"Just step over here with me, please."

With all three brows furrowing, Maks Leem followed the guard a few steps behind the scanner equipment. He stood with his back to the crowd. "Don't look around, don't look around. Just act natural. Make it look as if I'm going over your ID chip."

Master Leem looked at him blankly.

"ID," he said.

She handed it over.

He made a show of inserting it into his datapad. "Ma'am, sensors indicate that you are carrying a high-energy focused particle weapon on your person."

"I can explain that—"

"Most of the guys here wouldn't recognize that sensor signature," the guard went on, voice still low. "Not me. I know what it is. I know what you are. There's a group of us, we trade information, you know, but I never thought I'd actually see . . ."

"I'm not sure I understand," Master Leem said.

"Don't look around. Don't look. Just act natural. I

recognize the scanner sig," he said huskily. "You're Jedi, aren't you? I mean, the real thing?"

Maks Leem chewed twice. Three times. "Yes. I am."

"I knew it." The guard's voice was thick with emotion. "You're undercover, aren't you? People say the Jedi are only out for themselves now. They say they're just the Chancellor's secret police. I never bought that for a second. That's not the Jedi way."

"It most certainly isn't," Maks Leem said, genuinely shocked that anyone should think of the Order as the Chancellor's private band of thugs.

"On a mission," the guard said. "Don't look, don't look. Act natural. Just tell me what you need. I can help. Happy to help. Risk no object," he said hoarsely.

"Truly, you are a friend of the Order," Maks said.

"Tell me about it. You know how many times I've seen *Jedi!*—? Fifteen. Fifteen times. And I'm going with my nephew next week. Give me a mission. Just act natural and give me a mission," he said. "Risk no object. Anything to help."

"You've already done it," Master Leem said gently. The guard blinked. "Did you think it was an accident that you were working security today?" she said. "Did you think I came to your line by *chance*?"

He looked at her, awestruck. "By the Force!" he whispered.

"We know who our friends are, Mister . . . Charpp," she said, reading his name off his security badge. She tapped the handle of the lightsaber hidden under her cloak. "But remember, nobody must know. As far as everyone else is concerned, I'm just a humble traveler on her way out to Malastare to visit family. All you need to do now is act natural."

"Act natural." He nodded dutifully, making his chins wobble. "Of course, of course. But . . ." Here his voice grew very slightly wistful. "Is there anything else?"

"You could give me back my ID chip."

"Oh. Right." He shoved it back into her hands, the chip now liberally smirched with sweaty fingerprints.

"When the time comes, we will contact you," Master Leem promised. "In the meanwhile: may the Force be with you!"

Leaving him standing there with tears brimming in his eyes, Master Leem hurried over to the two Padawans. "I'm glad to see you made it through. But where's Jai?" she said. She frowned. "And where's *you know who*?"

Evan Chan hated to fly. Oh, not in the atmosphere. Tooling around the atmosphere in a lightflier was fine. Also, boats were good. As an environmental hydrographer—or "water boy" as his class of professionals were known in the environmental impact biz—he spent lots of time zipping across planetary surfaces and sampling their oceans, rivers, and lakes. It was getting to other planets in the first place that was the problem.

The whole idea of the jump to hyperspace—the atom-juggling, light-smearing, molecule-twisting jump—made Evan queasy. Not just nauseous and sick to the stomach—though it did that, too—but *spiritually* uncomfortable. And yet there was no way to carry out his work as a government-certified pan-planetary water evaluator without jumping. Traveling to any planet outside the

Coruscant system by sublight would take literally life-times.

Which is why he was in the men's refresher of the Delta Concourse at Chance Palp, sipping discreetly from his precious hip flask of liquid courage—SomnaSkol Red, in the 0.1-liter travel size.

He studied himself in the mirror over the sink. To tell the truth, he didn't look great. Faced with the prospect of a longer-than-usual hyperspace jaunt, he hadn't slept much over the last three days. His eyes were hollow and bleary, a two-day stubble shadowed his face like an unpleasant mold, and his knees were feeling distinctly jelly-like. He put his head in his hands and leaned forward over the hard white glare of the sink.

A droid came into the refresher, banging off one wall with the sound of a tin can hitting a ferrocrete sidewalk, and scooted into one of the privacy stalls.

Evan blinked. He was trying to remember if he'd ever seen a droid in a refresher before. Perhaps a custodial droid, but this had been an R2 unit, with no security insignia on it.

"Odd," Evan said out loud. Or at least, that's what he meant to say. As it turned out, the SomnaSkol had left his lips numb, and the word trailed out like the drool one got on oneself at the dentist when one's mouth was frozen.

Another R2 raced into the refresher. This one was wearing Chance Palp colors, black and tan, with a security logo. Its small metal head swiveled aggressively, pointing its cam around the white-tiled room.

The cam froze, trained on the stall where the first droid had gone. The door was open just a crack.

The cam aperture narrowed appraisingly.

Evan Chan shut his eyes very hard, and then opened them. The second droid was still there.

He took another shot of the SomnaSkol.

The security droid now wheeled stealthily—there was no other word for it—toward the suspicious stall. It was one of the big multipurpose stalls, with a toilet, urinal, trough, collection rods, and a telescoping drain with suction action. With infinite care the little security droid reached out with one metal claw, clamped soundlessly on the handle, and tugged the door swiftly to the halfway-open position.

Lights flashed, and the little droid rocked back and forth, wheeping and borping in consternation. Evan squinted, staring at the scene reflected in the mirror. The security droid's cam swept the floor of the stall. It was empty.

After a moment's hesitation, it rolled inside: and as it did, Evan's eye was caught by a flicker of motion in the mirror. The first droid was *floating soundlessly over the top of the stall door.*

Chirps and burbles of dismay. Most from the security droid, but some very definitely from Evan. He watched the first droid come floating noiselessly down behind the stall door. Now the two droids' positions were reversed, with the security droid poking around the stall in a bewildered fashion, and the fugitive droid in the main part of the refresher, hidden behind the stall door.

The fugitive droid stuck out its little arms. The bolt on the stall door shot home with a crack like a blaster rifle pulse, and then squeaked in the most uncanny way, as if the transparisteel rod was being tied into knots.

The security droid went berserk, whooping and beeping and banging on the stall door. Colored lights flashed over the white tiles. For its part, the fugitive droid made an even more horrible sound: a strange, hollow cackle, horribly unsynthetic—the sound of a Kowakian monkey-lizard laughing inside a barrel, perhaps.

Then Evil R2, as Evan had come to think of it, spun and rolled clumsily from the room.

Evan stared at the shaking stall door. He listened to the frantic wails of the trapped security droid. And then, with trembling hands, he took out his flask of Somna-Skol Red and emptied every drop into the sink, swearing he would never touch the stuff again.

6

Ventress took the Jedi courier group just after they dropped into Ithorian local space. *Last Call* was rigged with the best tech Geonosis could supply, including a "gemcutter" prototype built from plans the good folks at Carbanti United Electronics didn't even know had been stolen yet. The gemcutter had been built to counteract the cloaking effect of ships moving in hyperspace, so they couldn't suddenly materialize in the middle of one's fleet like a sand panther dropping from a tree onto the helpless herbivores below. Carbanti's prototype acted like a seismograph, picking up the fault lines a ship tore in the space–time continuum as it prepared to drop out of hyperspace. The warning was usually less than five seconds, but those seconds could mean the difference between life and death.

And of course if one put the gemcutter on a ship as fast and lethal as *Last Call,* flown by a pilot faster and more lethal still, one could entirely reverse the equation, so that, to continue the metaphor, the would-be panther found itself dropping onto a sharpened stake.

Beyond the last planet of the Ithorian system, space–time thinned; buckled; tore. Like a bead of dew condensing on a cold window, the first Republic fighter dropped through the rip and exited hyperspace. Asajj recognized it as an HKD *Tavya*-class armored picket, with an extra proton torpedo battery mounted on its undercarriage. Ignoring her tactical computer and *Last Call*'s HUD sighting reticle, she reached out with the Force, tenderly, entwining the picket like a lover in her embrace. She could see the pilot's eyes go wide with shock; feel the wild rush of adrenaline go screaming through his blood as his sirens went off. She could taste the sudden clammy sweat around his mouth. *"Last call, lover,"* she whispered. *"It's closing time."*

Laser cannons glittered in the silent vastness of space, and the picket ship drifted into splinters, like a Dantooine dandelion head gone to seed and blown apart. It was always strange how quiet death was in space, with no air to carry the thunder of explosions or the screams of the doomed. Even in the Force, one puny life lost made little difference, and the pilot's end came meekly, not with a roar in the mind's ear, but a flickering absence, like a candle going out.

Yoda's wingmates knew their business well enough. Two more pickets had crystallized in realspace. Instantly they understood they were under attack, and opened up with their forward cannons. They shot past Asajj on each flank, screaming insystem.

She tipped *Last Call* up and sent it tumbling, twisting between the deadly blinks of hardened light from the left *Tavya*'s laser cannon. The one on the right belched out two tracers—targeted proton torpedoes, moving nearly twice her current velocity.

Instantly Asajj juked and turned, forcing the torpedoes to bleed off speed in maneuvers. The harder she was to target, the more closely they would have to match her speed. She could sense their mindless little targeting computers, tirelessly reformulating interception angles with her every jerk and twist, and she laughed out loud, corkscrewing insystem after the first ship.

The gemcutter flashed, and a moment later the *Call* told her a *Seltaya*-class armored courier was punching out of hyperspace. Master Yoda had arrived.

She was gaining fast on the first of the Tavyas. He had one turret-mounted laser he could swivel around to fire backward at her, but he never came close to hitting her. On a good day, Asajj Ventress could walk between raindrops, and any day with a chance to bring Yoda's charred green head to her Master was a good one in her books.

The Tavya's pilot stopped firing abruptly, throwing everything he had into a wild dash for the first planet in the system, a lifeless frozen rock one would barely dignify with the word *moon*—but the Ithorians had armed it with a formidable battery of automated defenses as a deterrent for unwelcome visitors. He was hoping to run under the protection of its big guns.

Not that it would work. The *Call* was too fast. He had to see that. His readouts would be telling him. He had to try something new. Duck or rise, that was the question. He couldn't just stop. Asajj reached out through the Force, like another kind of gemcutter, surfing on the Tavya pilot's intention.

Down.

He would dive toward the rapidly approaching battery and hope she overshot. She could feel his heart racing; could feel him steeling himself to hold on, hold on, forcing himself not to commit too early.

She laid a couple of char lines across his wings just to make him twitch.

There—the dive! A fast drop, pulling ten crushing g's. Even his pressure suit couldn't adequately protect him from that. Asajj could feel blackout starting to close over him.

Merciful, really.

With the blood congealing in his veins from pressure, he was only dimly aware of *Last Call* shooting by *underneath* him and pulling sharply up. He didn't have enough extra consciousness to understand that Asajj, anticipating him, had already cut under his line. He couldn't pay *nearly* enough attention to notice the very tiny object trailing her.

The proton torpedo's new interception angle took it straight into the belly of the Tavya and detonated. The ship cracked open like an egg, spilling out white light and a red-stained yolk. Another little candle guttered out.

Yoda must have felt that.

The Tavya that had fired the proton torpedoes at her was banking away, heading back to join Yoda. She picked him off almost casually as another picket ship, the last of the four accompanying Yoda, dropped into realspace.

Three guards down, one to go, and then the Master himself.

Asajj frowned. It was singularly curious that Yoda

hadn't opened fire on her himself. Although he was usually quoted mumbling some piety about the inherent beauty of peace or life, the wizened old swamp toad was no slouch with a lightsaber, by all accounts, and from her reading about the battle on Geonosis, she would have expected him to come to the defense of his entourage with all cannons blazing.

As if in answer to her thought, his ship opened fire, but the shots were slow and wide of the mark. Either the old guy or his R2 unit was fighting the ship while suffering from some kind of damage, or else Yoda had a plan so subtle she couldn't grasp it at all. In a way, she was almost hoping for the latter. If he was sitting there in his cockpit gasping through a stroke, it lessened the glory of the kill very considerably, although she wouldn't, obviously, dwell on that when she reported back to Dooku.

Another few blinks of laserfire flashed off into the distance, missing her by a clear thirty degrees. If the old being had a plan, it was too deep for her to determine. Perhaps he was signaling for reinforcements, with some kind of code embedded in the pulse of his weapons?

Asajj shrugged and accelerated into a corkscrewing attack run on the one remaining picket. Best to get the distractions out of the way.

The gemcutter stammered a warning across her monitors, and a moment later the last of Yoda's protectors jumped right back into hyperspace. Asajj cocked one eyebrow. Better a live womp rat than a dead dire cat, as the saying went. So much the better. The stars knew that an overdeveloped sense of compassion was not one of her vices, but she got no particular pleasure from slaughtering defenseless bystanders.

Now for the Jedi Master himself.

She closed her eyes, feeling for him in the wide darkness of space. It was harder than she had anticipated. Dooku was a presence she could find half a planet away—a burning shadow, darkness made visible. From the Grand Master of the Jedi Order she expected no less . . . but when at last she felt the little frightened pinprick of life inside his ship, he seemed a weak and puny thing.

Perhaps age, that tireless hunter, had chased him down at last? She'd seen old beings wither thus, when the fire of life burned lower until they had no heat left for the great passions, love and hate and fury, but spent their last years in embers, able to support the little fires of avarice, peevishness, anxiety. Life's thin, pinched afterglow.

She felt out for him again, eyes open this time, watching his ship fall steadily under *Last Call*'s shadow. She rested her fingers on the firing buttons as her targeting computers locked down his thrusters, engine core, canopy. She had originally intended to go directly for the engine core, on the theory it would be best to be thorough, but if the old Jedi was going to go this easily, perhaps she should try just pricking open the canopy and letting the vacuum in. That would certainly leave her with a more convincing trophy to hand to Dooku than a series of archived spectrographic analyses that implied some organic residue left in a pile of debris.

The Seltaya juked and twisted mechanically in her sights, but there was no flair to its movements at all. Her fingers tensed.

No.

Ventress took her hands off the firing controls. She knew exactly what the Seltaya was doing. Its R2 unit was executing its factory-standard evasive maneuvers; she recognized them from a dozen previous kills.

Whoever was in that ship, it sure wasn't Yoda.

With a snarl Ventress snapped off a single shot from her lasers, picking off the Seltaya's rear stabilizer and sending it tumbling into space. Under high magnification, she saw the viewports of the Seltaya's cockpit go green. Whoever was in there—a decoy, obviously—was spacesick, and throwing up.

She had ambushed a decoy.

Score one for the other team.

Asajj took a deep breath, refocusing. What to do now? Killing the poor creature over there in a fit of pique would hardly be constructive. The decoy might well have been a child, come to think of it—she had seen the footage of him walking across the spaceport to the starfighter, and if he was more than a meter tall, it wasn't by much.

She shifted over to tractor beams and slowly stilled the tumbling ship. She could just let him go, of course. The R2 ought to be able to pilot him on to Ithor, although the descent would be tricky thanks to the damage she had done to his rear stabilizer. Once he got there, the local authorities could package him up and ship him back to Coruscant. What a farce.

Asajj shook her head. What a fool she felt. To think that the Grand Master of the Jedi Order could possibly go so easily into the long night.

Except . . .

. . . As far as the world knew, that was *exactly* what had just happened.

That cowardly fourth starfighter had seen her destroy the rest of the entourage. Remote surveillance from the Ithorian battery would confirm the engagement. If she were to let the decoy carry on to Ithor, surely the Republic would be a little embarrassed. But if she destroyed his ship in a way that would ensure blasted pieces went spinning insystem for the authorities to find . . . what would happen then?

Her cruel, pretty mouth twisted into a smile. What was it Dooku said to her once? *There are at least two things one appreciates more the older one becomes: excellent wine, and confusion to the enemy.*

She laughed, and dragged the hapless Seltaya in. "Confusion to the enemy," she said.

Obi-Wan Kenobi and Anakin Skywalker stood ankle-deep in the meltwater of spring on the Arkanian tundra, facing a third figure, a tall, imperious woman with the snowdrift eyes of her species. "Please," Obi-Wan said. "Reconsider."

"I have considered the matter long and carefully," the Arkanian said. Her name was Serifa Altunen, and she was a Jedi Knight.

Had been a Jedi.

Carefully she took off her Jedi cloak, folded it up, and handed it to Obi-Wan. "I follow the Force—not the law. I serve the people—not the Senate. I will make peace—not war."

"You swore an oath to the Jedi Order!" Anakin said.

She shrugged. "Then I am forsworn. But I must tell you, I do not feel it much."

"If every Jedi gets to choose which orders she will follow, and which ones she will not, it won't be long before we are all lost," Obi-Wan said.

Serifa's eyebrows rose. "I do not feel lost. The Force is as it always has been. It is the Order that has strayed from the path."

Which probably served Obi-Wan right for coming in philosophical with an Arkanian. Yoda managed to pull off these sage-like meditations, but they never seemed to work out quite right for Obi-Wan. Maybe one just had to be older.

"More to the point, the war will be lost," Anakin said angrily. "Say what you like about following your conscience, but if we divide our forces, the Trade Federation will win. If you think the Republic has strayed from the path of benevolence and wisdom, wait until you experience government by battle droid."

"So you care about winning this war?" the Arkanian asked.

"Of course I do!"

"Why?"

Anakin threw up his hands. "What do you mean, why?"

Serifa gave him that condescending look the Arkanians had been perfecting over the course of millennia. "Perhaps you, too, should examine your path—at least until you come up with a better answer to that question."

They watched her mount the hoversled she had ridden

to this rendezvous and peel away over the thawing tundra on it, raising twin fountains of icy meltwater. Scattered patches of snow and ice the same white as the Arkanian's eyes; white sun, too, glittering on the watery plain as if on broken glass.

Obi-Wan blew out a breath. "That didn't go so well."

"Does she really have influence on the government?"

"I have to think a respected Jedi coming forward to say she has renounced the Order and recommending that Arkania declare itself to be a neutral party in the war would carry weight. At the very best, it's diplomatically damaging, and a public relations nightmare." Obi-Wan turned and slogged back to their ships. They had landed far from any settlements, to avoid drawing undue attention to themselves, but for a weary moment Obi-Wan was missing a cozy bar with a good fire and a chance to drink off one tumbler of excellent Arkanian sweet milk—a demure term for a creamy mead that could leave a strong man under the table.

"Come with me for a moment," Obi-Wan said, waving Anakin away from his own ship. Anakin followed him into his starfighter. "Wipe your feet, or you'll get wet prints all over," Obi-Wan said. "You know the artoo hates that."

"When do we get your old artoo back?"

"When its repairs are done. Given the amount of fire it's seen riding shotgun with me, I'm sure it's in no hurry to report for duty," Obi-Wan said dryly, settling himself in front of the comm console. "You've been sending private messages back to Coruscant."

Anakin flushed. "You've been tracing my outgoing—" He stopped. "You just guessed."

"I am a wise and powerful Jedi Knight, you know," Obi-Wan said, allowing himself a small grin.

The little R2 rolled into the nav-and-comm area and wheeped unhappily at their wet bootprints.

An awkward pause.

"Since part of my duty as your Master is to pass on my vast wisdom—" Obi-Wan began.

"Here it comes," Anakin said.

"—I suppose I should officially remind you that a Jedi has no room in his life for . . . some kinds of entanglement."

"I'll keep that in mind."

"Nonattachment is a fundamental precept of the Order, Padawan. You knew that when you signed up."

"I guess I didn't read the Toydarian print," Anakin growled.

For the first time, Obi-Wan turned away from the holocomm transceiver. "How serious are you about this girl, Anakin?"

"That's not the point," Anakin said, still flushed and angry. "The point is, we are out here asking people to support a Republic that barely knows they exist, and backing it up with a, a police force of Jedi sworn not to care about them! And we wonder why it's a hard sell?" He waved out through the front viewscreen. "What if Serifa is right? What if we are the ones who have lost our way? I trust what I can feel, Master. That's what you have always taught me, isn't it? I trust the living Force. I trust love. The 'principle of nonattachment' . . . ? That's an awfully abstract thing to pledge loyalty to."

"Do you trust hate?" Obi-Wan said.

"Of course I don't—"

"I'm serious, Padawan." Obi-Wan held the younger man's eyes. "To follow your heart, to either love or hate, in the long run is the same mistake. Your judgment becomes clouded. Your motives, confused. If you are not very careful, Padawan, love will take you to the dark side. Slower than hate, yes, but no less surely for that."

The air between them crackled with tension, but finally Anakin lowered his eyes. "I hear you, Master."

"You can hardly help that," Obi-Wan said tartly. "It's whether you believe me or not that matters." He sighed. "For what it's worth, most Jedi make the same mistake. Learn from it; grow through it. If the Order were made up only of those invulnerable to love, it would be a sad group altogether." He turned back to his holocomm transceiver, scanning Arkanian news as he set the encryption key for the transmission he would send back to Coruscant.

"Does that mean there is a woman to be discovered in even Master Obi-Wan's past?" Anakin inquired. "Tall, I imagine, and dark-haired. Pathetically desperate to have anyone at all, *that* much goes without saying—"

"Anakin," Obi-Wan breathed, staring at the news flashing across his monitor. "Be quiet."

"I was only joking!"

Obi-Wan swiveled around in his chair. He had never felt so completely at a loss. "It's Master Yoda," he said. "He's dead."

"What?" Padmé cried.

"Ambushed just outside the Ithor system," her handmaiden said. "The Ithorians have confirmed debris from the Master's ship."

Thoughts of disaster hurtled through Padmé's mind like meteorites. The loss of Yoda was a crippling blow to the Republic—surely Dooku must have been behind it—what would it mean to Anakin? Anakin loved Yoda, of course they all did; but he also said the old Master never completely trusted him, always held him back—if it was true, who would take up the mantle as head of the Order? Mace was a soldier in a soldier's time, but he did not get on so comfortably with Chancellor Palpatine . . .

So her thoughts whirled madly, like snowflakes, drifting down to settle finally on one cold fact: Yoda dead, and the whole universe a little darker for it.

Courage, she told herself. *Hope. When the time grows dark, hope must shine the brighter. If I could trade my life for a chance of a brighter day for the next generation, would I do it?*

In a heartbeat.

"I'm going to the Senate chamber. The Chancellor will have the best and most reliable news." In the doorway Padmé turned to look back over her shoulder at her handmaidens. They seemed shaken and afraid—far more so than if the Chancellor had died. And who could blame them? After more than eight hundred years, it was only natural to think Yoda would be around forever. "I wouldn't write the old Master off yet," Padmé said. "I'll believe he's gone when I see them bring his body back. Not before."

"Thank you for receiving me, Chancellor," Mace Windu said tightly to the holographic image of Chancellor Palpatine projected in the Jedi Council Chamber.

"I am indeed extremely pressed for time, Master Windu, but I value your opinion exceedingly." Palpatine's intelligent face creased with a small, dry smile. "I think you may safely presume that given a choice between listening to the council of Mace Windu, or that of, say, the honorable Senator from Sermeria, with his startling ability to bring any topic under discussion to a close analysis of its impact on the trade in his homeworld's root vegetables, why, I would rather listen to you."

Mace Windu had his weaknesses, but an easy susceptibility to flattery was not one of them. "Thank you," he said briskly, "but may I ask why you have not issued an immediate denial of the reports about Master Yoda? I know—"

Palpatine interrupted him. "This channel is hard-encrypted, Master?"

"Always."

"I assumed as much, but my security forces tell me that Coruscant is presently infested with spies of every description, including the electronic kind. An unfortunate side effect of our policy of allowing unrestricted free movement to practically everyone, with only the flimsiest of security checks."

"The best security, Master Yoda once said, lies in creating a society that nobody wishes to attack."

"Of course! But having somehow failed to convince the Trade Federation, we must play the cards as they have been dealt," the Chancellor said. "This is not a perfect world, and not all our choices are easy ones." This was obviously true, and the kind of hard truth Mace Windu found more comfortable than the Chancellor's little sallies into gallantry and compliment. "Leaving the question of spies aside, I accept your assurance that this transmission is confidential. Carry on, Master Windu."

"I know Yoda was not in the starship destroyed by Asajj Ventress. You know—"

"It was Ventress, then? I think you sent me a file on her some time back."

"Yes, Chancellor. Or at least, it was certainly her ship. It's a distinctive design, patterned after Count Dooku's. We have analyzed the recordings from the fourth pilot—"

"Who will face a court-martial for cowardice by tomorrow evening, with a swift and public sentence," Palpatine said grimly.

"—And the ship is clearly Ventress's *Last Call*. My point being," Mace Windu said doggedly, "I know Master Yoda wasn't in that ship. I told you Master Yoda wasn't in that ship. So why, in the face of news reports of his death that are having a very bad effect on morale, does your office not come forth with a statement?"

For the first time, Chancellor Palpatine's tone held the trace of an edge. "Master Windu, you may recollect that you only thought to inform me that the ship publicly seen to be carrying Master Yoda was a decoy *after* it had launched. In effect, I have only your word that he isn't dead."

"My word," Mace Windu said deliberately, "is one of the few things in the galaxy that a Chancellor of the Republic can trust."

"Of course I trust you," Palpatine snapped. "It's not enough. We have due process for a reason. The Chancellor serves the people and the Senate, not the Jedi Order. The Jedi, likewise, cannot be seen to be my private army.

The people of this Republic must believe their government is directly answerable to them and them alone. It's Count Dooku's whole cry that the Republic is run by a handful of corrupt Senators and their cronies in the Order and the government bureaucracy. If I go before the people and say, *I know you've seen the footage, but my pals in the Temple tell me the whole thing was just a joke, that Master Yoda is still alive, but we don't care to produce him at this time* . . . how do you suppose that will play?"

Wearily Mace Windu rubbed his face. "You're the politician."

"I am, Master Windu. Not a profession you hold in much esteem, but I am a politician—a superb politician—and until such time as you hear me giving you helpful tips on how to wield a lightsaber, I beg you to consider I just might know what I'm doing."

After a brief silence, the Chancellor sighed and the asperity left his voice. "Master Yoda arranged for a decoy so he could travel undetected on his very delicate mission. Tragically, several beings have died to carry out that deception. Shall we throw away their sacrifice? Or shall we honor it, and give Master Yoda a few more days to travel in secret to Vjun, and perhaps end this terrible war?"

"Very well," Mace Windu said at last. "I just hope we're doing the right thing."

"So do I," Palpatine said gravely. "In the meantime, I would take it very kindly if you would take over, on a more formal basis, the daily briefings Master Yoda used to give me."

"Of course."

An aide appeared at the edge of the transceiver's view of Palpatine, telling the Chancellor in a low voice that he was very late for his next appointment. "Duty calls," Palpatine said, moving to cut the comm channel. Then he paused. "Master Windu, since we are being frank with one another today, let me add that in these briefings I wish to hear your own unvarnished opinions—not what you think Master Yoda would have said. He is a great being—perhaps the greatest in the Republic. But Master Yoda is a teacher at heart. You are a warrior. Regrettably, this sad age of the world may be your time more than his."

"Master Yoda is many things, and I am not his equal in peace *or* war," Mace said.

"That's too bad," the Chancellor said, "because right now you are all I have. I expect your best service."

"For the Order and the Republic, I will give anything and everything, including my life."

The Chancellor reached to cut the channel. "Good," he said. "We may need that, too."

"And in this time of crisis," Senator Orn Free Taa of Ryloth rumbled on, "of may I say *deepening* crisis, the apparent death, the willful assassination of the Grand Master of the Jedi Order underscores the urgent need for an entirely new level of security. The Jedi will naturally attempt to carry on their good work: but *they are spread too thin*. Master Yoda's tragic death makes that shockingly plain."

Muttered agreement throughout the vast Senate chamber.

"What we need," the Twi'lek Senator continued, "is a

massive, expert, committed security and counterintelligence force. My fellow legislators, a war such as the one we find ourselves in may be won in battle with great difficulty, but far more easily lost through treachery and sabotage. The resolution I place before you seeks to create such a large, dedicated, aggressive force, not under the jurisdiction of any of our innumerable, glacially slow bureaucracies, but answerable directly to the Chancellor's office and, through it, to us. It is time to put the security of the Republic *first*," he cried. "It is time to put the security of the Republic directly in the hands of her *people*!"

Meaning us, Senator Amidala thought, looking at her fellow Senators. All around her, her colleagues cheered, stomped, whistled, and applauded. Padmé's heart sank. Of course, everyone badly wanted to get some control over a situation that felt increasingly uncontrollable. But if the resolution passed—and it looked very likely to pass—then at some level, the charge of securing the Republic was being shifted from the cool, dispassionate, professional hands of the Jedi Order into the shouting, emotional, highly politicized mob of her colleagues.

Somehow, that didn't make her feel any safer.

The ship on which Whie, Scout, Maks Leem, Jai Maruk, and Master Yoda found themselves finally heading for the Outer Rim had originally been christened the *Asymptotic Approach to Divinity* when she came off her Verpine assembly line, intended as a pilgrim boat for a colony of mathemagi cultists. Unhappily, they had lost their communal savings in an investment banking scandal, leaving the *Approach* without a buyer. Rechristened the *Stardust,* she had gone into the glamour cruise business, taking well-heeled sophisticates on tours of exotic galactic sites and events, such as the Black Hole of Nakat, or the much-anticipated nova of Ariarch-17. Unfortunately, a miscalculation of the shock wave coming off the dying star had caused a dramatic and unexpected failure of the ship's artificial gravity, from which dozens of lawsuits ensued. The litigation lasted two generations, until the lawyers defending the *Stardust's* owners seized her in lieu of fees owed, renamed her *Reasonable Doubt,* and sold her off to Kut-Rate Kruises, whose maintenance protocols basically consisted of filling the ship up with breathable atmosphere and then waiting around in spacedock a couple of days to see how fast the air was leaking out.

The Verpine, though excellent starship engineers, were essentially two-meter-tall bipedal insectoids who communicated instantly through radio waves produced in their chests, and whose visual acuity was so extreme that they could distinguish between male and female lice in a nerf's fur at twenty paces. In consequence, the beds on *Reasonable Doubt* were no more than a hand span wide, the intercom system was nonexistent, and the ship signage, while no doubt screamingly obvious to other Verpine, was completely invisible to Scout. On their first day in space, it had taken her nearly an hour to find a refresher station, wandering the corridors with increasing agitation until she finally broke down and asked a crew member for directions. Embarrassing as that had been, coming out two minutes later to confess that she couldn't figure out which bits of plumbing to use had been worse.

Three days later she and Whie were lost, again, trudging through the labyrinth of corridors that were all slightly too narrow for human comfort. Master Yoda, who loathed being trapped in the R2 shell but was still trying to maintain his disguise, had sent them out to get food well over an hour ago. (Kut-Rate Kruise Lines had no time for frills such as room service.) Other luxury services—bedding, for instance—were also conspicuous by their absence. Scout had spent literally all her life dreaming of the day she would fly offplanet, escaping the Jedi Temple and crowded Coruscant for the wonders of the galaxy. But there had been some kind of mix-up in customs that kept them sitting at spacedock for hours, so that she had actually been asleep for the moment of liftoff, dozing fitfully on what was more like a plank than a bed, still dressed and wrapped in her cloak, aware of the great moment only because a sudden lurch had dumped her onto the floor. It had been a bit anticlimactic, and she had been grumpy ever since.

Plus she was now quite certain that Jai Maruk, her Jedi Master, didn't like her at all. But she wasn't going to let herself think about that just now.

As for the food . . . Scout shuddered. Master Yoda ate it without complaint, but then, perhaps he had evolved beyond ordinary mortal concerns.

Like smell.

Anyway, the last time she had seen the old Jedi with a bowl of food in the Temple rectory, there had been a tail hanging over the edge.

"I'm telling you, we're too low," Scout said. "We should have taken the lift tube to Level Fourteen. That's what the sign said."

"That wasn't a sign. It was a scuff mark on the lift tube wall."

"Sign."

"Scuff."

"Sign!"

Whie took a breath. "Perhaps it *was* a sign, and I am mistaken. Let's try Level Fourteen."

Scout stalked along the narrow corridor. "You know, the way you do that takes all the fun out of being right."

"The way I do what?"

"Give in. It's like even though I'm right and you're wrong, somehow you're just humoring me. Jedi serenity is all very well, but in a thirteen-year-old boy it's sort of creepy."

"What do you want from me?"

"Argue! Fight! Don't be this . . . this *pretend Jedi,*" Scout said. "Can't you just be human, for once?"

Whie's mouth quirked in a little smile. "No," he said.

The truth was, Whie was preoccupied. Master Leem had hinted they were going to Vjun to meet with someone very important—maybe Count Dooku himself, and possibly the famous Jedi-killer Asajj Ventress. Whie had done a computer look-up on her, and found himself staring at the woman from his dream.

Ventress would be waiting for them on Vjun. In a few days, a week at most, he would be standing in a room with a ticking detonator. Ventress would be smiling. Scout would turn to him with blood trickling down her shirt. "Kiss her," Ventress would say.

He wished he knew what he was going to answer.

* * *

They were standing in the cooked-food line—the lines for raw were far too long—when someone tapped Scout politely on the shoulder. "Passenger Pho?"

"What? I mean, Yes?" Scout said, belatedly remembering that she, Whie, and Jai Maruk were traveling as the Pho family, en route to a cousin's wedding on Corphelion.

She found herself looking up at a tall humanoid-shaped droid that had seen better days. If it had ever featured any markings—paint, interface instructions, or even a brand name—they had long since been worn away, so its whole body had a dull, scuffed, scratched look, as if it had been sanded down and never refinished. "The ship's purser asked me to fetch you," the droid said. "It seems one of your belongings has been turned in to the Lost and Found."

Scout blanched. It had become depressingly clear over their first few days together that Jai Maruk didn't think much of her. She could just imagine the expression on his lean, closed face if he heard she'd had to bail her lightsaber out of *Reasonable Doubt*'s Lost and Found. "What did I lose?"

"The purser neglected to mention," the droid said politely. "Will you come this way?"

She looked at Whie, who nodded. "Go ahead. I can manage." Still Scout hesitated. "Don't worry," Whie said. "I won't *tell*."

He isn't trying *to humiliate me,* Scout told herself. *It just works out that way.*

The scuffed droid turned and headed for the lift tube. Scout trudged after him. "Your finish is pretty worn," she said, making conversation.

"I am not a regular part of *Reasonable Doubt*'s crew," he explained. "I offered to work for them in exchange for my passage. Regrettably, my owner is dead," the droid went on. "I am responsible for my own upkeep."

The lift tube door opened. "I never thought of that," Scout said. "What would happen to a droid with no owner, I mean."

"I hadn't, either," her companion remarked dryly, "until it happened to me."

"What do you do about maintenance?" Scout asked. "Go back to the factory? Find a repair tech? But how would you pay for repairs?"

"Your grasp of the problem is admirable," the droid said. "As it happens, I was part of a rather small production run, now very obsolete. I am programmed to perform a good many repairs on myself, but spare parts are hard to come by, and correspondingly expensive, as they must be either bought as antiques or custom-built from my specifications. The challenge is considerable, as you surmised."

"Wouldn't cost you much for a couple of cans of metal paint, though," Scout said, glancing at her guide's scuffed bare metal surfaces.

"Ornamentation is not logically a high priority."

"Easier to get a job if you look smart, though. Think of it as a business expense."

The droid shrugged, a strangely human gesture. "There is some truth in what you say . . . and yet, there is something honest about this," he said, touching the bare metal surface of his cheek. "It seems to me that most sentients live in a . . . cocoon of illusions and expectations. We are full of assumptions: we think we know ourselves and those around us; we think we know what each day will bring. We are confident we understand the arc and trajectory of our lives. Then Fate intervenes, strips us down to bare metal, and we see we are little more than debris, floating in darkness."

Scout looked at him. "Whoa. You must have been a philosopher droid off the assembly line."

"Quite the opposite," he said, with a sharp inward expression. "Philosophy has come rather late to me." The lift tube arrived at Level 34, and the doors slid open. "After you, Mistress Pho," he said.

"My friends call me Scout." She stuck out her hand.

Gravely the droid accepted it. "I don't think I can count myself as a friend, yet. Just a droid with a job to do."

"Now you tell me your name," Scout prompted. "That's how this works."

"Certainly not. However trusting *you* are, I certainly don't know enough about you to give you *my* real name." Relenting, he added, "For now, you may call me Solis, if you prefer."

"It beats 'Hey, Scuffy!' " Scout had the distinct impression that if the droid's factory programming had included an eye-roll function, he would have deployed it. She grinned. "Solis it is."

The line in the cafeteria was interminable, even for cooked food, but after what felt like a galactic age Whie had finally placed his orders and paid for them. Now he stood looking uneasily over his haul. One large bubble-

and-squirt; five orders of vacuum flowers; half a dozen of what the menu called *Blasteroids!* and appeared to be double-fried chili dumplings; a bucket of crispy feet; and a sloshing half bucket of rank (extra gummy), along with five drinks and a handful of napkins. That ought to be enough, Whie thought. But how was he going to get it back to the cabin?

Would Asajj be the one who left Scout bleeding? Or would they be captured by guards and taken before her already hurt?

If he kissed her, would he taste the blood on the edge of her mouth?

Stop! Don't think about it.

Don't think. Don't think.

Whie's immediate instinct was to pile the food in a stack and trust to balance and a little judicious application of the Force to keep it from toppling over, but that seemed a bit conspicuous. How would an ordinary person handle this? *Awkwardly,* he decided, glancing around the cafeteria and watching a hefty female shouldering between tables with a tray on each hand and a sniveling toddler attached to each leg. Maybe he could grab one of the *Doubt*'s little service droids and get it to help carry trays down to their rooms.

"May I help you, sir?" said a tall droid painted with immaculate cream-and-crimson livery, appearing at his elbow as if conjured by his thoughts.

The Force is with me, Whie thought with an inward smile. "No, that's all right. I don't want to take you from your owner's duties. If you could help me find a ship's droid, though . . ."

The droid picked up the Blasteroids and the bucket of rank. "I insist, Master Whie."

"That's very k—" Whie froze. "I'm sorry. What did you call me?"

"Master Whie," the droid said, in a low, pleasant voice.

"My name is Pho—"

The droid shook its head. "It won't do, Master Whie—it really won't. I know a very great deal about you. It's possible I know more about you than you know about yourself."

Whie set the food on an empty table. His hand was light and tingling, ready to dive beneath his robes and draw his lightsaber. "Who are you? What are you? Who do you belong to?"

"I suggest," the droid said—and his voice was in deadly earnest now—"you ask yourself those exact questions."

Down in the ship's exercise room, Jai Maruk was working out in anticipation of his second meeting with Count Dooku, honing his body as another person might sharpen a knife.

Maks Leem was meditating in what had once been a storage closet, but was now officially listed on *Reasonable Doubt*'s directory as Cabin 523. Master Leem had her own room, next door to the others. Partly this was because she liked to meditate for several hours every day, preferably surrounded, as now, by a choking cloud of Gran incense that smelled, to the human olfactory system, like burning thicklube. But the chief reason the others had encouraged her to take a room of her own was that the Gran's four ruminant stomachs worked loudly and continuously all night long in a way that humans found impossible to sleep through.

Being at heart a social creature, Master Leem regretted being secluded from her human comrades, and in fact spent most of the waking hours with them. But now, with Jai exercising and the Padawans dispatched to the cafeteria, she had gone next door to her little snuggery. Surrounded by smoke thick enough to drop a small mammal, she was happily reestablishing her connection to the living Force that bound all things.

Next door, in Cabin 524, Grand Master Yoda was wondering what in space was keeping the Padawans. He wasn't worried for their safety. He was *starving*.

The whole point of travel, Scout reflected, was to learn about oneself. In that sense, this trip was going really well. She had learned all sorts of things. She had learned that being chosen to be a Padawan did not necessarily bring every happiness with it, as she had thought it would, if one's Master obviously viewed you as excess baggage. She had learned that her body was entirely too used to the comfortable and familiar food served at the Jedi Temple, and that the galaxy was large, and full of people who willingly ate the most disgusting stuff imaginable. And she had learned that she had absolutely no sense of direction at all, because it seemed as if her interminable trek with the droid Solis—whom she couldn't stop thinking of as Scuffy—must have taken her through the whole ship about three times. "Look, this is ridiculous," she finally said. "Have the purser send whatever it is to my cabin. If I can ever find my cabin again," she added.

"Here we are," Solis said imperturbably; and indeed, they had turned a last corner and stood before a small door marked PURSER'S OFFICE: SHIP'S PERSONNEL ONLY in Verpine signage, which was to say, so faint that Scout's nose was touching the door in her attempt to make out the letters. "Wait here one moment," the droid said, and he disappeared inside.

Scout waited.

And waited.

And waited.

"That's it," she growled. But at exactly the moment she was about to stomp away, the door hissed open and Solis returned.

"Good news," the droid said politely. "The missing item didn't belong to you. It has already been claimed."

"What?"

"It seems it was a handbag belonging to another Mistress Pho. A simple case of mistaken identity," the droid explained. "So sorry for the inconvenience."

The Jedi, Scout reminded herself, *is serene. She is not pushed lightly about by life's little whimsicalities. A true Jedi would not be imagining how this droid would look disassembled into three buckets of bolts and a heap of scrap metal.*

The droid's head tilted to one side. "Is there something amiss, mistress?"

"No," Scout grated. "Nothing at all. I'll just be getting back to my room now." She stalked away from the purser's office and turned a corner into the labyrinth of ship's corridors. Solis—whose hearing was based on the legendary Chiang/Xi audiofilament tech—listened to her footsteps recede for quite some time; stop; and slowly return.

"All right," she growled, turning the same corner several minutes later. "How in the name of crushing black holes do I even find my cabin?"

"Allow me to help," the droid said suavely.

"Charmed," the girl snarled.

Far away in third class, Taupe Corridor, Level 17A, the door of Cabin 524, registered to the Pho family, slid most of the way into the floor. The Verpine usually built their doors to slide downward, so that a room's occupant could see outside and if necessary converse with whoever was on the doorstep without embarrassment, even if wearing only a bathrobe. This door opened only *most* of the way, however, leaving a jutting lintel that any reasonably active five-year-old could have jumped over, because under the standing orders of the witty ship's engineer, maintenance cycles were only to be expended on third class if something was broken "beyond all Reasonable Doubt."

For a bipedal human, stepping over a lintel only fifteen centimeters high was no great challenge. To a squat, garbage-can-shaped R2 unit on wheels, however, the challenge was somewhat greater.

Routine security in the public spaces of *Reasonable Doubt* was handled by bottom-of-the-line Carbanti surveillance monads. Each monad was essentially a small cam and microphone slaved to a very dim little artificial intelligence. The making of efficient AIs was as much an art as a science, and the AIs assigned to surveillance monads were by and large the slowest kids in the class. Even by these standards, the mechanical consciousness monitoring the corridor in front of Cabin 524, Level 17A, was notably dim-witted. The whole range of criminal behavior, its patterns and motivations, was entirely beyond it. Several spectacular thefts and one rather amusing con game featuring a fish, a diamond, and two deaf-mutes had taken place directly under its cam without provoking the slightest urge to pass a Questionable Activity Report up to the larger and more intelligent AI that reported to ship security. The truth was, this particular monad had only one idea in what passed for its brain, and that idea was *Fire!* It had been waiting its entire existence, some seventy-three trillion processor cycles, for something to register on its infrared or smoke detectors. Then it would finally be able to break its eternal silence with a scream of lights and klaxons.

To say that the security monad on Taupe Corridor, Level 17A, *longed* for an event of fire would not be too strong a word. The never-flashed alarm lights and the never-rung klaxons were like seventy-three trillion processor cycles of a sneeze that wouldn't quite come. By this time, the little security monad would quite willingly have melted its own processors down to sand if only it could sound the alarm of *Fire!* first.

The sight of an R2 unit rolling up to the stuck door in Cabin 524, however, gave it no pause whatever—even when said R2 thumped painfully into the barrier and emitted a surprisingly unmetallic yelp, followed by a snuff of frustration. The sight of the little droid reaching out with one jerking mechanical arm to whap the stuck door repeatedly in what was, for a machine, a markedly petulant manner might have provoked some curiosity in an AI of greater intellectual accomplishments. In strict point of fact, the engineers at Carbanti would have said that even their least gifted security monad would surely have been struck by the sight of the same R2 unit rising slowly into the air *without the aid of any visible boosters or rockets.* When the droid settled back down into the corridor with a clang and rolled off with a decidedly puckish, questing air, it would not have been too much to expect a security monad with even minimal intiative to flag the little droid for linked follow-up observation.

But the monad in Taupe Corridor did nothing of the kind. The sad truth was, the only circumstance in which it would have paid the slightest iota of attention to this hungry, flying, bad-tempered R2 was if some helpful passenger had doused the little droid in lighter fluid and set it on fire.

Back in the cafeteria, long lines of bored passengers were still queued up for food. Children dabbled designs on the plastic cafeteria tables with bits of dipping sauce, or tried to convince their parents they had eaten their vegetables by hiding them under overturned cups. On the other side of the room, opposite the food service area, a giant holovid display was running endless coverage of the latest tragedies of the Clone Wars.

In short, there was nothing to show that the world as Whie knew it had slipped over some terrible event horizon, never to be seen again.

"You were born Whie Malreaux," the red-and-ivory droid said in its fussy, precise manner. "You came into this life on the planet of Vjun, after a difficult labor that lasted two standard nights and a day in early spring. You were a good-natured child, unlike your unfortunate brother, quick to walk and quick to talk. The one thing he did better than you was sleep," the droid said, still speaking quietly but holding Whie's eyes with his own. "For even as a very young child, you were troubled by your dreams."

"How do you know all this?" Whie whispered.

"I was there."

"But—"

The droid touched his livery of metal paint. "These are the colors of the House Malreaux, crimson and cream; blood and ivory, if you prefer. And I am a servant of that house."

Whie felt as if his mind had just made the jump to hyperspace. Into it leapt the image from his most recent visionary dream—himself and Scout and the evil woman standing in a rich house, the rich carpet under his feet, and under it, stretching away from the woven edges, a checkered floor of red and ivory tiles.

Home. The word a certainty in his heart.

He was going home.

"When the Jedi stole you from your home—"

"Stole! The Jedi don't steal!"

The droid brushed him aside with a brisk wave of his hand. "They found your mother in a weak moment, shocked by the death of her husband and so drunk she was half insensible. I urged her to reconsider, but nobody listens to a droid's advice." He sniffed. "The point is, the thing was done, and could not be undone. But within days your mother realized the Jedi had kidnapped the heir of a noble house. She sent me to Coruscant to watch over you, and wait."

"Ten years? Eleven?" Whie said, incredulous.

The droid shrugged. He was extremely well programmed—while still clearly a machine, his movements were fluid, natural, and precise.

"My name is Fidelis," the droid said. "I am programmed for absolute loyalty to the House Malreaux, which I have served through madness and war for twelve generations. Now I serve you."

"But, but . . . I don't want—" Whie stammered. "I am Jedi. I have no other family. I can't accept your service."

"Beg pardon, Master, but my service is mine to give. Whether you choose to accept it or not is outside the parameters of my programming."

"Then I order you to leave me alone!"

"Your mother is currently the head of House Malreaux, and while I respect your wishes, you do not currently have the authority to countermand her instructions. Beyond which," Fidelis said, "my ultimate loyalty is to the House Malreaux itself, and I am programmed with wide discretionary powers in deciding which actions best serve the family. In this case, I am very comfortable looking out for you, whether you wish me to or not. I can offer you some choices about what form that service would take," he went on soothingly. "I am most comfortable in my preferred role as your gentleman's personal gentlething, but if you would prefer a wordless bodyguard, or even a discreet assassin who simply haunts your travels, I am fully equipped to fill those roles."

"You don't understand," Whie said plaintively. "There's no such thing as a Jedi who runs around the galaxy with a, a, *gentleman's personal gentlething*!"

"There is now. Master Whie, consider your familial obligations. At this very moment you have a mother who waits for you in Château Malreaux, daily insulted and degraded by the odious Count Dooku."

"Dooku!" Whie said. "Dooku is at my house *right now*?" He sprang up from the table and loped toward the lift tube banks. "I've got to tell Y—I've got to tell the others right away."

Fidelis, humming to himself and turning over Whie's use of the phrase *my house*, gathered up the trays of food and drink and followed. He didn't have the Force to aid him, but he had waited table at the Château Malreaux for twelve generations, and in the matter of moving quickly while carrying vast amounts of food, it came to pretty much the same thing.

Across the cafeteria from Whie and Fidelis, the ship's holobroadcast was interrupted for a special news bulletin.

Meanwhile, in a turbolift moving briskly toward the Taupe Corridor of Level 17A, Scout and Solis were debating the conduct of the Republic and the Confederacy in the current conflict. "Honestly," Scout said with some heat, "do you really want to live in a world run by battle droids?"

Had Solis's manufacturer seen fit to equip him with eyebrows, he would have raised them.

"Oh," Scout said, looking at her own dim reflection in the scuffed metal plate of the droid's chest. "Well, I guess that would look different, from your point of—"

She stopped suddenly, her attention caught by the words *"Master Yoda"* echoing tinnily from the little holo-screen above the lift tube buttons.

". . . this video, shot from a defense installation at the edge of the Ithorian system, clearly shows the attacker destroying all but one of the Jedi Master's guard ships. The attacker's ship, a modified version of Count Dooku's notorious sailer, has been identified as Last Call, *registered to the notorious pirate and saboteur Asajj Ventress, who is wanted on eight worlds in connection with the deaths of eleven Jedi Knights."*

"Seventeen!" Asajj growled, shaking her head. "Can you believe that? And they call themselves journalists."

Palleus Chuff, lashed firmly into the copilot's seat of *Last Call,* assumed that this was a rhetorical question. Just as well. He was normally as glib as kiss-your-hand Palleus Chuff; considered quite witty in the better circles of the Coruscant actors' fraternity, which was saying a lot. But between the gag in his mouth and the unfortunate tendency to faint that had been coming over him at regular intervals since Ventress's tractor beams first gripped on to his ship, holding a conversation was more than he could currently manage.

". . . while a second clip released by Ithorian officials clearly shows a debris field now positively identified as

the remains of Master Yoda's ship. Chancellor Palpatine's office has declined to comment before a thorough investigation into the ambush has been completed, but privately, faces in the capital are grim, as the Republic must prepare for new Confederacy offensives without the Jedi who was not only her chief military strategist, but, in a very important way, her heart and soul."

"But that's not right," Scout blurted. "That's impossible." She looked blankly at Solis. "We have to tell them!"

"Tell them what?" he asked blandly.

"Um—nothing," she said, collecting her wits. "Nothing. Tell my friends, is what I meant. I have to get back to the room and tell my friends *right away.*"

"Certainly," Solis said. "We're almost there."

In the Kidz Arkade, Donni Bratz was watching his brother Chuck play his fourth consecutive game of Wookiee Warpath. "Is it my turn now?" he asked timidly. He tried to say it quietly, so as not to interrupt.

"Donni, shut it. I'm in the middle of the Gozar level, here." Chuck was playing hard now, using a little footwork and all the advantages his four thumbs could give him.

Donni thought Chuck was a god when it came to Wookiee Warpath.

Chuck had put his StarFries and Fizzy-Bip down next to the machine. Some very bad part of Donni considered tipping the Fizzy-Bip over, but he would certainly never do such a thing. Chuck, as Mom never stopped telling him, was the best big brother a guy could have. Besides, the last time he did something like that, Chuck had tied him to the old zink-sled with the missing right rear gimble and set it going until he threw up all over Mom's newly upholstered lounge chair.

Donni watched Chuck play, trying to be content with admiring his brother's skill, but after the Flying Knives and the Swamp level, and when Chuck had completely exploded all the Floating Toads of Doom, Donni couldn't help saying, "You *said* I could have a turn after you. You *said*. And that was four credits ago," he added under his breath.

"Don't be a pest, Meatface."

Donni's antennae slumped over. "Mom said you weren't supposed to call me that."

Chuck tore the arm off a green Wookiee with a smartly executed Twister Grab. "Well, Meatface, Mom isn't here, is she?"

Unnoticed by Chuck, who was in tense hand-to-hand with four berserk Wookiees, a short R2 unit lurched somewhat erratically into the Arkade and then stopped dead with its central video sensor locked in on the Fizzy-Bip. Donni watched, puzzled, as the little droid sidled up to Wookiee Warpath and reached for the Bip with one jerky mechanical claw. The claw snapped, missed, grabbed again.

"Hey," Donni said.

"Shut up, Meatface! It's not your *turn* yet!"

"But—" Donni gulped as the top of the little R2 swiveled around and locked on to his eyes. A queer, almost glassy feeling came over him, and then, as if by magic, two ideas popped vividly into his head, one after another. The first was that actually, when you got right down to it, Chuck was kind of a creep, and it would serve him right if some R2 unit stole his drink.

The second was: *What drink?*

On its way out of the Arkade, the little R2 paused, orienting to a small holoscreen by the door, where a carefully groomed news holoanchor, nearly inaudible over the simulated blasterfire, was saying, *"For a commentary on today's shocking news, we go to correspondent Zorug Briefly, who asks the question of the hour—What now, Jedi Knights?"*

Two bells binged softly in the turbolift bank at the bottom of Taupe Corridor, and two sets of doors slid smoothly down on either side of the foyer, so that Scout found herself facing the R2 unit. "You!" she said. "You're not supposed to be out! Where have you been?"

The little R2 dropped an empty Fizzy-Bip carton in what a careful observer might have called a furtive manner. Scout, bursting with her news, didn't notice.

The bare metal droid standing next to her did, though.

Scout was already running down the corridor. "It doesn't matter. Listen, we have to get a message back to—" She glanced at Solis. "—to *our friends* right away. There's been a terrible mix-up."

The R2 gave an unconvincing chirp and wheeled after her, taking the corner so fast it rose up on one wheel.

Solis watched the little R2 very thoughtfully indeed, and then, without appearing to hurry, moved swiftly after them.

Seconds later, Whie appeared at the other end of Taupe Corridor, running fast and shouting.

"Have you heard?" Scout yelled to him as she banged on the door of 524.

"He's on Vjun!" Whie said. "Count Dooku! He's on Vjun!"

The security monad mounted over the Taupe Corridor was not nearly a close enough observer to notice that this remark had been directed not to Scout, but to the little R2 unit.

Solis, on the other hand, was a very close observer indeed. He might not have the latest hologame downloads installed on his system, but Fate had given him an altogether more varied life than his companion, Fidelis, who now came trotting after Whie. Underneath his metal exterior, Fidelis was somewhat overwhelmed by the longed-for consummation of actually serving the Malreaux boy. Solis, who had no especial feelings for House Malreaux in general or this boy in particular, was more riveted by the fact that the tray Fidelis was carrying held five drinks, instead of four.

"Master Jai! Master Jai, open up! It's me!" Scout said, continuing to hammer on the door. "We have to send a message to the Temple!"

At this moment, a series of events occurred in quick succession. First, the door to Cabin 524 slid almost (but not completely) open, releasing a billow of steam and revealing Jedi Master Jai Maruk, looking considerably put out and wearing nothing but the towel he had grabbed on his way out of the shower. "This had better be important," he said, glowering at Scout.

As he spoke, the door of Cabin 523 slid down, and Master Maks Leem's worried face peered out through a cloud of dense black incense smoke. "Whie? What's all the commotion?"

"I just found out where Doo—"

Here Whie was interrupted by a loud crash as the little R2 unit careened—apparently by accident—into Fidelis, and the rest of the Padawan's words were drowned in the clatter and splash of dinner for five hitting the floor.

At the same moment, the Taupe Corridor security monad watched in electric ecstasy as the clouds of steam and incense in the corridor finally surpassed the hazard level on its built-in smoke detectors. Lights flashed and alarms sounded with all the passion of seventy-three trillion processor cycles of anticipation.

"Mistress Pho," Jai Maruk said heavily, "do you remember what the number one priority of this trip was?" He hitched his towel up with one hand and looked grimly from Scout to the flashing alarms, to the spilled food and the watching droids, and back to Scout again.

Scout gulped. "Yes, Mast—I mean, Father."

"And what was it?"

Whie and Scout exchanged pale looks before replying in unison. *"Keep a low profile."*

The extremely private comm console on *Last Call* chimed. "Yes?"

It was a droid. "I have some information you may be interested in acquiring."

"Not likely," Asajj said.

"I know where Yoda is. The real one."

Asajj sat up straight. "What do you mean? Don't you watch the news? Yoda is—"

"I can cut this link right now," the droid said. He was unmarked and unpainted, and his calm voice carried absolute conviction.

"No!" Asajj said sharply.

"You admit you are interested?"

"I might be."

"Would your interest extend to seven hundred and thirty-four thousand nine hundred ninety-five Republic credits?"

"A curious sum."

Her caller shrugged. "My treason tables are very precisely calibrated."

Asajj thought for a moment. "I think we might be able to do business."

When the terms had been negotiated and the communication broken off, Asajj set a course for Phindar Spaceport. After a moment's thought, she lifted a clip of the droid's face from the comm console's log of their communication and asked the computer to make a deep search, looking for a match for the droid's particular make and model. Such a search was rather slow, given the transmission lag between her current position and the 'Net, so she grabbed a quick lunch and administered an ampoule of adrenaline to her prisoner, whose tendency to stop breathing and pass out was becoming annoying.

The comm console gave a polite cough to announce the completion of her search. "Match found," it said, displaying a picture from the authorative *Peterson's Guide to Droids of the Republic,* Vol. VII: *The Great Corporate Expansion Era.*

THE LEGENDARY TAC-SPEC FOOTMAN DROID. PRODUCED AT ENORMOUS EXPENSE IN A LIMITED PRODUCTION RUN, MOST EXPERTS CONSIDER THE FOOTMEN THE DEADLIEST PERSONAL SERVICE UNITS EVER CREATED, COMBINING FANATICAL LOYALTY WITH A KILL RATIO THAT MAKES THE STATS OF MODERN-DAY ASSASSINS PALE IN COMPARISON.

Asajj came away from her console looking very thoughtful indeed.

7

Jai Maruk had always been a light sleeper, and at the first stealthy rustle he was wide awake. His hand was light and tingling, ready to sweep out the lightsaber from under his cot. He reached out with the Force, sensing the room: the Esterhazy girl was out like a log, making little snores. Even through the thin walls Jai could feel the gentle glow, like a banked fire, of Master Yoda, who now slept next door—Cabin 522 had opened up when another passenger had debarked two days ago.

Another rustle. Jai Maruk relaxed. There was no intruder; just Whie, stealing quietly into a set of robes. Wound up about something; across the room in the dark, Jai could feel him in the Force, his nerves jangling like the strings of a tri-harp.

Well, Jai thought, *no surprise there.* His first trip out of the Jedi Temple, and none of the challenges he was facing were the ones he'd been preparing for. Apprentices always thought the life of a Jedi Knight was all lightsaber battles and high-level diplomatic negotiation, because that's what they were trained for. There was no classroom work to simulate running into a servant who claimed you were some sort of long-lost prince of Vjun.

After the cleanup crews had made their sweep through Taupe Corridor, he and Maks Leem had met with Fidelis, the droid who claimed to serve Whie's human family, and his partner, Solis. At least it was clear to Jai that they were partners; he wasn't sure the Padawans had figured out that Tallisibeth's trip to the purser's office had simply been a ruse to allow Fidelis to get Whie alone. It was a curious business all in all, and certain to be distracting for the boy.

Jai had felt a fierce hope that the droid would be able to give them information about Dooku and his movements, but its information turned out to be strictly secondhand; it had not been back to Vjun in a decade.

Still, the droid's descriptions of Château Malreaux did match the glimpses Jai had gotten during his brief interview with the hated lapsed Jedi, Count Dooku, and his despicable lapdog Asajj Ventress. Jai had asked Fidelis for complete schematics on the château and its surrounding terrain, so they could prepare a plan of escape in case Master Yoda's negotiations with Dooku went badly. Exasperatingly, the droid had all but ignored him; he would only take orders from Whie. He certainly knew Jai and Maks were Jedi—a term that he clearly found roughly interchangeable with *cradle-robber* or *kidnapping cultist*.

It was one of the things they never quite mentioned in the Temple—how many people, even in the Republic, viewed the Jedi with distrust or even outright fear and hostility. The sentiment had grown during the Clone Wars, to the point that Jai hated going on the missions to identify new Jedi; as much as he knew the children they found were going to lead better, richer, and more useful lives than they would otherwise have had, the whispers of *"baby-napper!"* bothered him, as did the heartbroken eyes of the parents who watched their children being led away. Less painful but still ugly was the relief in the eyes of a different kind of parent, the ones glad to be rid of the burden of an extra mouth to feed.

One couldn't see that without wondering which kind of baby one had been oneself.

And now *"Palpatine's Secret Police"* was a whisper he was hearing more and more often—even, painfully, from schismatic Jedi who had left the Order.

But however unpleasant it was for Jai to see the word *Jedi* fill people's eyes with fear and distrust, instead of hope and gratitude, he was at least used to it. Maks Leem, who rarely left the Temple, and especially the young Padawans had been shocked to see just how mixed the public's feelings about the Jedi truly were.

And on top of all that, for Whie, there was the issue of the girl.

Tallisibeth was pushy and smart and pretty in an athletic way, and she was weak in the Force. A more disruptive combination it would have been hard to imagine, Jai thought wearily. Presumably Master Yoda had his reasons for bringing her along, but a stronger Padawan with a little less personality would have made life a lot easier. For one thing, Whie couldn't stop looking at her. This was normal, of course, in a thirteen-year-old boy forced into close quarters with a pretty girl for days on end: but it wasn't helping anybody focus. Scout didn't seem to have noticed the boy's habit of stealing glances at her, but to judge from Master Leem's affectionate little smirk, Whie certainly wasn't fooling his own Master. This would have been nothing but fun and games at the Jedi Temple—adolescence had its laughs at the expense of a few Padawans every year—but out here, on a mission to confront Count Dooku, it was one more distraction Jai didn't want.

Jai liked the girl, too.

He didn't want to, to be honest. With the war going as it was, Jedi lives were being risked far more frequently than at any time since the Sith War. A girl like Scout— *Enwandung-Esterhazy,* he reminded himself; *don't fall into the familiarity of nicknames, Jai*—a girl like that was going to be dead within a year.

That was going to hurt enough already. He didn't need it to hurt any more.

Whie had slipped into his robes. The room door slid down almost to the floor, revealing a dim hallway outside. The corridor lights had blown out when the fire alarm went off, and though Maintenance had taken out the hugely excited security monad, they hadn't gotten around to fixing the lighting.

Jai watched the boy step over the stub of door and close it again.

Jai would bet ten credits the boy was bound for the gym. Jai was pretty sure he had put in a few midnight workouts of his own as a Padawan, trying not to think about some girl . . . who was it? Jang Li-Li's red-haired friend. Politrix, that was her name. Killed in an ambush two months after Geonosis. Plasma grenade.

He remembered the fall of her hair, red ringlets around

her shoulders. The smell of it one day—they had been sparring in the exercise room, she pinned him and laughed, her hair dangling down to his cheek.

Gone now.

Jai felt a tear on his cheek and let it come. Grief, too, was a part of life: no use denying it. From a calm center he watched it, this grief. So much sorrow. So many of his childhood friends already gone.

It was getting harder now, to feel the grief without giving in to it. What had Master Yoda said once? *Too long sorrow makes a stone of the heart.*

So he tried not to like Scout so much, and at the same time he could feel himself pushing her, pushing her: willing her to be stronger and faster and more deadly because that's what she would need. She was brave enough, by the stars—even he would give her that. But brave wasn't enough. He'd been brave, standing before Dooku and Asajj Ventress. It hadn't kept him from failing.

Jai's breath came out in an exasperated hiss. So much for his Jedi serenity.

He lay in the dark a little while longer, then gave up all hope of sleep, slipped into his robes (far more quietly than Whie had managed), and followed the boy out into the ship, leaving Scout's strangely touching littlegirl snores behind.

As predicted, he found the boy in the workout room, going through the Broken Gate unarmed combat form—swing, stamp, strike, throw! He was good—better than good, he was quicksilver, letting the Force ball and surge in counterpoint to his movements, suspending it in a high flip, and then calling it down like a thunderbolt in the last stroke. Where the boy's feet had landed, the floor mat burst open, spewing out rockets of foam.

"Excellent," Jai said quietly.

Whie spun, flipped, and landed in a fighting stance, his open hands up, cupping the Force like chain lightning in his palms. "What do you want?"

Jai blinked. "Is that how you speak to a Jedi Master, Padawan?"

Whie stared at him, chest heaving.

"Padawan?"

"Would you kill another Jedi?" Whie said abruptly. "If you thought he had gone over to the dark side?"

"Yes."

"Just like that? Aren't we all supposed to be family?"

"*Because* he was family," Jai Maruk said. "A Jedi who has turned to the dark side is not a common criminal, Whie. His gifts and abilities give him a great power for evil."

"You wouldn't give him a chance to reform?"

"Once the dark side has you, boy, it doesn't let go." Jai cocked his head. Carefully, he said, "I hope, Padawan, you are not confusing a moment's weakness with a wholesale embrace of the dark side. We all have our vices—"

"Even Master Yoda?"

"Even Master Yoda! Or at least so he claims. I don't know what they are, though I will say that when Master Yoda is hungry, his temper does not sweeten." Jai grimaced. "My own temper is not well regulated. It might be described as angry and resentful. I am too quick to condemn and too slow to forgive. I have struck men in anger." Casually, now, careful not to place too much emphasis, "I have had feelings for women. This is natural. But though the dark side draws much of its power from such feelings, merely having them is not to have chosen the wrong path. Do you understand? It is the decision to dominate, to crush, to draw your strength from another being's weakness that signals a turn to the dark side. Dark or light is not a *feeling*, but a *choice*."

Some of the furious energy was draining slowly from Whie's tense body. His shoulders relaxed, and his arms fell to his sides. "I always thought I was a good person," he said quietly. "I could never see the point of . . . stealing food from the kitchen. Or cheating on exams. I was a good boy," Whie said heavily. "I thought that was the same as virtue."

"Amazing how easy it is to resist other people's temptations, isn't it?" Jai said dryly. He felt an unexpected surge of pity for the young man—one part sympathy for Whie, and one part compassion for his own remembered self at this age: pent-up and furious and barely aware of the fact. After a lifetime of pretending to be good, the boy was only now coming alive to the difficult choices of life—the ones that every shopkeeper's son had to face, let alone a would-be Jedi Knight. "Don't worry," Jai said. "There are ways Master Yoda and Master Leem know you better than you know yourself. Even I know a few things about you, young Whie. Life in this world is never easy, but all of us still see in you what you thought you saw in yourself: a fine man, who one day will make a fine Jedi Knight. Make your choices, Padawan. They won't all be right, but most will be, and none of your Masters has any fear that you will turn to the dark side."

Cautious hope came into the boy's face, along with relief. "Thank you," he said.

"Will you come back to your cot? You have some dreams yet undreamed this night."

It was not a happy turn of phrase. Whie's face darkened again. "N-no," he stammered. "I think I'll just stay up, thank you." He adjusted a weight machine currently set for a body type with flippers. "What about Scout? Do you think she would ever turn to the dark side?"

Jai shook his head. "Forgive me for putting it this way, but she hasn't had things as easy as you, Whie. She has lived with her temptations for years—to cheat, to peek at other kids' tests, to conspire against quicker students to make herself look better. She may not play by the 'regular' rules, but she has committed her whole soul to living with honor, despite her limitations. She will be fine, as long as she remains in the Order. If she were to be cast out, perhaps bitterness might drive her to the dark side. If she felt we betrayed her."

"That's what I thought, too," Whie said. "I always thought she'd be sent to the Agricultural Corps, but now I see why she wasn't. It's not just that Master Yoda feels sorry for her. It's that she's already passed the test the rest of us will be facing, with this horrible war."

"Scout told me yesterday that she found it very irritating that a boy so young should be so wise," Jai said. "I begin to see what she means."

Whie snorted and settled into the weight machine, pushing hard through ten fast repetitions. No use of the Force to move the weights: this was all the old animal body, burning in his legs, his breath getting deeper as his cells called for oxygen. It was good to push like this, meat on metal. The truth was, he'd had another prophetic dream, the worst one yet. Far worse than the vision of himself and Scout, bleeding, in a room with Asajj Ventress—

No. *Push the weights. Don't think don't think don't think*.

But as soon as he took his rest between sets, the images of his dream flooded back.

"Master Maruk?" he said, as Jai turned to go back to the cabin.

"Yes?"

"Are you afraid of death?"

"That is the one thing I do *not* worry about," the Jedi said. "It is my job to live with honor, to defend the Republic, to protect her people, to look after my ship and my weapon and my Padawan . . . My death," he said, with a little smile, "is somebody *else's* responsibility."

Phindar Spaceport, *Gateway to the Outer Rim*. The Phindians, known throughout the galaxy for their dour sarcasm, were tall and thin and mournful looking, with yellow eyes streaked in red and exceedingly long arms, so their luggage scuffed along the floor as they milled about the crowded space station. A vendor sold them balls of air-puffed flat bread and the stimcaf came in low-g squeeze bulbs instead of cups. Even the recycled

space station air smelled different, and the bland synthe-
sized voice that came over the speakers spoke Basic with
a sarcastic drawl that made their own Coruscanti pro-
nunciations seem clipped and brusque. *"If you want
your droids seized and searched by all means let them
wander around unaccompanied."*

"Hear that?" Scout hissed, pinging the R2 unit on the
head with her fingernails. "So *be good.*"

A muffled and rebellious snuff leaked out of the little
droid's casing.

They were standing in line waiting to buy tickets for
the next leg of their journey, from the Joran Station to
Vjun proper, this time as the Coryx family. "Business or
pleasure?" the attendant asked in a bored voice as Jai
Maruk stepped to the head of the line.

"Pleasure, mostly."

"On Vjun?" the attendant said. "Oh, *sure.*"

"I hope," Jai Maruk added, with a well-delivered
falter. "I'm a water chemist by trade, and I've always
wanted to study the famous acid rain. The kids are just
coming along to, ah, play on the beach and so forth . . ."

"Gee, *that* will be fun," the attendant said, glancing at
Scout. "Can't hurt her looks, anyway. By the way, I only
see one kid. Am I blind, or can you not count?"

"My son went to use the, ah, facilities," Jai said. "But
I have his ID card here."

The attendant took their docs. It was good work, best
Jedi forgeries, but Scout felt her heart speed up as he
frowned and thumbed through the stack.

*"If you want your droids seized and searched, by all
means let them wander around unaccompanied."*

"Everything is in order," Jai suggested.

"Wow, imagine my relief," the attendant said, handing the card back. "Put the droid on the scale next to your bags, please."

Scout jumped at a touch on her shoulder and found herself facing the well-worn droid she had met on *Reasonable Doubt*. "Scuffy!" His head tilted back. "I mean, Solis!" Scout said. "Shipping out?"

"In a manner of speaking. Actually, I was wondering if you could do me a small favor," the droid said. He pointed to the food court on the concourse above them. "I am supposed to meet a friend up there. It's no more than a five-minute walk, but apparently there was a Trade Federation attack at the Greater Hub spaceport two days ago, and consequently the Phindians are taking security very seriously at the moment." Scout looked blankly at him. "I would be traveling through the spaceport as an 'unaccompanied droid,' " he explained.

"Oh!" Scout said. "I hadn't thought of that."

"Phindar is notable for, among other things, the SPCB—Sentient Property Crime Bureau—given to the enthusiastic collection and resale of personality-bearing artifacts such as myself. As I would much rather not be seized and resold, I was wondering if you would walk with me to my rendezvous?"

Jai Maruk was busily lifting their indignant R2 onto the weigh scale at the ticket counter, but Scout caught Master Leem's three eyes. "Go ahead," the Gran said, smiling. "It will be your good deed for the day. And collect your brother on the way back, if you catch sight of him."

Solis bowed. "I am greatly obliged."

They set off at a brisk walk across the crowded concourse, Scout slipping through the throngs of Phindians with the droid at her side. "You're the same model as the droid who claims to be Whie's servant, aren't you?"

"You have good eyes."

"Did you—Wait a sec. Can droids get offended?"

"Not usually," Solis said ambiguously.

"Mm."

"Try me."

"Well, I was just wondering if you got, um, scrapped by your owner, and that was why you didn't have the shiny paint and so on. I have a morbid curiosity about this kind of thing," she hurried on. "I very nearly got sent to—got kicked out of the school I go to," she finished.

"I didn't get scrapped. Though I suppose you could say I lost my job." Solis indicated a flight of stairs, and together they started up. "We were both built as servant droids, Fidelis and I."

"A gentleman's personal gentlething," Scout said, grinning. "Whie told us."

"Just so. We were initially programmed to perform quite a wide range of . . . household duties. Makers of sentient property have typically found that if one has an intelligent model, equips it with a wide spectrum of skills and abilities, and sends it off into the world in a role requiring some foresight and initiative—if, in effect, one allows it to live—the property has a disconcerting habit of developing a personality and opinions of its own."

Scout couldn't be sure if that comment was supposed to be ironic.

"In our case, therefore, the bedrock of our programming was *loyalty*—a loyalty to our purchaser that was absolutely hardwired."

"Only the loyalty didn't run both ways," Scout said. "Since I guess your family let you go."

"In a manner of speaking," Solis said, reaching the top of the stairs. "They were murdered."

Scout didn't know what to say.

"It was a small war. Soldiers had found their way into the house. My family intended to use a secret escape passage. My mistress sent me down to the safe room to get the family jewels. I said I thought I should stay and cover their retreat. My mistress called me a fool and invoked the override. I got the jewels. But the family had been betrayed, and the secret passage was not so secret. The soldiers caught them and shot them before I returned. By the time I got there, everyone was dead. I dropped the jewelry on the bodies and walked away."

A tall, chitinous alien of indeterminate gender jostled Scout, who realized she had been standing, transfixed, at the top of the stairs. "Stars," she murmured. "What happened to the soldiers? The ones who caught your family?"

"I don't remember," Solis said blandly.

Yeah, right, Scout thought. She gulped, wondering exactly how the rest of that story had gone. They started walking again, toward the food court, and she found herself eyeing the gouges and scuff marks on the droid's metal body, wondering how many of them represented ordinary wear and tear, and how many more might have come from blasterfire, or needlers, or vibroblades.

"Fidelis still has a family, but other than that you're pretty much the same?"

"Not at all. My family was killed more than two hundred standard years ago. If you had a twin sister—and you might, you know—how different might her life have already become from yours, in just a decade?"

"Two hundred years?" Scout said, goggling. "How old *are* you?"

"Younger than your artoo," he said, with an uncomfortably penetrating glance. Scout felt suitably quelled, and not a little uneasy.

They came to the little circle of tables in the food court area. Whie, who was supposed to be off using the refresher, was instead sitting at a table with Fidelis, head down, listening intently. "Hey!" Scout said. "What are you doing here?"

Whie jerked around with a guilty start. "None of your business," he said. "Talking. It's allowed."

"None of my *business*? Did I just hear that come out of Saint Whie's mouth? It surely is my business if I catch you consorting with strangers and lying about it. Or have you forgotten who your *real* family is?" she said tight-lipped, jerking her head down at the concourse below, where Jai was laboriously counting out credits for their tickets to Vjun.

"From where I sit, it looks like we are consorting to the same degree," Whie said, getting himself back under control.

A funny sort of control, though: still angry and defensive. As quick as Scout could be to take offense, something about the whole situation was so strange she couldn't maintain the thread of her anger. "What is up with you today?" she said, genuinely puzzled. "You've been weird all day. I didn't mean to rattle your cage—to tell the truth, I didn't even know you could get rattled. I was just surprised, that's all. What's going on?"

"You're late," Fidelis said to Solis.

The unpainted droid shrugged. *Late?* Scout thought. *Late for what?*

A small platoon of armed Phindians in blue-and-white uniforms jogged into the food court carrying blaster rifles and grim expressions. The captain, a hard-faced Phindian with a rank badge on his shoulder, was the only one whose rifle was still slung on his back. "Stay perfectly calm," he announced to the staring diners. "I am Major Quecks, Phindar Spaceport SPCB. We have received a report of an extremely dangerous unlicensed droid onstation," he said, looking at Fidelis. "Make, model, and serial number, please."

"Master?" Fidelis said, looking to Whie.

Whie goggled.

"Are you the owner of this droid?" the captain said sharply.

"Yes," Fidelis said.

"No!" Whie said. "What is going on? Who *are* you?"

"Sentient Property Crime Bureau, Tactical Squad," Solis remarked. "Carrying regulation blasters and neural-net erasers." The attention of the Tactical Squad swung around and fixed on the battered, unpainted droid.

"This one's with me," Scout said.

"That remains to be determined. Are either of you carrying any weapons?" Major Quecks asked Whie.

Don't look at me, Scout thought, knowing he was about to. *Don't look around, just* lie.

Whie looked at her. "Scout?"

"You remembered to check your blaster cannon, didn't you, bro?"

"I *love* your sense of humor," Quecks remarked. "Those of us in security love jokes about blaster cannons from juvenile aliens traveling with dangerous droids. It's our favorite thing in the world."

His soldiers gripped their rifles more tightly.

Scout made eye contact with the major and summoned the Force as best she could. "No, we aren't carrying any weapons. Are we, Whie?"

Whie's eyes widened, and he followed her lead. "Nosir. We're just kids," he explained—and even Scout, who knew perfectly well that she had a lightsaber hidden under her cloak, felt how absurd it was that the major should be bullying two such obviously innocent children. The eight soldiers behind him looked around and lowered their guns.

The Phindian slowly relaxed. His arms were so long that his hands, hanging at his side, nearly brushed his ankles. "Very good, then. Remain seated at this table with the droids, please, until we sound the all-clear."

In the middle of the major's last sentence, Fidelis cocked his head to one side, as if listening for something. An instant later Solis did the same thing.

"What?" Scout said urgently. "What's going on?"

"The thing about spaceport security," Solis remarked, "is that it's designed to keep passengers from getting to ship personnel." Now even Scout could hear distant blasterfire, and smell the lightning-burn of ozone in the air. "As opposed to the other way around," the droid finished.

In a whirling blur of metal and high-tech ceramic, a platoon of battle droids came spinning down the corridors from the boarding area, blew through the security lines, and unpacked into full combat readiness with a deployed arsenal of blades, blasters, flechette launchers, and weapons Scout didn't even recognize. The droids themselves were half again as big as a human, built like sharpened exoskeletons, their lean hatchet-faced heads swept back to a scything point. The fluorescent spaceport lights glittered off every lethal surface.

The mixed throng of native Phindians and traveling galactics just passing through the spaceport stood for a long moment, transfixed, staring at all the hardware of death that had opened suddenly on them. A series of tinny beeps broke the eerie silence. "Look at that," Solis observed dryly. "They've set off the metal detectors."

Then mayhem broke loose.

Twin blades of light appeared as Master Maruk and Master Leem swept out their lightsabers, ready to deflect the battle droids' blaster bolts. *So much for disguise,* Jai Maruk thought. "DO NOT PANIC," he bellowed, drawing the Force into his voice so it lashed out in a tone of absolute command. Right now, the civilians could be as dangerous to themselves as could the battle droids, depending on exactly what this little welcoming party was here for. A Dooku double cross, or just plain bad luck? "KEEP DOWN AND HEAD FOR THE EXITS."

The terrified throng, held in some semblance of order by the force of his will, bent low and hurried like spider-roaches for the sides of the big main gallery, disappearing into duty-free gift shops, running for the turbolifts, or crushing into the refresher stations, searching for someplace to hide.

Six of the battle droids flanked out, knocking bodies out of their way, to take up crossfire positions on him and Master Leem. "Ohma-D'un super battle droids?" she asked.

Jai Maruk shook his head. "Confederacy assassin droids," he bellowed, shouting to be heard over the din. He recognized them from Anakin Skywalker's report on his mission to Jabiim. Anakin's foes had featured fairly generic armament—usually one handheld blaster and a shoulder-mounted backup. This squad had a much more eclectic array of weapons—aside from their built-in blasters, he could see a couple of flechette launchers, sonic grenades, two flamethrowers, even two fat, hollow tubes that he was pretty sure were tactical tractor beam prototypes.

A custom outfitting job. *Pretty much the stuff you might equip your battle droids with if you knew you were hunting Jedi and had heard they were good at deflecting blaster bolts,* Jai thought grimly.

Two of the assassin droids held up and triggered what looked like small antenna dishes, no bigger than dinner plates. Sudden thunder burst in Jai's skull—a keening explosion of sound, agonizingly loud, blew out his eardrums and dropped him to his knees. The noise was stupefying—loud enough to knock over the little R2 unit; so loud the sheer sonic assault hit Jai like an iron bar in the face. Maks Leem dropped her lightsaber. Her mouth was open and she was probably screaming, but Jai couldn't hear it. He suspected he wasn't going to be able to hear anything for a very long time.

Focus.

He couldn't think. His head was coming apart in plates, the bones of his skull rattling like dropped china. Hard-sound guns—he'd read reports about them, but nothing had prepared him.

Something wet on his neck. Blood. Blood was pouring from his earholes.

Focus.

A crackle of energy passed between him and Maks Leem as the tactical tractor beam smacked the R2 unit into the air like a tin can blasted by a slugthrower bullet. Then the beam steadied and slammed hard to the floor, the R2 can clamped tight in an electromagnetic vise.

The droids knew Master Yoda was in there.

They were hunting him down.

Beside Jai, Master Leem held out her hand. Her lips were pulled back over her long, narrow jaw in a grimace of concentration. Her lightsaber flew into her hand. With one swing she cut the head off one of the little metal poles that held the line-divider ribbons. The chunk of metal went spinning into the air. The Gran grabbed it in her other hand, spun, and hurled it through one of the two hard-noise projector dishes. It exploded in a shower of sparks.

Jai couldn't actually tell if the other one was still making noise. It was as if the auditory section of his brain had blown a fuse—everything happening fast, but sound-lessly. Finally the rattling feeling inside his skull sub-sided, and he managed to find a still point, an almost peaceful center to the maelstrom. A lifetime of training took over, and he was running, leaping, twisting in the air through a slicing hail of flechettes that opened a dozens cuts on his body. Everything crystal clear and soundless, as if it were happening behind transparisteel. Curiously impersonal now: the last battle of his life.

He dropped in front of the droid with the second hard-sound projector, and his lightsaber carved it into smoking ruin.

The terminal was a pandemonium of screams and shouts. The crowd, seeing Jai drop to his knees with blood streaming from his ears, had lost its tenuous sense of order, and people were now scrambling witlessly through the spaceport concourse like mermyns running from a burning nest.

Up on the second level by the food court, Scout tore her eyes away from the madhouse and started thinking again. *"Hey, Major!"* she yelled at the SPCB comman-der. "That looks like some pretty dangerous Sentient Property down there. *Start shooting!"*

The men looked uncertainly at the indecisive Major Quecks. One SPCB trooper raised his blaster rifle and sighted down into the main concourse. A Confederacy assassin droid looked up, and half a second later the SPCB trooper toppled forward with a burn crater where his face had been.

Major Quecks stared at the body. "That's it," he said unsteadily. He drew the neural-net eraser from his side holster and covered Solis and Fidelis with a shaking hand. "Take these units into custody and retreat until reinforcements arrive."

"That sounds like a good idea," Solis said. "Except for the first part." There was a brief blur of motion, inconceivably fast, like a repeating blaster striking, and suddenly the major was looking from the broken fingers of his right hand to the neural-net eraser now in Solis's comfortable grip. "Do you want to live?" the droid asked.

"Y-y-yes!"

"Me, too," the droid said, and he crushed the weapon into scrap. It wasn't a slow squeeze, metal buckling and shrieking. It was instant and effortless, as if the eraser had fallen under the gigantic footpads of an AT-PT transport.

The SPCB troops broke and ran.

Another troop of assassin droids came down the walkway from the docking terminals. A few little sirens and blinking lights saluted them as they passed through the spaceport metal detectors in two groups of four. Between them paced a lithe bald woman with a tattooed skull. She was smiling as she came. It was not a pretty smile.

The eighteen assassin droids—the full complement that *Last Call* could carry in her outboard crèches—now split into four distinct groups. Four of the newcomers stayed with Asajj. Four others peeled off and headed upstairs to secure the food court area. Five were closely engaged with the two Jedi, where the one Jai had taken down lay in a heap of smoking metal. Two were operating the tactical tractor beam, holding the R2 unit pinned to the floor a safe distance away, while two others approached just close enough to pitch sonic grenades to within centimeters of the droid's casing. The grenades went off with a churning, concussive vibration that buckled the floor underneath the R2 and made its casing writhe and ripple.

There was something anticlimactic about the business, Ventress felt. Part of her would far rather have taken on the old Jedi: Asajj Ventress and Master Yoda, lightsaber-to-lightsaber, winner take all. But Dooku, though an elegant man with a profound sense of the aesthetic, never confused flair with efficiency, and never accepted style in lieu of substance. Killing Yoda was the thing, and if it was messy and brutal and somehow perfunctory, it remained far better than giving him any chance to stay alive.

Still, it didn't make the next part especially pleasant. Asajj was not squeamish by anyone's standards, but she was not looking forward to seeing what a pair of high-decibel sonic grenades would have done to an old body trapped in such a metal shell—if indeed the little cripple had survived the opening blast of hard sound and subsequent tractor beam smack-around. But it had to be done. Flanked by her guard, Asajj approached the R2 unit, drew her twin lightsabers, and carved the metal canister opened with a flourish, so it fell slowly into pieces, like a flower shedding petals in the breeze.

It was a fine, dramatic moment, completely spoiled by the fact that the canister was empty.

Asajj blinked. There, where the bottom of the R2 unit should have been, was a neat circular hole. Yoda had carved an escape hatch through the floor and dropped into the dim ship's parking level below.

Ventress growled like a sand panther that had missed its kill and slashed another ring around Yoda's escape hatch so the assassin droids could fit through. "Get *down* there!" she snarled. The first of her droid commanders dropped into the hole feetfirst and disappeared.

There was a *thump*.

A flash.

A brief gout of sparks spurting up through the hole, followed by several clangs and a crash.

Silence.

"Assassin Droid A Seven Seven, report," said the leader of the assassin droids in its mechanical voice.

After a brief pause, A 77's head popped out of the hole, hit the terminal floor with a clatter, and rolled slowly to a stop.

Asajj studied the head, then kicked it furiously down the hallway. She took a deep breath. "Well, then. I guess we'd better make a bigger hole."

Time was slowing down for Maks Leem. She was bleeding from dozens of little cuts from the assassin droids' flechette sprayers. No one injury that severe, but she had to parry the razor flakes headed for her eyes first, and a few of the others seemed to nick her with every new spray of blades. She was a moving target now, no longer stunned by the hard-sound throwers, but the flechette launchers were a well-chosen weapon— impossible to parry completely, difficult to wholly escape. The flechettes themselves were light enough that the droids didn't have to worry about their own cross-fire at all; the tiny razors tinged and pattered off their transparisteel exoskeletons, leaving nothing but a few minor nicks. For flesh and blood, the danger was considerably greater. Sooner or later, if Maks got unlucky, one of the sprays would catch the tendons behind her knees, or ankles, and then the situation would become very bad.

She felt slow. Out of shape. Now, in the crystal clarity of battle, it seemed clear to her that her hatred for the war had manifested itself in a dull subconscious resistance to the whole idea of fighting. She had trained, of course she had. But not enough—not enough for this new scenario, in which the Jedi had been debased, falling from their true calling as peacekeepers to something very close to mercenaries.

She turned a high, twisting flip, taking the edge of a cloud of flechettes in her flank, coming down like thunder, her lightsaber a wand of lightning. The assassin droid's head was there for the taking, but she couldn't afford to do that right now. She lopped the arm off instead, grabbing it as her feet touched the ground. She cradled the severed arm into her body as she rolled past the startled droid, and came up firing the blaster still attached to it, her fingers closing over its metal fingers on the trigger, one shot, two, three four five into the back of the droid shooting at Jai Maruk, each pulse of diamond light hitting the exact same spot until its armor blew out from the inside.

Fire rushed like blood from its mouth and eyes.

In the midst of mayhem Jai looked fiercely happy now, at home, as if violence were his true element, and this moment a consummation long awaited. His face was streaming with blood but he gave her a quick grin and ran his lightsaber through the chest of another assassin. She wished she could feel that gladness. A little touch of battle madness would have helped, but she was not formed that way. As hard as she tried to retain her Jedi serenity, sadness kept welling up from the core of her body, leaking out from a hundred cuts to stain her robes.

Another volley of razors caught her from behind and she went down to one knee.

"Come *on!*" Scout cried. "We've got to help!" She put her hands on the railing overlooking the main concourse and started to jump over, only her muscles were thinking faster than her head and weren't ready to risk the eight-meter drop. She whirled and looked at Whie. "You go over from here—you can make it. I'll take the stairs—it's better if we come from different directions anyway. Solis, you come with me!"

"No," the droid said.

Scout turned. "What?"

The droid shrugged. "Not my fight."

"But they're *dying* down there!"

"Animals die. It's what you do," he said. "Machines, on the other hand, run for as long as they are kept in good repair. In the big picture, my life may not mean much, but I have worked and schemed and bullied and cheated for four hundred standard years to keep it.

I've become attached to my own existence, and I won't risk it for something as pointless as delaying meat's inevitable end."

Scout's expression of outrage faded slowly to something like contempt. "If that's your idea of life, you're welcome to it."

Fidelis shuddered in wholehearted agreement. "Shocking lack of values. There's one in every production run," he said primly, shaking his head.

Scout saved her breath for running, and sprinted for the stairs.

Behind her, Whie put one hand on the banister, scanning the fight below to decide where he would come out of his roll. Four of the new droids were making their way toward the stairs. All right—if the fight was going to come to them, so much the better. He could run along the top of the rail, take a flying leap, and come down on the two hindmost. Hopefully the distraction would give Scout an opening to do some damage to the two in front.

A steel band closed over his wrist. He looked down. Fidelis's hand was over his own, pinning him to the railing as effectively as if he had been nailed there. "What are you doing?"

"It's not safe," Fidelis said.

"But—"

"I didn't wait ten years outside the Jedi Temple only to let you throw your life away in a pointless defense of a couple of outnumbered Jedi," the droid said, as if explaining something to a small child. "If the droids don't get them, Asajj Ventress will."

"You're crazy!" Whie went for his lightsaber, only to find his other hand trapped inside the droid's iron grip.

"No, Master. Only sensible."

Whie heard Scout cry, "I'm coming, Master Maruk!" An instant later she came pelting down the stairs, taking them four at a time, lightsaber blazing in her hand. Did she even realize she was about to meet a party of four assassin droids? "Look," he hissed, "if I am your master, you have to do what I tell you, right?"

"Ah!" Fidelis chirped. "Now we are getting somewhere. You admit you are my master, then?"

"Yes, yes! Anything you say, but now you *have to let me go.*"

"Much better," Fidelis said complacently. "But I have to tell you, sir, in my capacity as your adviser—a not inconsiderable part of the role of gentleman's personal gentlething—entering this engagement is not a course of action I can recommend. The odds are very poor, sir. Very poor indeed."

Scout had pelted down to the middle landing on the stairs when she found four custom-armed assassin droids only ten meters away from her, and coming fast. She skidded to a halt, looking around for Whie. Her eyes met his and she stared at him, still safely back in the food court, with an expression of mingled fury and surprise and dawning fear.

If she died, Whie knew, that look would haunt every breath he took for the rest of his life.

Scout and the droids stared at one another for the space of three loud heartbeats. Then the girl turned and raced right back up the stairs, dodging and weaving, as blaster bolts whined and sizzled around her.

"Forgive me," Fidelis was remarking, "But I do consider giving advice to be part of my duties."

"*Let me go!*" Whie roared.

Fidelis hesitated, torn between his orders and his duty.

"I wouldn't," Solis said quietly.

But the moment of indecision was enough. Whie used the Force to lever open the droid's fingers, vaulted up into the air, and sprinted along the guardrail for the stairs. "I'm coming, Scout!"

The girl turned, distracted for a split second by the sound of her name. A blaster bolt caught her a glancing blow and she hit the stairs hard.

8

The docking bay deck was the dim underbelly of Phindar Spaceport. The big craft—commercial transports, passenger ferries, military troopships—hung outside the port proper, using small extendable walkways to off-load their personnel. Smaller craft, from single-pilot intersystem hoppers to luxury yachts holding up to thirty passengers, came in through the gaping jaws of the bay doors to dock inside the spaceport proper. After settling with a clang on the reinforced deck, they would wait for air and pressure to cycle into the bay, and then let the pilot droids park their craft according to their filed flight plans. Asajj Ventress, preferring a spot near the doors so she could make a quick getaway, had chosen not to utilize the docking service. In fact, a sprinkle of nuts, washers, scrap metal, and smoldering lubricant was all that remained of the valet droids.

The security cams hung from the ceiling like detached eyeballs, pitiful smoking tangles of wire with knobs of smoking glass at the end. Had they still been working, they would have beheld two rather remarkable figures moving toward one another. From one side, weaving swiftly through the parked starcraft, came Master Yoda, with a green light of battle gleaming dangerously in his eyes.

Yoda—a different Yoda—was also tottering down the ladder from *Last Call*'s cockpit. This Yoda looked rather the worse for wear, bruised, dirty, and dehydrated. His ankles and wrists were still bound together, and one of his ears had come unstuck, so it now hung sadly from the side of his head, furling and unfurling in little jerks and twitches.

The first Yoda held up his lightsaber like a glow rod and studied the battered parody of himself. "Hm," he snuffed. "Worse for wear, I look!"

"By the stars," Palleus Chuff croaked, "it's me! I mean, you!"

Somewhere in the murky distance came a flash of light, followed by a series of distinct thumps: one, two, three, four assassin droids dropping the eight meters from the main concourse to the docking bay deck.

"Now two of us there are," Yoda grunted. "Soon to be zero, unless move quickly we can." He wiggled his fingers, and Palleus Chuff watched, astonished, as the tape lashing his wrists and ankles together began to unwind itself. He yelped as the loops of tape suddenly tore themselves free, taking bands of body hair with them. "Might sting," Yoda added.

Metal footsteps clattered toward them in the dark.

"It's Ventress!" Chuff said. "She's come here to kill you. She took me prisoner, thinking I was you, but somehow she found out you were going to be here, and she's come for the real thing. She made one miscalculation, though," he gasped triumphantly. "Left me alone in the ship. Didn't think I could do her any harm, oh no! Not Chuff the puny actor. But I have programmed her horrible ship to self-destruct!"

A blaster bolt lit the darkness like sudden lightning. Yoda parried it. "Self-destruct?"

"Yes! I do the same thing in *Jedi!*—Act three, scene two, when you were escaping the Tholians . . ." Chuff paused. "Do you think maybe you should put that sword out? It seems like a natural tar—"

Yoda used the Force to whirl them both high into the air and over *Last Call* as a hail of flechettes pinged and pattered off the starship's side. "Set this to *explode*?" Yoda said again.

"Yes—I set a countdown to engage the hyper . . ." Palleus Chuff paused. "Although, you know, in *Jedi!* the ship is in open space and you have an escape pod. Do you think having *Last Call*'s engines fire and then boost for a random hyperdrive jump from inside the space station might be a *bad* thing?"

It was hard to get a thorough read on the Jedi Master's expression in the strobing flash of nearly continuous blasterfire, but Chuff, who had studied vids of Yoda for months, thought the old Jedi's crumpled face looked a trifle on the *sour* side.

Back on the main level, Whie leapt off the balcony railing with a loud cry, hoping to distract the assassin droid aiming a flechette launcher at Scout. The droid turned, the gun's throaty chatter roared out, and a hail of razor-sharp tracers came keening through the air at Whie. He twisted, using the Force to deflect the stream of metal up into the ceiling. The station's artificial grav-

ity was only 0.69g, heightening the boy's appearance of
weightless grace. He came down spinning, his lightsaber
a furious green blur. The four droids on the stairs scattered: two tumbled down below Whie; the other two
dived up toward Scout. One grabbed for her ankle,
meaning to crush it in its metal hand, only to have the
whining blue blur of her lightsaber slash the hand off at
its metal wrist.

The droid held up the severed stump of its arm.
Sparks jumped from its gears and wires. Scout lunged
forward, trying to skewer it through the heavily armored chest, but it turned sideways, letting her blade
pass harmlessly through space, and swung at her, a
tremendous blow that would have taken her head off if
the droid's hand had still been attached to the end of its
arm. As it was, its stump whipped past her face, hissing
and spitting sparks.

Years of training with Iron Hand kicked in. Dropping
her lightsaber without hesitation, Scout grabbed the
passing stump, tucked it close to her body, and dropped,
spinning, to the stairs, using the droid's own momentum
to hurl its massive body over the banister. It seemed to
hang in space, and then plunged with a crash to the floor
six meters down.

"Good throw," said a metallic voice. Scout turned
around just as the second droid's hand closed around
her throat.

Maks Leem lay gasping on the spaceport concourse,
bleeding from a hundred cuts. Her lightsaber lay where
she had dropped it when the last flechette pulse had
turned her sword hand into chopped meat.

Two assassin droids were left of the six that had been assigned to take out her and Jai Maruk.

Traveling incognito through the spaceport, she and Jai hadn't been carrying any weapons that could fire at range, and their opponents took full advantage of this fact. Stupid battle droids would press the attack with any available weapon; these super assassin droids had stayed maddeningly out of range, quite content to shoot from a distance, shielding themselves behind white-faced ticket agents or security guards they caught crawling away. Good programming, or good tactical briefing, or both.

The droid whose blast had finally brought her down threw aside the jump-shuttle pilot it had been using as a shield and approached to within five meters. No closer, of course. Blood dripped between the Gran's three eyes as she looked at her lightsaber. Not sure what point there would be pulling it to her with the Force. She'd have to fight left-handed, and the merciless droid would stay far away anyhow, waiting for time and numbers to tell.

"You will be disassembled," it remarked, raising its blaster.

"I know," Maks said. "But not by you." And she used the Force to make two quick tweaks in succession: the first, the hard one, crimping the barrel of his blaster. That was difficult: but once the metal squeezed shut, pulling the weapon's trigger and holding it down was child's play.

The blaster blew up, taking the droid's hand with it and knocking it on its back.

Then she did the same thing to the heavy-caliber

blaster built into its shoulder. That one blew its chest open, sending gobbets of hot metal rocketing through the concourse.

Jai Maruk turned at the first blast, grinning in fierce triumph. When the second explosion came, he was ready. He reached out with the Force, shaping the blast to guide the molten fragments of the exploding droid like smoking cannonballs into the body of the assassin that had been tormenting him. The impact knocked the droid back into a wall, banging a dent into the transparisteel sheeting. Jai used the Force to keep the droid pinned there, and raced over to him. Driven by a rage perilously close to the dark side, his lightsaber flashed and fell in a mighty cut, cleaving the assassin droid into two smoking halves.

He stood over his enemy, gasping, breath rough in his throat. There was blood in his mouth. He spat. *It's just a machine,* he told himself. *Just a tool.* His real enemy was the mind that had bought and briefed these killers.

A single pair of hands clapped lazily in the almost deserted complex. "Well done, Jedi," said a mocking voice.

Master Maruk turned slowly around. The big concourse was all but empty. A few people cowered, terrified, behind the ticketing booths and baggage carousels. Over by the information desk, Maks Leem had struggled to her knees. Splotches of her blood spattered the tile floor around her, red on white. The shattered forms of the five assassin droids they had destroyed lay scattered around the concourse. The sixth lay twitching and sparking on the floor by the stairs. It kept trying to stand up, but something was broken in its leg or hip joints. Instead of rising, it scrabbled around and around in slow jerky circles, like a child's broken toy.

There was no sign of Master Yoda.

In all the shattered scene, one figure remained brisk and erect: Asajj Ventress, as tall, slim, elegant, and deadly as he remembered her. "Ah—it's seventeen, isn't it?" she said pleasantly. A pair of sabers spat and blazed into hissing life in her hands. "Now I'm glad the droids didn't finish you off. That would have muddled my count."

"You number your victims?" Jai said. "That must take an army of accountants."

"Oh, I'm really a one-woman show, and I like to travel light," Ventress said, flexing her wrists and cutting quick arcs of brightness in the air. "I only count my Jedi, and I find dead reckoning is enough for that."

Down in the docking bay, Palleus Chuff had set *Last Call* to engage her engines after ten minutes. At least five of those minutes must have gone by, and the more the actor thought about those giant engines firing inside the enclosed bay, the more he thought that maybe the whole idea hadn't been such a great one.

Yoda was working very fast. The *Call* was anchored to the deck with high-pull magnets on the bottom of five support legs. The old Jedi was chopping them off one by one. "Why are you doing that?" Chuff asked, peering forward so his head was right under the corner of the ship now without support.

Yoda squeaked and puffed out his round cheeks with the sudden effort of using the Force to keep the *Call* from crushing Chuff into a grease spot on the docking bay floor. "Step back!" he barked.

"You don't have to get huffy about it." A stream of superheated plasma arced toward Chuff, curving mysteriously away at the last minute. "Whoa! That was lucky!"

Yoda snarled. He grabbed the actor's wrist and flipped him under the starship, letting the corner come crashing down where they had been standing a tenth of a second before. The air crackled and pinged as a line of flechettes tore into the ship's hull.

"Don't you think it would be better to take out these droids?" Chuff squeaked. "Not that I would try to teach you your business, but under the circumstances—"

A sonic grenade came bounding under the ship's belly. With a swat of the Force, Yoda sent it rocketing out again. "If the ship's engines fire, tear the spaceport apart it will," he grunted.

"Oh," Chuff said, crestfallen. "I guess I hadn't thought—"

"True!" Yoda grunted, and with another sudden twitch of the Force, the two of them were stuck to the ship's underside as a line of plasma fire swept the deck where they had just been standing. An instant later they dropped back to the floor, now hot underfoot.

"I will deal with the *machines*," Yoda said, eyes twinkling. He turned off his lightsaber and passed it to Chuff. "Take this. Cut off the last leg you must, so ship out of the docking bay I can push. Then get to the turbolifts."

"Me!" the actor said. "But—"

Yoda held Chuff's hands, clasping them around the lightsaber. "Live your part, you can. Be a Jedi hero, you must!" And somehow, strength and courage and confidence seemed to flow from the old one's hands, and Chuff felt more alive than he had ever been. As if courage were a fire, and he was standing too close to Yoda not to burn.

He felt his own eyes gleam and his own mouth curve up into Yoda's Merry Havoc smile. "May the Force be with you, Master Yoda."

The old Jedi cackled. "It usually is!"

Then the chattering sound of a railgun bit into the dim docking bay, gouging a line of sparks out of the floor, and Yoda was gone. An instant later one of the assassin droids was picked up as if by an invisible hand and hurled into a comrade. Tracers of railgun fire converged on a shadowy figure flitting away from Chuff.

How much time left, the actor wondered. *Three minutes? Two?* He drew a deep breath. Quietly he crept toward the *Call*'s last magnetic anchor.

The docking bay was filled with a grinding, scraping noise as a single-pilot stunt craft some distance away began to drag across the floor. Yoda was drawing the droids away.

Chuff limped over to the last leg of the ship. After days trussed up in Ventress's hold, his whole body felt stiff, sore, and awkward. The skin in the middle of his back was crawling, expecting the burst of blasterfire that would cut him down. He forced himself to ignore it, determined not to let Yoda down.

Muzzle flashes lit the far end of the bay like continuous lightning, and a sonic grenade went off, adding its bass growl to the whine and chatter of the railguns.

Without so much as a lightsaber, Master Yoda was giving the assassin droids all they could handle.

When Chuff got to the last stanchion, he had a sudden moment of panic, sure he wouldn't know how to turn the lightsaber back on. He tabbed what would have been the power button on the prop he had used for 1,437 performances of *Jedi!* To his delight the weapon hissed immediately to life. "By the stars," he murmured, feeling his best Knowing Yoda Smile creep onto his face, "the Force *is* with me."

Quickly he slashed through the support, turned off the lightsaber so it wouldn't give away his position, and threw himself backward as a sudden stuttering flare of tracer fire whined overhead.

The *Call* settled on the deck with a resounding crash, free of her magnetic constraints.

By the time Chuff made it to the turbolift, the countdown chrono running in his head said *Last Call*'s engines were going to roar to life any second now. He had a sudden image of what that would mean: rippling bands of magnetic energy and fusion bursts pulsing through the hold, the ship smashing blindly into walls. Energy building for the blind jump to hyperspace, and Force help anyone caught in a confined space with that.

Chuff swallowed. Playing the hero with Yoda's own lightsaber in his hands he had felt shaky courage everywhere, but now the courage was draining fast and only the shaking remained. He curled up in a corner and turned his face to the wall so he wouldn't see the first gleam as the *Call*'s engines flickered to life.

A hand touched him on the shoulder. He gasped, spun, and saw Yoda's merry eyes looking at him. Yoda grabbed Chuff and dived for the lift as a line of flechettes chopped into the wall where they'd been standing.

Lights flickered on throughout *Last Call,* and a deep humming throb began to build in her engines. The ship scraped across the docking bay floor blind, gathering speed, and then with a deafening metal scream punched into the space station wall. The *Call* jerked through the opening and tore free in a shower of transparisteel, insulation, and sparking wires. She picked up speed, angling away from the station as her preliminary thrusters kicked in.

Explosive decompression sucked all the air out of the docking bay, plucking chairs, papers, tools, small craft, and most importantly the four assassin droids, and flinging them into the black vault of space. The howling wind nearly jerked Chuff out of the lift tube to follow them, but Master Yoda's hand held him back. A pocket of air remained in the lift, held there by Yoda's will.

Out in the long dark of space, the assassin droids spun, tumbling slowly as they drifted farther and farther away, until their erratic blasterfire was only the twinkling of distant lights.

Yoda turned to Chuff. "Thank you," he said.

Back on the staircase between the main concourse and the food court, the killer droid's metal hand was cold around Scout's throat. She felt her vertebrae creak as it slowly lifted her off the ground by her neck. Whie was staring at her. Two other droids lay in pieces around him. "Put away your weapon," the droid told Whie.

"Don't do it," Scout gasped. "I'm not import—" The

droid's fingers tightened just a fraction, choking off any kind of speech. She could barely get air. With a lifetime's experience of choke holds, she figured she would be unconscious in thirty seconds. Unless the droid decided to squeeze once, hard, of course; then she'd be dead.

Whie studied the situation. For once he was even breathing hard. He gave a little nod, and the flame of his lightsaber guttered and went out. "Hurt her and I will . . . *disassemble* you."

"That is irrelevant," the droid said in its monotonous voice. "Only the mission is relevant. You must not interfere with the mission."

A faint black ring was forming at the edge of Scout's vision. She fought to keep conscious. The droid was standing sideways on the stairs, holding her out from its body with mechanical ease, a clear warning to Whie, who stood five steps below.

There was something odd about the side of the droid's head. Scout blinked and forced herself to focus. Yes, there it was: a tiny red dot, like the point of a glow rod beam, centered on the side of the droid's head. Odd.

"Is there a problem here?" Fidelis said, picking his way fussily down the stairs.

"Any interference with the mission will result in the termination of this unit," the droid said, emphasizing its point with a squeeze that wrung a strangled squeak out of Scout.

Fidelis approached slowly. "The girl is of no interest to me. I serve only Master Malreaux, who stands behind you. You and your comrades appear to have offered violence to him."

"He tried to interfere with the mission," the droid

said. It didn't seem to notice the little red dot on its fore-head. "Anyone who interferes with the mission must be suppressed. Stand back, or you, too, will be disassembled."

"That's hardly polite," Fidelis said. His fingers shot out, plunged through the assassin droid's eyeholes, and tore its head off.

At the same instant, the green blur of Whie's light-saber flashed, and Scout fell to the ground with the assassin's severed hand still around her neck. Half a meter away, she could see the severed gears and wires in the stump of its wrist trying to close the hand and crush her throat.

The headless, handless machine lurched to its feet.

"I think not," Fidelis said. The gentleman's personal gentlething plunged his hand down through the assassin droid's neck coupling and drew it back out holding the droid's innards, trailing tubes and wires like a heart ripped out with its ventricles still pumping. Fidelis tightened his hand with the same instant crushing force that had pulverized the SPCB soldier's gun, reducing the killer droid's innards to a gleaming lump the size of a sugar cube.

The droid crashed to the stairs like a pile of scrap metal.

"Cheap thugs," Fidelis sniffed. "Terribly underbred."

Whie was staring at his servant. "What *are* you?"

"Your gentleman's personal gentlething, sir."

"Um, a little help here?" Scout gasped. Whie stopped gawping and used the Force to prize open the metal fingers clenched around her throat.

Scout sucked in a great gulp of air. Stale, canned, recycled air it might be, but no ocean breeze had ever tasted so sweet. She looked at the pieces of droid scattered down the stairs. Whie had been doing some neat sword work while she was falling down and trying to break metal hands with her throat. "Thank you for the rescue, handsome prince."

Whie grinned. Scout decided that when he wasn't trying to be Serene and Above It All, he actually had a pretty likable face. He grabbed her hand and pulled her up. "All part of a day's work, princess."

They looked down from their vantage point on the stairs. There was no sign of the little R2 unit in which Master Yoda had been hiding. The spaceport concourse was littered with droid debris. The ferroceramic floors were gouged and charred. Near Maks Leem they were spattered with blood. A few Phindians were still trying to crawl from the area. Distant sirens were ringing. There was a great muffled crash from somewhere down in the docking bay.

Jai and Maks were in trouble. Master Leem was trying to force herself to her feet, but even from this distance they could see from her unsteady, swaying movements that she was fighting to stay conscious. Thirty meters away, Jai Maruk was in a fierce fight with Asajj Ventress, his one lightsaber, sky blue, matched against a pair of blood-red blades. Asajj was winning.

Whie and Scout looked at one another in dismay. "Let's go!" Scout said.

Jai Maruk was deaf, moving in a haze of white noise that grew gradually softer until it was just the faintest hiss, the sound of blood running under his skin.

He had never fought this hard in his life. The droids had been just a warm-up, a stretching exercise, costing him a cup of blood and a little mobility moving to his right, thanks to a flechette in his hip.

In the eleven and a half weeks since he had seen Ventress the first time, he had gone through their meeting again and again, cataloging every mistake, analyzing everything he could remember from that first savage encounter. Back on Coruscant, he had come to understand that he had underestimated her. For the first few passes of their encounter he had been looking to disarm her; by the time he realized his mistake, she had taken the initiative and was driving him back with a relentless attack. His parries had become wild, and eventually this overswinging had eroded his defensive posture and his balance.

He had imagined the rematch a hundred times: contemplated which opening stances to use, which attacks would be most successful, which of his strengths he could play to. Her mastery of the two-sword form was admirable, but in his experience such fighters tended to rely too much on their blades, and pay too little attention to the Force.

There was only one thing he had never fully admitted into his analysis. She was better than he was.

Just.

Better.

On the long flight home it had been easy to look away from that fact. As he lay on his cot in the Jedi Temple, planning combinations and footwork, he had forgotten this one, seemingly critical detail.

She was better.

Faster. More elegant. Better footwork. More precise with her blades. Succumbing to the dark side of the Force might be a poor life decision, but even her touch with the Force was better than his: more powerful, more subtle, more nuanced, and—this was the hardest thing to admit—more deeply understood. She understood her own nature and skills and weaknesses better than Jai knew himself.

Just better.

Like a dream, that knowledge had faded from him as soon as he left Vjun. It was nothing he could bear to believe. But now, like a nightmare forgotten during the day but creeping back at night, the profound truth that Ventress *was* going to kill him was piercing Jai Maruk's understanding, hard and sharp as a knife blade driving home.

After only three passes she had scored a long wound up his arm when his parry had been too late coming. By then it was already evident that skill was not going to save him. He tried trickery, using the Force to pick up a piece of a broken droid and hurl it at her from behind. Somehow she felt it coming, twisted like an Askajian dancer, and sent the chunk of metal screaming into him. He tried to bat it away but succeeded only in slicing the metal in two, and one of the halves had hit him very hard in the right leg.

He switched from trickery to pure will. He had won that way before, too. As a small boy in the Temple, sheer implacable will had been his trump card. He had won staring contests from the age of seven because he was simply willing to keep his eyes open while they burned and ran with tears, staring relentlessly until the pain was too much for his opponent. That was Jai Maruk. The Hawk-bat, they called him, because of that fierce wild stare.

It wasn't enough.

He hated that. This woman was evil. Despicable. He had dedicated his entire life to the principles of justice, to truth and knowledge, to honing his whole body into a kind of blade, a sword-spirit, keen and quick.

And it wasn't enough.

This woman, younger than him by five years or more, this spiteful mocking killer was just better than he was, and he hated that. With a black fury he attacked, driving her back, letting go of himself in a way he never had before, battering her down, half blind and mad with hate. He pressed her hard across the blood-spotted floor.

There was a great crash, the whole concourse rippled, and he lunged high, driving Ventress before him to where poor Maks Leem, that good, kind, dying partner, stood bleeding her life away at the edge of a pit cut into the floor. She was soft and she was going to die for it, because at the end of the day it was the killers who were hardest.

Ventress was smiling. Her mouth moved. He couldn't hear her, of course, but he could follow the motion of her lips. *Good,* she was saying. *That's it, seventeen.*

Ventress whirled, almost casually, and cut a smoking line across Master Leem's belly. The Gran sank to her knees. She didn't even look at the wound. She was staring at Jai, and her three eyes were sad, sad. Her lips said, *Don't, Jai.*

Another grinding crash: he couldn't hear it, but he felt it through the soles of his feet. Then there was a hurricane in the concourse, a mighty wind as all the air started to suck down through the hole in the floor. *The space station hull has been breached,* Jai thought.

Smoke curled up from Master Leem's belly. Still she stared at him. *Don't, Jai.*

Everything silent. Everything still.

Opening from the heart of stillness, a truth blossomed in Jai's chest: he was going to die.

He was going to die here. Now.

There would be no miraculous rescue. There would be no marvelous escape. They were both going to die, Ventress was going to kill them, and the question on Maks Leem's face was, Would he die as a Jedi, or would he spend the last seconds of his life giving in at last, forever, to the dark side?

Because that's where he was, right now. At the edges of this still place in his heart Jai could feel all his hatred. And despair, yes, that, too. The criminal waste of it, the horrible perversion that Ventress was going to win: it was all there, every reason he would ever need to admit the dark side was strongest. To give in.

There was the tiniest hesitation in his stroke. Maks Leem's body was being sucked into the hole cut into the floor. She couldn't look at Jai anymore, she was pouring the last of her strength into using the Force to seal the gap, to keep the station's air from running out. "I won't," Jai said. He couldn't hear himself. "I won't," he cried, and somehow he knew that Maks Leem, deaf and dying, heard him and was content.

Nobody would ever know how close Jai had come to giving in to the dark side. Nobody but Maks would ever know he had resisted at the end. In a few minutes they would both be dead, and to the universe, his choice would make no difference at all.

To Jai Maruk, it meant everything.

For the next thirty seconds he fought more beautifully than he had in his life, and when Asajj finally cut him down, he was smiling.

Whie had such phenomenal balance that he had managed to keep from falling even though he was racing down the stairs when the first blast of wind sucking into the hole in the concourse floor had hit. Scout was not so lucky. The gust knocked her down and dragged her tumbling down the stairs. She had to shake off a hard smack to the head before she could struggle to her feet. By that time, Master Leem seemed to be containing the breach, and Whie was far ahead, halfway to Asajj Ventress.

Scout had just started to run when Ventress killed Jai. Master Maruk had lifted his lightsaber to block a downward stroke from one of her blades; the other passed cleanly through half his chest in a scything cut that dropped him like a bundle of chopped burr millet.

The breath left Scout's body as if she'd been hit by a landspeeder. It didn't even occur to her to worry about herself. Jai Maruk was suddenly dead. Her Master, whom she was sworn to honor and defend. An hour before, she had been complaining about him, but when the true test came she had proved everything he ever said about her unreadiness was right. She had fallen on the stairs, she had dropped her lightsaber, she had wasted time because she let the stupid droid catch her by the throat: one ridiculous screwup after another, and each of them eating away the precious seconds that turned out to be all the time her Master ever had.

And now he was dying or dead already.

Whie faltered and stopped. "Stars," he whispered as Scout ran up. His face was deathly pale, and he was staring at Asajj Ventress. "This isn't right. It's not supposed to be here."

Another grinding crash came from down below. The wind no longer whistled through the hole in the floor.

The rigid concentration left Master Leem's body. She slumped by the hole, her breathing fast and shallow.

Ventress turned from Maruk's body and walked over to where Maks Leem lay. "That was noble, but someone appears to have patched the hull breach." She drove her lightsaber through Master Leem's chest. "Eighteen," she added.

With a yell of rage Whie lunged toward her, lightsaber blazing. Ventress stepped back. "Don't," she said calmly.

He attacked, blindingly fast. She was faster. He lunged: she stepped aside, turned his blade, reached out with the Force, and flung him into a ticket counter hard enough to drive the air from his lungs so all he could do was hang there, gulping, with his diaphragm in spasms. "I don't particularly want to kill you," she said, "but I will if you insist."

Air came back into Whie's chest with a whoop. "Not here, you won't," he gasped. "Not today. Are you Jedi?"

Deliberately, Ventress spat. "No."

"You carry a lightsaber."

"My first Master was a Jedi. The Order abandoned

him to torment and death. It's not a club I'm eager to join."

Whie laughed. It wasn't a good sound. *He's hysterical,* Scout thought. *Seeing Master Leem die has completely unhinged him.* "Usually you don't have to join the Jedi Order. Heck, I didn't. Usually they just . . . sign you up."

Ventress examined him, and then glanced, warily, at Fidelis, who came to stand at his master's shoulder. "The Force is strong in you," she remarked.

"So they tell me. I have a peculiar talent," the boy said. "I dream the future. Last night, for instance, I dreamed my own death. And this wasn't it."

Scout stared, wide-eyed. No wonder Whie had seemed so strange this morning. "Actually—and I think you'll find this amusing," Whie said, still on the ragged edge of hysteria, "I learned that I will die under a Jedi's hand. So I'm afraid you're out of luck," he said. "Doesn't mean I can't kill *you,*" he added.

"Do you want to?"

"You killed the person I loved best in the world," Whie said. "You stabbed her in the chest while she was helpless. I'd say my reasons are pretty good."

"I would agree." Ventress studied her fingernails. "But you're not really displaying the real Jedi sense of unattachment, are you?" Still watching him—and, rather more carefully, Fidelis—she began to pace as she talked, punctuating her words with the *click-clack* of her boot heels on the floor. "I mean, a real Jedi wouldn't attack, would he? A real Jedi would survey the tactical situation: respect his responsibility to the girl: respect his need to preserve himself as a valuable and expensive asset of the Republic. A real Jedi would try to find Master Yoda. A real Jedi would be a coward," she said. Nothing mocking in her voice now. Just thoughtful. Boots clicking, a steady tick like a pendulum, cutting time into seconds. "A real Jedi would leave their bodies lying here." She looked up at him curiously. "Do you want to be a real Jedi?"

He stared at her with hate.

"I don't think you do," Ventress said. *Click, clack.* "You are still young. You are not fully indoctrinated. And I think that deep down in your heart, you know the Jedi way is a lie. Do you *want* not to care that I killed your Master? Do you want to be the person who wouldn't care?"

Click, clack. Click, clack. Black boots. Slow strides. Voice calm. Strangely gentle. Strangely touched, as if seeing herself in Whie's pale fury. In Scout's horrified eyes.

"Let me tell you about the dark side," Ventress said quietly. "Typical Jedi propaganda to name it so. Let me give it another name," she said. *Click, clack.* "Let's call it *the truth.*"

She paused to study Master Leem's body with something like sadness. "The truth is, you do care that this one is dead. You should. The truth is, you would be less than alive if you didn't. The truth is, the principles that seem right to an eight-hundred-odd-year-old hypocrite who may live forever make no sense for the rest of us who live and suffer and die in this world. Our time here is so short: so precious: so sweet. To turn your back on it, to crawl into your monastery and teach yourself not to feel. What a waste," Ventress said. Her voice shook. "What a . . . *blasphemy.*

"If the universe loves the 'good' as the Jedi would have you believe—if the morality of the weak indeed governs the dance of the stars, if life is fair—why then am I alive, while your Master lies dead?" For a moment it looked as if she would touch Maks Leem's body with her foot. If she had, Whie would have killed her where she stood, or died trying.

Instead she paced on, always walking, that mesmerizing *click, clack* echoing through the empty concourse. "The truth is, there is no good, and no evil, either," she said with a wan smile. "There is only life . . . or not.

"The powerful always trick the simple with the promise of power. That's the easiest way to bring someone to see the dark side. 'Give in to your anger!' It's a simple trick, and an effective one, because it works. When people stop denying what they have always known in their hearts is true, they come to some degree into their own power. But that is not the end of the journey," Ventress said. "It is the beginning. That despair, that furious instant when your eyes open and see the world for what it really is . . . a necessary first step, that's all."

She looked from Whie to Scout and back again. "Behold: I give you the gift of life. Hate me, if you like. By all means hate this," she said, glancing at the bodies of the two Jedi. "You should. I give you the gift of my own heartbreak. If you learn from it, if you can face the emptiness of the universe, then you have some chance of growing up." She shrugged. "If, like scared children, you can't let go of old Yoda's hand, and you crawl back for his bedtime stories and his soothing lies, so be it. If having had a chance to see the truth, you willfully choose to live the Jedi lie, then I will know what to do when next we meet, and I'll do it with far less remorse than these executions."

A comlink beeped on her wrist. Asajj raised it to her mouth. "Yes? . . . Where are you? . . . You let yourself . . . you're tumbling in *space*? . . . No, I'm not going to stop to *collect* you," she said, rolling her eyes at the Padawans. She listened for another moment, and then snapped the comlink off and sighed. "Yoda has destroyed my ship and thrown my droids out the air lock. Several Phindian military cruisers are heading this way. Given the odds"—her eyes flicked curiously to Fidelis again—"I had best be stealing another ship before Master Yoda gets back."

With a shaking hand, Scout flicked the power switch on her lightsaber. "You're not going anywhere."

Ventress took what looked like a small dart gun from a holster at her side and fired at the wall. Some kind of contact corrosive or incendiary must have been packed into the tip, because where it hit the wall immediately buckled and blew out. "Hull breach," Ventress said brightly as the air started to scream out of the station again. "I'd fix that if I were you."

She turned her back on them and ran quickly back through the security checkpoints, heading for the cruisers on the station's docking arm. With a last look of fury, Whie turned his attention to the ruptured wall. Reaching into the Force, he concentrated on holding the breach closed until Yoda arrived.

"Scout?" The word a whisper of agony.

Scout whirled. Jai Maruk, not quite dead, was trying to form her name. She ran over and knelt beside him.

Asajj Ventress's killing blow had carved terribly into his chest. He was gasping, short shallow panting breaths.

He smiled at the sight of her face. Squinted at the blood, the bruises on her head and around her throat. His mouth worked. "Still . . . winning . . . the hard way," he whispered. He looked down at his ravaged body. "Me . . . too."

He was smiling. She didn't think she'd ever seen him smile before. Tears welled up inside Scout. "Don't try to talk. It will be all right, Master. Master Yoda will be here soon to take care of you." Tears dropped from her eyes onto his shattered chest. There was a long hitch in his breathing. His eyes closed. "Master Maruk? Master Maruk! Don't go," Scout cried. "Don't leave me!"

His eyes opened, and he smiled again. "Never . . . ," he whispered. ". . . my Padawan."

His eyes closed, and he was gone.

9

Count Dooku scooted his chair back from the dining room table at Château Malreaux, dabbing at the spilled wine dripping from its edge. As if she had been waiting for the spill to happen, half-mad Whirry lumbered into the dining room, settling a foxtail stole around the ragged shoulders of her dirty pink ball gown. "Which I can clean that up for Your Lordship, can't I, pets?"

Dooku sighed. In all reason—and he was a reasonable man—the spill was his own fault. He had been distracted, turning over the progress of the war. Things were going so well in the Outer Rim, the Republic press was urging action there, "before the whole Rim is lost to the Confederacy for good." Really, sometimes it seemed to Dooku that Darth Sidious's plots were needlessly complex. It was beginning to look very much as if Dooku could simply *win*: march his battle droids into Coruscant and claim the Republic outright.

Not that he would ever question the *power* of Darth Sidious. The dark secrets at his command. But each man to his own devices: give a problem to a soldier, and you will get a military solution; the same question will get you diplomacy from a diplomat, and clothes from a tailor. Darth Sidious had the mind of a *schemer,* and so he put his faith in schemes.

Dooku checked himself. The thought was unfair. Say rather, Darth Sidious, alone in all the galaxy, knew most intimately the dark springs that ran through creatures' hearts. He was an expert in personal disintegration—in the ways one came to betray oneself. It was no wonder, then, that even a clash of empires revealed itself to the Sith as fundamentally a *psychological* battle, to be won and lost at the level of each being's inner strength or weakness. Dooku himself—though certainly psychologically acute, both naturally and through his Jedi training, and more recently through the wisdom of the Sith—was also born to wealth and power, and had for years now commanded very large groups of followers, both in armies and corporations. It seemed to him that a being's inner nature, whether noble or debased, looked much the same as he or she was crushed under the tread of a tank. When one has sufficient force, there is no need for schemes.

"Uh-oh," Whirry said. She had reached out to dab at the spilled wine with an old rag—stars forbid she should risk a wine stain on the fancy Malreaux linen napkins—but her hand had stopped in midair, hovering over the splotch of burgundy on the table. "You're in trouble."

"Whirry," Dooku began severely, "I have told you before, I don't like—"

The comm console chimed. Glancing over, the Count saw who was calling and cut his sentence off short. "I'll take this in my study," he said.

* * *

For a long time Darth Sidious did not speak to him. Instead, he simply piped the breaking news story into Dooku's holoconsole. A smiling Palleus Chuff, bruised but modestly triumphant. Long panning shots of the interior of the Phindar Spaceport: reporters pointing excitedly at spent flechettes and plasma scorch marks. Quickly patched holes in the floor and wall. Head shots of Master Yoda—"another glowing chapter in his legendary career." Security footage of Trade Federation assassin droids running amok; two Jedi Knights bravely battling to save civilians before being cut down. Asajj Ventress, of course. A shot from external space station cams: *Last Call* tumbling heavily through space, accelerating, and then making a hyperdrive jump to certain doom. A state-of-the-art ship built at Dooku's own expense— the third one she'd lost, if one counted the craft Anakin and Kenobi had stolen from her.

Dooku wished Darth Sidious would speak.

It was Ventress's fault. The woman was impossible. She was talented, yes, but really, a battalion of droids was of more immediate practical use. At this rate, cheaper, too. He should terminate her.

The remorseless hooded figure flickered like a ghost on the holoconsole.

"I was not aware. Thank you for showing this to me. Needless to say, Ventress was acting on her own initiative." The arrogance—one might even say, the faint condescension—with which he had been thinking of his Master a few moments before had drained out of him like blood spilling from an open vein. "Nevertheless, the basic facts remain: Yoda is coming to me here, and here I will finish him, once and for all."

"So I trust." Darth Sidious smiled. Once, early in Dooku's Jedi career, he had arrived on a distant planet too late to stop a massacre—a long hall of wood and grass, tribal enemies inside, the outside doused with kerosene and a match thrown in. The flames, dancing, had looked like his Master's smile. "Of course, Count, I leave you to manage Ventress as you see fit: but would you like to know what I do, when my servants show enough . . . initiative?"

Dooku found his finger touching—just touching—the small red button on his desk. "Master?"

"I *crush* them," Darth Sidious said.

Jedi Council Chamber, Coruscant.

"Master Windu!"

"Chancellor."

"I give you great joy on the day's glad news! Wherever help is most needed and least expected, Master Yoda appears to save the day! A wonderful boost for morale: one day he is reported dead—the next, rising up on the other side of the galaxy with a glorious victory! Whoever said the public had lost faith in the Jedi must be eating his words tonight."

"We try, Chancellor."

A pause.

"You are grave."

"We lost two Jedi Knights, sir, friends I have known since my childhood in the Temple, and operatives of exceptional value. Master Yoda is now traveling, his cover broken, into the heart of enemy territory, accompanied by two apprentices who are barely more than children."

"Ah. Yes, I see. The politician is impressed with a victory on the battlefield of public relations; the military commander not so much. But I had anticipated you in this, at least somewhat. I tell you, Master Windu, I am not easy with Yoda's situation for precisely the reasons you describe. I should be happier if you were to replace the fallen with another detail. I'm not sure who, exactly . . . Well, why not Obi-Wan? Didn't I see in my last briefing that he had finished his last mission? Obi-Wan and young Skywalker. I would feel more comfortable if I knew they were on their way to Vjun. I think the world of Master Yoda, but he is very old, and perhaps not all that he once was. The idea of him facing Count Dooku alone, in the Count's stronghold . . . it makes my blood run cold. Yes, Obi-Wan and Skywalker would do very well."

"Is that an order, Chancellor?"

"Let's call it a *request*, Master Windu. A heartfelt request."

"This transmission was some time in coming," Dooku said, a twenty-centimeter-high hologhost, bright mauve, on the transmission deck of the cutter Asajj had stolen from the Phindian Spaceport docks.

"I've been a little busy, Count." Asajj tried to fix the console's color controls, wondering if the system was defective, or if the rig had been customized for some alien with ocular peculiarities that made mauve seem natural. Also, she was in no hurry to meet Dooku's eye. "I had to calculate a couple of hyperdrive jumps to shake Phindian security off my tail."

"You lost the *Call*."

"Yes. To Yoda."

"No, to an *actor,* apparently."

"What!"

"Perhaps I have more recent information," Dooku said. His voice was very calm. Very considering.

Asajj knew she was in bad trouble here. "The actor was doubling for Yoda. I caught him over Ithor."

"It would have saved time and trouble to leave him in the debris field, don't you think?"

Ventress's hands were getting clammy. She would a thousand times have preferred him ripping into her than this cool, surgical, distant voice. A fight would have been a dust-up between allies, between colleagues. This was more like a dissection.

"If I left him in the debris field, his remains would have been identifiably not Yoda's. I could have pushed him out an air lock somewhere else, but . . ."

"But what?"

She shrugged. "I have chosen my friends and enemies. To kill randomly, to kill for no purpose but spite seems weak to me. Undisciplined."

"If I had asked you to kill him?"

"Of course I would have done so."

"What about your scruples, then?"

"My loyalty to you overcalls them."

"But I did not ask you to kill him, did I?"

"Did you even know he was aboard the *Call*?" Ventress said. She realized the trap he had let her walk into the instant the words were out of her mouth. "No, you didn't. Because I never gave you a chance. I didn't tell you. Perhaps I should have." She squared her shoulders.

"I'll accept that responsibility. I was acting on my own initiative."

Some emotion, hard to read, flickered across his mauve face at the word *initiative*.

"Principles, scruples: this is somewhat the territory of the young. As one ages," the Count said, "one becomes more practical. I don't care so much about theoretical constructs of right and wrong. I care about timing, effect, precision. If I have a prisoner, or indeed an ally"—he looked mildly at her—"that is costing too much in resources, or introducing too many uncertainties into the scheme of things, I eliminate that person. Do you understand me?"

Asajj swallowed.

"I think," the Count continued blandly, "you had better convince me that you are a net gain to my efficiency, Asajj. You have lost two of my ships, one to Obi-Wan and the other to a second-rate actor from the Coruscant stage. Without consulting me, you broke in upon a chain of events I had put in motion to bring Yoda to my dungeons of his own free will. Instead of contemplating his head at this moment, I am watching a spike in Jedi popularity and a recovery of Republic morale that two days ago was nearing the breaking point. Right now, you are a very expensive ally, Asajj. Right now, you are costing me more than you're worth."

The cold burn of his words hit her like a splash of liquid nitrogen. He wasn't merely angry. Unless she did something right here, right now, he was going to murder her. She didn't even bother thinking about escape. If Dooku wanted to end her, he would. He had not taught her all the Sith lore he possessed, but even the slender connection between them made her terribly vulnerable to his arts. Besides which, he might well be the most powerful being in the galaxy, with nearly unlimited resources at his disposal. An amount of money that wouldn't even register as a blip in Dooku's accounts would be enough to keep her on the run from assassins for the rest of her short, miserable life, hiding out in jungles and living on womp rats, or passing herself through a series of chop shops, mutilating her features for the slim, desperate chance of disguise.

No. In every fiber of her being Asajj knew that running, hiding, defending was always the wrong strategy. In every engagement, one had to seize the initiative. In every engagement, the key was to *attack*.

"Kill your Master," she said.

Dooku blinked. "What?"

Well, at least he wasn't expecting it, Asajj thought, with a wild grin. She had made her gamble—nothing to do now but back it up. "Kill your Master now, with my help. Now while you can." She noted the tiniest flinch on the Count's face. "Sooner or later, every Sith apprentice tries to overthrow his Master. I know it. You know it. He knows it. Now is your time. You are an independent agent on a fortress planet. Armies are at your command. The wealth of worlds is at your feet. *Now is your time.*"

"I do admire the unexpected flair of your attack," Dooku murmured. "I have mentioned the benefits of age to you more than once, but it has its drawbacks, too. One gets settled in one's ways. But you . . . you still surprise me. You are still unexpected."

"How do you think this war is going to go?" Ventress said, pressing her tiny moment of advantage. "What happens if you win? Will you return to Coruscant in triumph? Will you sit at the great man's hand when the fighting is done? I don't think so. How can he let you live—Dooku, the conquering general. Dooku the wealthy. Dooku the wise. You must stand too much in his sun, Count."

"You are bluffing about things you do not know, Asajj. It is a brave show, but it will not do."

His attempt at a condescending smile did not convince her. "He will *use you up*," she said. "He will put you on the front lines when he can. He will throw Yoda at you, and his sycophants: Kenobi, Windu, Skywalker."

"With great ability comes great responsibility, Ventress. Not, clearly, one of your long suits."

"Fine, fine, take your shots," she said impatiently. "You're just buying time now, because I'm right. Ask yourself one question—ask it from the dark side, look at it clear-eyed, Count. Right now, your Master uses you because he is beset by dangers. *What happens when you are the most dangerous being left standing?*"

Through the comm channel, no sound but the faint static hiss of stars, burning and burning.

"If I told you to kill yourself, would you do it?" Dooku asked.

"No."

"What if I told you to come here, back to Vjun."

"I would come."

"Would you be afraid?"

"Terrified." Out here, in the deeps of space, she could hold him off. She could run away. But once she set foot in Château Malreaux, once she entered into the orbit of Dooku's power, she would never leave alive unless he willed it.

"But you would come?"

"If you order it."

Dooku regarded her. "I do."

So much for bluffing. "Will you have me killed, or will you listen to what I have to say?"

"That is none of your business."

"He's going to use you up, Count. He'll drain the blood from you and throw you aside. He'll pick someone younger, weaker, easier to influence."

"Someone like you?"

"I wish. No, when you go, I'll be swept aside," she said morosely. "I'm just one of your creatures, to him. Maybe to you, too. Loyalty runs stronger up than it does down, in case you hadn't noticed."

"Usually true," the Count conceded. "Master Yoda, perhaps, is the exception. His loyalty to his students runs deeper than theirs to him, I think."

"Admirable," Ventress said dryly. "But that doesn't do either of *us* any good, does it?"

Asajj Ventress sat before the nav computer on her stolen ship for a long time, trying to decide what to do, cursing softly but steadily. Finally she entered coordinates for Vjun. At the end of the day, running and hiding wasn't her style. Her chances of convincing the Count that they should work together would be better face-to-face. He liked her fire and her passion, and—though his iron self-control never slipped—she knew he thought her lovely, and that didn't hurt, either.

And if it went badly . . . better to be cut down quickly in person, blades drawn, than live in skulking misery for the rest of her days, feeling every stray gleam of sun on her back like a sniper's targeting dot.

All that being said, forcing her fingers to put in the Vjun coordinates felt like deliberately sticking them into a fire, and she was in a fairly filthy humor when the ship's comm console chirped. She ignored the signal. It wasn't, after all, her ship. But the hail kept repeating, over and over, until looking up with irritation she saw the call-up code for the Tac-Spec Footman droid, the one who had given her Yoda's location.

Oh, great. "What do you want?"

"I think you know," said the calm voice at the other end. "I want the rest of my money. We agreed on a certain price. Now I find only one-third of that sum has been credited to my account."

"I didn't get the target."

"My information was exact and correct, and that is what you paid for. Your inability to perform is no reason to penalize me."

"Yeah, well, life's tough all over," Ventress snapped. "As you must know, I am out the price of a starship. I don't have the credits to give you—to tell you the truth, I threw in the children's lives as a favor to you. Consider it payment in kind."

"They were not part of our agreement."

"Spoken like a cold-blooded droid, all right. Or should that be cold-oiled?" Ventress hunted through the ship's computer system, looking for the repair and maintenance manual. A service light had started blinking in the middle of her last hyperspace jump, a little icon of a purple jellyfish-thing with what looked like spears running through it and a big red bar; she had no idea what it might signify. "You know, haggling over money is not my favorite activity at the best of times, and to be perfectly frank, haggling with a tin can—a traitorous tin can at that—interests me even less."

"I may be a traitor," the droid said, "but I'm not a cut-rate one. I highly recommend you reconsider."

Aha! Ventress thought, scanning through the ship's manual—she had it! The blinking light was the fluid ligature spindling indicator. She read rapidly through the help section:

> . . . *when this light flashes, fluid ligatures may be in danger of spindling, or may already have spindled. Spindling may lead to excessive wear, loss of translight pressure, or weight gain due to instability in artificial gravity devices. Also, in rare cases, death.*

> *Occasionally, fluid ligature spindling indicator may flash for no reason.*

So here she was, heading back to Vjun in a stolen ship that might or might not have spindled fluid ligatures, in apparently imminent danger of a grav-induced weight gain, with the prospect of an interview with an angry Sith Lord waiting for her with execution on his mind.

"Tin Man, I gotta tell you—right now, you're the least of my worries."

Far away, in an anonymous comm booth, Solis, who had betrayed Yoda's secret and now was not even to be paid for it, stared at the CONNECTION CUT BY RECIPIENT message on the screen. "We'll see about that," he said.

At the same instant that connection died, another sputtered to life between the Jedi Council Chamber and Anakin Skywalker's ship. "Hailing."

"Master Windu!"

"Obi-Wan? Why aren't you in your own ship?"

Obi-Wan grimaced. "Repairs. Anakin agreed to give me a lift."

"I see. Current location?"

Obi-Wan rolled his eyes at Anakin, who grinned back at him. Mace Windu, supremely gifted in so many ways, was not much for small talk. "Inbound to Coruscant, flight plan as filed," Anakin said. "We're sublight for a day and a half for refueling and stores. Should be home in four days. According to local space news, reports of Master Yoda's death were greatly exaggerated."

"True. The same can't be said for Maks Leem and Jai Maruk," Mace said grimly.

"Oh." The Jedi looked at one another, their smiles fading. "We hadn't heard."

"Master Yoda is on his way to—this channel is scrambled?"

The comm protocols on Anakin's ship were permanently set for triple-encrypted hard code for any channel running to the Temple, but he double-checked. A gross malfunction in the ship's reactor drives could cost him and Obi-Wan their lives; much tinier slips in signal encryption could cost the lives of millions. "All secure," he said crisply. Mace Windu's grimness was catching.

"Master Yoda is on the way to Vjun to negotiate secretly for the possible defection of a highly placed Confederacy figure. *Very* highly placed," Mace said significantly.

"Master Yoda?" Anakin said, puzzled. "Surely there are more important things for him to be—"

He trailed off as Obi-Wan gave him a long look. "*Extremely* highly placed, I'm guessing," the older man said.

Half a second later, Anakin got it. "Dooku? He's going to negotiate with *Dooku?*—It's a trap. He must know it's a trap, right?"

"A trap, yes . . . but for whom?" Obi-Wan murmured.

"At the moment, Master Yoda is traveling to Vjun on a very important mission," Mace continued. "We wanted to keep it quiet, but obviously the secret is out. Equally obviously, your old friend Asajj Ventress is gunning for him. She killed both the Jedi traveling with him; only two Padawans remain. I would like—"

"Uh-oh," Obi-Wan said. "Why do I get the feeling we aren't inbound to Coruscant after all?"

"—the two of you to proceed to Vjun with all possible speed and give Master Yoda whatever help he requests and requires."

"Isn't there someone else?" Anakin said unexpectedly. "We were supposed to return to Coruscant three weeks ago. I've already broken one promise to be back . . ."

The words hung in the air, irrevocable.

"*Promise?*" Mace said. "To whom did you make this promise?"

"The students in Master Iron Hand's class," Obi-Wan said smoothly. "Anakin has been promising to teach them some tricks."

"Your chance to show off will have to be delayed," Mace said. His look of distaste was one with which Anakin had become wearyingly familiar. Mace's disapproval of Anakin seemed so general, so reflexive, it was hard not to resent even in a case like this, where there was actually far more to disapprove of than Windu knew. "Get to Vjun, please. Windu out."

Anakin colored a little, and did not look at Obi-Wan. "Thanks."

Obi-Wan shrugged it off, nettled. "I don't know why I bother sticking my neck out for you." He busied himself checking out a course for Vjun. "Especially since I feel, with every nerve in my body, that someday you won't thank me for it."

After the fight in the Phindar Spaceport, all Scout wanted to do was curl up in a ball and cry.

Yoda had other ideas.

He talked the station authorities into letting them take a rental to Jovan. Then it was a public shuttle to the low-rent end of Jovan Station, packed with used-ship dealerships and scrap yards. Yoda didn't want to take public transport anymore, he said. He pushed the Padawans from junkyard to junkyard, looking for a ship they could take to Vjun.

They'd had their choice of several decent-looking ships, but Master Yoda turned all of them down: too flashy, too new, too expensive. "Expensive?" Scout had asked. "You can use the credits of the Jedi Temple, can't you? Or the Chancellor's office, for that matter."

Yoda's face had sucked in and his ears had curled

down in an expression of repugnance. "So waste the people's money I should?"

Scout had thrown up her hands in frustration.

So the four of them kept looking—Yoda, Whie, Scout, and Fidelis, the gentleman's personal gentlething. They had seen no sign of Solis since the spaceport. No prizes for guessing why. Ventress had come there looking for them. Her droids had targeted the R2 unit right away. When Solis disappeared after the battle, it was obvious he had betrayed them. Scout's face went grim, remembering how the droid had set her up, dragging her away from the others with his story about needing a human escort in the spaceport. Whittling away their numbers. Maybe if she had stayed it wouldn't have made any difference. Maybe she wouldn't have been able to save Maks Leem and Master Maruk. But at least she wouldn't have been a hundred meters away on a staircase, watching their murders.

Fidelis had been inconsolable. At first Scout wanted him scrapped or abandoned, but his anguish at having brought along a confederate who had endangered the heir of the Malreaux line was so deep and obsessive, so obviously hardwired, that even she didn't believe he had been involved in their betrayal. They had thought about sending him away, but in the end that, too, seemed impractical. Having found Whie at last, nothing short of being cut in half with a lightsaber was going to keep the droid from following him. "If you refuse to let me come inside your ship, I'll just rivet myself to the hull," he'd said, and frankly they had believed him.

Yoda finally found what he was looking for in the fifth junkyard they visited on Jovan Station: a swaybacked old nag of a ship, an ancient B-7 light freighter with red blotches over the cargo bay doors.

"Rust?" Whie said. "How do you get rust with no air and no water?"

That got a big belly laugh out of the junkyard operator. "Naw, this little girl got held up by pirates, you see. Those red splotches aren't *rust,* they're—"

"How much?" Yoda said quickly.

Scout and Whie grimaced at one another. Master Yoda preferred not to use the Force for something as simple as arguing over a price. He said it was disrespectful to the Force, and to one's opponent in commercial combat, but the real truth, Scout privately thought, was that Yoda was a gleeful, cranky, relentless bargainer who thought haggling was *fun.* So much of bargaining is about patience, and bazaar-stand shysters on a hundred planets had learned to their sorrow that one doesn't know what patience is until one has tried to outlast an eight-hundred-plus-year-old Jedi skinflint. Whie and Scout had already heard Master Yoda spend hours dickering over price at the last two junkyards, only to stump away unsatisfied, waggling his stick and muttering, leaving the poor owners looking as if they'd been slowly crushed in a garbage compactor.

The two Padawans drifted away from the Haggling Zone. Whie looked terrible, Scout thought: gaunt and red-eyed from grief and lack of sleep. "Hey," she said. "You hanging in?"

"Sure."

"You're lying."

"Yeah." He gave her a long, searching look, almost

desperate. She saw his eyes flick toward Yoda, still haggling.

Scout jerked one thumb toward a little aisle between the B-7 and the next hulk, an old *Epoch*-class freighter with a single laser cannon turret, its barrel bent like a broken antenna. Obviously there was something on Whie's mind; Scout figured a little privacy might make it easier to talk about. As benevolent as Yoda was, there were some kinds of weakness, some kinds of doubt one didn't want to be confessing in front of the being with the power to make or break one as a Jedi Knight.

She ambled over to the narrow lane, running her fingers lightly along the Epoch's fuselage. Its hull was dinged and scuffed and pocked with a sprinkling of micrometeor punctures: the ship had probably spent her last few years as an insystem trader, swimming in dangerous solar space, murky with asteroid debris and other kinds of particulate matter. With starships, as with deep-water craft, only the lubbers loved the sight of land. To a sailor's eye, blue water or hard black space were the places to be, far from the perils of leeward shores and gravity wells.

When they were safely out of sight, Scout said, "All right, spill it."

Whie kicked absently at the old freighter with one space-booted toe. "Yesterday—was it yesterday, or the day before? I've lost track of the hours. It doesn't matter. The last time I slept, I had a dream." He paused. "A special kind of dream."

"The one where you . . ."

"Where I was killed by a Jedi. Yes." He swallowed and gave her a wan smile. "But it wasn't the only dream

I've had recently. There was another, just before we left Coruscant. You were in it."

"Me!"

"Yes." For the first time since Master Leem died, a little color crept into Whie's face. "We were in a room, a beautiful, terrible room. And you were bleeding—"

"Master Whie?" called the anxious voice of the Malreaux family gentleman's personal gentlething from behind the Epoch's hull. "Master? Where are you?"

"Here! What is it?" Whie snapped.

"There you are!" Fidelis came hurrying around the corner. "I was doing currency calculations for Master Yoda, and when I looked up, you had gone!"

"Twenty meters, Fidelis. It's not like I was abducted by space pirates."

"That's no fault of yours," the droid said tartly. "Please don't go wandering off alone. Don't you know what hangs around places like this?"

"Uh, nothing?" Whie guessed. "We're not exactly in the cabana quarters of Jovan Station. It's not like a bunch of naval ratings in spacesuits are going to roll out of a nearby bar and pick a fight with me."

"Though noble and accomplished, you are still naïve in the ways of the world," Fidelis said starchily. "A salvage yard like this is exactly where you might expect to find rogue droids. Runaways, looking to salvage parts. Masterless creatures that are not above taking a human hostage, if their programming has gone sufficiently awry."

"This warning's a little bit late," Scout said hotly. "Why didn't you think of that before you hired Solis?"

"The fact that I made an error in judgment is no reason to—"

"Fidelis, *get lost,*" Whie grated.

The droid drew himself huffily upright and retreated to the end of the aisle between the two freighters, pointedly maintaining eye contact.

"Do you suppose he can read lips?" Scout murmured.

"Yes," Fidelis called.

"Shut up, droid," Whie growled. Obviously the chance for a private chat had gone.

Scout blinked. "I don't think I've ever heard you be rude before."

"Sorry."

"Don't be." She laughed. "I think it's cute."

". . . *Cute?*"

Even Scout had to admit Yoda got a fantastic bargain on the B-7. "How'd you get it so cheap?" she asked, gaping at the smirking old Jedi as he stuffed a datapad into his belt. "You must have used your Jedi mind powers. I thought you said that was unfair?"

"Not interested in *fair,* am I. Interested in results," he wheezed. "Besides, Jedi powers used I not. Paid fair price I did."

Scout and Whie looked doubtfully at the shabby hulk. "What's wrong with her?" Scout said. "I mean, besides the obvious?"

Yoda rapped the outside of the ship with his stick, raising a little cloud of dust. And paint. And meta-ceramic. "Good hull. Good lines," he said.

"One laser cannon," Whie said. "No concussion missile tubes. No blaster cannon."

"She's got a Hanx-Wargel SuperFlow II aboard and a Siep-Irol passive sensor antenna," the junkyard owner said vehemently. "Backup generators, Carbanti active sensor stack, and almost new aft deflector shields, local-made but nothing wrong with them."

"What about bow shields?"

"If anything comes at you with a gun, you should run," the dealer said.

"If that doesn't work?"

"Surrender."

"Very encouraging," Scout said.

"I take it very hard, you talking down my beautiful little"—the dealer glanced quickly at the side of the ship where the name had been painted—"*Nighthawk*. I've a good mind to raise my price, you being so uppity."

"If she's got all these features," Scout persisted, "why were you selling her so cheaply? What *doesn't* she do?"

The dealer hemmed and hawed. Scout turned to Yoda, who smiled beatifically. "Fly," he said.

" 'A bargain it is!' he says. 'Fix it up in no time, we will!' Pass me the sonic wrench," Scout growled. Pale honey-colored fluid dripped from the engine-starter array she was trying to install, each drop drifting and spreading out in Jovan Station's comparatively light gravity.

"I think I've almost got these couplers installed," Whie said.

"Red ends up?"

"Yeah."

They worked side by side, installing the engine-starter unit Yoda had salvaged from a Corellian light freighter at the back of the yard.

"What's Master Yoda doing while we're working?" Scout grunted.

"Know that, I do not! He said something about supplies. Did you hear about the water?" Scout looked over. "Both for our use and coolant, ten five-hundred-kilo casks. We'll be loading it on ourselves," Whie said.

"Five hundred!"

"Master Yoda felt it would be wasting money to rent a lifter pallet for just one job," Whie said.

They exchanged looks.

Another fat blob of lubricant dripped free. This one had a dead bug in it, a metal borer with feathery antennae and mouthparts stained rust red. "Ew," Scout said.

"Pass me the solder-blaster, would you?" Whie was working about five meters away. Scout tossed him the tool in a gentle underhand. In the low g, it floated into his hand. She pitched him a stick of solder to go with it.

"Thanks."

Whie peered up. He had a mainplate off, exposing wires and tubes coiled like multicolored intestines. No wonder people talked about the "bowels" of a ship, he thought. He was working on the vaccum-pump housing; the casement was cracked, so the vacuum seal kept failing. Funny to think—a little hairline fracture causing all this trouble, because it let the *nothing* out.

A ship's vacuum like Jedi honor—nothing one could notice, until it was gone.

"Scout? Do you ever wonder if you're a bad person?"

"Wonder? I know," she said, laughing.

"Be serious. If you discovered you weren't a good person, that would bother you, wouldn't it?"

"I've never been a *good* person." Scout used the sonic wrench to pry open a nut that had rusted in place. "I just shoot for *good enough*. Why do you ask?"

"No reason."

Scout waited, not looking at Whie. According to the calendar, she was a year older than him, but he was so accomplished, so poised, that she usually forgot about the age difference. Today he sounded young, and she felt older than him by far. She remembered something Yoda once said—*Age more than a count of heartbeats is. Age is how many mistakes you have made.* Counting by screwups, she was an easy ten years older than Whie.

"I used to think I was a good person," Whie said quietly. "But then some things happened. I had this dream," he said. "And in this dream, I was thinking bad thoughts."

"Whoa there, boy. You're can't get down on yourself because of what you thought when you were *asleep*."

"You don't understand. This wasn't a dream, this wasn't my unconscious speaking: this *really happened.* Is going to happen," he corrected himself. The pain in his voice was obvious now, and Scout realized this was deadly serious to him.

Whie pressed solder into the cracked vacuum-chamber casing and ran the blaster-iron over it. Strange these sticks of metal, which seemed so hard and straight, could be so easily made soft. Inconstant. "And then there was the other dream. The one about dying. I've never dreamed about that before."

Scout waited.

"The whole thing was confused. I'm not sure where I was, or what I was doing. I was in my own head; there was a lightsaber flashing. I tried to defend myself, but the other was too strong for me. Too fast. Then the light like a bar across my eyes. Like a sun." The soldering iron sparked and glowed in the dim recesses of the battered freighter. "Then nothing."

"Just because it was a lightsaber, that doesn't mean it was a Jedi."

"Oh, but I knew. The dream was so short, I didn't even see who it was, but when I fell into the moment, I wasn't even frightened yet, I was just so *surprised*. I was thinking, *This is how I'm going to die?* Isn't that weird. Even having had this dream, my death is still going to come as a surprise, when it happens. I guess it always does," he added.

Scout gave the reluctant nut another shot of loosening solvent. "Maybe you got it wrong. Maybe you won't die. You didn't die in the dream, right? Not that you know for sure. Maybe it was a test, or an exercise. If you thought it was a Jedi, that's the most likely answer—a drill, or a tournament like the one we had just before we left," Scout said. "I bet that's it."

"Maybe," Whie said. She knew he didn't believe it. "Do you want the solder-blaster back?"

"Nah, I'm okay." Scout finally managed to pry off the rusted nut. "The dream you had with me in it. Did I die?"

"Not in the part I saw."

This was not as comforting an answer as Scout had been hoping for.

"Scout, I think I'm going to go over to the dark side," Whie said in a rush. "That's how it makes sense. That's why I'm thinking what I'm thinking in the first dream. That's why a Jedi cuts me down."

"That's ridiculous," Scout said, genuinely shocked. "You're the last person in the world to go over to the dark side. Everyone knows that. You're better than any of us. You always have been. I used to *hate* how good you were. There's no way," she said positively.

"I always used to think of myself as a good person," Whie said. "I was proud of it. But now, looking back, I was just *pretending* to be good. You know? Acting. It wasn't real at all. I was just . . . pretending to be a Jedi."

For the first time Scout put down her tools and sidled over under the belly of the ship. She put her hand on his arm. "Whie, listen to me. Sometimes pretending is all there is."

An hour later, Fidelis was setting ship's stores into the pantries of the freighter's tiny galley. Yoda had told him to buy enough food for a feast, and he had done his best. Programmed to please, he was distressed at the idea of cooking without knowing his guests' preferences—but, he philosophically reminded himself, all life was improvisation, and anyway the only cuisine Whie had ever known was what they served in the Jedi Temple cafeteria. If Fidelis couldn't exceed that standard, he deserved to be left behind with the rest of the scrap on Jovan Station. Besides, although his exposure to Whie per se had been slight, he had cooked for twelve generations of clan Malreaux, and of course he had the boy's complete genetic scan available. Gustatory development was still more art than science, but armed with this much information, it would be strange if he couldn't come reasonably near the mark.

As he set out his ingredients, he could hear Yoda in the forward cockpit, grunting and snuffing as he peered over the ship's manifest and owner's manual. Creaks, gasps, and bangs came from aft, where Master Whie and the girl were stowing the great casks of water.

Fidelis poked his head into the cockpit. "Pardon me, Master Yoda, but I would like to delay cooking for the time being and help stow the water. I shall be back in a matter of moments."

"No," the old Jedi grunted.

"I beg your pardon?"

"Go not. Padawans' job it is, to load the ship."

"Being considerably stronger, however, it would surely be more efficient for me to do the heavy lifting, particularly as it would eliminate the risk of muscle strain or injury on the young people."

"Use the Force they must. Good practice will it be."

"But neither of them has slept in more than a day."

Without bothering to look up from the ship's manual, where he was studying the B-7's rather odd protocols for coming out of hyperspace, Yoda reached back and whacked Fidelis on the leg with his stick. The droid made a pleasant ringing sound, like a brass bell. "Missing the point, are you, toaster-thing. Padawans need to work. If not working, think they will."

"Oh," Fidelis said.

Yoda turned, looking over his humped shoulder so their eyes met, sentient and machine. "Old are we, and strong; trees that have survived many frosts. But for these two, their Masters' deaths a first winter are. Work, let them," he said gently. "And eat. And cry. And maybe, just maybe, sleep after all."

The droid regarded him. "You are wise, Master Yoda."

"So they tell me," Yoda grunted. "But since here you are, tell me more of Count Dooku's quarters."

"They are hardly that," the droid said stiffly. "I trust the Count is staying as a guest of House Malreaux. The exact nature of the situation is unclear, as I have been on Coruscant for many years, and my communication with Lady Malreaux has been somewhat erratic."

Yoda studied the droid. "Jai Maruk mentioned to me a lady he saw in the house. A Vjun fox followed her."

"That would be Lady Malreaux. The fox is her familiar."

"Familiar?"

Fidelis shrugged. "So the servants call it. I do not care to speak to superstition, although certainly the Force is reputed to be very strong on Vjun, and House Malreaux, of course, has produced the finest adepts of its arts."

"Strong it is . . . in the dark side," Yoda murmured.

Fidelis shrugged. "Count Malreaux's attempt to apply genetic manipulations to the midi-chlorian bodies was, with the benefit of hindsight, perhaps overly ambitious. And yet, one must admire his scope and vision!"

"Must one?" Yoda said dryly. "An old saying is there, about playing with fire, gentleman's personal gentle-thing. But of your Lady Malreaux—Dooku's mad house-keeper is she now."

Even Yoda had rarely seen a droid look shocked: but shock was exactly the expression on the droid's metal face now. Shock, mortification, and something else that in a sentient one might almost call anger. "That cannot be."

"Washes the floor, Jai said she did. Also cleans refreshers," Yoda said. "Is it the wrong word, *house-keeper*? *Servant* would be better? *Scullery maid*?" he asked innocently. "*Slave?*"

"*Lady* is the appropriate term," Fidelis said sharply. "Or *Mistress*."

"Like to meet with Dooku, would I," Master Yoda continued blithely. "Convince him to come back to Coruscant I must. Not easy, though. Guards will be there. Followers, perhaps. Soldiers. Know you any private ways into Château Malreaux?"

"I do indeed," Fidelis said.

Three hours later, the *Nighthawk* was lumbering out of Jovan Station, beginning the long, slow run she needed to warm up for the jump to hyperspace. Her motley crew was gathered in what the B-7 owner's manual optimistically called "the crew lounge," a small bubble in the ship's throat between the cockpit and the galley, just wide enough to fit a small projector table suitable for playing hologames or screening holovids—as long as they had been encoded in one of two Hydian Way formats, neither one of which was the Coruscanti standard for Republic pictures.

The lounge's other amenities included two not-quite-full decks of cards; four secondhand bar stools of the sunken-middle design that had been fashionable twenty standard years before and made one feel as if one was sitting in an inner tube; and a foldout clothes-pressing board. Master Yoda was currently sitting on the ironing board, swinging his dangling legs. He was too small to sit on the stools without the risk of getting stuck in the hole in the middle.

From the galley, Fidelis emitted a surprising chime. "Dinner is served."

Whie set the projector table to the ship's external sensors, so the middle of the tiny lounge was now a starscape, deep blackness pricked by pinpoint suns, and their little freighter a glowing dot in the center. The boy's face was gaunt and exhausted, his eyes ringed with dark circles. "I'm not hungry," he said.

"Ah, but I have made crêpes Malreaux," Fidelis said, bearing two gently steaming platters of food into the lounge. "A recipe I created for the ninth Count. My gentlebeings have been so good as to commend it warmly these last eight generations."

"Smells delicious," Scout said.

"Obviously there were no acid-beets to make the customary side dish; indeed, I do not know that Vjun exports them any longer. I was, however, able to purchase a string of dried whip-smelt and some rather excellent cheese as an appetizer, along with a few Reythan crackers and a souse-mustard tapenade from an old Ortolan recipe that I hope will give satisfaction."

Fidelis placed the trays of food on the projector table. Whip-smelt in toasted cheese steamed gently amid the stars. "I took the precaution of supplying linen," Fidelis said, handing out napkins. "These are all finger foods; there's little room in the galley, and I thought it best not to ship much in the way of dishes."

"Tastes d'l'cious, too," Scout said thickly, through a mouthful of cracker and tapenade. "Stars, I didn't know how hungry I was."

"For you, Master Yoda, a bowl of the bottom-feeder

gumbo." Fidelis supplied a bowl of sticky, black, acrid stuff, with nameless pale blobs the color of tree lichen floating in it. It smelled extraordinarily like burning lubricant. "I did follow the recipe," the droid added anxiously.

Yoda leaned over the bowl and snuffed. His eyes rolled up in pleasure. "Most excellent!"

Scout's eyes were half closed in dreamy appreciation of a cheese-toasted whip-smelt. "Whoa."

Master Yoda held up his bowl. "Asked the toaster to make this feast I did," he said, nodding benevolently at Fidelis, "that we might share our food, and remember our lost Master Leem and Master Maruk."

Fidelis handed the Padawans beakers of a rich purple liquid that tasted like candleberries and rainwater and the smell of sweet stuff. It fizzed on Scout's tongue as she drank a toast. "Master Leem and Master Maruk."

"That's it?" Whie said angrily. "That's what you want to do? Eat? Maks and Jai Maruk dead, and all you can think about is filling your bellies?"

Scout looked up guiltily, licking cracker crumbs off the edge of her mouth.

"What about finding Ventress?" Whie demanded. "What about making her pay for what she did? Are the Jedi about justice, or dessert?"

"Profiteroles Ukio," Fidelis said quietly. "With a caramel ganache filling."

Yoda savored a spoonful of gumbo. "Honor life by living, Padawan. Killing honors only death: only the dark side."

"Well, much has the dark side been honored, then," Whie said bitterly.

"Kid, it's been way too many hours since you've slept," Scout said.

"Don't call me *kid*," Whie said dangerously. "I am not your little brother. I look out for you, not the other way around, Tallisibeth. Jai Maruk was right about you. If I hadn't been taking care of you back in the spaceport, I might have been able to get down to the floor in time to stop her from killing them both."

"Taking care of me!" Scout cried, outraged. "Who was pinned to the railing by his butler droid while I was trying to get down there? Who snuck off to hear stories about his so-called real family in the first place?" she said, white with anger.

Yoda set his bowl of gumbo regretfully aside. "Hear it working, do you?"

"Hear what?" Whie snapped.

"The dark side. Always it speaks to us, from our pain. Our grief. It connects our pain to all pain, our hurt to all hurt."

"Maybe it has a lot to say." Whie stared at the starscape hovering over the projector table. "It's so easy for you. What do you care? You are unattached, aren't you? You'll probably never die. What was Maks Leem to you? Another pupil. After all these centuries, who could blame you if you could hardly keep track of them? Well, she was more than that to me." He looked up challengingly. Tear tracks were shining on his face, but his eyes were still hard and angry. "She was the closest thing I had to a mother, since you took me away from my real mother. She chose me to be her Padawan and I let her down, I let her die, and I'm not going to sit here and *stuff* myself and *get over it*!" He finished with a yell, sweeping the plate of crêpes off the projection table, so the platter went sailing toward the floor.

Yoda's eyes, heavy-lidded and half closed like a drowsing dragon's, gleamed, and one finger twitched. Food, platter, drinks, and all hung suspended in the air. The platter settled; the crêpes returned to it; Whie's overturned cup righted itself, and rich purple liquid trickled back into it. All settled back onto the table.

Another twitch of Yoda's fingers, the merest flicker, and Whie's head jerked around as if on a string, until he found himself looking into the old Jedi's eyes. They were green, green as swamp water. He had never quite realized before how terrifying those eyes could be. One could drown in them. One could be pulled under.

"Teach me about pain, think you can?" Yoda said softly. "Think the old Master cannot care, *mmm*? Forgotten who I am, have you? Old am I, yes. Mm. Loved more than you, have I, Padawan. Lost more. Hated more. *Killed* more." The green eyes narrowed to gleaming slits under heavy lids. Dragon eyes, old and terrible. "Think wisdom comes at no *cost*? The dark side, yes—it is easier for them. The pain grows too great, and they eat the darkness to flee from it. Not Yoda. Yoda loves and suffers for it, loves and suffers."

One could have heard a feather hit the floor.

"The price of Yoda's wisdom, high it is, very high, and the cost goes on forever. But teach *me* about pain, will you?"

"I . . ." Whie's mouth worked. "I am sorry, Master. I was angry. But . . . what if they're *right*?" he cried out in anguish. "What if the galaxy *is* dark. What if it's like Ventress says: we are born, we suffer, we die, and that is *all.* What if there is no plan, what if there is no 'goodness'? What if we suffer blindly, trying to find a reason for the suffering, but we're just fooling ourselves, looking for hope that isn't there? What if there is nothing but stars and the black space between them and the galaxy does not care if we live or die?"

Yoda said, "It's true."

The Padawans looked at him in shock.

The Master's short legs swung forth and back, forth and back. "Perhaps," he added. He sighed. "Many days, feel certain of a greater hope, I do. Some days, not so." He shrugged. "What difference does it make?"

"Ventress was right?" Whie said, shocked out of his anger.

"No! Wrong she is! As wrong as she can be!" Yoda snorted. "Grief in the galaxy, is there? Oh, yes. Oceans of it. Worlds. And darkness?" Yoda pointed to the starscape on the projection table. "There you see: darkness, darkness everywhere, and a few stars. A few points of light. If no plan there is, no fate, no destiny, no providence, no Force: then what is left?" He looked at each of them in turn. "Nothing but our choices, *hmm*?

"Asajj eats the darkness, and the darkness eats her back. Do that if you wish, Whie. Do that if you wish." The old Jedi looked deep into the starscape, suns and planets and nebulae dancing, tiny points of light blazing in the darkness. "To be Jedi is to face the truth, and choose. Give off light, or darkness, Padawan." His matted eyebrows rose high over his swamp-colored eyes, and he poked Whie with the end of his stick. *Poke, poke.* "Be a candle, or the night, Padawan: but choose!"

* * *

Whie cried for what seemed like a long time. Scout ate. Fidelis served. Master Yoda told stories of Maks Leem and Jai Maruk: tales of their most exciting adventures, of course, but also comical anecdotes from the days when they were only children in the Temple. They drank together, many toasts.

Scout cried. Whie ate. Fidelis served.

Yoda told stories, and ate, and cried, and laughed: and the Padawans saw that *life itself* was a lightsaber in his hands; even in the face of treachery and death and hopes gone cold, he burned like a candle in the darkness. Like a star shining in the black eternity of space.

10

Château Malreaux stood on a high bluff on the north side of the Bay of Tears, a deep-water harbor guarded by sudden shoals. The River Weeping, which ran into the bay, had hollowed out a fantastic labyrinth of caves through the coastal cliffs. These features—a harbor friendly to those who knew her secrets, and death to those who didn't, and the chained galleries of caves that honeycombed the shore—had made the Bay of Tears the perfect smuggler's port. The first Count Malreaux had been a pirate, extorting his grant of nobility from the surrounding territory in exchange for a promise, only occasionally broken, to stop plundering passing ships.

The view from the bluff had a kind of bleak grandeur: the windswept point, bare but for the ubiquitous covering of Vjun moss, glowed a venomous green between leaden skies and a pewter sea. The wind blew hard, driving long rollers before it to smack heavily into the cliff face. Thin strings of rain bent and whipped in the air, mingling with spray blowing off the sea. A few pirate gulls, black with silver markings, wheeled and screamed over the little inlet.

The system of caves and tunnels that led up from the

beach had exits everywhere, including, of course, the cellars of Château Malreaux. One of these underground passages opened into the side of a tall hillock, crowned with thorn-trees, half a kilometer inland. From the cover of these thorns, an interested observer watched as an old B-7 freighter, accompanied by two wasp-winged Trade Federation fighter craft, came lumbering in, apparently intending to set down on the deserted landing pads in the ruins of Bitter End, a city on the far side of the bay from the château. Bitter End had numbered some sixty thousand souls before plagues and madness had rendered it a ghost town a decade before.

The freighter lurched suddenly, as if experiencing a problem with its attitude thrusters. It slipped rapidly sideways, spinning convincingly, and disappeared into a cleft between two rocky hills. A nicely judged performance, the observer thought. The Trade Federation fighters balked, jerked, and finally finished their descent into Bitter End.

One hundred twelve seconds later, the first landspeeders came screaming down the road from Bitter End to the cliff across the bay from Château Malreaux. The road ended there, at the famously scenic vista.

From his hidden observation post, Solis dialed up his T/Z telescopic sniperscope with the implanted reticle to identify the troops spilling out of the landspeeders and heading into the rugged terrain. Ten, twelve, fifteen humans in all, plus ten elite assassin droids like the ones Ventress had brought to Phindar Spaceport, and two platoons of grunt droids to help beat the bushes. There would be more specialized trackers in soon, no doubt;

this would be the reception committee Dooku had sent to be Yoda's "guard of honor."

There was a cave entrance within three minutes' hard scramble of where the B-7 had touched down. Yoda's crew should make it in plenty of time, Solis thought. Once inside the caves they should lengthen their lead, at least until the hunters brought in some pretty fancy sensors.

All in all, nothing unexpected—reasonable opening moves by both sides, each intent on a meeting, both preferring to control the time and manner of that encounter.

Solis nodded to himself. Time to head for the caves.

"You're late," Count Dooku said mildly as Whirry waddled into his study, flushed and gasping.

"Which I'm certain I'm sorry, for that I was looking for Miss Vix—but there she is, the pet!" Whirry cried, for the Count was holding the brindled fox. He had one large hand beneath the animal's chest, holding it, while with the other he stroked its red-brown pelt. The fox struggled and whined in his hands. It was gasping, and its eyes were round and terrified.

Dooku's fingers passed behind its ears, and his big hand ran over its thin shoulder blades, fragile as twigs. "I told you we had guests coming; one I invited, and a couple I did not." Dooku stroked the terrified fox. "I've been looking through some house records. When your husband went mad, you gave a child up to the Jedi."

"The Baby," Whirry whispered. "Which they stole him, the brutes. Took me when my mind was all ahoo. Blood all over my dress." She glanced absently down at her ball gown, looking at the splotches on the hem and cuffs, the dull stains darker than plain grime. "They stole him from me."

"There was a droid here at that time," Dooku said. "A Tac-Spec Footman who served the House Malreaux for twelve generations, but then mysteriously disappeared. No mention of it these last ten years. Curiously, Asajj met such a droid eight days ago, traveling with a Jedi Padawan on his way here."

Stroke, stroke: the little fox trembling and whining.

"Were you thinking of having a little homecoming without telling me, Whirry? That would be . . . disappointing."

"Which it was supposed to be a surprise, like," the old woman whispered.

"I don't like surprises."

"Oh. All right, then." She swallowed.

"You can communicate with this droid, I assume?"

"Yes."

The Count looked at her.

"Yes, Master," she said quickly.

Dooku ran his hand softly down Miss Vix's back. The fox twitched and yelped. Dooku lifted his hand. His fingertips were full of fur. "Hm," he said. He flicked the fur off his hand and returned to his stroking. Another yelp. More fur. He paused, as if at a sudden thought, and turned the fox, to show its mutilated pelt. "Here, Whirry—would you like to read your future?"

The housekeeper looked from her master to her fox and back, mouth trembling. "What do you want me to do?"

* * *

"What's wrong with your gentlegadget?" Scout asked Whie. They had been scrambling through the caves for some time, following the glow of Yoda's lightsaber, when the droid came to a sudden halt, as if his programming had hung.

"Fidelis?" Whie's voice, sharp and commanding. Echoes rattled away into the chambers on either side.

A whirring, clanking sound. Fidelis seemed to wake up. He shook his head. "Yes, Master Whie?"

"Is there a problem?"

"Not at all, sir. Just, ah, just running through my internal maps, sir."

"Come," Yoda said. "A large chamber there is. Rest there we will."

"I don't need rest," Whie said. His step, always graceful, was electric, and his voice hummed with suppressed excitement. "I need to get home."

It was all Scout could do to pick her way through these sinister caverns, eyes aching with the effort of peering into the gloom. She had already scraped her shins badly, twice, in the first dash into the cave system. Whie, on the other hand, was moving as if it were broad daylight. His eyes were bright, almost manic. "The Force is strong here," he said, and he laughed with the pleasure of it.

He was right about the Force. Even Scout could feel it: a nervous prickle running deep inside her, as if the world were full of magnets and she could feel them tugging on the iron in her blood. Whie found it exhilarating. Scout thought it was creepy. There was something edgy about the Force here: a sharp, unbalanced feeling, as different from the gentle glow of the Jedi Temple as the damp, acid wind of Vjun was from the air back home.

Whie bounded on ahead, with Fidelis pattering behind. Scout came up more slowly. Master Yoda took her lightly by the arm. "Soft now," he breathed. "Listen a moment, Padawan. Leave you here, I must."

"Leave us!" she hissed.

"Whether Fidelis may be trusted, I know not. Keep your fellow Padawan safe, I know he will: but Jedi business is a different thing."

True enough, Scout thought, remembering Solis's betrayal.

Yoda snuffed. "A way to the surface nearby there is; I can smell the air. Take it I will. You and the others stay in the caves. If all goes well, come to you, I will. If met in twelve hours we have not, head back to the ship, and send a message to the Jedi Temple, saying Yoda will not return."

"But—!"

The hand squeezed her arm. "Your fellow Padawan, watch you must! Vjun calls to the dark side in him."

"Check it out!" Whie called from somewhere up ahead. "Skeletons!"

"What am I supposed to do with him?" Scout whispered—but Yoda was gone.

Cursing under her breath, Scout scrambled up a series of limestone ledges. The only light came from the faint glow of Whie's lightsaber, far ahead. The floor was covered in a gray dust, fine as ash. Nothing grew here, although every now and then Scout saw small bones—animals that had fallen down a hole into the caves, or been carried here by floodwaters. Somewhere in the distance, water was dripping into an underground pool, drip, drop, drip: each drop with an echo that faded and died.

The idea got into Scout's head that each drop was like a life: swelling into being on the cavern's unseen roof; then life itself, a brief plunge ending with a smack into cold water; then echoes, like the memory left on those behind: faint, fading, gone.

"What do you suppose happened to Scout?" she heard Whie say in a strange, comical voice. "I better go check!" Whie answered himself, in a high, squeaky voice. There was a clatter, like old sticks clacking together. Just as Scout scrabbled up to the lip of the next cavern, a grinning white skull peered down at her. A bony arm reached out with a skeletal hand at the end of it. Whie was using the Force to make the frail bones hover in the air. "You look like you could use a hand," he said, in that high, squeaky voice, and the floating finger bones clutched around her wrist.

Scout screamed and smacked her arm down on the limestone. The bones snapped and splintered. The floating skeleton—no bigger than a child—held its hand, now missing its fingers, up in front of its empty eye sockets. "Whoa. Now I'm stumped," he squeaked in his little-boy voice.

A second skeleton, this one the size of a grown man, came bobbing through the air to join the first. "Careful there, junior," Whie said in an ugly parody of a mother's voice. "This one's *feisty.*"

Scout's heart hammered in her chest. "Whie. Stop it."

"Just having a little fun," Whie said, appearing.

"Scout, it's incredible. There's something about this place—can't you feel it? I've never felt the Force so strongly. Normally I would have to concentrate just to hold all these bones in the air, but here . . ." He hummed, waving his lightsaber like a conductor's baton. The two skeletons joined hands and began to dance.

"Put the bones down," Scout said, doing her best to keep her voice steady.

"Why? The original owners aren't using them."

"It's not respectful," Scout said.

"I don't see—"

"Whie. I'm begging you. Please," Scout said.

Silence.

"All right." Whie turned away. The bones dropped to the floor with a clatter. "I guess it's not nice to scare little girls."

Scout waited for her heart to stop racing. "Whie?"

"Yeah?"

"You know you don't sound right, don't you?"

Silence.

"I know."

"It frightens me," Scout said. "The Force is very strong here. If even I can feel that, I can only imagine what it must be like for you. I don't think it's a good idea for us to use it unless we absolutely have to. It's like . . . air with too much oxygen. The dark side is just waiting to catch fire."

"I've got news for you, Scout. The dark side is here," Whie said, tapping his chest. "We carry it with us wherever we go."

He flicked off his lightsaber.

Instantly the darkness was absolute. Somewhere a

drop of water gathered, fattened, dropped into a light-less pool. *Drip-drop-op-op-p.*

Silence.

Stars had come out in the darkness, little gleams of light spangling the cavern ceiling. "I've seen those lights before," Whie said.

"Glow-worms," Fidelis answered. "We used to come down here when you were an infant, Master. You and I and your brother and your father, before his, ah, ill-ness."

"What happened to him?"

Scout drew her own lightsaber and flicked it on at the lowest power setting, just to make a light.

"The better families on Vjun have traditionally had very high midi-chlorian counts," Fidelis said. "It was a mark of status. Vjun only established significant trade with the Republic in the last couple of generations; before then, the Jedi had not yet had a chance to—forgive me for speaking plainly—keep the inhabitants subju-gated by their usual practice of kidnapping all children of unusually high ability. In times past, Vjun has had some contact with the Sith, but the recent advances of the Republic marked the first prolonged exposure to the Jedi cult. Interest in midi-chlorian phenomena had al-ways been high, of course, but the arrival of the Jedi baby hunters naturally spurred the best families into thinking of how they could augment their own abilities and safeguard themselves from the threat posed by—" He coughed delicately. "—*outsiders.*

"The Count your father was part of a consortium in-volved in genetically enhancing the natural midi-chlorian levels of Vjun's populace. The experiment was, in fact, wildly successful."

"You mean they created a whole planet of Force-sensitives with no mental training for handling it?" Scout said, appalled.

"Oh, *that's* the smell in the air," Whie said. "*Madness.* They all went mad, didn't they? You can hear the rocks screaming."

Scout's mouth went dry. "Whie?"

"Can't you hear it? I can't make it *stop,*" he said.

"You're scaring me again."

"Don't worry. This is *my* place. My home. They know me here." He pushed his foot through the pile of bones. "A mother and child, I think. They came in here to hide from my father, didn't they?"

"Well, sir," Fidelis stammered. "I'm sure I couldn't say."

Scout held up her hand at the sound of distant footsteps, the clink and rustle of metal. Then, by some trick of the caves, a set of orders came through a crack in the rock as if the trooper giving them was only a few meters away. "*Spread out through the caves. Captives can be taken dead or alive.*"

Scout stirred. "Dooku's droids are coming after us."

"Time to get moving," Whie agreed. "Hey—where's Master Yoda?"

"He left. He said we should rendezvous back at the ship in twelve hours."

"I didn't hear that," Whie said suspiciously. "Why would he tell you and not me?"

"I don't know," Scout snapped back. "Because you're acting really weird right now?"

Whie started an angry reply, then bit it back. He nodded, tight-lipped. "Good answer. It isn't easy for me, being here. My thoughts keep spinning out: I have to cut them off. I've been using the Silent Meditation Master Yoda taught us back when we were all five. Do you remember that one?"

"Yeah." Eyes half closed, tongue curled up to just touch the roof of the mouth: the Force running in a wheel from the top of one's head, spilling down through one's spine, then the marrow of one's thighbones, then draining from the pressure point in the soles of the feet to discharge. *A child full of the Force like a cloud carrying lightning is,* he used to say. *Let the charge run through you to the ground, to the ground.* She could still hear his kindly old voice—*relax you must!*—and the sound of kids giggling around her in the sleepy sunlit classroom.

Whie's voice broke into her memory. "This is what happened to Asajj Ventress's Master, you know. He was marooned on a strange, violent planet, and the Jedi abandoned him. Master Yoda abandoned him."

"Do you really think that's the whole story?"

Whie shrugged. "Funny coincidence. That's all I'm saying. Fidelis, get us farther away from these droids, would you?"

"Certainly, sir. I know every crack and cranny in these caves. If you will follow me?"

The Padawans hiked after him, Scout second with her lightsaber shedding its pale blue gleam; Whie bringing up the rear, moving easily. The weight of rock overhead didn't seem to bother him, but Scout hated it: the crushing weight, millions of metric tons of stone, rotten with holes and apertures. A couple of mortar rounds or a concussion grenade could bring the whole string of caverns down, burying them alive.

Stop it, she told herself. *A Jedi—even a young, frantic Jedi—doesn't let herself panic. You worked all your life to take these risks, Tallisibeth. You earned this fear. What would Jai Maruk think?*

At the thought of him, grief and warmth stole into her. She remembered crying over him as he lay dying in the Phindar Spaceport. *Don't leave me, Master,* she had said. His answer—*Never, my Padawan.*

Behind her, Whie laughed. "Remember that thing Master Yoda used to say? *When you look at the dark side, careful you must be . . .*"

"*. . . for the dark side looks back,*" Scout said.

Drip, tap, drop, tick.

Count Dooku sat at the desk in his study, pretending to read the day's dispatches from the Clone Wars, but actually listening to the ceaseless Vjun rain tick-spattering against the windows behind him. Listening, too, with a sense other than hearing.

Yoda was close by.

He was moving carefully, quietly, hiding his presence in the Force; riding on its back like a leaf whirled gently down a stream. But on Vjun, the Force was bent mightily to the dark side, and every now and then the Master opposed its current. It was these moments Dooku was listening for. Once, several minutes ago, the old Jedi had misstepped, putting a foot against the current, and the shock of it had rumbled through the very bedrock beneath Château Malreaux, announcing the Master's coming like a distant groundquake.

Or maybe it hadn't been a mistake. Maybe Yoda wanted Dooku to know he was on his way.

Since then the world had been silent. The old Jedi was moving like a water-skeeter over the surface of the Force, with nothing to herald his coming but a faint sensation of heat on Dooku's skin, as if he were a blind man at sunrise, the dawn invisible to him but for a pale, spreading warmth.

He hadn't really expected the Master to allow himself to be brought into Château Malreaux under guard. *Combat timing is,* the Master used to say; *and the job of the warrior, to destroy his opponent's timing.* Even now Dooku could see the Master in his mind's eye, stumpy little form in brown robes on the first day of lightsaber practice, clucking and passing out the wooden practice swords, kids giggling, the smell of clean linen and matting, the Master shuffling out in front of them all, the long, snoozing sigh: and then the rush, the little figure calling the Force to fill him up, the pull of it so strong that Dooku and the other gifted children could feel it, like a current streaming from the corners of the room into Yoda's horny feet, running in electric streams through his legs and trunk, the fire in his eyes, the Force gathered at the tip of his wooden sword like caged lightning, and when he lifted his foot and stamped it back down into a wide ready stance, you could feel the whole Temple shake.

Tap, drop, tip.

No, it would be interesting to see Yoda again. Like revisiting one's childhood home. Not that Dooku intended to get caught up in nostalgic sentiment. Sitting here with the fate of millions in his hands, subordinates begging for orders, victims begging for mercy: naturally it was tempting to remember those earlier, comparatively care-free days, when he was a boy dreaming of the lives he was going to save, instead of counting his corpses by the thousands. Funny to think he had ever been so young that a single life seemed precious.

But he was all grown up now, and past such senti-ment; no longer a boy to be ordered around.

Except by Sidious, of course.

Ventress's words came circling back into his head. *How can he let you live? . . . He will use you up . . .* Talk-ing to get herself out of trouble, of course; but by the stars she had chosen her dodge shrewdly. One thing you could say for Asajj: her instinct for where to drive the knife home was impeccable.

You must stand too much in his sun, Count.

Dooku glanced at the holomonitors grouped on his desktop, many scenes vying for his attention: a view of the battle on Omwat; a panning shot of the devastation on Honoghr, six months after the toxic catastrophe there—part of General Grievous's proposal to step up use of bioweapons in the Outer Rim campaigns; a holo-feed from the Senate chamber of the Republic; an urgent interrupt showing a small ship coming hard into Vjun orbit, chased by two interceptor craft from the high-orbital pickets; real-time updates from the troops that had followed Yoda and his children into the caves; and a battery of surveillance views from the château itself: front grounds, main hall, servants' entrance, and the hallway outside this study.

The Count didn't like surprises.

Tap, drip, tap! Rain coming harder now, knocking against the windows.

He reached forward to magnify the view of the incoming ship his fighters were chasing, then stopped, examining his hand. The stupid thing was shaking again. The warm feeling on his skin intensified, like a blush of shame, and the trembling got worse. It was strangely as if he was afraid. His rational mind was quite calm, but for some reason his body was responding as if he were a schoolboy on the edge of speaking to a beautiful girl: fear and shame and longing and hope all jumbled madly together.

Tap, tap!

At last the Count realized *that wasn't the sound of rain*. He whirled around to stare out his study window. Perched impossibly on the thin ledge outside, five stories above the ground, Master Yoda was rapping on the glass with his stick. Rain was running down the furrows of his wrinkled face, and he was grinning like a gargoyle.

A Hoersch-Kessel *Chryya*-class modified very fast courier dropped through Vjun's atmosphere like a thunderbolt, with two Trade Federation pickets in hot pursuit. *Hot* being the operative word, as the pilot of the Chryya seemed to have skipped the unit on atmospheric braking in flight school. Instead of burning off speed in a long, shallow series of loops in the upper atmosphere, the very fast courier was coming down at a suicidally steep angle. Her thermal scalings were a deep, ominous, throbbing orange. A trail of superheated air and burning atmospheric particulates streamed behind her like a comet's tail.

One of the pursuing picket ships shot overhead into the distance, not daring to keep to that impossibly steep reentry angle. The other, glowing bright red, stayed doggedly on the Chryya, firing short bursts from her forward cannon that failed to hit their mark. The sky screamed as the ships tore it in half like flimsiplast. The Chryya jerked and twisted gleefully through the hail of incoming fire, swiveled her top-mounted laser to point straight aft, and let go with one continuous stream of fire.

For a long moment the picket ship's forward deflectors held.

When the end came, it wasn't the energy blast punching through her armor that killed her; it was the sheer ambient heat that reached the hull's melting point. For one eternal instant the ship's edges seemed to blur and run, hurtling toward the ground like a burning drop of blood. The pilot tried to pull out of the dive, but the enormous g forces tore the melting frame apart, and the ship dissolved, smacking into the ruined city of Bitter End like a fiery snowball.

A couple of kilometers away, the Chryya settled daintily on the ground one hundred meters from Yoda's abandoned B-7.

"What was *that*?" Obi-Wan Kenobi said, unbuckling himself from the turret cannon gunner's chair. "I thought you were going to get us shot. Then I was sure you were going to get us incinerated. Then I was positive you were going to crash."

Anakin bounced out of the pilot's chair, grinning. "Just a little thing I like to call—"

"Showing off?"

"Showing off! It's not just about winning, Master. Federation attack droids coming in two files from the B-Seven landing sight: six, seven, eight of them," he added carelessly, glancing at the Chryya's tactical monitor. "It's about winning with *style*." He put his hand on the lightsaber at his side and prepared to launch himself out the Chryya's forward hatch. "Ready?"

"No!" Obi-Wan dropped back into the turret gunner's chair and used the Chryya's laser cannon to blow holes through three of the attack droids hurrying down the path toward them before the others scrambled madly for cover. "All right. *Now* I'm ready."

Anakin drew two blasters from the gun locker by the forward hatch. "I *love* this planet. It's just steeped in the Force. I could feel it the moment we touched the atmosphere. I'm usually a good pilot—"

"Great pilot," Obi-Wan admitted.

"—But here it was like the ship's hull and my skin were the same thing. I could feel exactly how much heat she could take, how much torque, how many rolls . . ."

"Clearly you weren't using the Force to commune with my stomach." Obi-Wan, still looking a little green, picked up a blaster rifle and a couple of concussion grenades.

"The difference between Coruscant and here is like the difference between swimming in fresh water and in the ocean. I feel so *buoyant*."

Anakin tapped the hatch lock and launched himself outside with a towering leap. Bright glares of blasterfire sparkled around the hatch, but he was through, twisting in the air, a blaster in each hand, firing as he went, one, two, three, four shots—two droids holed through their video sensors, running blindly across the hillside, sparks shooting from their scrambled sensor arrays.

Anakin hung in the air for an impossibly long time, let himself fall at last into a shoulder roll, two more shots at a droid trying to sneak up behind him, taking off its weapon hand and blowing out a knee, and then he was standing, perfectly balanced, with the blaster pistols steaming in the thin Vjun rain. "I could walk on water," he said.

The droids began to retreat—a swift, efficient action for those still undamaged, though the two Anakin had blinded were stumbling and weaving around the terrain, emitting high-pitched shrieks that sounded like unnatural yelps of mechanical pain. Obi-Wan followed Anakin into the open, using his lightsaber to deflect a few blaster bolts sent at him by the retreating droids.

"Why are they making that *noise*?" Anakin asked.

"Echolocation. It's a last-ditch backup directional sense—they're squeaking like hawk-bats, trying to make an active sonar graph of the terrain." Anakin gave him a look. "I'm not joking," Obi-Wan said. "It was in one of the latest updates."

"Must have missed that one," Anakin murmured, watching the blinded droids clang into one another as they staggered back after their fellows.

"Come on. Let's see if they've got Yoda and the Padawans over there."

They ran after the retreating droids, stopping just long enough at the B-7 to make sure there were no Jedi captives there.

The droids scrambled up a hillside and withdrew into the mouth of a cave. "What do you think?" Obi-Wan asked, passing over a pair of electrobinoculars. The two of them were now lying flat behind a little mossy ridge, looking up at a dark slash, like a wound in the venomous green hillside above. They could see light sparkling on the tips of blaster rifles from droids lying flat in the cave's mouth.

Anakin considered. "Long run uphill to get to the cave's mouth. No cover. They'd be firing down at us from a shielded position. Kind of a killing field, when you get right down to it."

"That's sort of what I thought."

Anakin unclipped a dimpled sphere from his belt and hurled it uphill.

"Wait!" Obi-Wan said, too late. Anakin had already used the Force to guide the concussion grenade into the cave's mouth, where it detonated with a deep, flat sound, like a sound tube dropped from the top spire of the Jedi Temple hitting the stone pavement below.

One heartbeat. Two.

Metal debris blasted out of the cave mouth like confetti. A moment later, Obi-Wan felt a deep, percussive thud shaking the ground beneath his belly. Then another. Then more. The sound of falling stone roared out of the cave mouth, followed by a huge exhalation of dust, puffing from the opening like a giant's dying breath.

"Great," Obi-Wan said. "The caverns are collapsing on themselves."

Whole sections of the hillside buckled and slumped, going soft and dark like bruised fruit under the thin skin of Vjun moss. The rumbling sounds of crashing stone went on and on. The ground buckled as whole patches of the hill tipped slowly in on themselves and folded into the dirt.

The smile slowly drained from Anakin's face.

"I'm not sure a grenade was the best idea," Obi-Wan remarked.

"You don't suppose Yoda was in there, do you?" Anakin asked. "And the Padawans?"

"You better hope not." Seeing the young man's stricken face, Obi-Wan relented. "I'm sure we would have felt it in the Force if Yoda had been killed. But next time, think a little bit longer before rearranging the landscape, would you?"

"Yes, Master," Anakin said. Technically he was no longer Obi-Wan's Padawan, but he tended to slip back into sounding like one when he was acutely aware of having screwed up. "What next?"

Obi-Wan got to his feet. "Next, I think we . . . ugh!" he said, staring down. His Jedi robes were stained green, as if with the juice of some poisonous fruit, and where he had been lying on the Vjun moss, made damp with the planet's faintly acid rain, the thread was already beginning to rot.

"I know. I can feel my skin beginning to burn from the drizzle," Anakin said.

"What a horrible planet," Obi-Wan remarked. "I'd hate to be the minister for tourism here." He pointed to a magnificent manor house perhaps a kilometer inland, white stone bordered with blood red. "I think we head *there*. It looks to be about Count Dooku's style, and wherever Dooku is, Yoda will be close at hand."

* * *

Usually the Force only helped Scout predict her enemies' moves when they were face-to-face, but the air of Vjun was rich even for her, and a prickling premonition had danced over her skin seconds before the caves started to collapse. "Fidelis! Get us out of here!" she'd said, and the droid, responding to the urgent tone of command, had grabbed her belt and hauled her along. They pelted down a long, thin passageway at top speed. Then came the first explosion, a dull crack like blasters close at hand, followed by a rumbling thunder that did not fade but grew louder as the caves behind them began to crumble.

They stared at one another as the still air of the cavern suddenly began to puff and quarter, like a crazy wind. The floor of the passage shook beneath their feet. "Uh-oh," Scout whispered.

"Keep running!" Fidelis shouted. "We're almost there!" Moving swiftly in the gloom, he raced through another passage, carrying Scout so high and fast her feet missed the floor for steps at a time.

A rumble, a roar, a deafening crash. "One of the lakes has slid!" Fidelis said. Scout was still trying to puzzle out what he meant when a wall of water dropped suddenly on top of them. Some fissure must have opened up in one of the great underground pools, and what had once been a quiet and predictable little lake was suddenly a moving waterfall that dropped from above, smacking Scout's head against the droid's metal side so hard it made her ears ring.

"Master!" the droid cried. In the strobing flare of Whie's lightsaber, Scout could see him in flashes, knocked down by the sudden rush of water and swept back along the passageway. There was another titanic crash as the roof collapsed on the cavern they had just abandoned.

Fidelis threw Scout clear and darted back into the passage, which had now become a temporary riverbed. The current was driving Whie toward the edge of a newly created waterfall that thundered down into the abyss. Whie's pale face strobed up out of the freezing water and he stretched out a hand, grabbing for a bump in the rock to hold on to against the river pushing him to his death.

Ignoring the shock of the freezing water and the ringing in her head, Scout summoned all the strength she could and added her will to Whie's own, using the Force to pin his hand to that rock.

A few seconds later the danger was past. The pool of water had emptied, the current went slack, and Fidelis had reached his Master. The droid picked him up and carried him forward. Enormous relief flowered in Scout's chest.

"Thanks," Whie gasped.

"For what?"

"I felt you grab me. The rock was too slippery, I tried for it but I was slipping off. Then you grabbed me, and I held on." He smiled, gasping, face wet and bruised. "So, thanks for saving my life. Even if I am a pompous arrogant show-off."

"Yeah, well—you're *my* arrogant show-off," Scout growled. She was flushing with pleasure. "That's what Jedi do for each other."

The ground shook under their feet again, and somewhere uncomfortably close a few hundred more metric tons of rock collapsed onto itself. "Come on!" Fidelis said.

He pushed them forward along the passageway, past one side cave, a second, turning in at the third. Then along another thin fissure, so narrow Scout had to turn sideways to make it through, and suddenly there were flagstones underfoot. They were in a dark passageway, like an empty sewer. A few moments later, a door.

Fidelis pulled it open. "Quickly!" Brightness lanced out, dazzling to their dark-adjusted eyes, as the droid pushed them inside and closed the door behind them.

Blinking in the sudden light, Whie realized they were not in a dusty cellar or dungeon, but in a comfortably appointed room, with hangings on the walls and a fire crackling in a carved fireplace. There was a fine carpet on the floor, tapestried with a woodland scene in a border of crimson and cream.

It was the room from his dream.

It was the room from his dream, only there were six assassin droids waiting for them with weapons at the ready, and standing behind them, beside the door they had just stumbled through, was Asajj Ventress. "Master Malreaux," she said lazily. "Welcome home."

11

As long as anyone could remember, Yoda had spent most of his time in the Jedi Temple with the very young. Playing with them at ages two and three—hide-and-seek, dodge-bolt, Force tag. The early rambling lessons in the garden where he taught them the secret lives of vegetables, the irresistible burst of shoots, and flowers playing dress-up; clustering them around to watch an orb-spider weave its web, or a bee bumble its way into a mass of blossoms.

When the first combat training started, with falls and rolls and footwork games, Yoda led them. For one thing, he was just their size. The first touch of genuine combat Dooku could remember was playing a game called push-feather with the Master. The point of the game was to become aware of even the faintest, tiniest changes in pressure and balance, and to learn to counter one's opponent's force not by blocking with greater force of one's own, but by turning the opponent's energy back on him or her.

As one got better at the game—and Dooku was much the quickest learner in his year—it became more and more like sparring, with victory going to whichever fighter could make his or her foe lose balance first. As they got older, they more often started in a fighting stance, fingers lightly on one another's forearms. Dooku's first push would come light and fast, or slow and heavy; the energy would come up from below or drop from above, or come in a sudden thrust right to the chest. He won the Twelve-and-Under Tournament when he was nine, using the trick of starting with very gentle probes, as if feeling his enemy out in the kid's version of the game, and then suddenly popping the pressure point inside his enemy's elbow and attacking in the instant of shock and pain.

But as good as he got, he never beat Master Yoda. No matter what trick he tried—a Force push from behind, a slap to the eyes—the Master always felt the blow coming before it landed and twitched aside, like a stingfly dodging angry hands. Every time Dooku thought he had the old Jedi set up and made his final push, Yoda would melt away from the blow, and like someone walking down a staircase with two steps inexplicably missing, Dooku would find himself flailing, the old familiar lurch and loss of balance. The drop.

What made it more frustrating was that Yoda frequently lost these games of push-feather. He would shove out at some little boy or girl with half Dooku's talent, who would twist clumsily to the side, and the Master would pitch comically to their feet, making woeful faces while the kid giggled and shrieked with jubilation. He let them win on purpose, Dooku could tell. He was building confidence in them. But he never lost to Dooku, never once. It was *unfair;* blatantly unfair, and for six months Dooku attacked with greater and greater fury, trying anything to win, but at the same time making his own balance ever more vulnerable, so when he lost—and he always lost, always, always, always—he did it in progressively more spectacular fashion. He made a point of losing badly, painfully. Daring everyone else to notice how unfairly Yoda was treating him.

Dooku was twelve years old the last time they played. Yoda had been coming to the unarmed combat classes once a week or so, and that whole spring they had sparred through a long series of humiliating defeats in which Dooku found himself taking an increasingly proud, contemptuous, bitter kind of satisfaction. He was twice the Master's height now, and still Yoda had never let him win, not even once. Never admitted what he was doing, either, and Dooku would certainly never give him the satisfaction of crying about it, or complaining.

As they bowed to one another, Dooku decided that he would make this loss something spectacular: so blatant that everyone would have to acknowledge what was going on. He decided he would break his own arm.

They straightened from their bows. Dooku settled into his ready stance, calming himself and preparing for the pain to come.

"I win," Yoda said.

"What!" Dooku had yelped. "We haven't even started!"

"When one fighter his balance has lost, win his opponent has," Yoda said mildly. "I win."

—And at that instant, again, as always, the sudden lurch: the falling: and Dooku saw Yoda was right. As soft as Dooku had made his limbs, his pride was still stiff, and that's where Yoda had pushed by never letting him win, until he was so wound up in his rage and humiliation that he had gone into the match *intending to lose.*

The realization was so big he could hardly hold it. He blinked, dazzled by the genius of the Master's teaching: showing him a weakness he would never have found, no matter how many times he beat his fellow students. "Th-thank you," he had stammered, his insides all mixed up between rage and humiliation and abject gratitude: and the old Jedi's face had broken into a smile. He had gripped Dooku's hand and brought him close and hugged him, laughing. "When you fall, apprentice . . . catch you I will!"

That night, lying on his cot, two sensations were still mixing uneasily in Dooku's chest. The lurching, tipping, drop into space, unbalanced again, outfoxed and tumbling: and Yoda's tight, delighted hug afterward, a physical promise, delivered skin-to-skin—*when you fall, catch you I will.*

It was the lurch and drop, the loss of balance, and the sudden helpless fall that gripped Dooku again after all these years as he stared out in wonder at the ancient grinning goblin who squatted, dripping, on his window ledge.

He had a brief fantasy of letting go with a single blast of Force energy, shattering the window, flaying the old Master with the shards. He imagined Yoda tumbling through the air, bloody and insensible, dashing his brains out on the flagstones far below. Then it would all be mercifully over and Dooku wouldn't have to feel this strange, jumbled confusion. His hands would stop shaking and he would be dry inside and tight: dry and tight and empty as a drum, just a drum for Darth Sidious to play. How easy that would be.

But Yoda would be prepared for that; it would never be so easy. Count Dooku prided himself on his ability to see reality for what it really was.

He opened the casement window. "Master! Come in."

Yoda hopped from the window ledge to Dooku's desk, stamping through the various landscapes being broadcast to the holomonitors there and shaking like a dog, so a shower of Vjun rain spattered off him, splotching the desk top, and the spines of several of the more valuable titles in Dooku's outstanding collection of rare books. Yoda had his lightsaber, but for now it was still belted at his side. In one hand he held his stick—of *course* he had somehow clambered to a fifth-story window ledge without letting go of his stick. In the other he had a Malreaux rose, white petals trimmed in blood red.

"You've been picking the roses from my hedge?" Dooku said genially.

Yoda held up the rose. "Yes. A pretty thing it is," he said, examining the needle-sharp spines. Gingerly he tipped the cream-and-crimson flower head toward himself and snuffed. He closed his eyes and sighed with pleasure at the fragrance. It was an old, wild perfume: heady and sharp and tingling like a childhood secret.

"Actually, the roses are why I decided to stay here," Dooku remarked. "There are other mansions on Vjun that would have done as well. But we had roses in the great house on Serenno; I suppose these reminded me of home."

"Remember them, did you?" Yoda asked lightly.

"Obviously. I just said—"

"From before?"

"Ah." Dooku gave a little laugh. "As a matter of fact, yes. One of the very few memories I have from before I came to the Temple. It was a hot day, I remember that; a bright day, and the sun heavy in the sky. The rose smell was very strong, as if the sun were beating the fragrance out of them. Burning them like slow incense. I was hiding in the rose garden and my finger was bleeding. I guess I must have been playing in the bushes and pricked myself. I can still remember sucking the blood. The way it welled up from this hole in my finger."

"Hiding?"

"What?"

Yoda squatted down on Dooku's desk. "Hiding, you said you were." He stuck his short legs over the edge and let his feet swing. A holofeed from Omwat played unheeded on the back of his head. "Why went you not into the house to find a bandage, or get a kiss?"

"My mother got angry if I hurt myself."

Yoda looked at him curiously. "Angry?"

Silence.

"It's not our way," Dooku said abruptly. "The Counts of Serenno do not complain and cry. We are born to take care of others. We don't expect others to take care of us."

"And yet, your finger . . . *hurt*, did it not?"

"I don't expect you to understand," Dooku said. He

felt angry at the old Jedi, absurdly angry and for no reason.

Off balance.

There was a knock on the door. "What?" Dooku called sharply.

The door rattled open, and Whirry came into the room in an obvious agitation of spirits. "The Baby!" she said. "The Baby's back! But the land is all slipping too fast for me to read the fortune, and I'm worried your young lady will do him a mischief, begging your pardon, Count."

The little Vjun fox padded into the room from between her legs. It caught sight or scent of Yoda, stopped stiff-legged, arched its back, and hissed. Yoda glared down at the thing from the desktop, bared his teeth, and hissed back.

Whirry jumped with a little shriek. "Which it's one of they nasty cellar-goblins," she cried, staring at Yoda. "Don't worry, Your Lordship—I'll get a broom and knock it on the head."

"Master Yoda may be small and old and shriveled up like an evil green potato," Count Dooku remarked, "but he is my guest, and I would prefer you not hit him with a broom unless I particularly desire it."

"Oh! Which it is Your Lordship's guest, is it?" the housekeeper said dubiously. "Each beau his own belle, so they say. —But come, will you talk to your young lady with the knifing eyes and check her before she does the Baby any mischief? I did what you asked, Lordship; the droid brought them in right as whip-smelt in a net," she added piteously, and her large chest quivered with emotion under her grimy pink ball gown.

"At the moment, I am occupied," Dooku said sharply. "Asajj may play with her scrap mice any way she likes for all I care."

"But sir—!"

"Don't pretend you love him," the Count said. "If you loved him, you would have kept him."

Whirry looked at him, shocked. "Love the Baby? Of course I always loved—"

"You had a fine house, wealth, everything a person could desire, and you gave him up," Dooku said. "The Jedi arrived like beggars on your doorstep and asked for your firstborn, your heir, your precious Baby . . . and you gave him up." The Count's face was white. His traitorous hand was shaking and shaking. "You sent him away to a distant planet, never a letter or a message, sent him from the only home he had ever known and let them lock him up in the Temple and steal everything that should rightfully have been his, and *now* you have the impudence to come here and say you loved him? *Loved him*?" the Count shouted.

Whirry and her fox were backing from the room, frightened. Dooku mastered his voice. "Mother? Son? Love?" he said wearily. "You don't know the meaning of the words." He waved at her with his hand. "Leave us."

The housekeeper turned and fled. For a moment the fox stayed in the doorway, staring at Dooku and Master Yoda. Then it, too, turned tail and scampered away.

Dooku rubbed his forehead with a tired hand. "Forgive me. As you know, most of Vjun ran mad, and Whirry is no exception."

"Everyone on Vjun, goes mad I think," Yoda murmured. "Later or sooner."

"Forgive my comments on the Temple. You know I have never doubted your goodness," Dooku said. "But—and I say this with all respect—there are things you choose not to see, Master. The Jedi principles—your principles—are noble ones: but the Jedi have become a tool in the hands of a corrupt Republic. If you truly want to see real justice—"

Yoda looked up and met Dooku's eyes with a look of such infinite, distant boredom that the Count's speech staggered to a halt. "No lies for me, Dooku," Yoda said, knocking a rather fine statuette off the desk with a lazy whack of his stick. "Through the motions, do not go. No Sora Bulq am I, to be caught in a web made of ideals. Pfeh. Thin stuff. Save it for the young.

"I am not young," he said, turning his deep green eyes wholly on Dooku. "The old, easily bored are. Even Yoda, though I try not to hurt feelings by showing it. But come across the galaxy to hear *you* tell *me* about nobility and justice?" Yoda laughed. It was by far the tiredest, bitterest, most unpleasant sound Dooku had ever heard him make.

He had thought he was beyond shock: but the disgust in Yoda's voice was shocking to him.

Yoda looked down at the floor, making little patterns in the air with his stick. "Something real, tell me about. Show me another way we can end this war. Tell me something Dooku knows that Yoda does not." The Count looked at Yoda, baffled. "Come across the galaxy I have for one thing, Dooku."

"Yes, Master?" Dooku said, hating the words as soon as they were out of his mouth. He only had one Master now, and a jealous one.

"Obvious, is it not, Dooku?" And then Yoda was doing it to him again—the unexpected lurch, his balance gone, and the world turned inside out as Yoda said, "*Turn me,* Dooku. I beg you. Show me the greatness of the dark side."

Far below, in the Crying Room of Château Malreaux, Scout snarled and reached for her lightsaber.

Ventress raked her with a vicious clawing strike across the head, knocking her to the ground. "Stay still until I tell you to move," she said.

A fire burned in a grate across the room. The wood was wet, making the flames gasp and sputter. Thin strings of bitter smoke crept from logs and drifted toward the ceiling.

Scout gasped, crouched on her hands and knees, waiting for the stars to clear from in front of her eyes. Blood trickled from the cuts in her forehead and scalp, dripping onto the richly embroidered rug. Little red drops, *pit-pat.* Red spots appearing on the carpet.

Pit, tick, *pat,* tock, *drip.*

"Thank you," Asajj said, glancing at Fidelis. "Who doesn't relish a nice spot of gentleman's personal gentle-treason? Oh, don't look so shocked," she said to Whie. "Did you think it was just your bad luck I was waiting here?"

Whie turned to Fidelis. "But . . . you're supposed to look after me."

"Indeed, sir," Fidelis said, looking embarrassed. "But your lady mother is still the head of House Malreaux, and she represented to me that it would be best for you both—in the long-term interests of House Malreaux overall, if you follow me—for you to come to an accommodation with Count Dooku and his, ah, representatives."

Ventress chuckled. "You just can't get good help these days. Do you know what you're playing with, boy? This is a Tac-Spec Footman. *Very* dangerous. The hardware alone would retail for the cost of a small planet these days, for the right collector." She frowned. "As it happens, I could do with a bit of cash. The price of a small planet is looking pretty good. Present arms," she added absently. The assassin droids instantly took a bead, every one of them, on Whie's chest and head.

"What are you doing? I demand to speak to Her Ladyship," Fidelis said. "Put those things down, or I will be obliged to *take steps,*" he added meaningfully.

"Don't be ridiculous. Even you couldn't take me and six droids out before we killed the boy. And I *will* kill the boy if you cause me any trouble. I gave him his chance to live the last time we met."

Scout lurched heavily to her feet, wiping the blood out of her eyes with her sleeve. She watched Fidelis, wondering what the droid would do. Numbers and diagrams poured in a flickering glow across its eyes as it sized up the tactical situation.

Asajj pulled out a blocky hand weapon. "Do you know what this is?"

The Padawans glanced at one another blankly. Fidelis shifted, coughed. "Neural-net eraser," he said.

"That's right," Asajj said pleasantly. "Take it." She held it out. "Come on, droid. Take it, or else." Her eyes flicked over to Whie.

Woodenly Fidelis reached out for the ugly weapon.

"Put it to your head and pull the trigger," Asajj said.

Tip, *drip*, tap. More blood trickling down Scout's face.

"Come on, droid. Put it to your head and pull the trigger, or I blow the boy's head off. What are you *waiting* for?" she asked. "Is this the legendary loyalty I've read so much about? There is a clear and present threat to a Malreaux here."

Whie licked his lips. "Fidelis. Don't. I won't die here. I can't. I can only be killed by a Jedi. I saw it in a dream. Don't throw your life away."

"That would be risking a lot on a dream," Asajj said. "And even if it's true, why do you suppose that is? Because Fidelis is going to save your life. He is going to make the ultimate sacrifice, like a good little droid. He knows his duty, doesn't he?"

If the droid had been programmed to hate, he would have looked at her with hate. Instead he lifted the neural gun to his head. "Only remember, I served the House Malreaux," he said.

"Fidelis, no! Don't!"

The droid blinked. "I didn't think it would end like this," he said. Then he pulled the trigger.

Scout and Whie screamed together. The droid's eyes went blank and his body toppled to the ground, jerking and twitching. Blue lines flared along his circuit maps as the nano-burn ran along his processing conduits, searing them out like thin streams of acid. For a long time the droid jerked and spasmed, and then, at the end, he emitted a horrible, chattering mechanical sound, like a vibro-weapon blade skittering and grinding into piping:

a horrible parody of a human scream that went on and on, until finally the body lay still—nothing but a pile of hardware on the floor.

Asajj looked down and nudged the dead machine with her boot. "Loyalty," she said philosophically. "It'll get you every time."

The great thing about Einblatz/Docker ultrahigh-fidelity auditory sensors with built-in real-time sonographic analysis software and HyperBolic™ directional virtual-mike capability, Solis thought savagely from his hiding place on the other side of the cellar door—as Fidelis's death scream went on and on—is that one can set them to mute.

Solis hadn't been programmed to hate, either, but he was a fast learner.

"You want me to tell you about the power of the dark side?" Dooku said wonderingly.

Yoda had the dragon's eyes again: half closed, gleaming under heavy lids. "Strong, *strong* the dark side is in this place," he murmured. "Touch it you can, like a serpent's belly sliding under your hand. Taste it, like blood in the air . . . Tell me of the dark side, apprentice."

"I'm not your apprentice anymore," Dooku said.

Yoda snuffed: laughed: stirred the air with his crooked stick. "You think Yoda stops teaching, just because his student does not want to hear? Yoda a teacher is. Yoda teaches like drunkards drink. Like killers kill," he said softly. "But now, you be the teacher, Dooku. Tell me: is it hard to find the power of the dark side?"

"No. The lore of the Sith—that is another matter. But to touch the power of the dark side, to begin to know it, all you have to do is . . . allow yourself. Relax. We carry the dark side within ourselves," Dooku said. "Surely you must know that by now. Surely even Yoda has felt it. Half of life, dark to balance light, waits inside you like an orphan. Waiting to be welcomed home.

"We all desire, Yoda. We all fear. We are all beset. A Jedi learns to suppress these things: to ignore these things: to pretend they don't exist, or if they do, they apply to someone else, not us. Not the pure. Not the Protectors." Dooku found himself beginning to pace. "To know the dark side is merely to stop *lying*. Stop pretending you don't want what you want. Stop pretending you don't fear what you fear. Half the day is night, Master Yoda. To see truly, you have to learn to see in the dark."

"Mmmmmmmm." Yoda hummed and grunted, eyes nearly closed now. "The dark side, power would give me."

"Power over all. When you understand your own evils and the evils of others, it makes them pitifully easy to manipulate. It's another kind of push-feather," the Count said. "The dark side will show you the stiff places in a being. His dreads and needs. The dark side gives you the keys to him."

"Hmph. Very fine that is, but Yoda has power," the ancient Master said, examining his hairy toes. "I live in a palace bigger than this one, if I count the Temple as a palace. Dooku is a master of armies: but Yoda is a master of armies, too. So far, we are even."

"Is there such a thing as too much power?" Dooku mused. "For instance," he continued carefully, "there was a day when your power was clearly greater than mine. Today, however, I have waxed as you have waned. You stand in my citadel. I have at my command servants and droids and great powers of my own that I think would overwhelm even you. It is possible that at a single word, I could have you killed. And without you, how long would those dear to you last? I could have them, one by one: Mace and Iron Hand, Obi-Wan and precious young Skywalker, too. Surely you would feel safer if this were not so."

Yoda cocked his head to one side. "Like Anakin, you do not?"

"Perhaps he reminds me too much of myself at the same age. Arrogant. Impulsive. Proud. I realize humility is high among the Enforced Virtues, the ones no one acquires by choice; but that being said, if Fate is looking for an instrument to humble Skywalker, I confess myself willing to volunteer."

Yoda reached behind his back with his stick, trying to scratch a spot just between his shoulder blades. "Power over beings, need I not. What else can it give me, this dark side of yours?"

"What game are you playing here, Master Yoda?"

Yoda smiled at the use of the term *Master*—curse him—and shrugged. "No game. Wasteful, this war is. Even you agree. Sent you the candle, did I: you know there can be coming home for you. Know this, both of us do, and if come back to the Temple you wish, I will take you there."

"Very kind," Dooku said dryly. "Decent of you to give me an arm to lean on."

"*Always* catch you will I, when you fall," Yoda said. "I swore it."

Dooku flinched as if stung.

"But another way to solve the war there is. If you will not join with me, perhaps join with you I should. Tell me more," Yoda said testily. "If power over beings need I not, what else can your dark side do for me?"

"What do you want?" Dooku snapped. "Tell me what you want and I will show you how the dark side can help you achieve it. Do you want friends? The dark side can compel them for you. Lovers? The dark side understands passion in a way you never have. Do you want riches—endless life—deep wisdom . . . ?"

"I want . . ." Yoda held up the flower in his hand and took another sniff. "I want a rose."

"Be serious," Dooku said impatiently.

"Serious am I!" Yoda cried. He bounced to his feet. Standing on the desktop, he was almost as tall as Dooku. He held the flower imperiously toward his former pupil. "Another rose, make for me!"

"The dark side springs from the heart," Dooku said. "It isn't a handbook for cheap conjuror's tricks."

"But like this trick, do I!" Yoda said. "The trick that brings the flower from the ground. The trick that sets the sun on fire."

"The Force is not magic. I can't create a flower out of thin air. Nobody can—not you, not the Lord of the Sith."

Yoda blinked. "My Force does. Binds every living thing, the Force I understand."

"Master, these are games of words. The Force is as it has always been. The dark side is not a different energy. To use it is only to open yourself to new ways to command that energy, that have to do with the hearts of beings. Want something else. Want power."

"Power have I."

"Want wealth."

"Wealth I need not."

"Want to be safe," Dooku said in frustration. "Want to be free from fear!"

"*I will never be safe,*" Yoda said. He turned away from Dooku, a shapeless bundle under a battered, acid-eaten cloak. "The universe is large and cold and very dark: that is the truth. What I love, taken from me will be, late or soon: and no power is there, dark or light, that can save me. Murdered, Jai Maruk was when the looking after him I had; and Maks Leem; and all the many, many more Jedi I have lost. My family they were."

"So be angry about that!" Dooku said. "Hate! Rage! Despair! Allow yourself, just once, to stop playing at the game of Jedi Knight, and admit what you have always known: you are alone, and you are *great,* and when the world strikes you it is better to strike back than to turn your cheek. Feel, Yoda! I can feel the darkness rising in you. Here, in this place, be honest for once and feel the truth about yourself."

At this moment Yoda turned, and Dooku gasped. Whether it was the play of the holomonitors, beaming their views of bleak space and distant battles, or some other trick of the light, Yoda's face was deeply hidden in the shadows, mottled black and blue, so that for one terrible instant he looked exactly like Darth Sidious. Or rather, it was Yoda as he might have been, or could yet become: a Yoda gone rotten, a Yoda whose awesome powers had been utterly unleashed by his connection to the dark side. In a flash Dooku saw how foolish he had been, trying to urge the old Master to the dark side. If Yoda ever turned that way, Sidious himself would be annihilated. The universe had yet to comprehend the kind of evil that a Jedi Knight of nearly nine hundred years could wield.

From the shadows, Yoda spoke. "Disappointment like I not, apprentice," he snarled, in a wicked, wicked voice. *"Give me my rose!"*

There were roses carved in the wall of the Crying Room, and thorns, too, wonderfully lifelike. Wonderfully sharp. The blood seemed to be running off Scout's face a little faster. *Not serious,* she told herself. *Head wounds always bleed a lot. Doesn't make it serious. Pat-drip-drip-drop:* blood spill-trickling slowly down her cheeks and running the line of her jaw; droplets dropping away like grains of sand in an hourglass. Running down. Running out.

Drip, drop. From the fireplace, the smell of wet wood burning. Flames gulping and shuddering. Where the flames passed, welts and blisters blackened the pale bark.

"What are you going to do to us?" Whie said.

"We're not going over," Scout growled hoarsely. "We won't—"

"You don't need to talk to your betters," Asajj said softly.

Crackle. *Drip*.

Scout struggled to speak, but Asajj held the Force like a clamp around her throat.

Drop.

"I'll let you know when the time is right to speak," Ventress said.

Scout's eyes burned as she fought for air.

Drip. Crackle. *Drop*.

"Don't do that to her," Whie said.

"Her? The Force is weak in her," Ventress said. "Live or die, she hardly matters. Killing her would be tidier, but I don't insist. You, on the other hand, interest me very much." Asajj reached out with one hand and touched, just touched, Whie's cheek. "There are things you want," she said. "Why not take them?"

"I don't know what you're talking about."

"I'm not your mother," Asajj said softly. "You don't have to be . . . *nice,* for me. I feel the dark side very well, here. Very well." She glanced at Scout. "I've seen the way you look at her."

"You're making this up," Whie said hoarsely. "You think you can kill my droid, hurt my friend, and then talk me over to your side?"

"That's exactly what I think." Again, with just the back of her fingers, she touched the line of his cheek. "I killed your droid and I could kill the girl. Life isn't a storybook, boy. The good guys don't always win. Sometimes the bad guys don't even know they're on the wrong side. You *do* know you're on the wrong side now, don't you?" Her voice still soft and lazy. "In this world the only rule is power: who has it, and who is willing to use what they have."

"I'm not like you," Whie said, but his voice broke as if he were on the point of tears.

"Don't think so? You told me you were going to die under a Jedi blade," Ventress said. "Sounds to me like you're due to change sides."

The fire hissed.

"You're fighting me with everything you've got," Ventress murmured. "As if I'm trying to hurt you: when all I want is to set you free." She was standing so close he could feel the heat from her body. Her voice a whisper, light as a spider crawling into his ear. "What you want, you can *have*, boy. What you desire, you can *take*. This is all yours," she said, gesturing around the room. "The room is yours, the manor house is yours. The Jedi took it from you, but it's yours and you can have it back. The fire belongs to you, too. This is all for you, and with it, anything else you care to take. She can be yours, too," she added, glancing at Scout. "You can have her if you want."

The bitter smell of damp wood burning.

"Tell him it's all right," Ventress whispered to Scout. And to her horror, Scout felt Asajj use the Force to pull her lips into a smile.

Drip, drop.

"Kiss her, Whie." Blood trickling down Scout's face. Her collar wet with it. "Kiss her." And he wanted to.

Asajj smiled. "Welcome home," she said. "Now choose."

"Your hand is shaking," Yoda said.

"Yes." Dooku frowned down at it. "Age."

Yoda smiled. "Fear."

"I don't think—"

Yoda came out of the shadows. The vision of him in his Sith avatar faded. It was only Yoda, the same as always, taking Dooku's hand and studying it intently, as if he were mad Whirry, trying to read the future in the pattern of liver spots. "Feel the trembling, even you must."

Behind him, broadcast on the holomonitors, the attack on Omwat played out. "I tricked you into coming here," Dooku said. "This is a trap."

Yoda said, "A trap? Oh, yes it is."

His old touch was warm and firm. *If you fall, catch you I will.*

No. Not *if* but *when.* Yoda had said, *When you fall, catch you I will.* Had he known even then, seventy years ago, that this day would come? Surely even Yoda could not guess that his star pupil would fall so very, very far.

"To the dark side I do not think I shall go," Yoda said conversationally. "Not today. Feel the pull, do I? Of course! But a secret let me tell you, apprentice."

"I'm not your apprentice," Dooku said. Yoda ignored him.

"Yoda a darkness carries with him," the Master said, ". . . and Dooku bears a light. After all these years! Across all these oceans of space! All these bodies you have tried to heap between us: and yet call to me still, this little Dooku does! Flies toward the true Force, like iron pulled to a magnet." Yoda cackled. "Even the blind seed grows to the light: should mighty Dooku be unable to achieve what even the rose can do?"

The Count said, "I have gone too far down the dark path ever to return."

"Pfeh." Yoda snapped his fingers. "The empty universe, where is it now? Alone are you, Count, and no one your master. Each instant the universe annihilates itself, and starts again." He poked Dooku in the chest with his stick, hard. "Choose, and start again!"

Far below, Whie was standing centimeters from Scout's bloody face.

And then Scout smiled for real, because she knew, she *knew* what he would do, and the Force welled up in her and she broke Asajj's grip around her throat. "It's all right!" she gasped. "You're going to make the right choice!"

"I am?"

"Yes!"

Relief spread across the boy's face like daylight flooding into a dark place.

"What are you doing?" Asajj said angrily.

Whie laughed and snapped his fingers. "Waking up!" he said. "Scout, Scout, you're right! I'm not going to give in! I'm not a bad guy!"

"You're going to be a *dead* guy," Ventress said. Her two red lightsabers flashed to life.

Whie laughed again. "Honestly, that scares me less than the idea I was going to . . . to turn into *you*," he said. "No offense."

"None taken," Asajj drawled. "Droids, kill th—"

A hail of lightning came through the door, reducing it to smoking splinters. On the other side of the room, where six assassin droids had been standing with their blasters leveled, there were suddenly two badly damaged assassin droids, one on either side of a heap of molten slag.

"What was that?" Ventress asked.

"Rika/Moab mini rail cannon," Solis said, walking through the space where the door used to be.

"That's not in the Footman specs."

He shrugged. "Upgrades."

Then he liquidated the remaining droids.

"I didn't know there were two of you," Ventress said, eyeing him warily. "I thought this was the one who called to give me Yoda's location." She tapped Fidelis's corpse with one foot.

"No—that would have been me."

"Why would you rescue us?" Scout said, bewildered.

"You're not rescued yet," Asajj said tartly.

"She backed out of a bargain. One can't let that happen too often," Solis said. "It's bad for business. I saved you because the odds of taking her down are better if all three of us are alive and fighting."

Scout looked at him narrowly. "I don't think that's it at all. I think you just didn't like the thought of us dying."

Solis sighed. "I didn't want you to die," the droid said. "I never got very attached to the boy."

Scout drew her lightsaber, a pale blue wand of flame. "I like the better-odds thing, too."

Asajj leapt high over the sudden death spitting from the cannon attachment at the end of Solis's arm. A cabinet exploded in a shower of debris. Ventress was swinging for the girl, but the Force was strong in Scout, too, in this place and hour, and her parry was there before the killing blow could fall.

Whie swept out his lightsaber. The room was bedlam and fire, the smell of smoke and hot metal.

Another prickle of premonition shivered up Scout's spine and she gasped, seeing Ventress use the subtlest of Force grabs to lift the forgotten neural eraser from Fidelis's metal hand. "Solis!" Scout screamed, as the trigger punched down. "Behind you!"

Too late.

Lines of blue flame streaked along Solis's spine. "Run!" the droid shouted. He fired at Ventress with mechanized speed and accuracy, sending a stream of superaccelerated metal through her left leg. The neural-net eraser took hold and he was shooting behind her; and then he was shooting at nothing at all as his limbs jerked and spasmed. Whie, white-faced, watched him start to die.

"Come on!" Scout shouted, grabbing him by the collar. "We've got to get out of here and find Master Yoda!"

She dragged him through the far door, and the two of them raced up into the unfamiliar house. Sirens were going off and bells were ringing. They turned down a corridor at random and Scout sprinted toward an archway that seemed to lead into a large entry hall. She stopped dead as a burst of blasterfire came spitting through the arch. "All right—next choice," she gasped, and they picked a different door.

Behind them, Asajj Ventress tore a length of cloth from her own shirt and wrapped it around her bleeding leg, growling. The wound wasn't critical, but it hurt, and she meant to make the Padawans pay for it. She pulled the makeshift bandage tight and sprinted after them, growling deep in her throat. She darted down the same passageway, following the sound of blaster-fire, and leapt through the doorway into the great entry hall of Château Malreaux. "*Now* I've got you!" she snarled . . .

. . . And found herself face to face with Obi-Wan and Anakin. "True as you tell it," Obi-Wan said, ever urbane. "But what are you going to do with us?"

Behind him, Anakin's lightsaber hissed into sizzling life.

Ventress turned and ran.

"Blowing up, your house is," Yoda remarked, peering at the various holomonitor displays with interest. A light blinked on the comm console. A special, red light. Dooku stared at it, then tore his eyes away.

"Message," Yoda said helpfully. "Answer it, should you?"

Sweat was running freely down the Count's face.

"Or maybe someone it is you do not want me to see. Your new Master calls. Dooku, ask yourself: which of us loves you better?"

"I serve only Darth Sidious," Dooku said.

"Not my question, apprentice."

The red light blinked. There was another explosion from downstairs. A siren went off, and several of the holomonitors began to flash.

"Come," Yoda said urgently. He put his hand once more on Dooku's arm. "Catch you, I said I would. Believe you must: more forgiveness will you find from your old Master than from the new one."

A rush of panicked footsteps, and the housekeeper

burst into the room. "Master, which there are Jedi in the ballroom. They're *coming to take my Baby*!" she shrieked.

Dooku flicked through the security monitors until he found the ballroom. "Ah," he said. Something in his face seemed to freeze, and die. "I see you brought your protégé."

"Understand you, I do not," Yoda said.

"You didn't mention bringing young Skywalker," Dooku said, pointing to the holomonitor. "And Obi-Wan, too. That changes the odds considerably. There's your Wonder Boy now, fighting the assassin droids I have standing sentry duty at the front door." His hand was wonderfully steady now. "Your new favorite son."

"Bring him, I did not!"

"And yet, there he stands, with Obi-Wan. A miracle and a prodigy to be sure. I suppose you left him under cover. Perhaps you missed a rendezvous. So easy to lose track of time, chatting with old friends," the Count said.

In the entryway, Whirry was shifting from foot to foot in extremes of agitation. "Please, Master! Don't let the Jedi steal my Baby again! Do something for me, for all my hard work, Master?"

Dooku glanced up. "Do something for you?" His eyes flicked to Yoda and the lightsaber at the Jedi Master's belt. "Of course I'll do something for you."

With a flick of his hand, he picked up the heavyset woman with the Force and hurled her through the window casement. Yoda's eyes went wide with shock. "You might want to help her," Dooku said.

With a bound, Yoda was at the casement. Whirry was windmilling down through the black air, screaming and tumbling toward the flagstones. Narrowing his eyes, Yoda reached out through the Force and caught her not three meters from the ground.

Instantly he was in the air himself, spinning away from Dooku's vicious attack before he was even consciously aware it was coming. The blinding scarlet blur of Dooku's lightsaber split the air, slashing a burning line along Yoda's side before chopping his desk in half.

Yoda whipped out his blade while trying to set Whirry gently down on the cobblestones below. "Wish to hurt you, I do not!"

"That's odd," Dooku remarked. "I intend to enjoy killing you."

As Yoda released Whirry from his mind's hold, and let her spill gently onto the flagstones far below, the tip of Dooku's lightsaber scored a burning line across his shoulder. The Count's blade was quick as a viper striking. Among the other Jedi, perhaps only Mace Windu would have been his equal on neutral ground: but here on Vjun, steeped in the dark side, his bladework was malice made visible—wickedness cut in red light. "I've hurt you!" Dooku cried.

"Many times," Yoda said. He considered his pain: let it drop. Now he had nothing but Dooku to focus on, and his lightsaber gleamed with the same fierce green light that flickered from under his heavy-lidded eyes. "But killed me you did not, when you had the chance. A mistake, that was. More than eight hundred years has Yoda survived, through dangers you could not dream."

"I know how to kill," Dooku hissed.

Yoda's eyes opened wide, like balls of green fire. "Yes—but Yoda knows how to live!"

Then their blades clashed together in a lace of fire, green and red: but the green burned hotter. Slowly, slowly, Dooku gave way: and in the dark, drunken Vjun air, Yoda was terrible to behold.

"Yes," Dooku whispered. "Feel me. Feel the treason. All those years of teaching me, raising me. Trusting me. And here am I, the favored son, butchering your precious Jedi, one by one. Hate me Yoda. You know you want to."

Count Dooku lashed out with his lightsaber. Yoda took a quick step back and felt the heat of the red blade as it sliced the air centimeters from his tunic. He jumped, spun, and struck at Dooku's back before he landed. Dooku turned aside at the last moment, whipping his blade across the space where Yoda was seconds earlier. Facing each other again, their blades met, clashed, froze.

"Cunning, are you," Yoda said, breathing hard.

"I've had excellent teachers," Dooku said.

Yoda dropped and rolled to the side, his lightsaber blazing, reaching for Dooku's ankles. Dooku leapt up and flipped backwards landing lightly to face Yoda squarely. On his feet again, Yoda whirled and struck at Dooku, his green blade meeting Dooku's and pushing him back. Dooku attacked with reckless abandon fueled with hatred. Their blades hummed together, hissing and sparking.

Dooku brought his blade down toward the diminutive Jedi Master and Yoda parried, locking his blade against Dooku's. Yoda breathed, calming himself. "And yet, even here on Vjun, where the dark side whispers and whispers to me . . . love you enough to destroy you I do."

Pushing Dooku back yet again, blades flashed and flared stutters of light, blood red and sea green.

Sweat ran in streams through Dooku's beard as he countered Yoda's every move, and his lips were white. Holobattles raged around them as the consoles showed Obi-Wan and Anakin clashing with wave after wave of battle droids. Dooku shot a quick glance at the red button on his desk and, with a Force push, he punched it in.

Yoda cocked his head. "A choice made, have you, Count?"

"I notice I am no longer your *apprentice*," Dooku said between breaths. "There was always a chance you could overpower me, of course." Yoda attacked: Dooku parried. "So I put a missile in high orbit, slaved to this location. It's falling now. Gathering speed." Dooku stepped warily back to the open window casement. "Can you feel it dropping? A thorn, a needle, an arrow. Faster all the time." He paused to get his breath. "Obi-Wan and your precious Skywalker and your little Padawans will be wiped out when the missile hits. So what you need to decide is, what means more to you, Master Yoda? Saving their lives—or taking mine?"

And with that he leapt backward, out the window. Yoda bounded after him. In the dark Vjun air it was all he could do not to leap after Dooku, to fall on him like a green thunderbolt and annihilate him utterly.

. . . But already he could feel the missile, too, dropping in a red scream through the atmosphere, two hundred armored kilos of explosive aimed for Château Malreaux. With a snort, Yoda turned his eyes to the sky and picked out the glowing dot racing in from the horizon.

Below him, Dooku landed softly on the ground and melted into the rose gardens.

The missile was coming in with terrible speed and power: too much coming at Yoda too fast ever to wholly stop it, even if he had time and perfect peace. But he reached out to pull up the Force binding even Vjun's bitter green moss and twisted thorn-trees, and let it flow through him like a wind: the breath of a world, gathered and released in a push-feather game with all their lives on the line, not to oppose the missile's force with force, but to touch it gently on the side—just enough to send it screaming by the broken window casement to plunge a kilometer offshore into the cold and waiting sea.

A long instant later, water fountained from the ocean in a blaze of light three hundred meters tall, and then fell back.

The château and all those inside it had been spared: but Dooku was gone.

Moments later, Yoda trotted down into what had once been the great entryway of Château Malreaux, now a shattered and smoking ruin.

Obi-Wan was thoughtfully toeing the remains of a prime combat droid that his partner had cut in half. "Nice work, Anakin." He looked around generally, surveying the carnage. "If you were considering a career in interior decoration, though, you might want to take a few more classes."

"Oh, no," Anakin remarked. "This is the New Brutalism. I think it will be all the rage if these Clone Wars don't end soon."

"Master Yoda!" Obi-Wan said, running across the hallway as the old one came down the great curving staircase. "Are you all right?"

"Sad am I, but unhurt." The old Jedi sighed. "So close, I was!"

"Did you almost kill Dooku?" Anakin said sympathetically. "How frustrating!"

Yoda gave him an odd look—almost angry.

Anakin didn't notice. "Perhaps we can still catch him—he must be around here somewhere. I thought we were going to get Ventress once and for all, but she gave us the slip. This place is crazy—honeycombed with secret passages."

"And battle droids behind every wall," Obi-Wan added. The familiar rumbling sound of a starship engine coming to life started up in the distance. Obi-Wan headed for the front door.

"Masters!" Anakin hissed. He put a finger over his lips, signaling the others to keep quiet, and edged along the wall of the entry hall until he came to a doorway that led into the mansion's interior. Touching his lightsaber to life, he leapt into the corridor with a blood-curdling yell—at exactly the same moment that Scout and Whie leapt from the other direction. For a long, comical instant the three of them were frozen in battle stance, lightsabers glowing, screaming at one another.

Yoda doubled over, wheezing with laughter.

Anakin was the first to recover. "Hey—it's the small fry!"

"Glad to see you, am I!" Yoda said. "But hurt you

are," he added, his long ear tips furled with worry. Whie's robes were scorched and slashed by stray fire from Solis's death throes, and Scout's hair was clotted with blood.

"It's nothing," Scout said, grinning. "We couldn't be better."

Whie laughed and threw his arms around Anakin in sheer joy. "I'm so glad you're not coming to kill me!"

Anakin clapped him on the back, bemused. "Me, too." Looking back over his shoulder, he said, "You might want to check this one for a head injury, Master."

"Anakin?" Obi-Wan said.

"Yes?"

"You remember that the first time I met Asajj Ventress, I stole her spaceship?"

"On Queyta, right?"

"And then we met again, and we took her ship again?"

"Right. Why do you mention it?" Anakin said, coming to stand in the doorway beside Obi-Wan.

Together the two of them watched their lovely Chryya rise slowly into the weeping Vjun sky and head for space, accelerating hard. "Oh, no reason," Obi-Wan said.

12

Obi-Wan's hands played over the controls of the secondhand Seltaya Yoda had purchased in the Hydian Way. After hours of haggling, the Master had gotten an excellent price, once they included the trade-in value of the two Trade Federation gunships they had hijacked to get off Vjun. "Ready to drop out of hyperspace?"

"More than ready," Anakin said.

The older Jedi glanced over at the young man, who was grinning with anticipation. *I envy him,* he thought, surprised.

"What are you thinking, Obi-Wan? I saw you smile."

"Do you remember Yoda's little maxim about humility?"

"Humility endless is," Anakin quoted.

"That's the one. Did you ever hear Mace Windu's translation?" Anakin shook his head. *"You're never too old to make another big mistake."*

Obi-Wan set the controls for the drop into subspace. "Coming out of hyperspace into Coruscant space on three: two: one."

The starship lurched as if taking a wave, the smeared stars collected back into twinkling points, and Coruscant hung burning in the blackness before them as if lit by the souls of her billions.

Anakin looked hungrily at the image of the planet growing larger on the viewscreen, as if, even from the very edge of the solar system, he could almost pick out a particular street, a certain residence, one lit window where another pair of eyes looked up into the stars, waiting for him. "I'm so glad to be home," he said.

At the far end of the ship, Scout and Whie were looking at the same viewscreen image. Scout shook her head. "Funny to think we'll be back in the Temple tomorrow. I wonder if it will all seem like a dream." The instant she said it, she regretted the word *dream*.

"No, we're awake now," Whie said quietly. "The Temple was the dream."

"Maybe . . . maybe it won't come true, your last vision," Scout said. "Or maybe you misunderstood."

"Maybe." She could tell he didn't believe it. "But it's all right. I'm afraid of dying," Whie said. "But I was even more scared that I was going to . . ." He trailed off. "Still, that didn't happen, thanks to you. What you said—it was like you gave me myself back. You gave me permission to be good."

Scout shook her head. "No mind tricks here, Whie. I didn't do anything. I just knew which way you were going to choose."

Whie smiled. "Have it your way. Actually, it's kind of interesting seeing you be humble. I think it's . . . *cute*."

Scout Force-slapped him upside the head, but only a little. Not nearly enough to stop him laughing. "Vermin," she said with dignity.

Yoda bustled in from the galley carrying a tray with a bottle of something amber-colored and three glasses. "Worry not," he said. "Chances to be bad will you have again." He cackled, pouring out a glass for each of them. "And good. Every instant, the universe starts over. Choose: and start again."

Scout lifted her glass and peered dubiously at the contents. Yoda snuffed indignantly. "Something nasty Master Yoda would give, think you?"

Scout and Whie exchanged looks. Gingerly, they tilted their glasses and sniffed. The fragrance of fine Reythan berry juice stole through the little cabin, sweet as sunshine on millaflower. "Almost home," Scout said, bravely tilting her glass and sipping. The juice went down like honeyed summer rain.

"Thanks to you," Whie said grinning. "I can't wait to tell everyone how you commandeered those ships at the spaceport to get us off Vjun. 'Quick, Lieutenant—the Jedi assassins are getting away in their Chryya! We've got to scramble up some ships and follow them!' "

"It was you guys doing your Mind Thing that sold it," Scout said modestly, flushing with pleasure. It was nice of Whie to make her feel as if she had really contributed to the mission, rather than being nothing but the excess baggage Jai Maruk had expected her to be. *Jai and plenty of others,* she thought, remembering Hanna, her white Arkanian eyes full of contempt during the Apprentice Tournament. She sipped her juice. "Whoa. I just found myself missing Hanna Ding."

"The Arkanian girl who gave you such a hard time?"

"She's worried she might be killed in this war," Scout said, surprising herself. "She doesn't want to die for nothing. The Jedi matter to her. To all of us. The Order is the only family we have."

For the second time in as many minutes, she clapped her hand over her mouth. Whie gave her a pained smile.

Yoda snuffed. "Hard it was, I think: to meet your mother after Dooku had fled."

"All those years she had been waiting," Whie said. "But the funny thing is, it wasn't me she was waiting for. Not really. What she lost was her baby, and that baby is gone. When she saw me, she saw a stranger."

"It was like that when everyone went to Geonosis," Scout said unexpectedly. "The Temple was just deserted. We tried to do our lessons and be good, but really we were just marking time, waiting for them to come back. Only they never did." She sipped the juice. "I don't just mean the ones who died. Even the ones who survived came back different people. Grimmer."

Whie swirled his juice around in his glass. "Do you think we'll . . . *fit*, when we get back? I just can't imagine doing the same classes, talking to the same people as if nothing had happened. Everything feels different to me," he said, and his voice was troubled.

He has changed, Scout thought. He used to be the boy who knew everything. Now he sounded much less certain, but it made him seem older. He wasn't a boy pretending to be a Jedi anymore; he was a young man beginning to grapple with the shifting, uncertain, grown-up world in which a real Jedi Knight had to live.

Whie glanced over at her. "So—are you still worried about being sent to the Agricultural Corps?"

And to Scout's surprise, she found she wasn't. "Nah,"

she said comfortably. "I think the Jedi are stuck with me now."

"I guess we can learn to live with that." Whie smiled, but his eyes were haunted. "You know," he added, after a moment of silence, "I chose to leave Château Malreaux. I chose to come back to Coruscant. I was hoping it would feel like home to me—like Vjun did when I first stepped on the planet. But it doesn't."

He looked at the planet rapidly swelling in the viewscreen. "It feels as if I've come *unstuck*. I don't belong on Vjun, I know that: I couldn't go back there now, no matter how much my mother wanted me to. I'm not Viscount Malreaux, I'm me, Whie, Jedi apprentice. But I don't feel like I belong on Coruscant, either. Is that a Jedi's destiny?" he asked Yoda. "To wander everywhere and never be at rest? If so, I accept that. I pledged my life to the Order and I won't take that back, but I guess . . . I guess I didn't know it would be so hard. I guess I didn't know I could never be at home."

Yoda refilled Whie's glass, and sighed. "*Never step in the same river twice can you*. Each time the river hurries on. Each time he that steps has changed." He furled his ears, remembering. "On many long journeys have I gone. And waited, too, for others to return from journeys of their own. The Jedi travel to the stars: and wait: and hope, with a candle in the window. Some return; some are broken; some come back so different only their names remain. Some choose the dark side, and are lost until the last journey, the one we all must take together. Sometimes, on the darkest days, feel the pull of that last voyage, I do." He threw back his glass of juice and glanced at Whie. "The dark side within you is: you know this."

Whie looked away. "Yes."

"But other things, inside you there are." Yoda tapped him gently on the chest. "The Force is inside you. A true Jedi lives in the Force. Touches the Force. It surrounds him: and it reaches up from inside him to touch that which surrounds." Yoda smiled, and Scout felt his presence, warm and bright in the Force, like a lantern shining in the middle of the cabin. "Not a pile of permacrete, home is," Yoda said. "Not a palace or a hut, ship or shack. Wherever a Jedi is, there must the Force be, too. Wherever we are, is home."

Scout raised her glass, and clinked it gravely against the others': tink, *ting*. "To coming home," she said, and they drank together.

Far, far away, on a minor planet in a negligible system deep behind Trade Federation lines, Count Dooku of Serenno walked along the shore of an alien sea, alone. He had established his new headquarters here, and in an hour he would be back in the camp, surrounded by advisers, droids, servants, sycophants, engineers, and officers, all vying for his time, all presenting their schemes and stratagems, sucking like bees on the nectar of his power. Possibly Asajj Ventress, his protégée, would be there, clamoring to be made his apprentice. He had a meeting scheduled with the formidable General Grievous, who was even more powerful than Ventress, but a great deal less interesting as a dinner-table conversationalist. And of course at any time his Master might summon.

What are we?

On the surface of the bay, water heaped and rolled, landing with a white crash to run hissing up the cold sand.

What are we, think you, Dooku?

The sea foamed up around his boots and then withdrew, leaving an empty shell half buried in the sand. Dooku picked it up. He had a sudden vivid memory of doing this back on Serenno when he was still a tiny boy, before the Jedi ever came. He could remember the smell of the sea, the thin salty mud trickling from the shell as he held it to his ear: and in this memory something wonderful had happened, something magical that filled him with delight, only he could not now recall what it had been.

He shook the shell to dry it, and held it up to his ear. An old man's ear, now: that child he had been had lived long ago. He felt his heartbeat speed up, as if—absurd thought—he might hear something in the shell, something terribly important.

But either the shell was different, or the sea, or something inside him was broken beyond repair. All he heard was the thin hiss of wind and wave, and beneath it all the dull echoing thud of his heart.

In the end, what we are is: alone.

Alone, the shell whispered. *Alone, alone, alone.*

He crushed the shell in his hand, letting the fragments drift down to the beach. Then he turned and started walking back to camp.

Whie's mother sat in the big study chair in the broken shell of Château Malreaux, looking at the sunset. The window Dooku had smashed with her body had not been repaired; ragged spikes of glass showed around the edge of the casement like teeth in a howling mouth. The glass had slashed her pink ball gown to ribbons and spattered it with blood. She didn't care. The Baby was gone.

When she first read her future in the broken glass, she wept. Then the time for tears was past. There was nothing left, now. Nothing to do but sit at the window.

The sun sank. With the coming of night, the wind turned to a rare land breeze, and the ever-present clouds rolled back. The sun touched water: floundered: drowned. Darkness crept over the sky, clear for once. The stars overhead like chips of ice. Her boy out there, somewhere. Never coming back.

Full dark fell, but she did not move to put a light in the window.

Dark now, and colder still. The little Vjun fox whined and nosed around her stiffening legs.

By morning, it, too, was gone.

Light.

Gray at first, touching the spires of the Jedi Temple, the tall peaks of the Chancellor's residence. A soft light the same color as the sleepy trantor pigeons just sidling from their roosts in the great ferrocrete skyrises of Coruscant. The low, continuous hum of traffic began to swell as the first commuters hurried to their early-morning jobs at bakeries and factories and holocomm stations. Then the rim of the sun peeked up over the horizon. The light turned pale watery gold, splashing across windows.

Dew sparkled on parked fliers; their sleek metallic sides took on the day's first blush of warmth.

Dawn on Coruscant.

A bell rang in the depths of the large suite housing the Senator from Naboo, and a few moments later the second handmaiden of Padmé's entourage hurried into the main room, still struggling into her dressing gown, to find her mistress standing at the window. "You rang, m'lady?"

"Put on some water for tea and set out a suit of clothes, would you? Something I can wear outside, but it must make me look *wonderful*," Senator Padmé Amidala said, and she laughed out loud.

The second handmaiden found herself grinning. "Wonderful it is, m'lady. Can I ask what the occasion is?"

"Look!" A kilometer away, a ship had settled on the landing platforms of the Jedi Temple. Little figures came down her ramps; other little figures ran forward to greet them. Padmé turned. The smile on her face was radiant. "They're home," she said.

Read on for an excerpt
from the exciting prequel to
Star Wars: Episode III
Revenge of the Sith

LABYRINTH
OF EVIL

by James Luceno

Capturing Trade Federation Viceroy—and Separatist
Councilmember—Nute Gunray is the mission that
brings Jedi Knights Obi-Wan Kenobi and Anakin Skywalker, with a squad of clones in tow, to Neimoidia. But
the treacherous ally of the Sith proves as slippery as ever,
evading his Jedi pursuers even as they narrowly avoid
deadly disaster. Still, their daring efforts yield an unexpected prize: a unique holotransceiver that bears intelligence capable of leading the Republic forces to their
ultimate quarry, the ever-elusive Darth Sidious.

Swiftly taking up the chase, Anakin and Obi-Wan follow clues from the droid factories of Charros IV to the

far-flung worlds of the Outer Rim . . . every step bringing them closer to pinpointing the location of the Sith Lord—whom they suspect has been manipulating every aspect of the Separatist rebellion. Yet somehow, in the escalating galaxy-wide chess game of strikes, counterstrikes, ambushes, sabotage, and retaliations, Sidious stays constantly one move ahead.

Then the trail takes a shocking turn. For Sidious and his minions have set in motion a ruthlessly orchestrated campaign to divide and overwhelm the Jedi forces—and bring the Republic to its knees.

Darkness was encroaching on Cato Neimoidia's western hemisphere, though exchanges of coherent light high above the beleaguered world ripped looming night to shreds. Well under the fractured sky, in an orchard of manax trees that studded the lower ramparts of Viceroy Gunray's majestic redoubt, companies of clone troopers and battle droids were slaughtering one another with bloodless precision.

A flashing fan of blue energy lit the undersides of a cluster of trees: the lightsaber of Obi-Wan Kenobi.

Attacked by two sentry droids, Obi-Wan stood his ground, twisting his upraised blade right and left to swat blaster bolts back at his enemies. Caught midsection by their own salvos, both droids came apart, with a scattering of alloy limbs.

Obi-Wan moved again.

Tumbling under the segmented thorax of a Neimoidian harvester beetle, he sprang to his feet and raced forward. Explosive light shunted from the citadel's deflector shield dappled the loamy ground between the trees, casting long shadows of their buttressed trunks. Oblivious to the chaos occurring in their midst, columns of the five-meter-long harvesters continued their stalwart march toward a mound that supported the fortress. In their cutting jaws or on their upsweeping backs they carried cargoes of pruned foliage. The crushing sounds of their ceaseless gnawing provided an eerie cadence to the rumbling detonations and the hiss and whine of blaster bolts.

From off to Obi-Wan's left came a sudden click of servos; to his right, a hushed cry of warning.

"Down, Master!"

He dropped into a crouch even before Anakin's lips formed the final word, lightsaber aimed to the ground to keep from impaling his onrushing former Padawan. A blur of thrumming blue energy sizzled through the humid air, followed by a sharp smell of cauterized circuitry, the tang of ozone. A blaster discharged into soft soil, then the stalked, elongated head of a battle droid struck the ground not a meter from Obi-Wan's feet, sparking as it bounced and rolled out of sight, repeating: "Roger, roger . . . Roger, roger . . ."

In a tuck, Obi-Wan pivoted on his right foot in time to see the droid's spindly body collapse. The fact that Anakin had saved his life was nothing new, but Anakin's blade had passed a little too close for comfort. Eyes somewhat wide with surprise, he came to his feet.

"You nearly took my head off."

Anakin held his blade to one side. In the strobing light of battle his blue eyes shone with wry amusement. "Sorry, Master, but your head was where my lightsaber needed to go."

Master.

Anakin used the honorific not as learner to teacher, but as Jedi Knight to Jedi Council member. The braid

that had defined his earlier status had been ritually severed after his audacious actions at Praesitlyn. His tunic,
knee-high boots, and tight-fitting trousers were as black
as the night. His face scarred from a contest with Dooku-
trained Asajj Ventress. His mechanical right hand sheathed
in a tight-fitting glove. He had let his hair grow long the
past few months, falling almost to his shoulders now.
His face he kept clean-shaven, unlike Obi-Wan's, whose
strong jaw was defined by a short beard.

"I suppose I should be grateful your lightsaber needed
to go there, rather than desired to."

Anakin's grin blossomed into a full-fledged smile.
"Last time I checked we were on the same side, Master."

"Still, if I'd been a moment slower . . ."

Anakin booted the battle droid's blaster aside. "Your
fears are only in your mind."

Obi-Wan scowled. "Without a head I wouldn't have
much mind left, now, would I?" He swept his lightsaber
in a flourishing pass, nodding up the alley of manax
trees. "After you."

They resumed their charge, moving with the supernat-
ural speed and grace afforded by the Force, Obi-Wan's
brown cloak swirling behind him. Victims of the initial
bombardment, scores of battle droids lay sprawled on
the ground. Others dangled like broken marionettes
from the branches of the trees into which they had been
hurled.

Areas of the leafy canopy were in flames.

Two scorched droids little more than arms and torsos
lifted their weapons as the Jedi approached, but Anakin
only raised his left hand in a Force push that shoved the
droids flat onto their backs.

They jinked right, somersaulting under the wide bodies of two harvester beetles, then hurdling a tangle of barbed underbrush that had managed to anchor itself in the otherwise meticulously tended orchard. They emerged from the tree line at the shore of a broad irrigation canal, fed by a lake that delimited the Neimoidians' citadel on three sides. In the west a trio of wedge-shaped *Acclamator*-class assault cruisers hung in scudding clouds. North and east the sky was in turmoil, crosshatched with ion trails, turbolaser beams, hyphens of scarlet light streaming upward from weapons emplacements outside the citadel's energy shield. Rising from high ground at the end of the peninsula, the tiered fastness was reminiscent of the command towers of the Trade Federation core ships, and indeed had been the inspiration for them.

Somewhere inside, trapped by Republic forces, were the Trade Federation elite.

With his homeworld threatened and the purse worlds of Deko and Koru Neimoidia devastated, Viceroy Gunray would have been wiser to retreat to the Outer Rim, as other members of the Separatist Council were thought to be doing. But rational thinking had never been a Neimoidian strong suit, especially when possessions remained on Cato Neimoidia the viceroy apparently couldn't live without. Backed by a battle group of Federation warships, he had slipped onto Cato Neimoidia, intent on looting the citadel before it fell. But Republic forces had been lying in wait, eager to capture him alive and bring him to justice—thirteen years late, in the judgment of many.

Cato Neimoidia was as close to Coruscant as Obi-

Wan and Anakin had been in almost four standard months, and with the last remaining Separatist strongholds now cleared from the Core and Colonies, they expected to be back in the Outer Rim by week's end.

Obi-Wan heard movement on the far side of the irrigation canal.

An instant later, four clone troopers crept from the tree line on the opposite bank to take up firing positions amid the water-smoothed rocks that lined the ditch. Far behind them a crashed gunship was burning. Protruding from the canopy, the LAAT's blunt tail was stenciled with the eight-rayed battle standard of the Galactic Republic.

A gunboat glided into view from downstream, maneuvering to where the Jedi were waiting. Standing in the bow, a clone commander named Cody waved hand signals to the troopers on shore and to others in the gunboat, who immediately fanned out to create a safe perimeter.

Troopers could communicate with one another through the comlinks built into their T-visored helmets, but the Advanced Recon Commando teams had created an elaborate system of gestures meant to thwart enemy attempts at eavesdropping.

A few nimble leaps brought Cody face-to-face with Obi-Wan and Anakin.

"Sirs, I have the latest from airborne command."

"Show us," Anakin said.

Cody dropped to one knee, his right hand activating a device built into his left wrist gauntlet. A cone of blue light emanated from the device, and a hologram of task force commander Dodonna resolved.

"Generals Kenobi and Skywalker, provincial recon unit reports that Viceroy Gunray and his entourage are making their way to the north side of the redoubt. Our forces have been hammering at the shield from above and from points along the shore, but the shield generator is in a hardened site, and difficult to get at. Gunships are taking heavy fire from turbolaser cannons in the lower ramparts. If your team is still committed to taking Gunray alive, you're going to have to skirt those defenses and find an alternative way into the palace. At this point we cannot reinforce, repeat, cannot reinforce."

Obi-Wan looked at Cody when the hologram had faded. "Suggestions, Commander?"

The ARC made an adjustment to the wrist projector, and a 3-D schematic of the redoubt formed in midair. "Assuming that Gunray's fortress is similar to what we found on Deko and Koru, the underground levels will contain fungus farms and processing and shipment areas. There will be access from the shipping areas into the midlevel grub hatcheries, and from the hatcheries we'll be able to infiltrate the upper reaches."

Cody carried a short-stocked DC-15 blaster rifle and wore the white armor and imaging system helmet that had come to symbolize the Grand Army of the Republic—grown, nurtured, and trained on the remote world of Kamino, three years earlier. Just now, though, areas of white showed only where there were no smears of mud or dried blood, no gouges, abrasions, or charred patches. Cody's position was designated by orange markings on his helmet crest and shoulder guards. His upper right arm bore stripes signifying campaigns in which he had participated: Aagonar, Praesitlyn, Paracelus Minor, Antar 4, Tibrin, Skor II, and dozens of other worlds from Core to Outer Rim.

Over the years Obi-Wan had formed battlefield partnerships with several Advanced Recon Commandos—Alpha, with whom he had been imprisoned on Rattatak, and Jangotat, on Ord Cestus. Early-generation ARCs had received training by the Mandalorian clone template, Jango Fett. While the Kaminoans had managed to breed some of Fett out of the regulars, they had been more selective in the case of the ARCs. As a consequence, ARCs displayed more individual initiative and leadership abilities. In short, they were more like the late bounty hunter himself, which was to say, more human.

In the initial stages of the war, clone troopers were treated no differently from the war machines they piloted or the weapons they fired. To many they had more in common with battle droids poured by the tens of thousands from Baktoid Armor Workshops on a host of Separatist-held worlds. But attitudes began to shift as more and more troopers died. The clones' unfaltering dedication to the Republic, and to the Jedi, showed them to be true comrades in arms, and deserving of all the respect and compassion they were now afforded. It was the Jedi themselves, in addition to other progressive-thinking officials in the Republic, who had urged that second- and third-generation ARCs be given names rather than numbers, to foster a growing fellowship.

"I agree that we can probably reach the upper levels, Commander," Obi-Wan said at last. "But how do you propose we reach the fungus farms to begin with?"

Cody stood to his full height and pointed toward the orchards. "We go in with the harvesters."

Obi-Wan glanced uncertainly at Anakin and motioned him off to one side.

"It's just the two of us. What do you think?"

"I think you worry too much, Master."

Obi-Wan folded his arms across his chest. "And who'll worry about you if I don't?"

Anakin canted his head and grinned. "There are others."

"You can only be referring to See-Threepio. And you had to build him."

"Think what you will."

Obi-Wan narrowed his eyes with purpose. "Oh, I see. But I would have thought Senator Amidala of greater interest to you than Supreme Chancellor Palpatine." Before Anakin could respond, he added: "Despite that she's a politician also."

"Don't think I haven't tried to attract her interest, Master."

Obi-Wan regarded Anakin for a moment. "What's more, if Chancellor Palpatine had genuine concern for your welfare, he would have kept you closer to Coruscant."

Anakin placed his artificial hand on Obi-Wan's left shoulder. "Perhaps, Master. But then, who would look after you?"

**The *Star Wars* adventure doesn't end here!
Read *Star Wars: The New Jedi Order*.**

THE COMPLETE NJO SERIES

VECTOR PRIME by R. A. Salvatore

DARK TIDE I: ONSLAUGHT by Michael Stackpole
DARK TIDE II: RUIN by Michael Stackpole

AGENTS OF CHAOS I: HERO'S TRIAL by James Luceno
AGENTS OF CHAOS II: JEDI ECLIPSE by James Luceno

BALANCE POINT by Kathy Tyers

RECOVERY by Troy Denning (eBook)

EDGE OF VICTORY I: CONQUEST by Greg Keyes
EDGE OF VICTORY II: REBIRTH by Greg Keyes

STAR BY STAR by Troy Denning

DARK JOURNEY by Elaine Cunningham

ENEMY LINES 1: REBEL DREAM by Aaron Allston
ENEMY LINES 2: REBEL STAND by Aaron Allston

TRAITOR by Matthew Stover

DESTINY'S WAY by Walter Jon Williams
YLESIA by Walter Jon Williams (eBook)

FORCE HERETIC I: REMNANT by Sean Williams & Shane Dix
FORCE HERETIC 2: REFUGEE by Sean Williams & Shane Dix
FORCE HERETIC 3: REUNION by Sean Williams & Shane Dix

THE FINAL PROPHECY by Greg Keyes

THE UNIFYING FORCE by James Luceno

WWW.READSTARWARS.COM
Published by Del Rey/LucasBooks • Available wherever books are sold

While the Clone Wars wreak havoc throughout
the galaxy, the situation on the far world of
Drongar is far more desperate. . . .

STAR WARS® MEDSTAR 2: JEDI HEALER
A CLONE WARS NOVEL
BY MICHAEL REAVES AND STEVE PERRY

The threatened enemy offensive begins as the Separatists employ legions of droids in their attack. Even with reinforcements, the flesh and blood of the Republic forces are no match for battle droids' durasteel. Nowhere is this point more painfully clear than in the steaming Jasserak jungle, where the doctors and nurses of a small med unit face an impossible situation. As the dead and wounded start to pile up, surgeons Jos Vandar and Kornell "Uli" Divini know that time is running out. Even the Jedi abilities of Padawan Barriss Offee have been stretched to the limit. Ahead lies a test for Barriss that could very well lead to her death—and that of countless others. The conflict is growing, and for this obscure mobile med unit, there's only one resolution. Shocking, bold, and unprecedented, it's the only option Jos and his colleagues really have. The unthinkable has become the inevitable. Whether it kills them or not remains to be seen.

WWW.READSTARWARS.COM
PUBLISHED BY DEL REY/LUCASBOOKS
AVAILABLE WHEREVER BOOKS ARE SOLD